BLOOD OF MY BROTHER IV
Behind the Mask

By
Zoe Woods & Yusuf T. Woods

PUBLICATIONS

Taking you Beyond the Read!

BLOOD OF MY BROTHER IV: Behind the Mask
Copyright © Zoe Woods & Yusuf Woods, (2012) Master Expressions
Publications, 2019.
All rights reserved.

www.MasterExpressionsPublications.com
Master ExpressionsPublications@Gmail.com
Instagram.com/MePublications
Copyright © 2012 Zoe Woods and Yusuf Woods
ISBN: 978-0578094151

Printed in the USA

5 6 7 8 9 10

DEDICATIONS

Yusuf

I would like to dedicate this book to the woman that my heart is so devoted to, my lovely wife Zoe. Words can't describe how much I admire you for the way that you love me. I treasure the way you continue to push yourself to be the best mother, woman and a wife there is. I guess what I'm trying you say is thank you for just being you. And to my children, you are my motivation in life.

Zoe

Without question, I express this dedication to my husband Yusuf. You are a force to be reckoned with. What you have given me in this life are the greatest and most valued things that are irreplaceable, with the blessing of God. We get greater, wiser, and love even harder with time. You hold the title of being my husband, a father, a business man, and a King, I love you.

To our lovely daughter Brooklynn, a future author; I could not be more privileged. There is no greater gift than a child...and for that beautiful gift I thank God, my husband Yusuf, and you. Continue to be your best, be unique, and intelligent...you're on your way to excellence.

This dedication is extended to my late Great-Uncle, Mr. Phillip Jackson, whose sun set on June 8, 2011. You have given me a lot in presence; your spoken wisdom remains in my heart and mind. You were strong even as you passed into paradise and you will forever have my admiration.

ACKNOWLEDGEMENTS

Yusuf

First and foremost, all praise is due to Allah without him I am nothing. I would like to give thanks to the fans that supported the Blood of My Brother Series, it is because of you the reader that I write as hard as I do. The love that I receive let's me know that it's okay to push the bar a little and give my readers something to really think about in order to understand a plot or to write in ways that are not conventional or always identical to the past. Your support is greatly appreciated. I would also like to acknowledge Aziz *(big boah I got you)*, Butter out of Riverside Delaware *(don't worry it's almost over. In a second it's back to them big cars and long trips these cats be lying about but you do it for real)*, Kevin Black, *4o (Cuz congratulations on your new born)*, Jasir Hines *(You're up to bat)*, Vincent Lofton *(My main man, I can't wait to hear you talk that talk all up in the missile)*, Mikey Raw, Ski, Fly Ty from 60th N Reinhard St. and last but not least I would like to give acknowledgements to the many men we have lost so soon from our life's. This is truly sad. Yes, I write about death and the street life and so much more because it's real. But if I could stop it all today I would and never write another book about it…because I've touched a dollar with Manny, who we lost too soon … I've touched a dollar with Sonny, who we lost too soon…Slap Shot, we use to live in the same house, we lost you too soon. Artie from Delaware, we lost too soon…Little Pittman, come on man! It has to stop.

I can continue to list names for days of the good men that are gone. Then I could go on writing for months about the families this madness affects. The children that are left behind with unanswered questions or grow up riding back and forth to the penitentiary to be patted down, all in the search of affection….I can't judge anybody because I've been there and have made life altering errors. I just pray that some one will learn from my mistakes… This is the reason that Behind the Mask was so needed…please let it *Take you Beyond the Read!*

1

A Calling from the Grave

Just a week after Mr. Holmes' death and as his will requested, his funeral was small but lovely with only the few people he took care of and that took care of him present. The location was a little local church in North Philly. Roc sat in the back row, not believing he deserved to be in the front row with the rest of his family because for the past week his mind had been all over the place as he recited Mr. Holmes' words in his head a hundred times and they still hadn't made sense to him. Then there was Mr. Holmes' smile at the moment of his death as if it was an abstract message that he didn't get.

"Roc, baby...Roc," the gentle touch of his mother's hand brought Roc out of his daze. "Baby you look so drained, you're even losing color in your face. I know how much you cared about him but dear, that man didn't mean us any good in the end. So don't trouble your head over spilled milk."

"I know mom but I didn't think he really meant to hurt me at all. Even when he died, the gun in his hand was on safety and he doesn't make mistakes like that, ever!"

"If he wasn't trying to harm you, then what?"

"That's what got me."

"Well come on and lets pay our respects to the person that helped you become the man you are today, he deserves that much," Mrs. Miller held Roc's hand tightly as they walked down the aisle to the open casket. Unbeknownst to them, Travis observed Roc's every move closely. Roc was known for being hard all his life, literally since the age of thirteen. But at the sight

5

of his mentor who held so much life in him, in his clean cream Armani suit and white tie with matching shoes...Mr. Holmes lay there in a permanent still, like Roc had never seen him before. Roc didn't fight the tears running towards his mouth as he talked, "Damn old head. The bull shit ain't nothing; you know I would do anything for you. This should have never come to this." While talking, Roc could feel the stares of Stevie Blue, Sammy 'Big Block' Gators and Money Bags Merrick, who really didn't know what happened but they wanted to place their pain as well as their anger on Roc, and take action. The only thing that stopped them was Mr. Holmes having told them that everything was cool between him and Roc before he'd left for Miami.

Roc resumed, "Somehow I feel there's more to your side of the story that you haven't told me but how and you're gone? Please know old head, even with everything that happened...I love you. I know you taught me better than to be up here crying like a bitch but nothing could have prepared me for this feeling of losing everything I knew." Roc slowly turned from the casket, removing his tears with the back of his hand, missing Travis' sudden movement, who met him just as he completed his turn.

Travis swiftly removed something from his back pocket and stuck it to Roc's chest. Roc, not caring anymore just looked Travis in the eye, emotionless, prepared for his fate. "Here, he wanted you to have this." When nothing happened, Roc looked down to see a brown envelope resting on the center of his chest. "Read it when you're alone." "Thanks," Roc stated. With the letter in his hand he could feel the power of Mr. Holmes once more.

The sun shined high in the sky as Roc's Maybach led several vehicles through the steel gates with one man standing on the side, "Wait, stop." The driver touched the brake with Roc lowering the window and asking the unrecognized guard, "Who are you and where are David and Marc?"

"They came down with the pig flu, I think you call it. I'm not for sure, I'm new to America."

"And you are?"

"Kotov sir, the new protector I would call me."

Roc thought, "*Alright,*" while giving his driver the okay to proceed. The cars continued to go through the private cemetery slowly and stopped along side the clear road. Mr. Holmes' body was lowered into the ground as twenty white doves were released into the air to represent a moment of peace at the end of the life of a true Don. Once the two hour event was finished, one by one each visitor said their goodbye's to Roc who was standing in a trance, staring down at the fresh dirt that now covered the new home of his mentor.

Mrs. Miller saw enough of the mental hurt in her son's face and headed for Roc when Billy D stopped her. "Wait Carmen, let him be."

"No Billy D, that's enough. He must leave so he can begin to heal."

"And he will when the man is ready and not a moment sooner. So take your family and his friend and go home. I'll make sure he gets there safely. Plus they're scaring me," Billy D looked in Boggy's direction as Boggy had his eyes dead locked on him with his hand in his pocket. Billy D was sure there was a powerful weapon in there.

"Billy D, are you positive my baby's going to be fine?"

"Carmen, do you remember the day you had Roc and we was all there?"

"Yes, it was you, Top Dollar, Mr. Holmes and Odell. We were so proud."

"Do you remember what Odell said when he first let me hold Roc?"

"That Roc would be the one, but you know Odell like any father, he praised his first born."

"Well to this day he hasn't lied to me," Billy D walked off and stood next to Roc in silence as Mrs. Miller got everyone into their car. "That goes for you too, Boggy. I said he's going to be fine, now come on!"

"Okay Mrs. Miller but if he's not…"

"I know baby, you're going to kill the whole world and I'm going to help you. Now will you help an old lady to her car?"

After an hour of preparing himself for the last conversation he would ever have with Mr. Holmes, Roc slowly raised his head from his daze, sensing the presence of Billy D and asked without looking in his direction but focusing on the sky, "Do you ever feel like you were forced into a game that you had to play to win and the very moment you didn't give it your all, you would lose everything?"

"All the time," Billy D answered truthfully, understanding Roc's pain way too much. Roc turned to make eye contact with Billy D, "Then why is it when you become victorious it hurts worse than when you lose yourself?"

"Roc, you know a lot of times we lose sight of our goals and begin to live for others that are near to our heart, so when they lose..."

"Our heart knows no difference," Roc finished the statement.

"Exactly, but always remember this," Billy D placed his arm around Roc's shoulder as they headed for his black Phantom with Foxy behind the wheel. "Leadership is the art of getting someone else to do something that you want done because he wanted to do it."

Not really understanding the reason, Roc paused asking, "Why did you say that?"

"I just thought I would."

The two reached the vehicle when the sound of a roaring engine of a Bugatti descending through the private cemetery came to a stop along the road. Roc watched Todd intensely and became shocked to see his tearful eyes as he stopped in the same spot that he was just standing and questioned Billy D, "Who's that?"

"You don't remember him?"

"No"

"Are you sure?"

"I'm positive"

"You will; he's the newest member to our Corporation"

"I thought we were voting Rafael in?"

"I know but there can only be four and as the rules state, when a member is killed and hasn't been voted out, his power and position go to his next male offspring."

"So he's Diego El Sovida's son?"

"No...Mr. Holmes'"

"What!" Shocked, Roc's mind quickly flashed to Mr. Holmes smiling as he said, "How else would he get a chance at power."

Todd bent down placing a few flowers on top of his father's grave. "Rest in peace Pop, but I swear to you if there is more to the story that Billy D told me, I'm going to handle it."

"Well, you won't have to wait long," a stranger's voice said from behind that had Todd standing up immediately, coming face to face with a man in a cemetery uniform. The hatred in Todd's eyes was evident as he asked, "And who the fuck are you?"

"I'm Kotov but my few friends call me Cyrus…the same as your father."

"You knew my father?" Todd inquired anxiously.

"Yes, and he wanted me to give you this. Once you're done reading, we shall begin." Cyrus handed Todd a brown envelope. Todd looked down at it and smiled seeing his father's handwriting.

From the back seat of the Phantom Roc was hidden by the tint, watching Todd receive the same envelope he had sitting on his lap and questioned, "What's his name?"

"Todd"

"Todd…Todd, Todd," as the name rolled off Roc's tongue, his eyes darkened while he remembered the letter he spotted at Billy D's on the locker, computer and table. He asked, "So it was him that was supposed to replace me as the next coming?"

"Yes"

"So what happened, why didn't I know about him until now?"

"Because once your name began to buzz in the street and I saw that you were a step ahead of what I had planned for you, I pulled his training against Holmes' wishes. Holmes then sent Todd away to get some of the best schooling around the world. The whole time he'd stated that he hoped I made the right choice. The last I heard, Todd had become wealthy as the sole owner of his father's company."

Roc slowly removed the envelope and began to read the front as his mentor's voice played ever clearly in his mind, just

9

as Todd did the same. They started to read out loud, "Are you my begotten son?" Simultaneously they answered, "Yes," while ripping open the letter.

"Dear Son,

If you are now reading this letter, you may feel that our journey together has finally come to an end...but truly it has just begun. I know my recent actions may have left you confused with thoughts that I had mishandled your trust which you have positioned so deeply within me and replaced it with disloyalty, going against everything I have taught you to believe in. A man's word is all that he will ever have in life, but son you'll come to realize that I have been nothing more than loyal, entrusting you with everything, even my life...literally. Together we will continue to fulfill whatever is meant to be of your destiny. I have left several notes behind. Through them you will find support as your vision will become clearer of my actions and the reasons for them.

I know that I have taught you that no man should ever have to explain himself, for an excuse is only to satisfy someone else's interest. But in this case, son you deserve it. Furthermore, you'll need it if you choose to accept in the near future the last and ultimate chess match that will change your life forever.

The board has already been centered and I have set the pieces in play. In the end, there will only be one person who will remain to run the corporation and that will be my true begotten son.

I will begin to explain...I know what you must have been thinking over these last few months and to answer your thoughts, yes, I used you. I'm sorry son, but I needed for you to believe my actions were one way, so that your reaction would be destructive and unreserved. Therefore, when the corporation came after me, you along with Adrian Cortez and Sunan Kudari would believe it was what had to be done and not what I wanted you to do."

Roc paused from reading to rethink Billy D's previous statement, "Leadership is the art of getting someone else to do something that you want done because they wanted to do it."

Now understanding their reason, Roc questioned, "But why?" as he continued to read...

"Thanks son, for being understanding. You of all people know we survived as long as we have in this dangerous society because we followed the rules passed down to us without any emotional attachment and anyone that crosses them ,whether it be you, my mother, or your brother, they must perish. Therefore I deserve to die by the barrel of a gun like that of a true soldier with the mud still fresh on his boots from combat instead of this disease that's slowly killing me."

Together, Roc and Todd yelled, "Disease!" both puzzled as well as outraged, for neither of them knew that the man they loved and held such high regard for was even sick. The letter continued...

"On September 27, 2007, I received a call from Dr. Woods who informed me that I had Alzheimer's. After forcing him to sworn secrecy, he stated it was a degenerative brain disease that had been eating away at my brain for several years. Mentally, there wasn't a drop of doubt in me that I would defeat it. I dreamed to live to see who would be victorious, on one hand there is Roc who has the criminal mind state to do business and on the other hand there's Todd with the business mind that was raised by a criminal.
Within a short amount of time I began to forget the small things like how to lace my shoes or where I placed my keys. After searching for hours, there were times when the keys would be right in my hand. While I have retained the memory of every pressure point to kill a man with one exposed hand at close range, clearly as if he was dying in front of me. Down to old Boon coon, the only man I ever regret not killing for the disrespect he had once revealed to me as I inscribe this letter. Yet the average everyday tasks were so easy to forget.
With the clock ticking on a soldier's sanity, I was forced to make a sudden decision. A resolution that would uplift my people as a whole and in doing so I used the both of you...

11

Roc and Todd, the power you now both hold, sadly to say won't be enough if you chose to defeat Adrian Cortez and Sunan Kudari on your way to becoming the one. Over the years I have studied each of these men's strong and though not many, weak points that they possess. The whereabouts of each of their several mistresses that they believe no one has knowledge of, the numerous offshore accounts as well as much more, thanks to Billy D. These secrets you will receive in parts from Travis as you did this one. Excluding the approval of your teachers Billy D the Paramount businessman and Cyrus the absolute criminal as they make the each of you equal. In the end it will be your individual skills that will dictate your survival. You now have 72 hours to being your training under the watch of each of your helpers, with the choice of who will become your target once finish. Remember I'll be watching. This will end the first letter of several to my true begotten son..."

Todd was the first to complete the letter. Looking down at his father's grave he said, "Thanks Pop, for believing in me and giving me the chance to prove they've made the biggest mistake of their life by not choosing me in the first place." Todd turned to Cyrus with his dark brown eyes transitioning to an amber coloration, indicating his anger and willingness to win and asked, "What are we waiting for?"

"I think we'll get along on this journey of death just fine, Todd. But first you must meet someone." Cyrus set his watch to a count down of 71 hours and 58 minutes. "Anything to prove my father didn't die for nothing and why are you looking at me like that?"

"To be honest I wanted to see if you would kill yourself for me. Now come on, we don't have a second to waste."

"Why, what would happen if we're late?"

"You'll become the hunted...instead of the hunter."

Cyrus, using his photographic memory started back down the trail from which he came, without turning to see if Todd would follow. Todd paused, studying the strange man with the deep foreign accent carefully with the headache that shortly occurred slowly fading. He thought, "Wait! There's something mysteriously risky about this man...thanks again, Pop." With a smirk lit with evil he yelled out, "Hey Cyrus, wait up man! And what about my car, it cost too much just to be sitting on the side of the road?"

"Leave it, we walk. Now you'll begin to understand the struggle plus if you're successful there wouldn't be anything you can't buy a million times. If you fail, you won't need it...you'll be dead."

Roc slowly concluded the letter with his body temperature rising over each word as his gray eyes once again darkened. He set Billy D directly in his sights, holding back the intense anger that grew in the depth of his soul, which quickly repaired his broken spirit due to the loss of Mr. Holmes. He inquired, "You knew about this the whole time?"

"A little."

"Well know this also...Mr. Holmes was a great leader but not as good as you may have thought because I'm out! That's it...I said it, my family has suffered enough. It's over. So if this is about whether or not you've made the right choice, I can tell you now that you didn't." Roc knocked on the tinted divider to get the driver's attention and the two inch sound proof glass slowly lowered with the driver asking, "Yes Mr. Miller, what can I do for you?"

"Take me home."

"And what about your dinner meeting?"

"I suddenly lost my appetite."

"Are you sure?"

"I'm more than positive."

Foxy looked to Billy D who gave a slight nod before sliding the glass back up, "Will do."

"Roc, I understand that you're upset," Billy D stated, "But you must not make a decision based off of anger and frustration."

"I'm not, that would be counterproductive. Actually, I'm relaxed now more than ever."

"That's not the story your eyes tell."

"No, my vision reflects the sad memory of why I'm done. Because of this game I lost my father who was murdered by a junkie and left to die in the streets when I was only 13. My family was left penniless as I watched my mother struggle for

13

months to keep food on the table. There were times she didn't eat, insisting that she had so that my brother and I would eat in peace. One day the food stamps stopped..."

Billy D leaned in closer; concentrating on Roc's every motion intensely as he noticed his eyes darkening, as if they were black. His veins pulsated on the side of his neck as he spoke, "I was ordered by my father shortly before his passing to never let a man stop me from feeding my family. So that night after stealing food from the local store for my family, I eased into his old room and gripped his 22 revolver. For the first time I studied the same weapon that I witnessed him take a life with."

Roc paused with the reminiscent smell of his father's cologne taking his mind deeper back in time. "Just moments before I would take my first, it was at that very instant that this so called game replaced my stomach's hunger for food with a hunger for death. Indeed my family grew from rags literally, to riches publicly. But the cost in the end was too unbalanced. If the paved alleyways could talk, they would say that my father was a slave to them until his death. Then I became one so that my mother's youngest boy wouldn't have to. But instead, I unknowingly gave him the blueprint to become a master slave by allowing him to watch me, which he followed without swaying and damn near got himself killed in his pursuit of trying to kill me. This is my fucking life, what I had tried so hard to establish for him ended in failure. Now you look me in the eyes with that staring game you're always playing nigga and tell me why I should give another drop of pain and sorrow to this game that ya'll believe in? Because I truly don't believe in it...not anymore. Mr. Holmes may have been willing to give his life for the corporation's future and I don't want to let him down because I need for him to rest in peace for he deserves that, but I'm not willing to do the same."

Roc waited for an answer, refusing to remove his fixed stare on Billy D. He was well aware that there couldn't be a grain of weakness or doubt in him when it came to his decision. Moments went by without a word before Roc broke the silence, "I thought so nig..." Billy D placed a single finger in the air, which demanded an unseen respect that stopped him in mid-sentence. Billy D poured two glasses of Brandy, adding one ice

14

cube to each, handing one to Roc. He then took a long sip before speaking.

"Roc I'm a very secretive person. I possess a soul that has passed through a time that many people feared to make it out of, let alone cared to remember. So I will act as if you didn't ask that question and just call and cancel the meeting." Billy D released the car phone from its cradle when Roc forcefully gripped hold of his hand, slamming it back down and said, "You're not getting off that easy! You're going to tell me something. What did Mr. Holmes know that I don't and you better not speak of fear again to me? What the hell can you tell me that I haven't already heard or did?"

Billy D, still in excellent shape snatched his hand away from Roc's grasp with ease as his sparkling green eyes inflamed suddenly turning pitch black that revealed his own anger. The cold wickedness of his face forced Roc to break his stare for a second, unsure of what he was witnessing. "The beginning, ha-ha," Billy D laughed before sitting his glass down and continuing, "You can't possibly believe that you're the only one this game has changed. I wasn't always accused of a thousand murders. We're gangsters! Somewhere along the line you forgot that. But...if you must know to bring you back to the fucking reality of the life we live, I will remove this mask I wear and one day you'll put on that shields the blood, tears, and scars of my past to give you a glimpse of what lies beneath for you to understand why you have no choice but to continue," Billy D finished, keeping the last statement to himself, *"Or you will become number one thousand and one."*

15

2

*I*nside the walls of Roc's mother's brownstone located in the heart of north Philly, where she refused to move no matter how much money her son's hands possessed a cloud of sorrow and mixed emotions filled the air for the loss of a true legend. Boggy, who was Roc's second in command and first to go to when it was time to kill, sat off by himself in the far corner of the well furnished living room. He made certain that he was away from Top Dollar, Lil Mac, NayNay and Fox of the Get Money Click as well as isolating his own men Mohammed, Raja, M Easy and Haffee as he watched local hustler after hustler hug Mrs. Miller with words of kindness thinking to himself, *"Look at all these fake ass niggas in my man's mom's face talking that bullshit. Knowing that Mr. Holmes didn't even fuck with them... he played with G's not fleas."* Boggy replaced the bottle of coconut Ciroc to his lips that was now passed halfway gone and he had just opened it, *"Man fuck this, if Roc or Mr. Holmes was here this wouldn't be happening and your sitting there like the shit cool"* Boggy slowly got up from his position feeling not drunk but slightly buzzed. He made his way to Mrs. Miller staring Lil Mac in the face with a look of degust as Pretty Tony, a quickly growing major player in the game, told her, "Sorry for your loss, if there's anything I can do please don't hesitate to a--"

"Man, shut the hell up and get the fuck out of here. You lying ass nigga, what can you do?" Boggy interrupted. "You lucky Mrs. Miller's here or I'd shoot you in the face nigga, can you stop that?" Boggy's free hand slid to the Mack 11 resting in his waistline.

"I-I-I—"

"I know nigga, now everybody get the hell out!! If you're not family I don't want to see your face or I'm going to put a bullet in it. Mohammed, get the door and if one of these faking ass lames pauses... down him." Boggy demanded, meaning every word.

"My bad Boggy... but we still on tonight at Soldi II right?" pretty Tony asked on his way out the door too scared to wait for an answer.

"Boggy, it's ok dear they can stay, they mean well baby."

"No Mrs. Miller it's not alright. Mr. Holmes ain't ever eat with these lames and now that he's gone they're sitting around here chilling and shit amongst us just on the strength of his death."

"I know baby but they're still our people."

"They're not m—"

"Let it go Boggy, she said they can stay. Why don't we go down into the basement and put some of this sours in the air?" Lil Mac questioned, as his hand lightly gripped hold of Boggy's arm. Boggy slowly began to calm down realizing that the pain he in fact felt was for the man who didn't only look after Roc but treated him as a son as well may have gotten the best of him. He gradually turned and saw Lil Mac, when his blood pressure shot straight to the roof. "Nigga get the fuck off of me!" Boggy yelled, pulling his arm loose with a strength that knocked Lil Mac off balance. "You're the reason behind all this bullshit to begin with trying to be somebody the fuck your' not." Boggy, with the instinct of a killer embedded in him moved in for the kill as he swiftly passed the bottle of Ciroc off to Mrs. Miller while unlatching his other gun in the same motion from his shoulder, making her a conspirator in her own son's murder.

The cloud of sorrow quickly faded as a serious midst of tension flowed in, thickened by the second. These men trained for situations like this, each out of impulse quickly chose their side mentally as they watched Boggy's steps place him inches away from Lil Mac. "Oh it's on!" Fox stated, jumping to his feet just as Mohammed stepped in between Boggy and Lil Mac. Mohammed, who's an ex-military soldier that lost his brother on a street in Iraq with a name he barely could pronounce, begun his own war against the powers that be at that very moment. Shortly after, he was returned back to the states dishonorably discharged for acts of over aggression on his fellow soldiers. Sense then he and Roc have been a match made for destruction.

17

Mohammed always knew it was hard for Boggy to comply with Roc's request of leaving the issue with Lil Mac behind, even among the gifts of cars and money, for no true soldier who wasn't complete in essence could live with himself knowing another man had put a bullet in him and was still breathing. What ever the case may be, Mohammed decided this instant was not the time. "Fox you sit back down and you too," Mohammed said to Boggy and Lil Mac, "I understand that ya'll situation one day will have to be handled... just not today or at least not now."

"Yeah and I'm sure everyone is a little emotional and stressed due to the fact that we lost someone dear to us all but ya'll are not going to tear up my damn house to help you get over it, and Boggy put that gun away you're not going to kill nobody in here dear," said Mrs. Miller, taking a sip of Boggy's Ciroc her self. "Child, you kids will work an old lady's nerves." Boggy stared at Lil Mac with eyes of hatred as he gave Mohammed a light head nod in respect saying to Lil Mac, "You know I'm not the one for you to be testing."

"It's cool Boggy, I know this isn't you, you're just upset. But to set the record straight, you know I'm not the one to be testing."

"What's going on here?" questioned Roc, interrupting Lil Mac. Roc could smell the danger in the atmosphere as he softly walked up on Boggy and Lil Mac unnoticed; a skill he'd learned from Mohammed. Lil Mac was the first to speak, answering with a smile that Roc couldn't read. "It's nothing big, I was just telling Boggy here that we're family now that's all and I would never try to hurt family, hurting him would be like spilling the blood of my brother... and I would never do something like that."

"Good because we have a bigger problem at hand," Roc stated, while thinking to himself, *"Did he just threaten Boggy while using me as an example in my face? Nah he wouldn't...not after all we've been through. The sad thing is that I can't tell...damn he's getting good."* Roc turned his attention to Boggy making a mental note to study Lil Mac more closely as he asked, "What's good baby boy?"

18

"You know me the same old shit, ride or die on any of these niggas without question. I have no cut cards in me. You either skip town when it's on or you know what's going to happen." Boggy was speaking to Roc but talking directly to Lil Mac before shifting gears so Roc wouldn't be the wiser. "But pay me no mind because I'm dying for some action, I just can't believe that old Holmes isn't with us no more and these lames are. Now if you would please, tell these bitch ass nigga's amongst us to step so we can get back to business. I'm dying to hear what this sick ass cat Billy D had to say."

"Don't worry he will continue to live through us," Roc whispered, so only Boggy could hear before turning to the rest of the room and stating, "Thank you everyone for showing your respects. But if you're not a part of my immediate family I must now ask you to leave. The rest of you meet me in the basement in five minutes...for the game as we presently know it, has changed." Roc pulled M Easy off to the side and said, "This cat Billy D. may be untrustworthy, I need you to have the Wiz run this name giving me the information and research on it, yesterday!"

"I'm on it, in ten minutes you will know everything about this clown from where he was born to who will ride for him."

"Great, but make it five," Roc demanded then approached his mother with open arms kissing her on cheek questioning, "How you holding up pretty girl?"

"I'm fine dear. Being black on this earth for sixty some years has allowed me to witness a lot of great men pass in my days. Even though there was some that deserved to go, I believe after your father's murder my heart just became numb to the reality of death. So you just make sure you're okay love and give your mind the time it needs to nurse back to good health; because you have to be on point when it comes to dealing with Billy D and I believe Mr. Holmes would want it that way," Mrs. Miller answered. Roc watched his mother's lips slowly connect with his as a little smirk crept from the corners of her mouth as she departed. The smiled forced Roc to wonder if she knew about Mr. Holmes' plan and was she in on it from the very beginning. His body shook to get rid of the chilling parts of the

19

Legend of Billy D. But being permitted only to hear part of it, Roc's blood started to boil with anticipation for tonight when he would continue to learn the rest of the details about the man whose name many were afraid to mention. "Thanks again Mr. Holmes I'll never forget you old head. The pawn has been pushed and I have now gained control of the center of the board...against Billy D just as you planned," Roc whispered with a smile as he headed toward the basement to join his soldiers and get his own game plan air tight. He knew undoubtedly that this match would only be won by whoever made the least mistakes. Roc reached the door of the basement but paused, replaying his philosophy of what unexpectedly occurred moment's ago in the car.

As Billy D's words ended and the cold wickedness that was within his eyes slowly faded, Roc continued to watch his every movement while his mind deliberated on what he'd just heard, witnessed, and now thought about the man he knew would surely try to kill him once Todd and the rest of the corporation were finished. Roc smiled in the reminiscence of his mentor amongst receiving this much needed gift, because only Mr. Holmes knew his true weakness of needing to understand the past of his enemy so that Roc could feel that he had the ability to stop them from reaching their future. Roc mulled over Mr. Holmes' words back when he was only 14 years of age as he gripped the handle of his father's 22 pistol and pointed it out the window of an abandon building aimed on the brother of the first man he ever killed in a robbery. Although Roc was young, and his face showed a mask of hardship while his trigger finger held firm, Mr. Holmes could still sense his fear and pressed, "Go ahead and finish what you started Roc, I know he has done nothing more then possess the blood of a man you murdered but in the rules of life we live... that's enough. One day he may follow the nature of man and avenge his loved ones death. Now end this chapter!" Roc's finger tightened around the trigger then paused. He asked, "What's his name?"

"Dead man, now put a period behind it." Mr. Holmes insisted. Roc took a deep breath and adjusted his aim to the

man's head, inquiring, *"What if he has a half brother some where?"*

"I'm sure he doesn't," Mr. Holmes said as he lowered Roc's gun hand down from the window. *"What's with all the questions?"*

"O.G I know you mean right by me but my dad said everything in life is about information and research... he's the information now I must do the research."

"Ok, if you must."

Roc could still see the look of disappointment on Mr. Holmes face as he removed the man's rap sheet from his inner jacket pocket handing it to him, *"Here kid, but there's not always going to be a sheet to go with your target because some people's pasts are so secretive that only your enemy will know the answer. Then what will you do...let him kill you?"*

"I don't know."

"You'll figure it out, you're a natural. All you got to do is get close enough to listen." Roc's smile widened with pride for his mentor as he opened the door, whispering, "I'm close enough and I'm going to listen to every word...once again it's on!"

3

A few yards away, unaware to many, Detective Michael and undercover officer Dell from 39th station parked on Roc's mother's block in a tinted Charger. Detective Michael rotated his personal amplified listening device trying to reconnect to Roc's voice. "Damn it! He was getting deep, whatever's going down Dell, it's big and I'm not just saying it this time I really mean it. But with this cheap piece of shit I lost him again. Wait, someone's coming out from the back of the house. Look, ain't that the crazy bastard Mohammed?"

"Yes that's the maniac, do you want to go after him?" Dell questioned as him observed Mohammed jimmying open a car door. "No because whatever's going on in there is big and he's just a small part of it."

"Well, keep trying to hear something," undercover Officer Dell insisted.

"No, who are we fooling? There is no way anyone can bring a man of Roc's status to justice with any devices you can buy online, we need the big stuff."

"Yes, but to do that we will need Detective Brian and are you sure we can trust him again?"

"You know Dell, to be honest I don't know who the fuck I can trust but I'll do anything to get this bastard." Det. Michael wanted Roc and anybody that was connected to him so badly he could taste it. For years, the Philadelphia police department wanted Roc, but there was no success until Det. Michael and his partner Det. Rayfield were able to bring Roc's second in command along with Haffee his instructor, in on a weapon charge.

That would be the moment the detectives' life took a turn for the worse. The first day of their trial, Det. Rayfield mysteriously went missing. There wasn't a doubt in Det. Michael's mind that it was the doing of Roc. Sadly the body of Det. Rayfield reappeared a year to the very day of the start of their intense investigation as if some hidden sign, burned to a crisp lying on the steps of the 39th station. Refusing to give into the pressure, Det. Michael and Det. Brain after an 18 month investigation tracked Roc's personal assassin Mohammed to a basic row home. There, they surrounded him in the midst of his evening prayer. With no sign of an exit, Det. Michael grinned underestimating his opponent when the room suddenly went pitch black. Det. Michael pulled his trigger to the sound of return fire. He awakened the next morning in the hospital to find that Mohammed had gotten away and he had been shot by his new partner Det. Brain. Even with the investigation clearing Det. Brain of any wrong doing, Det. Michael still promised to never trust anyone from now on but his gun. "Call him."

Moments earlier, in the basement full of killers there was dead silence as the vibration of Roc's voice echoed off the sound proof walls. Roc stood emotionless with his arms folded watching the soundless second hand of his Rolex swiftly glided toward the number 12. Reaching it, he gave a nod to M-Easy who stopped the iPad that was playing the recording of Roc reading pages of *"The Art of War"* before clicking on the debugging device that stopped anyone from eavesdropping on their conversation.

"Five minutes of that should be long enough for them pigs to feel they're getting close to putting these wrists in cuffs. Only if they knew that if I were to ever slip, there's no other option than shooting it out. Because I too will die resembling a soldier with mud still fresh on his boots from combat as I deserve."

"Damn Roc where did that come from? First we lose old head. Holmes now you're talking about dying. Fuck that we're going to live forever and I put that on these," Boggy placed his matching Mack 11's onto the cherry Oakwood table moving his sights from Roc to Lil Mac and back. "Cause I'm going to die from cancer or pussy that's the only way the boah Boggy the killer of Philly is going out and the only reason I'm saying that is because some dirty pussy got Al Capone back in the day." Laughter filled the room.

"I wish that was true Boggy but I'm damn sure going to try, and for the record we haven't lost Mr. Holmes, well at least not yet." Roc tossed the letter onto the table for everyone to read saying, "At this dreadful moment, that paper is stronger than any weapon we ever possessed but our minds."

Roc studied the response of each person as their eyes testified to a story that they would never acknowledge while moving over the words of the letter that now dictated their survival. Roc entered into deep thought as his sight stopped on Haffee who was the first to get analyzed. *"Haffee...I see you're prepared to fight, but you have doubt that we can be victorious against such a powerful individual.* Roc's eyes rotated ..... *"Top Dollar I notice you can't wait to see it happen old timer and I know you will be there every step of the way to ensure that I make your old friend and partner, my father, proud..."* Roc continued his silent evaluation moving counter clock wise when his eyes slightly widened. *"Fox, oh shit you're afraid. NayNay, my down ass lady, if I didn't know Lil Mac I would swear that killing turned you on more then he did."* Roc's vision rested on his friend and partner... *"Boggy my ride or die associate, no matter how much money we get, if it's not the front line you're on...you're not there and at this very moment your eyes say this mission will be no different. But there will be change old friend cause after the training with this cat Billy D, I'm going to be right next to you with fresh blood on my hands from anyone that stands in the way of me being what I was bread to be by my father, the true one and only."*

Roc knew why his lil brother was last to be read, *"Lil Mac, you had to be the final one didn't you? But I know you lil brother... it was only so that you could learn the response of everyone else while studying my reaction to their reply. Now you're trying to conceal your own reactions from me. Mac you're good but you still have a lot to learn, just doing that move told me more than what you tried to hide. For one it lets me know you're aware that I'm watching and I can read you. Two, that you did use me as an example to Boggy earlier... but why? The thing I do know is I will never fall in the same hole twice no matter who's digging it."*

Roc grinned as Lil Mac slid the letter back to him avoiding eye contact before addressing his team that in the near future would accept to do what has yet to be done. "A true leader is only as good as the men that follow him and Mr. Holmes knew this, therefore he was able to play us all," Roc confirmed. "Was he really playing us Roc?" Manny questioned, "Or was he just putting us in a position to win, Allah willing?"

"What? Nigga we been winning," Boggy cut in, now not knowing how he really felt about Mr. Holmes after the letter. "That nigga had top game, the kind of fucking cleverness we'll need if we're going to defeat Adrian Cortez or Sunan Kudari because Holmes was smooth enough to play us in our face by using us to kill his old ass to put his son in position just in case we're not good enough. And Roc you know there's more to this shit; we just can't see it yet. So if this training Billy D is talking about is on that level I think you should do it and while you gone, me and *Mr. "We're like family"* here will hold the blocks down." Boggy shot Lil Mac a look that stated if you slip that's your ass, then continued, "The only thing that gets me is how we been around Holmes damn near our whole lives and we didn't sense this shit or even know he had a son."

"I did." The whole room turned to face Top Dollar as he stood to his feet adjusting the black Versace suit on his back until it lay on his frame just right. "Roc may I?"

"The floor is all yours," Roc answered, he's been waiting for the day that Top would take charge without being forced and the moment had arrived. "I knew Holmes had a son and he loved him dearly. So dearly that he thought Todd was above the teaching of the book, which some of you may have heard of, *The Victory of the Mind*. In it, it states that a soldier should be constructed from a deep depressed struggle of any nature then slowly schooled into a man. But Holmes disagreed even though he knew that hardship built a powerful inner passion and drive. He felt that Todd could do the same with a higher education alone."

"So that's what this is all about... who's right or wrong?" asked Lil Mac.

"No it just makes it a little more interesting. It's about who's the very best. Always has been, it's the way of man," answered Top Dollar.

"You're wrong nigga, you wrong," Boggy said, grinning at Lil Mac.

"The Victory of the Mind," Roc repeated with the words automatically flowing from his tongue as if it had an understanding of it's own to show respect, "I have read a few pages on the count of Mr. Holmes. The knowledge that lies within the dept of its spine is indescribable. There was a moment I even witnessed him writing in the interior."

"And so will you, but not until your soul tells you that you have found the next leader to fill your shoes after you're announced as the one," Top Dollar informed.

"That will be me," stated Boggy and Lil Mac simultaneously. The two again made eye contact for third time this evening with hidden messages smuggled beneath the surface.

"Stay in your lane you youngin. You may have killed a few to get your name popping. So now your peers praise you like you're Lil Wayne. But niggas know that Roc's a smoother Jay-z in this game of war who possesses seasons of bodies under his belt that's about to retire. And I'm the new caretaker in charge like Kanye nigga and you are now watching the death throne," Boggy vindictively winked.

Lil Mack staying true to the structure of a gangster when in the region of a enemy quickly decoded Boggy's message thinking, *"You can forget it, the time of you riding on Roc's coat tail is over and the moment he steps down I will be there to place the crown onto my head. What the hell you think I'm here for, to be another man's shadow? That never did sit right with me... did it? Ha –ha,"* Lil Mac laughs to him self while running his hand over the long scar where the colostomy bag once was to remember his own struggle, before putting his attention back on Top Dollar who was speaking about the book that just placed a new spark within Roc. "Whoever will succeed you Roc, you must write down in the book the things you have learned while in power."

"This, in turn will make each person stronger then the leader before them," Roc added seeing Billy D's motive for him more clearly, so he thought.

"Correct. It's said that a slave was the creator of the movement that has us in this room at this very instant with the chance to be one of the most powerful teams in the world. He was brought from Africa and held in captivity for 11 years until he began to fight back."

"You mean he was like a male Harriet Tubman?" Fox questioned.

"No, much more," Top Dollar informed, "He was a man that understood the weaknesses and strong points of life and proceeded to write them, leaving behind to his student his sorrow, pain, mistakes and corrections as well as many other chronicles ending at the moment with Billy D's. There is only one original book which has the account of every man who ever touched it, Roc as you follow the book you will learn that you will have to make copies, but only giving people what they need to know to satisfy your interest at the moment."

"Oh shit, the chronicles!" Roc quickly got up from his seat rechecking his Rolex seeing that it was only 9:00 and began to relax knowing that his meeting with Billy D wasn't until 11:30.

"Roc is everything alright?" Top Dollar asked.

"Yes, it's just that in every war I have fought I only had to trust my own instincts to win. Now I have to trust this cat Billy D to teach me just to have a chance to fight."

"The two things I know about Billy D is that if he thinks you're the one he will teach you everything he knows."

"And the other thing Top?"

"Oh, if he doesn't... he will kill you."

"Then I guess we'll see at 11:30," Roc affirmed fearlessly, being at the point in his life that he was willing to face whatever it had in store for him.

"What's at 11:30?"

"My meeting with Billy D..."

"Oh there's one other thing I remember about Billy D."

"And what's that?"

"That you're late."

"Impossible I h—"

"R1 there's a black Maybach approaching the block, do you copy?" a voice erupted from the walkie talkie on Roc's hip.

"Roc, you of all people should know there's nothing that's impossible. He's always hours ahead of his watch," Top Dollar grinned knowing that his mentor Billy D hadn't lost a step.

27

"R1 here, I need you to stall him," Roc screamed through the speaker smiling, also thinking *"I would have done the same move if I was dealing with the enemy,"* before demanding to his team "Triangle offence." Roc then questioned, "M Easy, the Wiz's report?"

"It's right here. The target is in his mid sixties, last known address was a few blocks from here on Lincoln St. in the heart of North Philly. Mohammed just left there and reported that the house is empty but still owned by the target."

"Is there any possible threat?" Roc asked out of routine because he had already finished reading the report and previously thought of a way to get around the four treacherous men who's names where written in it. "Yes, for years our target was a loner; mostly hanging around women until he met this one man here who may give us a fight. I'm not saying anything big, but a fight. And I know you Roc; if a person will throw a rock back at us you want to know about it. These three men may follow up after his death."

"That Billy D is slick!" Roc commented before asking his next question, "Do we have anybody on our team that's connected to any of these men?"

"Yes, Boggy and it's him," M-Easy's finger slammed on the name of one of the dangerous men in the city. Roc laughed saying, "They say killers hang together…the sad part is this one has to die first before the rest. Boggy!" Roc yelled into the walkie talkie. Boggy appeared shortly after with his gun gripped tighten questioning, "Who you want me to kill?"

"God, am I getting that predictable?"

"Only when your game face is on cause your particular opinion is death," Boggy informed.

"Well I'll have to change that," Roc answered with certainty, "But not today, I need you to get all over him… yesterday!" Roc slid the name across the table. Boggy recognizing it said "Will do, but tonight I got my man's party."

"Then you'll just have to cancel but a party sounds like a great idea; M-Easy make the calls needed and have Mohammed find me the weakest link."

Roc walked down his mother's steps at 9:15pm heading toward Billy D's Maybach as he watched NayNay through his peripheral vision rotating the barrel of her gun along with Foxy's every movement from the rooftop on the opposite side of the street. Foxy opened the back door as Roc got comfortable behind the tinted window in the plush interior. "The boss is on the move," stated Haffee sliding the stolen Lexus into drive. Billy D greeted Roc with a firm a hand shake and a smiled, "Glad to see you could make it."

"I don't think I had much of a choice. Not only that but I'm dying to hear the rest of your story."

"Nice selection of words, but enough about me for the moment lets converse about you."

"Ok let's start with where are you taking me?"

"That's easy, to the meeting with Todd. You have to know your enemy first before you kill him or have my Intel let me down?" Roc remained silent with a poker face while speaking only to him self, *"How does he know; did Holmes tell him?"*

Billy D interrupted his thoughts. "I know you're asking yourself how can I be familiar with your shortcomings and who leaked it. Don't worry there's not a drip in your corporation. I got the information the same way I know we're being followed in the triangle offence formation, or how that pretty young girl would have killed poor old Foxy if she would have made a wrong move...all by having the same weakness as you. The need of doing the research about every move and decisions I make. Earlier today when I dropped you off I used your need to know of my past by feeding you only enough of my history until I could memorized every color and model of car on your block. If you can recall the night working postman who was kissing his wife when we pulled up?"

"Mr. Thomson, he drives a new Grand Prix ... which is easy to get," Roc said fully understanding when he had been out smarted.

"Yes, and if you look out the back window closely you will see one right behind your hit man in the white Lexus. All that was needed was a postal hat and your lookout with the walkie talkie let him right on the block without notifying you."

"Then he just sits there and watches my team get in place... damn I'm slipping!"

"Kid you're not slipping; you're just no match for me. But you are the one!"

"No match?" Roc's hand promptly eased onto the 9mm hidden in his suit jacket lining, and then paused. "Did you say I'm the one?"

"Yes"

"You believe, so this means we won't have to fight to the death this evening?"

"No, what I'm going to do is teach you to be the best. You will eventually be fighting the battle of your life against these men once I'm done preparing you. Although they are not as skilled as you, they do have the mind state to destroy you."

"That just means I will have to destroy them first!" Roc stated as his eyes slowly faded to black.

"Wrong! What I'm about to teach you is the true definition of leadership; using their mind state to destroy themselves while wanting to do it."

"Like Mr. Holmes did with me?"

"Yes, but please don't feel any less of your self. This ability has been used on some of the most powerful men in society. How do you think we got a black president today? It was the ability to make the other side believe now was the prefect time to prove the blacks didn't have what it takes to run this country if they give it to him in it's worst condition," Billy D smiled. "Oh, watch how we fool them. Yes it looks bad now but "O" is going to get it together. The key is to take control of a person's life that has power over the lives of others."

"That way I will be in command of many, through only one person and my worker could never put me into the picture because they wouldn't know my face."

"Do you know why?"

"Because I will be working from behind the mask," Roc envisioned.

"Correct, I will show you how to shield your feelings, reasons, emotions and actions to the point where it well become so automatic that your mind will even conceal its actions from your own heart so there won't be any emotional attachment involved. You can take control of any one life for good or bad whatever the reason you choose but it has to be done from a distance."

"Excuse me Billy D dear," Foxy's voice interrupted from the interior speaker. "We're here."

"And the white Lexus?" Billy D inquired.

"I lost it four blocks back."

"Great, now the fun can begin."

The two exited the vehicle and to Roc's surprise they were at his club, Soldi II. The name stood for money in Italian. To be present in his club, customers needed to have deep pockets. This place was for the top ballers only. Charging fifty dollars just to get through the doors, there wasn't another club around like it in the whole city. The place was packed as usual as on looker watched as three bodyguards aggressively fought their way to the front. "Right this way Mr. Miller, your elevator to your office awaits you."

The two well dressed bosses were led to a side entrance where double stainless steel doors closed behind them. Stepping out into Roc's lavish main office they spotted Gizelle, Roc's wife sitting at his desk with her arms folded looking pretty and mad. "Roc, where have you been? This place is overcrowded and it's not even twelve o'clock yet. You've got too much going on. There's the welcome home party for Boggy's home boy, which I just found out about and Boggy can't even come to it because now everyone thinks he is in jail thanks to you. One can only think of what you're putting together." Gizelle shook her head for the senseless act but she still loved her husband to death. "Then there's the men you flew in from the ATL making it rain and shit like they're the new BMF, that are about to get robbed. Didn't you tell them it's a recession in Philly? These nigga's out here will put a hole in there head for one third of that."

"Ok, then go to the safe and get them some more money to throw. I dare someone to disrespect my place. I swear I'll make it a living hell for him and everyone they know."

"Alright love," Gizelle said while heading for the door, cutting her argument short at the sight of the seriousness in her husband eyes. "Oh and before I forget…there's two fellows that said they had a meeting with you tonight. At the moment they're in the V.I.P. while Raja is running their background check. But if

31

anything comes back off the mark you will not have to worry about a meeting." Roc's vision raced over the several surveillance cameras until he spotted Todd sipping on a glass of wine thinking, *"He looks relaxed for a man whose life is on a count down."* Roc picked up the phone demanding, "Raja the two men in section 16, bring them to me and don't let them out of your sight for a second." Raja responded, "In motion."

Shortly after, the door opened to Roc's office with Todd and Cyrus walking in. "Gentleman please have a seat and make yourself comfortable," Roc said, positioned in a large leather chair.

"Why the fuck would I do that?" questioned a displeased Todd, who wanted this very moment to set the record straight. "None of you before thought I was good enough to sit at the table with you. And now that my father has given his life to prove you wrong, you want me to get relaxed…I'll be damned. The only reason I'm allowing you in my presence at the moment is because I need you now as much as you need me because you own the streets and I need to learn the struggle of the book. And I just happen to run one of the biggest companies in several cities and you need to be a businessman. Once that's complete you will kill Adrian Cortez and the other I will take to his grave the same way they did my father… then I will come for you."

"Why wait?" Roc said, without hesitation removing the 9 mm from his waistline while throwing a hard right jab at Todd's chin to give him space to fire. Todd, educated in the art of Judo stared at Roc with confidence as he slipped the sharp jab aimed for his face and retrieved his own gun. Simultaneously, they raised their weapons both now looking down the barrel of a gun. Billy D and Cyrus looked on as each man's finger inched back on his trigger knowing within seconds that someone would be dead. "That's enough," Billy D yelled. "There will be time for that in the future if you're both successful."

"Oh I will be successful," Todd declared.

"I believe you both have the power to win," Cyrus stated. "But you must learn more if you're going to do so."

"Anyone can put up a fight and shortly meet their maker," Billy D cut in. "The skill ya'll receive will take years but in the end if you can gain the knowledge of it, there will be nothing to stop you but you...."

"Boom - Boom!" a hard knock connected to Roc's door with Raja rushing in behind it. "Roc come quick, they're shooting outside the club." Roc couldn't believe his ears as his eyes moved back in front of the surveillance cameras spotting a man diving for a gun and coming up firing. "How dare you disrespect me!" Roc yelled. Billy D, seeing the fire dance in his eyes whispered into Roc's ear, "I notice your anger; your lesson must start now, let's go!" A hidden diabolical grin appeared on Roc's face. "You will rest in peace old head."

4

*T*wo years later inside Club Soldi II, Roc waited in his freshly redesigned office with a new mature swagger about himself as he observed Isha exiting from the V.I.P section until she enter the lady's room out of sight of his surveillance cameras. She stood in the bathroom mirror looking at her reflection as she said to her self, "I got to stop doing this shit." Isha was built as close to perfection as you could get. God blessed her in all the right places and with just the correct size. Her breasts were a lovely C cup with a back side that stood so far out you could witness it from the front. Tonight she had on a pair of tight black Gucci pants that fit her shape to a tee. The Eli Tahari blouse that she wore brought out her beautiful green eyes and smooth caramel complexion. Isha was fixing her makeup when Kim came through the door.

"Isha you better get back out there girl. That nigga Pretty Tony is on you hard. He even sent me in here to get you, like you're going to leave with someone else," said Kim. "He doesn't have to worry about that, I'm going to give him everything he wants tonight," Isha replied. "I know you are. You see all that ice them niggas is wearing? I know I'm going to sex the shit out of that nigga Simon tonight and when I'm done, it's a wrap for the rest of them bitches." Kim and Isha laughed then gave each other a high five. "So come on and get your ass out that mirror so these niggas don't get away cause you know how I do," shouted Kim as she held the bathroom door open.

Isha applied a little more lip stick, "Girl, go ahead. I'm coming. This champagne is running right through me." Isha walked into one of the stalls and locked the door. She made sure Kim was gone before pulling out her cell phone and dialed. "Hello?" a male voice answered.

"Yeah it's me, Soldi II in 20 minutes."

"I got you."

Isha checked herself one last time in the mirror before she stepped out.

She knew club Soldi II was owned by a man named Roc who was one of the most respected and dangerous players in the city and for that her lust grew. The club had three different levels with V.I.P. rooms on every floor. The closer your room was to the top, the more it cost. Within V.I.P. Pretty Tony accompanied by his men Martin, Simon, and Mall sat in the third section on top floor. They usually obtained the very best but tonight that wasn't possible due to 50 Cent being back in the city.

Gizelle sent over two bottles of Rozay on the house for the inconvenience. The scent of Purple Haze filled the room as females walked around half naked trying to get their attention and a whole lot more. Pretty Tony exhaled the blunt smoke and said, "Kim where's your friend at? I know she's fine and all but you see these women in here trying to get at the kid. I might have to take a rain check."

"Come on; don't even play yourself like that. You've been after my girl for months, now she's finally gets the heart to come out here with you and now you're going to try and play her? If you do, she will never talk to you again," explained Kim.

Isha stepped off of the glass elevator still under Roc's close observation as she made heads turn as always. The way she moved her hips gave her the sexiest walk without even trying. Men called out to her as she past by. *"Damn baby where you going?"*

"Hold up love, let me holla at you for a second sexy." Isha had heard it all before and most of the time she never stopped, but to keep from being rude she would wave or just smile. Isha entered the V.I.P. room with more then half of the eyes in the club on her as she started to make her way to Pretty Tony's table when a handsome 6'6" 220 lb. dark skinned man dressed in a three button Bernard Moore suit stepped in her path. "Excuse me beautiful, my name is Claude. I don't usually stop women in clubs because of my status but your beauty called to my soul."

"There goes my girl right there Pretty Tony. So if you want a rain check it's okay because there's always someone trying to play fair if you don't want to." Kim was talking to Pretty Tony but was looking Simon straight in the eye while sliding her hand between his legs. "Damn that's you, Tony? Man, she is major. If you don't want that, let me know and I'll

35

pay for that ass off the top!" Mall assured. Pretty Tony turned around to see Isha, as beautiful as the first time he saw her.

The N.B.A. player was refusing to let Isha by. "Kim, go get your girl and get that nigga out of her face," Pretty Tony demanded. "Don't worry Tony, Isha is a big girl. She knows how to respect who she's with." As the words left Kim's mouth, Isha excused herself and made her way to the table where bottles of Rozay and plates of lobster sat everywhere. Pretty Tony pulled a soft leather black and gold chair out for Isha to sit in while he took in her beauty from behind. He thought about the things he would do to her tonight before he spoke, "Isha you can't keep me waiting like that. I was starting to miss you already."

Isha leaned over and put her hand on Pretty Tony's leg as she whispered in his ear. "I'm sorry baby; I will make sure it doesn't happen again…I promise." Pretty Tony instantly became rock hard from the light brushes of Isha's tongue across the inside of his ear. Isha knew she had him right where she wanted. Pretty Tony stood to his feet pulling out a bank roll of hundred dollar bills and dropped half of it on the table. "Well players, the night has been lovely and I hate to end it like this but I got to do what I got to do." Pretty Tony helped Isha out of her chair and then gave her his arm. "Damn Tony, it's only a little after one and you're leaving already?" asked Mall.

"Come on Mall; make sure you don't ever wear that suit again. It doesn't look good on you."

"Nigga this is 2013 Prada, nigga's ain't going to witness this until next year. What you talking about?"

"Fuck Prada, I'm talking about that hater suit you got on."

The whole table burst out in laughter while saying their goodbyes. Kim pulled Isha to the side and demanded, "Girl make sure you call me in the morning and tell me everything. I need to know if he can lay that pipe as good as he looks."

"Kim you need to stop," Isha replied.

Outside, a low whisper could be heard, "Here they come now," said Rich, speaking with the two other men in the all black Tahoe as Pretty Tony and Isha entered the parking lot. Pretty Tony pushed the button on his remote control to unlock his pearl white Cadillac Escalade. He made the sunroof ease back while

36

he pulled out into the night traffic. The soft voice of Mary J. Blidge's *'Sweet Thing'* caressed the air while he laid his mack down.

"Honey, can I ask you a question?"

"Yes Pretty Tony, you can ask me anything."

"Why did it have to take this long for me to have you in my presence, is it something that I did or is it that you just don't like pretty people?" Tony moved his hand up and down Isha's thigh as he talked.

"Tony please, it has nothing to do with you at all. Look at you, you're handsome and caring, you know what you want out of life and you go get it. A woman couldn't ask for anything more in a man. It's me...I have my own baggage, like my situation with Dro. I tried to tell him it's over but he won't listen. Even though he's been locked up for two years, his friends still ride for him. It was to the point where I felt like I'm caged in. They watched me as I would go places and I didn't want to bring you into that after everything that happened with you and Dro in the past." Pretty Tony gripped the steering wheel tightly... just the mention of Dro's name gave him a headache. He thought back to the very first time he laid eyes on Isha...

~ • ~ • ~ • ~ • ~

She was alone waiting for her food at the counter in Max's Deli while Pretty Tony and his men sat in the booth at the Eagle Bar watching the Sixer's game. The two places were connected so Pretty Tony didn't have to walk far as he stopped right behind Isha. He was so close that he lightly brushed up against her firm backside. Isha smoothly slid out from in front of him and turned to face him. With a fake smile she said, "I would watch that if I were you. I don't think my man Dro would like that."

"Where is he at sexy?" Pretty Tony asked. Isha pointed out to a red Range Rover where Dro sat watching the movie *"300."* Pretty Tony had heard the name Dro before but he knew that the little man in the S.U.V. couldn't be the same one he heard so many stories about. So he pushed on while taking Isha's smile as an invitation, "Well he should know better than to leave someone as gorgeous as you alone for even a second." Isha looked over Pretty Tony's shoulder and saw Dro now watching

37

them. She knew Dro had a relaxed temper but when it was awakened someone was sure to pay.

"Excuse me miss, your order is ready," the lady said from behind the counter. The words were music to Isha's ears. She turned and quickly paid for her food, said bye to Pretty Tony and walked to the door. Just then, Pretty Tony grabbed her arm, "How are you just going to leave like that without giving me your name and number?" Isha tried to pull back before Dro saw the contact but he was already out of the truck, "Please...please let me go," Isha begged. "So that's a no I can't g..." At that moment a voice interrupted saying, "Come on man, and ease up off of her." Isha closed her eyes at the sound of Dro's voice knowing shit was about to hit the fan. Dro stood at 5'9" and 190 lbs. His frame was very muscular from all the training he was doing to become a pro boxer. Dro had a light complexion and hazel eyes; you would have thought that he and Isha were brother and sister. Pretty Tony released Isha's hand and said, "Little man, you better handcuff something as fine as she is before a real nigga like myself gets that up off you."

Pretty Tony was standing in Dro's face when Dro stuck his hand out to put distance between the two. "Yeah you right," Dro replied sarcastically, while opening the door and proceeding to walk out with Isha in the lead. "Nigga, don't you ever turn your back on me," Pretty Tony shouted, grabbing the back of Dro's shoulder. The people in the deli saw that something was about to go down and rushed off in different directions to get out of the way. Mall was the first person from Pretty Tony's team to see the situation unfold.

"Yo, I know that's not Tony...oh shit it is, come on," Mall said, pushing away from the table. On contact Dro spun around pushing Pretty Tony's hand off of his body. Then he threw a left hook that landed hard to Pretty Tony's body, followed by a quick over hand right to the chin. Tony's body fell hard to the floor in the deli. Dro stood over top of him and stated, "Understand that this didn't have anything to do with my girl. I'm a man and I don't fight over women, there are too many ways to go about that, believe me. Plus they'll do what they want anyway, but don't you ever put your hands on a man!"

"Back the fuck away from him before I drop your ass," screamed Simon. Dro looked up to see Simon with a Mack 11 automatic in his right hand and two men at his side. Dro smiled before he stepped away from Pretty Tony. "Stay put Champ and don't move," Simon demanded as Mall was helping Pretty Tony up off the ground. Dro looked Simon right in the eyes with the same sly grin and walked straight out the door to his truck and pulled off not knowing that someone was right behind him.

"Why didn't you shoot him?" Pretty Tony asked.

"Do you even know who that was?"

"I don't care who that clown was, he put his hands on me and that's a violation. He must get it!" Tony Screamed.

"Nah, you're lucky you didn't get it without question, that cat was packing heat," Simon replied.

"Damn, you talk like that nigga's God or something," Pretty Tony stated.

"No there is only one God and he's up there but down here, one of the next best things is Dro when it comes to putting that work in. He moves with them A-One cats and they don't play games. You read the newspaper; they've been beating bodies all over the city. It's four of them; him, Rell, Bo and Gotti. I heard they've been riding together since they were five. They're on that clean up the street shit so you had to be on some bull shit. It's because the man moves with integrity and respect that nobody is running to testify against them. You saw the nigga didn't budge at the sight of the Mack, he just smiled at me," Simon tried to explain.

"Fuck that nigga, they bleed just like us," replied Pretty Tony while he was putting a hundred dollars on the bar before he walked out.

A week later Pretty Tony pulled up to his baby mom Amanda's house on 42nd Street knowing that he was God's gift to women. He blew his horn and after waiting five minutes he knew something was wrong. Pretty Tony walked to the front door and rang the bell, yet there was still no response. "Where the hell is this girl at?" He walked around the house to find the back door unlocked. Inside, he checked every room he past when a noise coming from Amanda's bedroom got his attention. The door was cracked a little and Pretty Tony couldn't believe his

39

eyes. Amanda was on all four taking it roughly from the back as Dro pumped away. Pretty Tony looked back and forth from Amanda to Dro, in shock. Dro was staring back at him when their eyes met. Dro winked and then kissed Amanda on her back. Instantly, Pretty Tony charged through the door.

Dro was on his feet within seconds and grabbed his gun off of the night stand, holding it level with Pretty Tony's chest stopping him in his tracks. "Make a move and your finish. See, the problem is, you playa's now a days can't stand what ya'll do. You open doors but you don't want nobody to come in. And I must say, it is lovely inside," Dro smiled glancing at Amanda then looked back at Pretty Tony who's face became red as he inched a little closer to Dro. "Go ahead. I don't want to, but if you take another step and I'm going to blow your head off," Dro said very calmly sliding back into his clothes and walked out. Dro hit the last step outside coming off of the porch as the front door busted open with Pretty Tony following it. "Dro if you didn't have that gun, I swear I would smash your little ass."

"I know you would," Dro said pulling his gun from his waistband. He pushed the button on the side to release the clip as it fell to the grass. Then he cocked it making the bullet come flying out of the 45 mm chamber. "As you were saying?" Tony rushed down the step while Amanda pulled at his arm, "Tony stop please...I'm sorry. He didn't mean anything to me. I love you." The words were too late; Pretty Tony wanted blood and it showed. Dro's level of respect for Pretty Tony shot up a little because any man that wanted to see him in hand to hand combat had to have heart. Dro just hoped that his cause for fighting wasn't Amanda's love box.

Pretty Tony threw two strong punches at Dro's head. Dro knocked the first one down with his right hand and slipped the other. Dro quickly back pedaled in a half circle when Pretty Tony hastily turned to face him. Dro then slammed a solid right hook to the body sending Pretty Tony down on one knee. He then stared into Tony's eyes stating, "It's not you, it's your mouth," before placing a sharp blow to Pretty Tony's temple knocking him out cold.

~ • ~ • ~ • ~ • ~

"Tony...Tony," Isha shouted to bring him out of his nightmare and back to reality. Ever since that very day Pretty Tony swore that he'd get back at Dro and tonight was only the second part of his plan. "My bad baby, I was out there in deep thought. You know how it is; I got to keep my mind on my money. So what were you saying?"

"You passed the hotel parking lot." Pretty Tony circled the block and pulled in the parking lot of the Comfort Inn at the Philadelphia airport.

"I know I was playing hard to get but I really like you Pretty Tony. I can't wait to get to know you better." Isha leaned over and kissed Pretty Tony softly on the lips and with each touch the kiss became more passionate. Tony worked one hand on Isha's breast when her cell phone vibrated. She eased her way apart to open her Dolce & Gabbana purse. Pretty Tony released his seat belt, when his driver side window blew into pieces.

Ricky reached through and placed his 44 magnum to the side of Pretty Tony's face. "Open the fucking door," Ricky demanded as Isha screamed at the top of her lungs. The touch of the cold steel made Pretty Tony fight back his pride to resist, "Okay, okay I'm opening the door. Don't shoot." The second masked man ran to the other side of the truck pulling Isha out and tossing her roughly down to the cement. The third, who was the quiet one out of the three, slammed Tony up against the side of their Tahoe. He then placed the stainless steel hand cuff's tightly around Pretty Tony's wrists. "Wooooo," Tony bucked wildly trying to fight his way free while refusing to be thrown into the back of the truck. 'BOC' "Aaaaahhhh!" the pain from the gun shot ran through Pretty Tony's body as he crashed to the ground. "All right, all right," Tony said. "I know all right...or the next shot will be in your brain," Ricky yelled. Isha closed her eyes and hoped they didn't kill her next. The men swiftly picked Pretty Tony up and tossed him into the back of their truck. Then they all jumped in and pulled off, leaving her face down in the parking lot as Mohammed watched her fake tears in the shadows from a distance

41

5

*T*he next morning at her three story house located in South Philadelphia, Isha rested on her queen sized bed. She worked for a law firm nearby as a paralegal assistant. It was 7:45 am as she dreamt of Dro's firm hands caressing her body as they touched lips just when the bedroom door flew open and two people rushed toward her bed. One by one they leaped on top of the cover. Dashon put his hand around Isha's neck as he kissed her on the cheek. Rasheed, the shy one laid his head on her chest and was just happy to be next to her. "Mommy, get up," Dashon demanded. Isha tried to fight being brought back to reality as Dro's next kiss touched her inner thigh. Isha knew where this was leading; it was like she could actually feel Dro lying against her body. But this was a battle she would not be winning. Dashon started jumping up and down making Isha and Rasheed's body bounce. "Get up Mommy; it's time to go see Daddy." Isha quickly opened her eyes to check the clock on the night stand, making sure she had not overslept.

"Yaaayyy...mommy's up!" Seeing that it was only ten minutes before eight, Isha closed her eyes again knowing she still could get an hour of rest before getting ready. Dashon wasn't going to be refused. "Mommy, I want some pancakes," "And I want some crunch berries," the two requested. Isha just smiled at her two beautiful children and then started to get out of bed when her mother, Mrs. Smallwood entered the room, "Now you two little knuckle heads come on out of there and let your mother have her rest. She has a long ride ahead of her today."

"But grandma I want some pancakes."

"Ya'll just come on and I'm going to make what ever my two little strong men want."

"Grandma I'm the strongest," Dashon claimed.

"No you're not," replied Rasheed.

"Yes I am," Dashon shouted as he pushed Rasheed in the back of the head, sending him flying out into the hallway. "Stop that boy! One day Rasheed is going to beat your ass if you keep messing with him," stated Mrs. Smallwood. She softly closed the door and said to Isha, "Baby go ahead and get your rest. I'm going to get them ready to go."

Isha knew she didn't have to say anything because she and her mother had been through so much together. When they didn't have anything, they had each other. Still Isha moved her lips to say, "Thanks mom, I love you." Mrs. Smallwood was 5'7" and 155 lbs with the same beauty that she'd blessed Isha with. She was an ex-Black Panther like Isha's father Nate and that is how they met. The love that they shared for helping black people brought them together. In the 60's and early 70's they did their best to help the black community but when Elijah Mohammed died in 1975 things fell apart, making Mr. and Mrs. Smallwood no strangers to the struggle and hardships; they'd even served Fed time together. She did five years in Danbury Federal Correctional Institution for women, charged with conspiring to commit bank robbery and attempted murder. Nate received thirty years along with his other partner, Ace.

The fact that Mrs. Smallwood found out that she was three months pregnant with Isha after being in jail for two months, crushed Nate's heart. He begged her to point the finger at him so that Isha would not be born in a cage controlled by his oppressor but Mrs. Smallwood would not hear of it. She was taught to always stand by her man. At the time of her incarceration, she was twenty-three and refused to let Nate stand alone. After their lost of trial, with Billy D and Mr. Holmes present, Mrs. Smallwood held her head high when the judge handed down her sentence. Tears rolled down Nate's face as he stood next to her, but not a signal tears were for him. Nate knew that at anytime the black man would be sacrificed but not his love and child. Before the judge could finish, Nate screamed out, "I swear on my unborn that you're about to put in a cage, when the black man's turn comes to be the oppressor, you'll be more then oppressed and if that takes too long I will kill you myself for this you cracker or I'll be laying in a box for trying."

Back then, in the feds a person only had to do 1/3 of their time and women could keep their child in jail with them until they became two years of age. Mrs. Smallwood used every one of those seven hundred and thirty days to build with Isha.

Once released, Mrs. Smallwood with the help of Mr. Holmes rented a two bedroom apartment on 123rd in Harlem.

By the age of thirteen, Isha's bond with her father was amazing after all the letters that they shared. Nate told her about the ways of this cold world and how nobody would give her anything. If she wanted something, she would have to get it herself. Nate returned home and put all the knowledge he had into action with her. Together they would ride for hours and talk about everything. One day Nate drove down 125th in his new money green Buick with Isha riding shot gun. "Baby, as your Dad you know you're always going to be my Lil' Princess. "I know Daddy."

"But I'm also aware of the fact that you're becoming a woman," Nate said after coming home from work and called Isha, "Anita," which was her mother's first name. He couldn't believe it when she turned around and saw that it was his little girl and she was built like a grown woman.

Now he knew this talk was needed as he continued, "As you become a woman, boys are going to start to come into the picture."

"I don't talk to boys Daddy, they stink."

"I know but you will and when you do, I'm going to be over protective because you're my baby. I know that I can't tell you who or how to love, but hopefully I can show you what to look for when you find a person that you may like. Baby make sure he looks into your pretty eyes when he speaks to you. It shows that he has confidence and a person can't make it in this world without that. Please make sure he loves you for the person you are inside and not just your beauty."

"Dad when I meet someone I am going to make sure that we love each other as much as you and Mommy do if not more I promise." At that moment Nate was so proud of Isha that he couldn't take the smile off of his face as he wrapped his arms around her shoulders and pulled her closer. "I love you princess."

"I love you too, Daddy."

6

Nate witnessed first hand what the crack epidemic in the 80's was doing to Harlem as him and his men tried hard to clean up the streets but in the end it was either the drug dealers or the drugs themselves that were taking his team out. The neighborhood became so bad that Nate decided to make one more move from his past life and then move his family to Philly. Isha was now sixteen and enrolling into a South Philly High School in the 10th grade.

Isha had a few boyfriends but never anything serious and up until that day she had only been kissed once. That didn't mean the boys didn't try. Isha had men of all ages and sizes coming onto her. With her 32-26-34 frame, who would have thought that she was still a teenager? Isha was so used to being hit on that she came up with many ways to let people down without being rude. Her first day of school was also another student's first day, a girl named Kim.

Though they were in all the same classes, Isha didn't like the girl because she was loud and always asked a million questions. *"Girl where'd you get that, girl you got a boyfriend cuz my friend likes you, when we go to lunch can I sit with you?"* Isha never said no, so they began eating lunch together and before she knew it, three months had passed.

One day a couple of girls waited on Isha to pay for her meal and as she headed back to the table, someone whispered, "Here she comes now, Shy." When Isha went to sit down, the girls surrounded her with Shy in the front standing in Isha's face. "Bitch, what were you doing talking to my man at your locker today?"

"I wasn't talking to your man, he was talking to me and I would like it if you would tell him to stop because I don't like him," Isha replied. People saw that a brawl was about to take place and called out, "Fight!" as they formed a circle surrounding Isha and the group of girls.

Isha was aware that she was out numbered and didn't care. Nate taught her everything she needed to know to survive. She didn't want any trouble but was willing to show that she was a good learner. "I know you're not trying to clown me, because I'm not having that, ho!" said Shy. Isha just shook her head and tried to walk away then Shy's partner blocked her path. "It's not going down like that, you better get out of my girl's way, bitch!" Kim demanded, grabbing the girl by the hair. They started to fight and Isha smacked Shy across the face, then threw a right hand jab that connected in the same spot like she were Ali himself. Shy fell back against the lunch table, holding her face. Isha tried to rush Shy when her other partner grabbed a fist full of Isha's ponytail that laid down her back.

The girl was pulling so hard that Isha thought her brain might come flying out of her head. She fought in pain and moved her body around until her face lay at the girls' knee. Isha spit a razor out of her mouth into her hand and swung it hard and deep into the girl's calf. "*Aaaaahhhh my leg!*" The girl screamed as the pain pierced through her, forcing her to release Isha's hair. The girl fell to the floor with blood pouring down her leg. Shy picked up a tray and was about to throw it when Dro grabbed it out of her hand.

"Now you lovely girls got to stop all this fighting shit before ya'll mess up one of those pretty faces," Dro said as he and three of his friends; Bo, Gotti, and Rell broke up the fight. The crowd was disappointed at Dro's actions but being one of the toughest people in the school when he talked, people listened.

Dro walked over and stood next to Isha and spoke in a low tone, "Drop it in my hand." She just looked at him as the school security guards raided the cafeteria. "Drop it now or you're going to jail for assault," Dro said to Isha again. She let the razor fall into his hands. He then smoothly placed his arm around her waist and made his way to the exit. Isha stopped next to Shy, who was still holding her face and said, "Harlem bitch! And don't you ever forget it!"

"Yeah, don't you forget," Kim added.

"Kim, you're from North Philly," said Shy.

"So, she said don't lose your damn memory and that's what it is."

Isha's heart was beating a mile a minute as a security guard approached them. "Dro, what's going on here?"

"Man I don't know, why don't you do your job and go see," Dro answered, squeezing Isha tightly as they departed. This was the start of their togetherness but no one could have dictated it would turn out like this...

The clock now read 8:50 and Isha just finished getting dressed when she heard the sound of her Beyonce ring tone. Seeing that it was Kim, she sent it straight to voicemail. She knew that she had to tell Kim something but now was not the time. Isha walked into the kitchen to see her beautiful family having an enjoyable breakfast and asked her self, *"Why do I keep doing this?"*

"Mommy look, Grandma made us blueberry pancakes."

"That's nice Dashon, but what did Mommy tell you about talking with your mouth full?"

"Ease up on my little soldier princess and come give me my morning sugar," said Nate. Isha walked around the table and kissed her mother, "Good morning mom," and then her father. "Now, that's better princess." Nate put down his morning paper and pushed his chair back to get a better look at his only child.

"Turn around and let me see you. Where are you going, looking so beautiful?"

"It's Saturday, you know I'm going to see my baby today."

Just the thought of his young revolutionary made Nate proud. He instantly dug in his pocket and pulled out some money. "Give Dro this and tell him that right after we talked on Monday, I took care of that. It's a done deal, and young lady what did I tell you about being out so late? You know there are killers out there in them streets. I'm telling you, my heart isn't as good as it used to be and you got me up all night worrying about you. I'm going to have a heart attack one of these days."

"Aaawww, I'm sorry Daddy but I'm a big girl and I can take care of myself," Isha said taking her morning meds to relax from the tension of the night before. "Plus we have to get going so I'll talk to you when I get back," Isha said in her best baby voice. Nate was in great health after getting out of jail. He maintained to Workout, as ran two miles when he got up at 5 am every morning before hitting the gym, ending with three rounds of pad work with Matty.

7

*I*nside the thick walls of Graterford penitentiary Dro stepped out of cell 128 on D block with a razor sharp hair cut that made his jet black curls look like silk. His brown D.O.C. uniform was tailored and pressed meticulously as usual. His footwear only consisted of one thing; Jordan's and he owned over twenty pair. D block housed 830 inmates on its tier with only two Correctional Officers to keep the order, if there were any. This block, like the other four was a world within itself and there wasn't anything you couldn't get for a price.

"Yo, get your faggot ass away from my cell!" yelled Dro. "Ain't nobody by your cell," said Apple, speaking like a female as he and another gay guy nicknamed She-he stood three cells down. "Man, what did I say? I don't want to see you gay ass niggas anywhere around my cell. Take that shit on the other side of the tier or at least thirty cells down. If I catch you standing anywhere around this end I'm going to put something up in you alright," Dro said as he flashed his 10 inch knife which still had blood on it from his last victim. The two gay men took off down the tier with one of them saying, "Oh no he didn't!"

Dro hated gays more then he hated cowards, and he couldn't stand them, for he saw how down low brothers were killing their families. They would be in prison sleeping with men without using protection, then go to their visits or back out into the world and be with their wives and kissing their kids. Dro shook his head as he walked down the tier that was about half a city block long, thinking to himself how he got trapped in this nightmare he was now living. His vision was so clearly as if it was only a moment ago and not two years.

~ • ~ • ~ • ~ • ~

"Throw the jab, that's right. Jab your way out. Stop dropping your right hand," yelled Matty who was Dro's corner man and trainer. "Time" Dro exited the ring slowly, exhausted from the ten rounds of sparring.

"Put some life in your step kiddo, the biggest fight of your life is in three weeks and after we win that, what is it?" Matty asked.

"The title fight."

"What?"

"The title fight!"

"So act like it. I want you to give a hundred and ten percent at all times, not only in the ring. I need that same effort and determination when you're on your way to the gym, running, hitting the bag or if it's when you're just walking out the ring."

Matty leaned in and whispered the rest in Dro's ear, "You're going to be the next champion of the world and that's without question in my eye, but the only person that can stop you is you. I'm telling you this because I love you. Dro, we have come a long way together. When you first came in here you didn't know the difference between your right cross and an uppercut. To top it off you were in those damn streets, but we worked through it. I kept you out of the street and you kept me out of the old folk's home."

They both laughed. "Seriously kiddo, I'm saying this because you have two lovely children and a wife who loves you. You worked hard for this big pay off that you're about to get but those streets can smell money like the white man can smell oil and they both don't give a damn what they have to do to get it. So stay on your square kiddo and stay away from those two right there because they don't mean you any good." Matty looked in the direction of Bo and Gotti as they waited on Dro. "Don't worry about them Matty they're just some old friends that stopped by to say what's up."

"Old friends? Where were they when you were cleaning up Pop's gym at night just so that you could train there after you worked an eight hour shift? Where were they when you were fighting at the Blue Horizon or when you were fighting people 30 lbs over your weight class for a thousand dollars to split it three ways? Now you're about to get three hundred thousand per fight and we've got old friends. Just watch yourself kiddo, that's all I'm saying. Now hit the shower."

Dro hit the shower and then stepped out into the warm crisp Friday night air. "Damn nigga, you was always nice with

49

the hands but you look like Mike Tyson in there the way you were fucking that boy around the ring," said Gotti giving Dro a handshake and half hug and then Bo did the same.

"You know how we get down. I can't let anybody out shine me in my own gym. So what brings Batman and Robin all the way down here, where it's cold at?"

"Man we're down here because of Rell."

"Rell? What's up with him? Is he alright, did he get the money I just sent him... man what is it?"

The silence was killing Dro inside. They all were best friends for over twenty years but him and Rell were closer to each other, like Bo and Gotti. When Dro ran the streets they did whatever it took to make a dollar, from robbery, selling drugs, kidnapping, and shootouts. You name it, they did it until they met Mr. Nate and he showed them how to get money with respect and clean up the streets. There were many times Dro had close calls with his life and Rell was always on time to bail him out. Six months after Dro stopped moving in the streets to focus on his boxing career; Rell caught his first case for attempted murder and couldn't beat it. His was sentence to 10 to 20 years.

Being that Dro was still willing to keep his connections to the street, he quickly found out with the help of Mr. Nate, where the man whose testimony put Rell away was staying. He was secretly tucked away in protective custody. Two weeks after finding the right location, the man with a great deal force signed the affidavit stating that he lied and that the police forced him to say Rell shot him. That was over three years ago and they were waiting for Rell's appeal to go through. Dro never got over the fact that he wasn't there for Rell when he needed him the most, so if there was anything he could do now to help, he did it without question.

"Ya'll clowns still aren't saying shit." Five minutes had passed and neither Gotti nor Bo said what was going on with Rell. They just sat on the top of the black Lincoln Navigator with 26 inch shoes, blowing haze smoke from the blunt in rotation when suddenly the back door of the Lincoln opened up and a pretty dark skinned woman exited wiping her mouth with the back of her hand. Dro knew he was slipping; he had been out there for over twenty minutes and never thought to check his surroundings. That would have never happened when he was in the game. What he saw next was even more unbelievable.

"Nigga, if you would just shut up, I would have been out." Seeing the man's face, Dro rushed to the truck. The man fought to keep his pants from falling down as Dro lifted him up in the air. "Damn man; let me button my pants up first. You know a pretty young dame just took care of the kid." Dro released the man as a tear of joy slowly rolled down his face. "Rell, when did you get home and why didn't anyone tell me?" Dro looked back at Bo and Gotti. "Don't look at them; I said I didn't want you to know because of this right here." Rell pointed to Dro's left cheek.

"You're all teary eyed and shit. I know how you get, wanting to throw a party and I needed to slide into town as quietly as possible to find out a few things before people know I've touched down."

"What type of things, you all right...do you need me?" Dro asked.

"I'll holla at you later on that. Your boy's home and we're going out to do it big, you with me? Because it can't be a home coming if you're not coming," Rell replied.

"I wouldn't have it any other way," Dro smiled.

Two hours later they all met up at Soldi II dressed to impress, the only way the A-One team knew how to do it. They were sitting in a lovely back end booth table on the second floor. Soldi II was packed as usual with three live performers on stage. "Now this is what I'm talking about. There's ass everywhere up in here. By the end of the night I might have three kids," Bo said jokingly. "Yeah it's on up in here. I'm glad you decided to come here instead of your favorite spot, Touches," said Gotti while watching some light skinned woman bend over and touch her toes before she dropped it like it was hot.

"Yeah, what made you want to come here Rell?" Dro asked.

"When I came down to the county jail on writ for my appeal I met this good dude and he said he owned a piece of this place and when I made it out he would make sure they rolled out the red carpet," Rell stated.

51

"Where is this good dude at now because this is alright but it sure ain't no damn red carpet?" said Bo as they all laughed.

"I think he's still in the county. One night he was just gone. I believe they moved him to another block or snuck him out," answered Rell.

"What's he in for because the man I hear owns this place is bigger than a made man. They say he's the sole reason the streets are getting so much money in this recession. The word is that his connection shorted him a few keys so he killed them and took all their coke and money. Now he buys straight from the Columbians," Gotti explained.

"I think they were in on a gun charge," Rell answered.

"There were two of them. Man, get the fuck out of here, two niggas on a single gun charge and they didn't make bail? Something's fishy with that, if they did they wouldn't be there but your man owns a piece of this...be real," said Gotti who was unconvinced.

"Man, I'm telling you these dudes are real. Ya'll know if anybody could pick out a major player in a room full of nickel and dime hustlers, it's me. While I was in the county I didn't want for anything, ya'll kept me straight because real people do real things. But main man had the jail on smash and me being who I am, he put me right in. The man got his ear to the street. It's like he knows everything. You know those same cats that did me dirty and I asked you about Gotti."

"Yeah I'm still working on finding those clowns."

"Excuse me, my name is Gizelle, I'm the manager here at Soldi II and I believe a mistake has been made," the attractive woman interrupted.

"A mistake?"

"Yes, your name is Rell correct? You're a friend of Boggy?"

"Yes."

"Well, please follow me."

As they got up from the table, Bo started to grab the two bottles of champagne off ice when Gizelle stopped him, "Sir, you can leave those there. From now on you can order whatever it is that you'd like; bottles of Moet, Rozay, or lobster...it's on the house."

Gizelle was looking lovely as ever while she led them to the top V.I.P. floor. Soldi II had a section taped off with Rell's name on it. As soon as Gizelle removed the tape, six barely dressed women came and stood at the entrance, two black females, two white and two Asian. "They're for you all. Do as you wish. Through those doors down there on the left where the two body guards are standing, is a room with a shower and top of the line clothing if you should need to change. If there is anything else that you need please don't hesitate to ask and oh, before I forget, Boggy said to tell you it will always be two faces one tear."

Dro couldn't keep his eyes off Gizelle as she left. He had a thing for beautiful women and she was most definitely a natural beauty. The V.I.P. room was packed with top hustlers, basketball players, rappers and pimps. "What did I tell you? I don't mess with no suckers; I only deal with the real."

"Rell all you kept saying was my man this, my man that. If you would have said it was ride or die Boggy, there wouldn't have been anymore rap. Everybody knows the killer of Philly," said Bo who was being led away by a woman he'd been watching. They went to a back room followed by Gotti who was with a woman that had an ass that would put Buffy to shame. More women came but Dro and Rell refused, they needed the time to talk alone.

"Dro, watch those niggas dog, I'm telling you."

"Watch who?"

"Who the hell do you think I'm talking about? Bo and Gotti, those niggas smiles aren't real. You haven't been in the street so you don't have a clue and I didn't want you to come back so I didn't say anything. Not only that but it was late when it all went down and I didn't have it all together until Boggy's people helped me put the connection in place. One day Gotti called me and said he had this big score on some shake down cat in West Philly. Mind you, you're not there so by now I'm doing my own thing on the side alone, just a step up from hand to hand. I wasn't hurting for anything though so if the numbers weren't right, I was going to pass. Gotti says it could be anywhere from 400 to over a half a million in cash and drugs and I would get a bigger piece if I put up the buy money, which is fifty grand, so I was like, bet. We staked out the cat, some Italian dude named Cesar for three weeks we watched his every move. By then we had him down pack, so it was time to make the direct connect; the way to do that was..."

"By moving with one of the people that are being shook down," Dro interrupted. "I guess you haven't been retired that long."

"Some things you can't forget no matter what you try to do."

"Well the person that was being shook down is right there, just like Boggy said he would be," Rell pointed to Pretty Tony who was sitting in the corner section with about ten people surrounding him, listening to him talk. "Rell I know you weren't putting no work in with that lame ass nigga. While you were gone I had to teach him an old lesson about when you disrespect someone, always make sure you can't be disrespected."

"I knew he was a clown but it was Gotti's call. So we all posted up at the top of the old graveyard in North Philly. It was me, Bo, Gotti, Pretty Tony and two of his people. At the time it was winter. Caesar rolled up in a brand new Audi A8 and got out with two big greasy haired, pizza eating dudes and started talking big shit."

He said, "Hey Tony let me speak to you for a minute over here."

"It's okay Caesar, this is all family. Whatever you got to say you can say in front of them."

"Really it don't matter, you know them extra keys you said you couldn't handle. I'm led to believe different so they'll be an extra 30 in this shipment with a little rise in price and don't make me wait any longer than usual because we wouldn't want to mess up this pretty snow out here. It's all nice and white and we want to leave it like that. Red would just mess it up."

"Caesar then pulled off and five minutes later the shipment arrived and the shit was pure butter. A week later Pretty Tony made the drop of 600 G's to the same two slick haired cats. After the drop, me, Bo and Gotti followed their van to the same small row house that we tailed Cesar to on several occasions so the exit routine was already set. Bo hit the front after me and Gotti rushed through the back. I picked the lock and then slid into the kitchen. I could hear Cesar talking to about four other people saying, "I told you that nigger Tony was a work horse, you just got to ride them niggers hard into the ground and as soon as they can't race anymore you kill them...bang, bang. Two in the back of the fucking head and forget about it."

They started laughing. "I bent down low in the doorway that led to the living room and pointed the infrared on my black Mack 11 to the side of Cesar's head and pulled the trigger. The bullet made contact blowing off the side of his face. One of his body guards yelled "What the hell?" And before anything else could be said I put two hot slugs into his chest. Gotti entered the living room with a chrome 45 automatic in each hand. He shot the first man to his left with four shots while simultaneously taking out another body guard. The last man stood still shaking as hot piss rolled down his leg."

Gotti questioned him, "Are you ready for hell, just say the word and I'll send you there." Bo watched from the window with his guns ready in case something went wrong. I let him in after making sure the house was clear. The man told us where the rest of the money was. In the end we were looking at 25 bricks, $800,000 in cash. The mark sat in the middle of the three of us when Gotti said, "Look here you pasta eating bastard. You did what I asked so I'm going to let you live but the next time I see your face, I'm going to put two bullets in it."

"Thank you I promise you'll never see my face again."

"Bang, bang...two in the back of the fucking head," said Bo in his best Godfather voice as he quickly pulled the trigger twice, killing the man. "Now let's get out of here."

"We put the money in the back of Gotti's Tahoe and raced for the exit. The escape time was ten minutes flat. I was behind the wheel making record time with only two blocks before hitting the highway when a Ford Explorer sat parked in the middle of the alley, stopping our escape. We could hear the cops in the distance as the police scanner reported they were about three blocks away heading in the opposite direction but that still wasn't good enough for me. I hit the horn, at the two men talking. The one standing said, "Yo, let them get by," the driver looked back at the truck and replied, "Fuck them, they can get by when I'm done." I could read his lips so I cocked my gun

55

back and jumped out. I approached with my gun tucked behind my leg. The man standing must have felt something wasn't right because when we made eye contact he just walked off. When I made it to the driver's side window I was looking into the face of a masked man with a 12 gage shot gun pointed at my head. The rest happened so fast I couldn't believe it. Another black Explorer raced down the alley blocking us in.

Knowing that it was a set up, I wasn't going out like a sucker. I grabbed my gun tightly then kicked off the truck to give myself room to level my gun off when, "Drop it or I'm going to put your thoughts on the window," was called out.

I closed my eyes, mad at myself as I let the gun hit the ground like a cold sucker while another masked man's gun rested on the back of my head. They pulled Gotti and Bo out of the truck and tied us all up and dropped us off in an abandoned field. At first I was thinking that they just caught us slipping but there were too many loose ends. Like how did they know we were going to be there unless they'd been watching us as we watched Cesar? The only ones that knew were Bo and Gotti, they're blood so I was like fuck it. But two months later I'm at the car wash getting the Benz a bath and I see him.

"See who?" asked Dro slowly as he was feeling good after taking down a bottle of red Moet.

"Allen, he was the one talking to the driver. This cat was there washing a brand new 300 C with 23" shoes on it. I grabbed my gun and called Mark, my little cousin over to get the Benz."

"Mark... the wild young boy that was in the paper for the shooting?" Dro questioned.

"Yeah he's going up state for it but that's my heart. He just wouldn't listen when I was trying to tell him there's another way to get money out here, but he just loved the plan street life.

Anyway, Allen was sitting on the driver's side with his door open blasting his system on some young boy shit. I put the burner to his face, "Move the fuck over." I pulled off in his shit and this clown started crying like a woman. He was talking about, "I didn't have anything to do with it I swear." I asked him who did and he said he didn't know. I pushed down harder on the gas and let one fly, 'BOOM,' he started screaming, "All right

56

it was Pretty Tony. He said he had a smooth move working on the inside. I just had to supply him with a few young cats that busted their guns and he'll handle the rest."

Allen cried as blood ran out his gut, "So who was the inside man that crossed me, Bo or Gotti," I asked as my body became hot with anger. "I don't know...it's the one who states it is what it is all the time." Man what the hell are you talking about? "One day I was with Pretty Tony and he stopped at a dope house he had doing numbers and the dude was there. That's when he inquired about the plan and all he kept saying was *it is what it is*."

"So if you saw him, could you identify him?"

"No they were in another room. Yo, I got to get to a hospital before I die...please."

"You don't have to worry about that."

Dro I swore I killed him, I hit him at close range three times in the chest, that nigga had nine lives. I left him in a Wal-Mart parking lot to die after I got the rims from the car. The next morning the cops kicked my door in before I could see that nigga but I got his ass tonight and he's going to tell me which one of my so called partners for life sold me out for a dollar."

"Rell, you know I'm with you. You already know how we do," said Dro. "We cry together, we die together, we chill together, we kill together," they both said in unison.

"I know big brother, that's how we used to do it. But while I was in that cage all I did was read about how my main man could be the next big champion and that's what you're going to be. These streets aren't yours anymore and to be truthful I wish I had the heart to leave when you did," Rell confessed.

"You can still get out Rell and you know I'll help you."

"It's too late family, my soul has tasted blood, it's calling for it and I'm going to give it some starting with that nigga Pretty Tony and anyone else that has something to do with crossing me. If I had to pick which one it was, I would say..."

"You two niggas still here with all that ass they're giving away behind those doors? It's off the chain in this joint; your man Boggy is doing it so big. I had to take my hat off to him," said Bo as he threw an unused condom on the table making everyone laugh. They all partied for a few hours while Rell watched Pretty Tony's every step. He noticed that he was about to exit and quickly rose to his feet saying, "It's getting late fellas and I have to make some moves early in the day, so ya'll go ahead and enjoy yourselves. I'll catch ya'll in the AM."

"Come on with all that, we came together so we're leaving together," said Dro who could feel that something wasn't right.

Outside of club Soldi II, was almost as crowded as the inside with people and cars moving everywhere. Rell, refusing to be denied swiftly slid his Mac 10 automatic out of his waistline and down beside his leg when he saw that Pretty Tony was now talking with two women. He then checked his surroundings; Bo was off to the left talking to some female that looked like Mary J., while Gotti went to get the Jeep from the parking valet. Dro pulled up to Rell's side so nobody could hear and said, "Man what are you going to do with all these people out here?"

"I'm going to show you right now. If you forgot how to put that work in, this is going to be a flashback you won't forget."

"Rell stop, you don't..." Dro pause in mid sentence seeing that it was too late. Rell was already half way across the street waiting on a row of cars to pass. There were three cars to go before Rell would make someone pay for the nights he had to sleep with his knife taped to his chest to fight off killers in order to keep his manhood. As the last two cars approached, Rell aimed his vision at Pretty Tony and Pretty Tony at him. "Yeah, nod your head because it's me pretty boy and you're going to tell me what I want to hear or you're going bye- bye," Rell said to himself.

The last car was an old Ford Taurus that came to a stop right in front of Rell's path. "Hey my man, can you tell me how to get to the highway from here?" the driver of the car asked. "Just make a right at the first light, and then bang a hard left and you're right there."

"Thanks because I'm going to need it after I kill your nosey ass." *"BOOM-BOOM-BOOM,"* E-Money let off three shots, two of which hit Rell in his chest. The power from E-Money's desert eagle knocked Rell off his feet. E-Money

58

quickly placed the car in park to finish off the job he was paid to do.

Dro heard the shots and looked in time to see Rell fall on his back a few feet away. "Nooooo!!!" Dro yelled and took off running as two men with guns jumped out of the car. "E-Money handle your business and I'll get this brave heart ass nigga," said Dirty Rich as he took aim at Dro's head and fired. Rell saw E-Money approaching and looked for his gun that was no longer in his hand. He saw it several feet away. Rell fought the pain in his chest to get to the gun and then it was gone. "What the fuck?"

Dro could feel the bullet whiz by his head as he dove in the air landing not far from where Rell laid gripping the gun and came up firing. "Boc-Boc-Boc-Boc," Dro's first two shots were way off but on the next ones he started to get his groove back, hitting Dirty Rich in the neck. The following shot told him he was all the way there. The slug crashed dead center into Dirty Rich's forehead. "Sweet dreams," Dro was busting on E-Money before Rich's body hit the ground, "Boc-Boc-Boc," E-Money bit down hard on his lip until tasted blood then he squeezed the trigger "BOOM-BOOM," hitting Dro in the leg forcing him to one knee. Dro tried to put the feeling of the pain out of his mind as he got back up on both feet. He returned fire, "Boc-Boc-Boc," E-Money raced to his car realizing he was now out gunned when a bullet slammed into his shoulder. Bo's next shot was aimed at E-Money's head but before he could fire, E-Money was racing down the street.

"Rell, come on talk to me man. Come on...we cry together we die together. You can't leave me!" Dro screamed. "Dro, come on man we have to get up out of here. The cops will be here any minute," Bo shouted, hearing the sound of sirens getting closer by the second. Gotti's jeep came to a stop right beside Dro, "Get the hell in the truck now. The cops are right behind me." Bo grabbed Dro by the arm. "No I'm not letting him die in these streets alone like this. The same way I wouldn't let you die like this," Dro protested.

"Ya'll got to do something, they're right here." Bo looked up to see the black and white police car turn onto the block. "I'm sorry Dro," Bo ran and jumped in the truck as Gotti hit the gas forcing the truck passed 90mph down the block. Five

59

police officers surrounded Dro and Rell with their guns drawn. "Drop the weapon now." Dro was about to go out in a blaze of bullets when Rell, with the last drop of physical strength grabbed his slowly rising gun arm. Dro looked at Rell to see why he stopped him but Rell's face was now the face of Rasheed and Dashon. "Don't they need you?" said Rell. Dro dropped the gun slowly as he raised his head at the same speed, feeling an odd sense on his left; Dro turned and locked eyes with Roc who was standing in the distance at the edge of the crowd.

~ • ~ • ~ • ~ • ~

The press was having a field day with Dro's case. The front page of the C.V. Daily Scoop read, *"Up and coming Boxer tired of fighting. Local Boxer Jonas Brown was involved in a shootout outside of Club Soldi II Friday that left one person dead and another in I.C.U. on life support. Three others suffered minor injuries. Story continued on page four."* When the smoke cleared, Dro was charged with third degree murder. Many people spoke up for Dro at his sentencing hearing and being that it was his first offense; the judge sentenced him to 2 ½ - 4 years in prison.

"You okay, man?" asked old man Scotty, snapping Dro out of his daze as a tear descended down his face for Rell. "Nah, I'm good Scotty I was just thinking about finishing the ending of a story told to me by a good friend when the time is right. Why, what's up?"

"They have been calling you for a visit for the last ten minutes and your team is looking for you too. I don't know why you spend so much of your time helping those two crazy young boys anyway," Scotty spat, speaking of Mark and Forty. Dro answered, "Because they were my man's peoples, now they have become mine." Scotty just shook his head as Dro walked off.

8

Dro entered the visiting room and gave C.O. Dickenson a nod, then walked right by him without stopping like other inmates had to. The reason being was that Dro was now back to the person he tried so hard not to become again...a killer. Dro continued to walk around the visiting room that was split into two sections. The first side was an area where children could play amongst themselves while the adults could have a lovely visit with a little less distraction.

Dro proceeded to move down the back wall and cut through the open door to get on the other side where anything went for a hundred dollars and the C.O. wouldn't see anything. Dro thought he was at an x-rated movie as he watched a woman with her dress pulled half way up, riding her man like a pro. She threw her hips into every bounce while she gripped the front legs of the chair for support, thinking she saw Dro as well as another man whose girls face was in his lap watching when it became evident they were, she started putting on a show that they would never forget.

She picked up speed while releasing the chair and placing one hand on her large breast and the other on her clit. Locking eyes with Dro, she licked her lips before removing the two fingers from her clit and putting them into her mouth. "And what the hell do you think you're doing?" Dro turned around and was face to face with Isha. "Aawww baby that wasn't about nothing, I was looking to see if you were sitting back here," Dro replied. "Don't play with me Dro, you know I would never disrespect myself like that and if it wasn't about anything, why is man-man awoke?" Isha yelled while pointing to Dro's rock hard manhood. Isha rushed back to her seat without saying another word.

Before Dro could make it half way to his seat, Dashon and Rasheed raced full speed across the visiting room floor, "Daddy, Daddy." A big smile appeared on Dro's face as he scooped them up into his arms. "How are my two big men doing?" Dro asked.

"Fine," they both yelled.

61

"Daddy I made the honor roll again."

"That's great Rasheed but how do you keep getting a B- in gym?"

"I don't know."

"It's okay Ras, I'm always going to love you no matter what you do or get on your report card. You hear me big man?"

"I love you too Daddy."

"I see you're not saying anything about your grades Dashon, when I opened up your report card all I saw were C's and D's."

"Dad it wasn't my fault. The kids keep messing with me in my class and when I…"

"Boy I'm the one that taught you how to throw that right hand jab since you were five. Is it still fast?" Dro asked his son Dashon.

"Like lightening," he replied.

"Let me see." Dashon jumped out of his seat and threw two left jabs and a quick right. Dro gave him a high five.

"Moving that fast I know there is no one messing with my next champ, am I right?"

"You're right, Dad."

"So you're going to stop playing around in class and bring those grades up right? Or I'm going to tell your mom to stop letting you go to the gym with Mr. Nate, you hear me?"

"Yes Dad, I'm sorry and I'm going to get all A's next time."

"You better."

Dro talked with the kids for almost two hours, until they couldn't take any more of watching the other kids play so they took off to participate too. Isha still hadn't spoken. "Damn baby girl, I know you're not going to sit there and reject the love I have for you."

"Dro don't try to sweet talk me, I saw the way you were looking at that dirty ho in there disrespecting herself."

"Isha that was a look of lust from an animal let out of his cage, looking at meat he hasn't eating in years. That look could never have anything to do with what we have. What we have is love, respect, and understanding for each other. Your pain is my pain and you're hurting me right now."

"How am I hurting you Dro?" Isha quickly questioned.

Dro licked his lips real slow before answering, "You're not hurting me love."

"I thought so!"

"No, you're hurting my soul; its begging for your kiss. If you listen you can hear it calling for you to be in my arms so that it can be reconnected with its mate. Baby I have never asked you to disrespect yourself and I never will because I don't mess with those kind of woman. If they disrespect themselves they will disrespect me and I will never tolerate that." Isha got up and sat on Dro's lap and wrapped her arms around his neck. "Dro you know I would never disrespect you." They kissed with intensity until they both needed air.

"Dro I miss you so much, it's like these last six months are taking forever to come to an end."

"Don't worry my sweetness; I'll be there soon to ease your pain."

"I know baby, and so does everyone else. I'm getting calls from Gotti, Bo, the newspaper; Molly Weiss of in these mean streets and so many other people at home. Bo dropped some more money off for you and every time Gotti sees me with the kids he tries to buy the store for them."

"Isha how many times do I have to tell you not to take anything from them niggas? The only reason I'm still talking to them is because when I get out they will give me answers," Dro explained.

"But baby they're like family," Isha insisted.

"Family my ass! Family doesn't leave family in the street to die; you and I are family do you understand?"

"But ya'll were like brothers and all they do is ask about you."

"Isha what did I say?" Dro interjected firmly.

"Okay Dro. But I still think it's sad." Isha shook her head hoping that in time she could change Dro's mind.

"Is everything a go for when Mark comes home?"

"Yeah it is all in place, I talked to Rell's sister Thursday and she said that the parole people came by the apartment we got and gave their approval." Just then an announcement came from

C.O. Dickenson, "Excuse me ladies and gentlemen, will you please wrap it up, visiting hours are now over."

"Oh baby, I meant to tell you...Daddy said he handled that and Matty said he didn't understand your letter but he has the fight lined up for you anyway and that you have had enough time off," said Isha.

"Don't worry about anything Isha, there are going to be things you will not understand about me, but believe me I have everything under control. Now let me feel those sexy lips of yours." Dro hugged his family saying his good-byes and right before he walked through the door he turned and said, "Oh, before I forget...stay out of places like Soldi II late at night. I hear it's not safe." Isha's heart almost stopped. So many thoughts were running through her mind at once; *how much did he know, did he know anything and if so how did he find out? He couldn't possibly know everything or I would be dead. I have to get a hold of myself.* "Baby I was just..." Isha realized that Dro had already left before she could explain anything.

9

*D*ro moved through block D, heading to his cell when he felt eyes were watching him. He thoroughly checked out his surroundings as he moved past people looking for any sign of danger. Dro had a lot of connections with people and made a few friends but in a prison where people die every day, you can never be too sure of anyone. As he approached his cell he understood his feelings and decided to play along.

Dro watched the two open cell doors on his right before he spoke. "What did I tell you two stinking ass fagots about being on this tier?" Dro yelled out. One of the guys named She-he said, "I don't know who you think you are but my man told us to wait here and what are we going to do Apple?"

"Wait here," replied Apple. They both stood there just past the second open door that was three cells apart from each other. "We'll see, after I knock one of you punk's faces off if you still want to wait there." Dro headed straight at them, passing his cell while grabbing for his knife as he neared the first open door when he found he didn't have it because he'd stash it for his visit.

"It's too late to stop now," Dro thought to himself as he kept walking and looked into the open cell. He couldn't see in because a sheet hung from a string on a pole inside in order to block the view of eye hustling. The moment he turned his head a knife came protruding through the sheet, missing him by inches and pierced another inmate in the back. The other inmates that witnessed the brutal act of violence walked off minding their own business as if nothing happened. The sheet fell to the floor as a muscular man about 6'1, 250 lbs rushed out the cell with a sock that contained one of the locks used for lockers in it swinging it recklessly at Dro's head. The man pulled his arm all the way back with every swing to maximize the force of the blow. "I'm going to teach you nigga's to start keeping your mouth shut around this joint," said Q.

Dro ducked just in time as the bottom of the lock touched the tip of his head. Dro was back in his boxing stance doing a light bounce, changing pressure from one foot to the

65

other. He faked a left jab at Q's head that made him swing the lock when it passed Dro's shoulder. He threw a three piece combination to Q's rib that made Q scream with each contact *"Aaaahhh,"* as the punches forced him down to one knee. "Oh my God he's killing him, somebody help!" screamed Apple. Before Q could get back to his feet, Dro bounced to the side and let go a powerful left upper cut to his chin followed by a sharp overhand right to Q's eye.

Everything went black for Q as he fell flat on his back. "Nah, there's no sleeping out here," Dro said as he sat down on Q's chest with his feet holding Q's head still while he punched him in the face repeatedly. "That boy is going to catch a body," said Scotty as he dipped off. Q was brought out of the stars of unconsciousness by the force of Dro's right hand and then put back out by his left hand.

"Yo, back the fuck up," said Mark.

"You heard my man, move out the damn way, where they at Scotty?" asked Forty. Scotty dipped his head in the direction of the Mayhem, and then stepped off not wanting to be a part of any repercussions. He only told them what took place because he liked Dro and he didn't want Dro to kill Q and end up with a life sentence like him self.

The crowd of people parted like the Red Sea when Mark grabbed Apple from behind his back at the waist as Apple screamed, "Oh no please" and kicked his feet that were now airborne. Mark, with his 6'2" 280 lb build slammed Apple back over his shoulder firmly as he came crashing down to the cement floor, cracking Apple's shoulder blade. She-he tried to run when Forty gripped him with one hand around his skinny neck, "Where do you think you're nasty ass is off to?" She-he stuttered, "I-I-I-I." Forty's grip was so tight that She-he could barely breathe let alone answer him. "Aaahhhhh," tears rolled down She-he's face as Forty pulled out the 10 inch jailhouse knife made of steel from a day room chair and said, "You want to be a woman, now bleed like one." Forty stuck it in his ribs and She-he's feet gave out. He then threw She-he into the open cell and then slammed the door.

"One time, one time," an inmate called out who was giving everyone a warning that the Correctional Officers were

66

coming. Forty could see them in the distance and they were moving quickly, "Lets go, time to move," Forty told Mark, pulling his arm. Mark let his construction Timb's find Apples face one more time before he helped Forty peel Dro off of Q.

"Q, that pimping shit is over. I want you and the rest of these damn freaks off this block by count time or I'm going to put ya'll in a box under the jail," Dro promised before he slowly walked off. Far in the background Scotty shook his head, knowing that Dro was no longer the soft spoken man that walked into these prison walls two years ago and if he made it to the street, there was going to be hell to pay.

10

On Roc's number two block the flow of money move rapidly back and forth as Isha sat behind the wheel of her white Lexus ES300 waiting on Kim. She was still trying to put the pieces together about what Dro knew. "I have to slow down, it's been fun but my baby is ready to come home so it's a wrap." Isha said to herself while just a few feet away on a row house step sat Lil Mac accompanied by his two personal body guards ordered by Roc. They posted a short distance away on each side of him looking for anything that seemed out of placed. Lil Mac knew he didn't need them but Roc insisted. "Come on Roc, you can't be serious about these two? I can guard my damn self."

"I hear you but if I'm going to give you and Boggy the power to take over all twenty of my blocks and to supply the top fifty major players until I learn the influence of my own mask, they must come with it. Not only that but there's someone I need you to look after in my absence, but be easy on him, he isn't cut from the same clothe as us."

"Okay but I still think it's corny." Lil Mac stated.

"I know it, but when I started to touch that kind of money out here I had them." Roc said speaking of his past personal body guards that he sadly had to kill. He continued, "The same way I know muthafucka's don't care how many people we kill before them. If they're hungry and we're eating, they'll still try anyone of us. The same way if every drug dealer in the world went to jail today. A crack head is still going to want that hard gray shit. The same way I couldn't stop you from wanting this life style no matter how hard I tried."

"But Roc you don't understa---" Lil Mac started to explain when Roc planted a single finger in the air that demanded a unseen respect as Roc smiled saying, "don't, It's life Mac, the facts are harsh but real."

"So when will you be back in charge because I don't know how long I can keep working with Boggy?" Lil Mac questioned.

"That's just it; we don't know who really killed Omar Kadafi, we just have the knowledge of the pawn that pulled the trigger."

"Roc what the fuck is you talking about?"

Roc looked at his watch and grinned and said, "That you don't have to be seen to be in control and if I was you I'd answer that."

"Answer wha-?" *BBBrrrr-BBBrrr,* the vibration of Lil Mac's phone interrupted his words as Roc laughed. "That's my man Tywan... he just got back in town. Take care of him alright; he's a young boss in training." Roc smiled walking away, "Damn I'm getting good. Oh and Mac you don't have to like working with Boggy all you need to know is that he won't turn you in and that he would die first in any confrontation before letting anyone on his shift down. Who can ask for anything more..."

Lil Mac stood to his feet at the sight of a disagreement taking place in the middle of the block as he continued to think of how much Roc had changed in the past 24 months. In the short amount of time Lil Mac witnessed the ambition to be the best grow within Roc. As Roc followed the close instructions of Billy D by purchasing failed businesses and turning them around for a profit, he attended school by day and worked at Holmes' construction company by night, quickly transforming himself from a top criminal into a genuine businessman.

Lil Mac ended his thoughts as he neared the dispute to hear Todd's voice now stripped of its proper English that it once held proudly saying, "Listen man, fuck what you're talking about. If I'm the one that's Betty Crockering this shit, the work is going to come back short."

"And how the hell is that if you're telling me it's all pure coke?" asked a mad youngin. "Nigga if you can add I'll tell you. It's because I take one gram off of every seven nigga, that's four off of every ounce, which leaves you a hundred and fourteen in a quarter pound and you're copping two keys. So that's eighteen hundred and twenty four grams you get nigga. If you want the whole two thousand you got to cook it up it your damn self because my kitchen costs. I know Obama just passed that new crack law but damn, it's not that sweet," Todd stated hastily

69

checked the repeated beep on his phone. Lil Mac who became closer could tell by the bulge on the young man's hip that he was packing enough fire power to kill an elephant as he became angrier by each passing second. "Why did Roc tell me to look after this clown?" Lil Mac said speaking of Todd while slowing down his speed. Todd continued, "Dog, what you still standing there for with your face twisted up? This is a drug strip not Starbuck's, cop and roll."

"You Bitch ass nigga, what you just say?"

"I said get the fuck off of the block, you think you can question me because these cats really don't mess with me out here and they couldn't care less if you killed me with that 45 automatic on your hip and the 9mm in the center of your back. The funny thing is that I'll literally kick you in the face, knock you out and take your gun off your hip before you hit the ground. Then I'll let my quiet Russian friend across the street have a pleasurable time killing you real fucking slow." The youngin looked Todd up and down and said, "Get the fuc-" as he reached for his weapon. His right palm landed on the butt of the gun gripping it tightly when the force of Todd's round house kick shot his head forward. Todd knew the kid was out on contact but still followed all the way through with the motion as he swiftly removed the weapons with his right and left hand seconds before the kid kissed the concrete. The hard thump sheltered the sound of Cyrus' footsteps, who suddenly appeared out of nowhere at Todd's side with a submachine gun rotating at waist level, making sure that no one made any sudden moves. He demanded, "Continue...continue now!!" *"BOOM-BOOM"* Todd pulled the trigger aggressively without pause, willing to do what ever was needed to complete Cyrus and Billy D's testing to move on to with his father true mission.

Lil Mac reached Todd unfazed by the killing because sadly it was an everyday event in North Philly. He was more taken by the Wall Street book smart man that arrived two years ago who started as a look out. Then progressed to selling two for five dollars bags of powder follow by dimes and now there Todd was this thug with death in his eyes that stood before him. *"Damn he's getting good,"* Lil Mac thought before ordering,

70

"Get this body out of here and clear the block, its shift change. Where the hell is Boggy, he's a half an hour late to cover?"

Lil Mac was on his hunt, "Sexy, you see Boggy?" Lil Mac asked NayNay through the walkie talkie who was posted at that top of the block with Top Dollar in a tinted Buick. "No but knowing him he can be anywhere on the block, crack house, alleyways and on the roof anywhere."

"Yeah" Top Dollar cut in, "That's one thing you can utter about the kid Mac, he's on every inch of this block and there's not too much that he miss, you dig."

"Yeah I dig; I dig that he better get a watch." Lil Mac said disconnecting the conversation as his body guard who waited until he was finished to inform him, "The block is clear but there's this bum lying on the sidewalk that's refusing to move. You want me to force him to go Boss?"

"Where is he?"

"Right over there…on the ground a little behind that white Lexus with that woman in it."

Lil Mac looked at the bum closely, smirked then commented before walking in a crack house in search of Boggy, "If I was you I'd leave him lying right there or you may be in his place but not breathing." Inside, Lil Mac had to hold his breath due to all the weed, crack and laced joint smoke in the air. He reached the kitchen where a light skinned man sat at the small table; his finger tips were as black as coal and raised a crack pipe to his lips while striking three matches at the same time. Lil Mac stared as the man inhaled deeply sucking the frame through the thin metal until its gray color faded into a bright orange. The scent of burning skin overwhelmed the weed fragrance, despite the fact, the man continued to pull until the match stick disappeared. He paused holding the smoke in his lungs until he was on the edge of passing out, then exhaled. "Lil Mac, Boggy is coming in now." Fox's voice erupted through Lil Mac's walkie talkie.

"Okay, make sure he doesn't leave."

"I'll try Mac but its Boggy."

"Well at least follow him then," Lil Mac demanded heading for the door.

"Wait, let me get that for you," the man said routing towards the exit when he froze like a statue with one foot stuck in the air. Lil Mac shook his head saying, "A crack head is still going to want that gray shit."

Boggy pulled to the curb with Kim in the passenger seat of his black Benz s55 listening to the sound of Meek Mills' I'm a boss. *"Look I be ridin threw my old hood, but I'm in my new whip, same old attitude but I'm on that new shit, they say they gone rob me, see me neva do shit, cause they know that's the reason that's gone put 'em on a news clips."* Placing the high priced vehicle into park Boggy said "Give me that shit," while snatching the blunt from Kim's lips.

"Oh shit, oh shittt!" Kim screamed, as she jumping around in her seat, trying to put out the sparks of fire burning through her silk Gucci blouse from the blunt. Boggy just shook his head, *"Women,"* he mumbled, taking a deep pull of the exotic weed as he watch his two personal body guards approached his automobile from both sides. Getting out Boggy stated, "This is a lot of bull Roc got me going through with you two lames. I don't need this shit; I'll rock the both of you to sleep before you even think about touching your gun." Boggy felt that Roc had him doing something that was less than a man. Because he truly believed with all the blood in his veins that any man that couldn't put in his own work needed to be dead or give up what ever he had that people wanted to kill him for.

"I'm with you Boggy but you know what Roc said, no matter how on point we are there's always someone willing to die for the life we have," Lil Mac affirmed stepping out in front of the body guards at the edge of Boggy's car door with Todd. "What? That's the shit he tells you so you can sleep better. He knows I'm going to be on a nigga's ass before he even thinks about making a move on one of these blocks. I'm just doing it not to make you look bad nigga," Boggy stated letting out a cloud of gray smoke through his nose. "If you don't want to make me look bad, just be on time," Lil Mac said slamming the Kindle Fire into Boggy's hand that's secretly held the block's info spread through out the charters of the thousands of books on it. "Nigga I been here, you need to start listening more to what Roc is really saying and fuck them words coming on of his."

72

"Boggy you all high, you don't even make sense," Lil Mac rebutted walking away shaking his head thinking, *"This dude done lost his mind."* When he heard Todd say, "Boggy that was good looking on that text earlier about that kid coming to rob me. So when he was talking I knew he wouldn't be leaving."

"Yeah, I heard it in the air that he was getting his plan together so I just relayed it. Now that kick was something major. I wouldn't it do it, but its still was major."

"So he was here...what the hell is going on that I'm missing," Lil Mac continued to think to himself. *"Boom Boom....*Girl, open the damn door!" Kim yelled, before Isha released the lock. "These niggas out here don't care, they just be gripping your ass and shit. I don't know why Boggy stays down here with these wild young boys with all the money he has anyway. I told him if he wanted anymore of this suction cup pussy that it's the Marriott or better because I am not coming back down here. Then he gave me another fifteen hundred dollars so I had to give him another taste," Kim said while laughing.

"Isha...Isha? Hello, earth to Isha."

"Oh I'm sorry what did you say, Kim?" Isha asked pulling away from the curb as Mohammed got up off the ground racing to his stolen car pulling out right behind her.

"Isha you have been tripping lately and who were you just talking to before I got in the car, yourself?"

"Nah, I was singing with the radio," Isha lied.

"So what happened with you and Pretty Tony, you must have put it on him something good because Simon has been calling me all day asking if I have seen ya'll. He said that they were supposed to meet and Pretty Tony never showed up," said Kim.

"Girl that fool started talking crazy and on top of that I took a quick feel and he was only working with about five inches and that's a no-no," they both said in harmony. Their rule was that anything less than seven inches was a no go.

"So I faked a headache and told him to take me home."

"Girl his money is so long, he could have had three inches and I would have been right on it," Kim said, rocking her hips back and forth.

73

"You talking about me? What did you and Simon get into after we left?" Isha asked even though she really didn't care. She just wanted to change the subject.

"Oooh Isha that man is a cold freak. He was with it all; he even tried to get all three holes on the first night. You know I'm not going out like that."

"I don't know Kim," Isha looked at her suspiciously.

"Don't look at me like that, you know that only happened twice and I was on them E pills. I know I should never have even told you about that...anyway," Kim rolled her eyes and then continued telling Isha what happened, "I worked Simon so hard I had him over heating, talking about hold up let me get something to drink and when he came back I had something for him to drink my box." Kim closed her eyes and smiled from the thought of last night. "And his head game was unbelievable; it had me in another world. I was climbing the head board and all but I'm going to have to teach him how to stroke it if I'm going to keep him."

Isha pulled into the parking lot of Club Touches, "Damn it's packed out here. I thought we were going to Soldi II again tonight?" Kim questioned.

"No, I heard that this place is lovely also and I wanted to give it a try," replied Isha as they exited the car.

"Girl you only come out every couple months and you know all the hot spots. I don't know how you do it but you stay on baller point," said Kim, speaking of all the clean luxury cars that filled the lot like Lamborghini, Benz, Porsche, BMW, Land Rover, and Aston Martin.

Inside, the D.J. had the club rocking to the sound of Drake's *'headline'*. They moved quickly through the crowd when a light skinned man gripped Kim by the arm, "Damn girl where you rushing off to without me?"

"Boy pleases! You're cute and all but I'm a high priced ten and a half baby and you got on Roca wear gear, which means we don't mix. So when you upgrade yourself, then I'll let you upgrade me." The man was saying something but Kim never stopped to hear him. Kim was 5'9", 135 lbs. She had a nice brown complexion with jet black hair that fell just passed her shoulder. Everything she wore was top of the line and had to fit her body perfectly.

"Let's sit over there," Kim pointed to a booth in the middle section. "No we're going to V.I.P."

"How are we going to do that, you see that line over there? And I don't know the bouncer."

"Harlem in the building, come on." Inside, Bo and the whole A-One team held the VIP room hostage just like their blocks in South Philly. Anything you needed they had. The bar was priced out and there wasn't a bottle of Champagne left in the building because they were all on ice surrounding their booths in the back.

Indeed Bo had come a long way. Just two years ago he was a small time stick up kid and hand to hand clean up the street hustler. Now he was a 50 brick a week mover hoping to become a major player one day. With the help of his mystery girl Maria, anything was possible. At first their relationship was just about the sex, then it became a lot more. It started when Bo saw her crossing the street looking as beautiful as ever with her head held low. 'Beep Beep' Bo hit the horn on his Chrysler Sebring convertible and she looked in his direction. Bo could tell she had been crying as he waved her over to the car.

As she approached, Bo's mind went into action," Sorry to stop you but I just saw that you looked as if you were having a bad day. I was wondering if I could be of any help."

"Come on Bo, I know I've been crying but it's me, Maria. Damn do I look that bad that you can't tell who I am?" Maria said.

"Maria?" Bo said puzzled then jumped back on his pimping, "Don't do that...you look lovely today. Where are you going, can I give you a ride someplace?"

"No thank you, I'm working today. I'm just taking my lunch break and I didn't feel like eating anything so I came out for a walk and some fresh air."

"I feel you. Sometimes we all need quality time to ourselves to clear our mind in this cold world. However if you need anything or just someone to talk to, here is my number, and if you're up to it I'm having a little get together on Sunday. It looks like you need a night out."

75

"We'll see. It's getting late so I have to go, bye."

"You go ahead and take care of yourself," Bo replied. As Maria was walking away she turned around and said, "Hey...thanks for caring." A few weeks later Maria was still feeling down from the loss of her love and decided to call Bo.

"Hello."

"Hi, may I speak with Bo please?"

"This is him."

"It's me Maria. Is that invitation still open?"

"Yes, the invitation is definitely still open. Where are you?"

Maria gave Bo the address and he was there within an hour. They were having a great time together at a nice jazz lounge in N.J. The night was full of dancing and deep conversation. "Bo I'm having a nice time and all but it's getting late. I think I should be getting home now."

"Okay, let's just have one more drink before we bounce."

"That sounds good, why don't you order for us both while I go to the ladies room." While Maria was gone, the drinks arrived and Bo looked around to make sure she was not yet on her way, then he quickly placed four crushed E pills into her drink just moments before she returned. "Let's toast to a lovely night, between two friends." Maria closed her eyes and then tossed the drink straight back.

As they crossed the bridge from New Jersey back to Philly, Maria's body started feeling the effects of the E.

"Bo, are you hot? I'm hot as hell."

"Take that hot ass coat off," Bo replied. She removed the coat but still felt heated so she started to unbutton the top three buttons of her silk blouse.

"Why are you touching my leg?" Maria asked.

"Girl what are you talking about? I'm changing the C.D." Bo placed on some Keith Sweat. Listening to it blast through the 10 speaker Kenwood system, Bo licked his lips knowing it wouldn't be much longer.

"Damn you got some big lips Bo."

"Yeah I do. And I know what to do with them too," Bo commented as he ran his tongue slowly over his lips again. This

76

turned Maria on even more. "It's really hot in here." Bo slipped out of his shirt, leaving nothing on but his Polo tank top to show off his muscular body. Maria couldn't take it anymore; she squeezed her breast and gently massaged her nipples until they became hard. Then she slid her other hand into her pants, touching her wetness. The bass vibrated Maria's seat while she tried to imitate the rhythm massaging her clit. Maria couldn't explain the feeling of cold and wet lips on her nipples. Bo was now parked and kissing all over her upper body. Their tongues danced with lust for minutes until they both needed more. "You want to go inside?" Maria looked up to see the sign that read Holiday Inn and smiled. "He don't want to see me...why not."

In the room, Maria pushed Bo's chest hard forcing him down on the bed. She ripped his tank top shirt off and unbuckled his Gucci belt. "I'm going to need this," she removed it and worked on taking off the rest of his clothes. Bo was completely naked as Maria took the belt and wrapped it around his wrists. "Hold up...what you are doing?" questioned Bo. "Shut up and give me your other hand you big baby," Maria demanded. Bo loved a woman who knew how to take charge so he went along with the plan.

After tying Bo to the bed post, Maria took off her shirt and gold lace bra. Then she removed the white marble handle 9mm from the center of her back. Bo looked as though his eyes were about to jump out of his head. Fear was written all over his face but also becoming more attracted to her as his manhood stiffened even harder. "Wh-wh-what are you going to do with that?"

"Don't worry bitch...if I wanted you dead you would've been gone already." Maria said, stepping out the rest of her clothes. *"Damn this woman is cold,"* Bo thought to himself, looking at Maria's naked body as she placed the gun on the nightstand. "So you know what to do with them?" Maria said, stepping onto the bed with her back facing him. She did a slow seductive dance by moving her hips from side to side as she lowered herself on top of Bo's face. Bo worked the middle like he had something to prove. "That's it nigga, right there...right there. Oooohh, oohh I'm going to cum in your mouth." Maria grinded her hips back and forth at a fast pace until she came harder than ever before. Leaning forward but still riding Bo's lips, she took his manhood deep into her mouth and worked it in and out of her warm wet mouth until she knew he was about to cum. "That's enough for you. Time to take it for a test spin before you blow your tire," said Maria. "Please don't stop baby, you feel so good...please."

"Don't beg nigga, that's why I never gave you any of this gold before...I knew you couldn't handle it. I always saw the way you looked at me. Now you got me and it's please don't stop."

When Bo didn't respond Maria knew she had become his weakness and he would become her new pet and do whatever she said once she was done. Maria gripped his manhood tightly while guiding it inside her pussy inch by inch. She smacked his balls with both hands before squeezing each of his nipples while riding him at top speed. She was so hot and moist inside that Bo couldn't hold back after only two and a half minutes his body began to shake. "I know you're not going to, shit?" Maria said as she jumped off and proceeded to work her hand at the same pace jerking Bo off, making him cum several seconds later. Bo closed his eyes, disappointed at him self for all the times he wanted a real woman instead of the hood rats he'd dealt with. This was his big chance to step up and he knew that he just blew it. Maria would never want to see him again. Bo opened his eyes, feeling Maria's soft lips against his. "Its okay baby you'll do better next time."

"What are you saying? You're going to see me again?" Bo asked. "Yes I'm going to turn you into a man in no time but you know my situation so you can't be sweating me. When I call you, come running. Bo I know you bust your gun and all, but from now on if you ever try to disrespect me by putting something in my drink...I'll kill you." Slowly but surely Maria did just what she said she would. As a result of Bo telling her about the block and the rest of A-Ones business, Maria would instruct him on how to handle different situations. Now it wasn't about the team or cleaning up the street, it was about the come up.

11

*B*o was now sitting and talking to a couple of pretty women when a man questioned, "Yo Bo can we buy a bottle of champagne off you?" Bo looked up at the man and another young fella standing in front of him with a small amount of jewels and different colored Rocawear suits. Bo shook his head at the poor sight before asking, "Do you know how much a bottle costs?"

"No, how much?" asked the man with a little attitude. "Eleven hundred nigga, put the money on the table and grab one." The two men looked at each other and then walked back to their table. Bo stood up on a chair saying, "This is what I'm talking about. These niggas in here are faking it. The only time they spend a G is when they're lying to a gangster."

Laughter filled the V.I.P room as Bo pulled two bottles off the ice and let the cold water drip onto the two females. "Come on Bo, that shit is cold." Bo paid them no mind as he popped the bottles, held them up in the air as the foam raced down his arm over the platinum iced out Rolex and onto the silk Prada shirt he wore. "Somebody tell them petty ass nigga's to get some paper cups or something. Matter of fact, how the hell did they get in here anyway? This is V.I.P am I right?"

Bo didn't wait for an answer before he kept speaking, "That means very important people, so get them the fuck up out of here." Several members of A-One rushed the two men and then tossed them over the red velvet rope. The tall one landed right at Kim's feet. "Damn Isha, this is what I'm talking about. These cats are off the hook up in this place." Kim stepped over the man's body that tried to talk to her earlier without hesitation and stopped next to Isha who was talking with the bouncer.

"I'm sorry beautiful but nobody else is getting in," the bouncer explained. Before Isha could protest, a man laid his arm around the bouncers shoulder and lightly placed two hundred dollar bills in his top shirt pocket. "Now I know you could make an exception for these two lovely ladies." The bouncer quickly removed the velvet rope. "Come on, I have a nice spot in the cut to keep the suckers out of your face."

"Thanks Bo."

"You know how I roll Isha… that goes without saying. Plus we go too far back for that."

Their seats were at a small booth off to the side. Bo raised his arm and the barmaid came running. "Give these ladies whatever they need for the rest of the night, on me."

"Okay sir." Bo admired every curve on Isha's body while licking his lips as he held her chair out for her. "You're my man's girl, so if I got it you got it. How is ole' boy doing anyway? Did he take the money this time?"

"Yeah he took it now because he didn't have a choice. I put it on his books. What I don't understand is what happened, ya'll were so close." Isha looked as if she was lost in space as she tried to relive the moment that Dro and her were so happy. Kim saw the look and understood her pain from losing her own love of her life. "Isha no disrespect but Dro got soft and changed after he started boxing. Then after what happened to Rell, it's like he wasn't a part of A-One anymore. It was like the street life is beneath him and on the real, when there was nothing…there was us and there's no ending without us."

Everyone present at the table could see that Bo was hurt over the person he wanted so badly to be. Bo fought back a tear as he continued, "I still got mad love for my dog so the next time you go see him let him know that anything he needs, he got it. When he comes home, there's always a spot in A-One for him. He started this and we never forget our people."

"I hear you and you're right, Dro did change but never for one second think that he got soft," Isha stated. Bo laughed and replied, "I hope you're right about that." He then walked back to his table. "Bo, what was that all about? And why were you looking at her like that?"

"It's nothing Gotti, damn I was just saying hi."

"That's all it better be," Gotti replied while he observed Bo closely talking to E-Money.

"Girl that's the cat Bo and they say he's holding big money now not bigger then Boggy but big," Kim said to Isha.

"So what's that got to do with me?"

"You mean to tell me that you didn't see how he was just looking at you?"

"Kim you need to stop, he wasn't looking at me and if he was...I'm taken!" Isha stated.

"What did I tell you, here he comes now and he's got somebody sexy with him."

"Excuse me once again ladies, this here is my right hand man E-Money and he was just dying to meet you Isha," Bo smiled slyly.

12

*T*wo months later, Mark was sitting alone in his cell saying a prayer. "Lord, since I was born it seams the angel of death has been upon me. There were times he was so close he even had his hands on me. At these moments I thought I would never make it but here I stand, still. When I was ten and barely a man you took my father away, but I didn't cry, didn't even ask you why. I stood strong because he let me know every man must die. With him gone, there were many nights when I had nothing to eat and I didn't ask you to feed me. As my soul wanted to cry, I kept a dry eye as I watched my mother put a needle in her feet to get high. Having nobody to turn to, I ran to the streets for affection and a hug. I couldn't fight so I took a couple of losses, started hustling, got my money up and bought a 9 and a couple of slugs. Then, one by one I let them fly, begging you as I squeezed the trigger that they all would die. More will fly but this time it's for Rell so before I go, many are going to come with me. This is hell on earth and I'm going to be firing when the angel of death comes to get me. I just hope I'm high when they hit me. Amen." Mark stood to his feet and out stepped onto the tier with a yellow folder under his arm.

"Man what was taking you so long? If I was going home today I'd be beating down the door," said Forty.

"He acts like he don't want to leave us," Dro commented as they walked Mark to the front desk. "You remember what you got to do, right?"

"I wouldn't forget it for the world, this is for Rell," Mark assured before strolling outside the huge gun tower walls into the warm 80 degree summer day. He looked around the parking lot for his ride. There wasn't a car in sight but Mark could hear the sound of the Notorious B.I.G's 'Warning' vibrating in his ear. Shawn's Benz SUV pulled to a stop and he jumped out and gave his partner a pound with a hug. "Damn nigga, you're big as a house. You must have been hitting that weight pile heavy," Shawn said. "You know how I do, where are the keys?"

A few hours later, Mark pulled up to Dro's old gym. Inside, Mark thought he was back in Graterford. Dro had the same set up there from the two rings in the middle, the speed bags on the right and the punching bags on the left. Activity was going on all over the gym as Mark watched a two hundred pound man dripping off sweat working the punching bag. As he looked on, Mark started to move his body to defend himself from the punches automatically out of reflex. Shawn was surprised to see how smoothly Mark moved. When they were growing up, Mark would get into fights twice a day for his drug pack and never once won a fight but still he would never give them up.

A man watching, thought he knew Mark's style of fighting and said, "Young man, it looks like you know what you're doing. You here to sign up for ring time or are you looking for a trainer?" Mark wiped away the little bit of sweat that was on his forehead and laughed. "Nah, I got a trainer I'm just here to pick up a bag for a good friend from Matty...do you know him?"

"Maybe, it depends on who this good friend of yours is," the man said.

"Oh he is the man of this joint, Dro."

"I never heard of him but if you can show me something on this here, I could get Matty to give you that bag." The man told the person on the bag, "time kiddo, go ahead and hit the shower."

"You've never heard of him? Come on Shawn, this nigga's tripping." Mark walked off leaving the man standing there holding the punching bag. He then approached a trainer helping a boxer free his hands from his gloves. "Excuse me, could you tell me where I can find Matty?"

"Yeah in that office right there," the trainer pointed to the only office in the back of the gym.

As they walked, Mark took notice of all the pictures on the wall. There were boxers from every time frame, Joe Louis, Muhammad Ali, Frazier, Foreman, Tyson, and Hopkins. But the one that held his attention was of Dro with a man holding his hand up in victory. Mark turned around and stopped next to the same man, now holding the punching bag for another man. He tapped him on the shoulder, "Let me go for a second." When the man stepped aside Mark went to work. Slowly he brought himself into a nice rhythm hitting the bottom of the bag with a

83

five piece combination, then the middle with six. As if he were standing right there with him, Mark could hear Dro's voice saying, "I don't care if you don't know how to fight. You have the heart to fight and that's all that matters because you have the heart of a man and this punching bag here is your enemy. The bottom is his ribcage, the middle's his chest, and the top is his chin...now work. Don't ever stand still when you're throwing punches because someone is always throwing them back."

Mark worked the bag, his feet and his head all at the same time. He side stepped the bag, landed a hard eight piece, and then he was back on the opposite side throwing a left to the ribcage. He ducked his head while sending a sharp upper cut down the middle. People gathered around to watch him work. The man holding the bag was having a hard time keeping up because he felt the force of every punch Mark threw.

In a zone, Mark called out his combination, "Five middle, four chin, six rib, four middle, upper cut, upper cut and hard right." Mark backed away soaking wet as people started to clap and making remarks, "Man he's nice."

"Did you see that?"

"Man fuck that nigga, I'll knock him straight out"

"Who's his trainer?"

Mark stated to the man holding the bag, "Now can I get what I came for Matty?"

"Yeah, yeah whatever you want kiddo. Follow me. That was amazing, your timing was on point...it was like you were in another world. Do you have a manager?"

"No I just need the bag," Mark replied. Inside Matty's office Mark and Shawn sat while Matty went to the back in search of the bag. "Here you go kid, but you don't have to put them gloves and shoes to work elsewhere. I've got a spot with a trainer and all for you right here." Mark grabbed the bag and was about to walk out the door when he turned around and said, "No thanks Matty. And by the way, my name is not kid it's..."

"Mark, I know kid. I know you didn't think you could come in here and get something of Dro's and I not know ahead of time," Matty stated. "So why did I have to hit the bag?" asked Mark, looking down at his still wet shirt. "Because Dro said you were going to be the next champ after him, now I know why."

84

13

*D*riving in Center City, Shawn made a left on Chestnut St. "Man, where the hell are you going? You said you were going to show me the new block," yelled Mark. "I got you but you have to see your probation officer first."

"Probation officer? Man if you don't make this right, right here!"

"But what about him?"

"Fuck'em and if he don't like it he can try and come and get me."

Mark opened the bag he'd gotten from Matty and threw the shoes and gloves on to the back seat that covered the top to reveal over sixty assault weapons. "Yeah let him come and get us," Shawn laughed as he made the right turn. They walked down 10th and Walnut passing the blunt between themselves. "Damn, it's flowing out here like water," Mark said as he watched the customers coming from everywhere. "What ya'll doing like 20 grand a night out this bitch?"

"More like an easy ten. We're moving two keys a week, all from break down but with you back at my side I know we can get ten keys once Bo and Gotti hear you're back. They're going to throw us at least another five keys at a lower price just on the strength of Rell," Shawn hoped.

"So that's the new connect you've been writing me about, those A-One cats?"

"Yeah, but I tried Lil Mac first because he's doing the pussy out here heavy but my money's not long enough yet to deal with me."

"I'm hip, so you getting money with them A-one niggas now?"

"Man I'm trying to get money with you, it's your call," Shawn corrected.

"That's what I wanted to hear!" Mark filled Shawn in on part of Dro's plan to find out which one of them crossed Rell and the way to go about it. "Listen, first for us to get close enough to sit next to them, we've got to step our money up like theirs, we can't get it by them fronting us coke because a real nigga is never going to truly respect someone who works for him. We've got to buy it and lots of it, so how much money you sitting on now?"

"They just hit us off plus what we had left, we've got two and a half keys," Shawn explained.

"And how much cash?"

"I'm not going to lie, I've been messing my bread up chasing these ho's and buying cars. I only got forty thousand plus the twenty I have for you."

"Sixty and two and a half keys, that won't do. Yo, take me down South Philly to 7th and King. My man Bone got it on lock down there. He said he would have something nice for me when I touched, now I'm going to see if he's a man of his word. If not, I got something for him."

On the way there, Mark thought to himself how dumb Shawn was and the conversation that he'd had with Dro before.

~ • ~ • ~ • ~ • ~

"I'll tell you Mark, you young cats out there are in the way," Dro stated.

"How the hell are you going to say some shit like that Dro when my team busts their guns."

"Yes they bust their guns but for what reason? Some cars and jewelry because ya'll damn sure aren't stacking. Look around at all these young cats sitting in here with murder cases facing life plus forty with a public defender as their lawyer. They will sit there and put their lives in the hands of a person who gets paid by the same people that want them in jail because they have no other choice. They don't invest in anything, no property, no stock, a store...nothing. This may become too deep so I'm going to put it in layman terms for you Mark."

"Come on with the bullshit man," Mark said, not wanting to hear the truth.

"For real, ya'll don't even invest in family but will ride around in a ninety thousand dollar car yet their mothers are on section 8 somewhere in the projects but when ya'll get knocked off, they're the first person you'll call. Then it's stupid how ya'll disrespect the same old people that sit there and watch you sell drugs 24/7 in front of their homes who knew you since you were a baby. That's the only reason they don't call the cops and you

86

still won't move out the way when you see them coming or help them with their grocery bags. Yet you'll invest in a girl that you probably hit the first night you met her in a bar. You'll buy her everything, let her know where your money and drugs are and 95% of the time, when you get locked up they tell and take all your money, then jump on the next cat with a Benz dick. That's the difference from when me and your Uncle Rell were in the streets, we took care of our family and we understood what a friendship was. If I called you a friend, I was there for you one hundred percent. I didn't try to sex your girl as soon as you got locked up; we did what we had to do for bail money. We didn't tell the police everything you did at the first sign of trouble and we would make the suckers who had no respect pay and show them how to really be disrespected. We were in the streets for a reason, even when I was doing no good I showed the heart of a man trying to make a difference."

~ • ~ • ~ • ~ • ~

"Yo, there goes your man Bone right there sitting on that pretty white quarter to eight B.M.W," Shawn said pulling up next to Bone as Mark's thoughts came back to the moment at hand while he slowly lower the tinted window. Before the window could fully drop Bone's young bulls were on point; they gripped their guns and pointed at the Benz from all sides. Bone never looked up until he finished counting the knot of money in his hand while ending the phone call on his ear piece. "You was right Roc, that call just came through…will do."

"Bone I don't have all day to be sitting on this hot ass block." Mark's voice was like music to Bone's ears. "Marky Mark…what's up baby, long time no see? Ya'll clowns put them guns down and show some respect to a cannon."

"That's not about nothing, I just touched down and I'm trying to get my hands dirty but I need a little help," Mark explained.

"Enough said, now get out of that little ass Benz and I'm going to show you how we look out for family down here."

Bone was the person Mark caught the shooting for when he stopped two men from trying to rob him. They'd been friends since they were locked up in a juvenile detention center together. Bone set it out like he said he would, he passed off 2 keys of raw

87

cocaine to go along with the thirty thousand he had in a brown paper bag.

"That's half of what they would've gotten and this is on me," Bone threw Mark the keys to the 745il B.M.W.

"What's this for?"

"That's you, now you can get out of that little ass Benz."

For a month, Mark and Shawn put in around the clock shifts on the block. They wore the same clothes for days, until Mark had all he needed to put his plan in effect. As the months moved by, Mark cut over half the block workers for being disrespectful in anyway; and he still was moving more product by the week.

Mark made sure that if there was an old person that needed something like their electric kept on or heat fixed and they were good people, they got it. Mark changed the way they bought their product. Now whatever they got fronted from A-One, they bought also. When they finished he would send all the money to Lil Mac and Boggy for a quick flip doubling up the profit before seeing A-One again. Their money grew as well as their status and A-one couldn't but notices.

There were moments when everything wasn't always sweet and at those times, Shawn and Mark never hesitated to let their steel bring a situation to an end. To clear his mind, Mark went to the gym and worked out with Matty and tonight as he exited "good night Matty," His phone vibrated.

"Hello?"

"What up go getter?"

"It's nothing Bo, what's good?

"I called because I need to holla at you tomorrow."

"Don't worry, we'll be ready, and I need two more this week so bring twelve and whatever ya'll toss I got it."

"I know, you're always on time but I need to holla at you alone. You understand?"

"I feel you"

"Alright I'll see you." Hanging up the phone, Bo laid back in a Four Season private residence in New York, with Maria on a soft king sized bed with eight pillows around them after another wild sex escapade. "Maria, I need you to handle this one last move for me and I promise you I will not ask you for nothing else."

"Baby I would but you knew my situation from the start and I'm not going to do anything that will get in the way of that," Maria said, expressing her strong feelings about it.

"I know and I respect that but we have come too far."

Bo moved behind Maria pulling her in between his legs and started massaging her shoulders while placing soft kisses in between each of his words, "To...stop...now...you like that?"

"You know I do, that's my spot."

"I thought you would."

"But pleasure will not get you anywhere this time, plus I believe he is onto us and if he finds out, he'll kill us both."

"That's understandable sweetheart, for someone as beautiful as you, who wouldn't take another one's life but this is your plan and if we don't handle all the loose ends we will be dead anyway," Bo explained. "Is it we or more like you? Oh, don't look so shocked. Please believe I know more than what you think," Maria corrected.

Bo was caught off guard by Maria's words. Over the years they'd been together, Bo had built up his self confidence and started making some of his own moves on the side. He prayed that they had not caught up with him just yet. Thinking quickly on his feet, he bent over the side of the bed and grabbed the bag he'd gotten from Tiffany's for his other girl Neshonda. "I bet you didn't know this." He put the 4.2 carat pink and white diamond necklace around Maria's neck. She jumped up and ran to the full sized mirror and couldn't believe how lovely the chain was or how it made her eyes glow. "Bo it's so beautiful! But what did I tell you about buying things, how am I going to explain this...say I found it?" Bo was now standing right behind her, sucking on her right ear lobe and said, "Give it back then." When he tried to remove it, Maria smacked his hand hard.

"So does this mean you're going to help me?"

"Why wouldn't I? It's my plan; I just wanted to see you sweat some. This is how we got to do this because the last time the target's team was all over me. There's one that still has not stopped asking me about him. Gotti leaves town for Texas in two days and how long is he going to be gone?"

"For five days and he leaves on Thursday and will return on the following Tuesday," Bo stated.

"That's it; we'll handle it that weekend while he's gone. Make sure you have people you can trust this time so we don't have to go through this again."

"Is there anything else you need me to do Ms. Monarchy?" Bo joked.

"I may be able to come up with a few things for you to do." Maria turned around to face Bo and then pushed him down to his knees. "But as far as he goes, mmmmm that's it right there. I already got him eating out of my hand from the first day you introduced us."

14

On June 28th, 2011 at 6:30 am, Dro walked out of his cell without taking anything. He moved down the tier saying his goodbye's only to the real men on the block. "Basil, hold your head up man, keep fighting with that case law and they will have no choice but to let you go one day. But until then do the time and don't let the time do you."

"I will and you maintain out there and be who you need to be to stay away from this place that's nothing but death. Don't come back talking about it's hard out there like the rest of these fellas."

"I heard they wasn't lying, it's hard out there."

Basil's face became tight instantly after all the books and talks he had with Dro about banks, the stock market and how to make it out in the free world as a convicted felon. Basil knew it should be easy for him to survive; now Dro tells him this. Basil wished he didn't have a life sentence from a mistake he made to show them how it was done. He caught his first and only case at the age of forty five. He was a successful baker with three stores who came home one day and found his wife in bed with the mail man. Blacking out, he removed his 38 special he carried every day for his safety and killed them both. Basil had been in jail ever since and that was thirteen years ago.

"Lighten up old head; it's hard for them because they're suckers. A real man finds his way in, and then makes his own exit."

"Don't play with me like that. You know I really, really dislike seeing my people in cages and chains no matter if they're gold, diamonds, or shackles. That's why I took my time with you because you're a good kid at heart under all that rough stuff. That I also comprehend you sometimes use that to get through the time they give us." Basil fought back a tear as he continued; "Now go ahead out there son and take care of your family and your friends. Then I will handle my part." They hugged and Dro promised himself that he'd see Basil's partner Patterson soon.

Dro's next stop was to cell 112 where Meshane agreed with Biggie that it was the spot of a player. When Dro stepped in, Meshane was all smiles when he spoke, "Damn playboy what took you so long to holla at your real old head? I saw you down there talking to that square that makes the cakes and pies and shit when I'm sitting here with some hot news for you."

"Come on Shane, why you so hard on Mr. Basil, is it because he don't sell drugs?"

"Now you know I don't give a damn how a nigga gets to a dollar as long as he gets there. I just don't like you talking to that nigga because his outer appearance looks so strong. He's intelligent, soft spoken; stays out the way and on top of that he's a murderer, now let's go inside. The man comes from a rich background so he didn't have to go through the things we did that led us here. He had the proper schooling, even went to Paris to be a cook. I heard he was offered a head chef job at one of the top restaurants over there but his woman Betty didn't want to stay. So he came back to the states and a few years down the line he killed the bitch. Now put that all together, he passed up on a life I would have given my left arm for. Why? Because he's emotional and any man that makes moves with his heart and not with his brain needs to stay the hell away from my people, you feel me?"

"I feel you," Dro answered. "But later for that clown, you asked me to do something and I did it."

Meshane was 5' 10", 230 lbs with black hair. He was locked up for trying to buy 150 keys of cocaine off of an undercover cop on tape. Then at the time of his trial the tape mysteriously vanished, forcing the D.A. to offer him a sweet deal of five to ten. But being behind bars didn't stop anything for him; He was more than well connected, if you needed anything Meshane was sure to make it happen.

"I looked into them A-One boys like you asked and they're running kind of heavy out there now. When you first came in they wasn't doing anything major. Then your man Bo got some ambition from somewhere and started making some smart moves, you know; rubbing elbows with the right people until he found a strong connect who happened to be my young buck Tywan from North Philly. I raised the boy until he moved to Cali for a few years and when he returned, he made it snow with coke. He said Bo scores with about a quarter mill so Bo could be your man. I didn't want to talk on my cell phone so the next time he comes up here, I will make sure to let you know everything son."

"Thanks Shane. Since I've been here you never let me down. That's why I will never let you down. Get me a piece of paper to write down my info for you."

"No need, you're family. Where ever you're at Dro, believe I will find you and that other thing you asked for is a go. All you got to do is call. Now go out there and be the man you said you are, Champ." While Meshane watched Dro leave, Blue slid up on his right side saying, "Damn Shane you look down that your man's leaving. Don't worry I'm going to be here for you."

"Nigga you going to be here you're damn self. His date before mine so I need him to leave so I can go, then maybe you can follow." Meshane said looking Blue dead in the face. Dro walked out the cell to the sound of the C.O. calling his name. "Dro, there you go. I've been looking all over for you. They've been waiting on you in R and D," said C.O. Harper who stood there impatiently. "Alright let me say goodbye to Scotty real quick and I'm out."

"No, there are no more goodbyes shit, I want you off my count now."

"What? Who the fuck you think you're talking to like that?" Dro stepped into Harper's face. "I'm talking to you. Now how bad do you really want to go home?"

Dro's fist tightened and you could see his veins start to pop out the side of his neck. Thoughts of madness raced through his mind for Harper who felt that every black man on earth should be in jail. *"I can't believe this coward finally came at me after all these years. His racist ass never said one word to me, now he got a heart. Fuck it, he wants it I'm going to go ahead and knock him out and try to crack his face."* Dro smoothly drop stepped his right foot behind his left, placing him into the half man fighting position. His right hand rested nine inches away from his front pants pocket ready to strike. "Not like this," Scotty said in Dro's ear as he moved in between the two. "Really bad Mr. Harper, he wants to go home really bad."

93

"Man, what the hell is going on here?" asked Forty while looking from Dro to Harper, feeling the tension in the air. He slid his right hand onto the knife in his pocket.

"There's nothing going on boy, we're just going to walk Dro to R and D so he can get out this hell hole, right?" asked Scotty hoping that Dro didn't lose his cool so close to freedom. Dro was still looking Harper straight in the eyes when he answered, "Yeah Forty, this isn't about nothing. If it was, I think C.O. Harper would have been said something. Am I right Harper?"

"You're absolutely right, so you go ahead and talk to Scotty and enjoy your freedom, now if you will excuse me," Harper said to Forty who was standing so close to him that Harper could feel the heat from his breath on his face. Forty didn't move until Dro gave him a head nod. The three made their way down the hall to R and D. "See Dro, you in there talking to that nigga Meshane who wants to be the 2012 Nino Brown and after hearing that mess you come out here and almost let that man pull you back in here before you had a chance to leave."

"Don't worry about that Dro, I'm going to handle him before the week's out," stated Forty. "You're not going to handle nothing!" Scotty said. "Dro, you see what you're leaving me with? But I am going to make sure he stays out of trouble so he will come right behind you. Just do what we talked about and I'm going to keep you posted on my part of our plan. Please make me proud again and show the world what real men are made of."

Scotty gave Dro a big hug and as they embraced he whispered to Dro so that Forty couldn't hear, "Watch yourself out there. They say your young gun Mark might be playing on the other side. After E-Money got killed he became Bo's number one go to man and the boy is making so much money, if he is gone it would be next to impossible to get him back, so you know what to do." Dro closed his eyes then stepped back before reopening them to look at Scotty, "No I don't know Scotty, what are you saying?"

"What I'm saying is you're going to handle this situation then get your life back on track and if he's playing the fifty don't hesitate to put him with the rest of them."

94

"I know you're right Scotty, I just pray that you're wrong," Dro replied.

"Me too, I know how much love you got for him. Check this, the fellows asked if you would let Q and those funny boys come out the hole. They said the drug flow is not the same and they're willing to pay because it's harder to get it in with them off the compound."

"I said what I had to say about it but I'm leaving so it's now up to Forty."

Dro said his goodbyes then laughed to himself as Scotty and Forty disputed on their way back down the hall. "Tell those niggas I want ten thousand a week or I'm going to kill a faggot every day they're late with my money."

"Come on Forty, be reasonable. We both can make some real money off of this move."

"Fuck what you talking about Scotty. I don't need any money, Mark's hitting me off crazy plus my man just walked out the door and you know how he's going to do it. I'm the next king of this shit so with the ten I need some weed, some dope, and coke...all that shit."

15

"*T*hanks," Dro said, passing C.O. Dickenson back his cell phone. Two hours later Dro stepped into his first taste of freedom in years. Mark was sitting behind the wheel of his brand new Mercedes S55 with Shawn in the passenger seat. At the sight of Dro, Mark rushed out of the car. Dro immediately went into the half man stance as he looked Mark over. Mark had on a $300 Kiton T-shirt with a pair of blue Prada jean shorts that were about the same price. His shoes were a pair of retro Jordans, however what caught Dro's attention was the forty karat handcrafted Aximum diamond link chain with two hands praying. That coordinated with his yellow and white diamond Audemars Piquet watch and ring.

They embraced, "Look at you looking as clean as P. Diddy."

"Look who's talking, you're not too dirty yourself." Dro's attire was tailored black Gucci pants with a silk black and white Fendi shirt and belt. His feet rested in egg shell white ankle high gator boots. "You know I'm not into all this materialistic stuff, this is Isha's work." As they walked toward the car, Shawn watched Dro's every move. Dro was twenty feet away when Shawn slid his arm under the seat. "Mark you still got it or has all that money gone to your head?"

"What?" Mark threw a quick two piece that Dro slipped with ease.

"Well we're going to find out, time to clear our mind. Dickenson said the closest hotel is fifteen miles from here so tell your man you'll get with him later and let's get it."

Dro dropped the bag from his shoulder to the ground. Then he unbuttoned his shirt, leaving on his tank top. In the bag he removed his state boots that had over 100,000 miles of track on them and put them on. "Now that's better," said Dro. Mark handed Shawn his jewelry when Shawn asked, "How am I supposed to give it to him now if he's not getting into the car?"

"Yo, keep your voice down and just chill. You can give it to him before the party tonight then you'll be in like me. I promise."

Shawn pulled off mad as he watched Dro and Mark start off down the dirt road at a nice pace. "I know you're not going to just leave them gators in the parking lot?" Dro turned and took one last look at the hundred foot walls that held him captive for 912 days, hoping this was the last time he had to see the sight of it as he answered, "Why wouldn't I?"

"Because they cost two grand."

"And....this is all I need to fight my way to the top," Dro said.

With that, he picked up speed, making it hard for Mark to keep up. Dro enjoyed the feeling of fresh air deep inside his lungs. The sight of the trees passing by with the sound of birds singing was music to his ears. Dro took in everything, not paying Mark any mind until he heard Bo's name. "What was that you just said?" Dro slowed down his pace to be right next to Mark when he answered, "The operation is totally different from when you and my Uncle Rell used to run A-One on that safe street shit."

"And how is that?" Dro asked.

"Now they are getting money hand over fist all over the city. They're not doing stick ups no more to eat and if people don't like it they have two choices; break bread or fake dead because Bo's not having it."

"So A-One is now the Get Money Clique every body is talking about?"

"Nah, that's Top Dollar and Solo, but they are family. Bo gets money with them too but Roc wouldn't play with him but in the end he will. A-One is still the same, only instead of sweating blood and losing men over a street that don't want to be clean; A-One is trying to become the street."

"And you feel that's right?" Dro sped up again then turned around and started back pedaling to look at Mark's eyes as he answered, "It depends on how one looks at it. I know how you feel from the many nights we talked and I respect and understand the meaning. You'll see how your words didn't go in one ear and out the other from how I run my eight blocks. But Bo and Gotti do have a good point about it being our community. Why keep letting our people kill each other and doing long jail sentences for the white man to keep getting

97

richer. Either it's the D.E.A. coming and taking anything they want then calling it drug related or it's the bank that's foreclosing on home loans early because of this new law or any reason being there are no jobs. Whatever it is, A-One's not having it. If you need money to help with your bills until you get on your feet, see us. If you need that work dropped off at your door step, it's sad... but see us. If you're trying to start your own business and you can't get the city to give you the proper permit, we'll get it done. Dro, they're well connected and Bo wants you to have your top spot back."

"Like he could stop me," Dro smiled while turning around before taking off running at full speed, trying to figure out all the information he'd gotten so far before he put his next move into place. His first thoughts went back to the three men of wisdom, Scotty, Meshane, and Basil. The importance of these men even though they couldn't stand each other because they were so different, was to put them together and they could rule the whole city and Dro knew it. Basil was an inmate not a convict. The difference was that an inmate did what he was told and tried hard not to break the rules because he or she truly believed they deserved to be there. Convicts did what they wanted and took the consequences that came with it. Basil didn't talk to many people so it took Dro over six months to get a real conversation out of him after Scotty told him Basil was a co-owner of a bank that was sponsoring his last fight before he came to jail.

Basil may be a sucker for love but he was far from stupid. What Meshane didn't know was that Basil was a baker by choice, after finishing college at the top of his class with a promising future as a stock broker. In just two years he made 1.2 million off of great investing. A month later he put his own money on the line which landed him in Paris three years later with 21.5 million and the time to start cooking duck. Once they became friends, Dro learned Basil was the co-owner of several banks but Dro was only interested in one, The Bristol Bank of the Nation where Bo and Gotti cleaned their money. Dro smiled at the thought.

Next it was Meshane and his words, *"Yeah my young bull Tywan is their connect."* Dro knew he had to jump face first

98

back into the game to get the answer for Rell and the only way for that to happen was to play for keeps on the next level. In doing so, he needed Scotty to school him on the fact that Meshane was the person to get close to. The times they cooked, talked, and ran the track together paid off for Dro. Now all he had to do is make one phone call and Tywan would pass off fifty keys to any place he wanted within an hour with no money needed, he could pay after he pushed the work. Just off the word of Meshane.

Then there was Scotty who was arrested for a bank robbery where he made off with $250,000 which was never found. He was captured after one of his neighbors recognized his face from the banks camera shot in the newspaper. Scotty was convicted and sentence to 6-12 in the beginning but the news of his son pushed him over the edge. The next day he had an argument with a ticket runner over whether he had hit the ticket. He left and when he came back he had two knives taped to each wrist and killed the runner. After that he went off looking for the bookie. Scotty found him in his cell sleeping. He walked out as smoothly as he went in, after he put the seventy two holes in the bookie's body. Now he got high to escape that madness of life in prison and the reality of not being there for his only boy Rell. He still didn't miss a thing. If there was dirt on any person and they didn't want anybody to know, best believe Scotty knew. Scotty would use the information to maximize his power to help Dro find out who betrayed his best friend and his son. Dro built a close relationship with these three wise men, for years on the inside and now that he was free, he laughed at the person he had in his pocket to stay connected to all of them, C.O. Dickenson.

16

Dro entered the Comfort Inn parking lot with Mark right on his heels, dripping off sweat while Dro remained dry. Dro spotted Isha's white Lexus as she stepped out looking flawless, wearing John Ashford from head to toe. Her button up white see through top would have bedazzled any man as her breasts rested in a white and gold push up bra. The pants fit her hour glass figure impeccably and to top it off she had her toes out because she knew Dro loved pretty feet.

"Damn, I could never forget that body, that's the girl."

"Isha's my wife so watch your mouth," Dro slowed his pace into a walk. When Isha saw him, her heart stopped and if there was any doubt in her mind who she wanted to spend the rest of her life with, there wasn't anymore. She took off running at full speed then jumped right into Dro's arms. She wrapped her arms around his neck and her legs around his waist as tears raced down her face. Isha kissed his lips, neck, ears, eyebrows…anywhere she could before she laid her head on his shoulder. In his ear she whispered, "Baby I love you more than life itself. I couldn't believe my ears when Mr. Dickenson called me and said to be here. I thought I was dreaming. Now I'm scared to let you go, too afraid you may leave me again."

"Isha, look at me," Dro spoke in a soft smooth voice. Isha picked her head up to look into Dro's eyes that melted her heart. "Baby I'm here and I'm not going anywhere, you hear me?" Dro caressed her face as he wiped away her tears, "But I am going to need you to be patient with me for a few months until I get to the reason why I just did the last two and a half years of my life in hell. Can you do that?"

Isha was about to speak when Dro put his finger to her lips and stopped her. "Isha I love you as the person who stands before you, a real man and real men make choices then take what ever comes with them. I made mine and I would love for you to be by my side for this last run. If you can't, I can understand that also, and I wouldn't love you any less no matter what your answer is. I promise my family will never want for anything."

Isha, being a strong woman that understood that life was hard, tried not to make decisions based off of her emotions. But when it came to Dro, she was still like a little girl. He was her hero that always kept her safe. The reality of Dro's words hit her heart like a Mack truck. A few tears rolled down her face, when Dro went to remove it she said, "No, leave it. I need you to see the suffering you put me through when you're gone. Yes I'm going to be right by your side but this time to make sure it never happens again." They kissed passionately, "Thank you," he replied. "Dro you know I could never leave you. Now come on, I'm going to show you why that nasty girl couldn't have nothing on me." Isha ran the hotel key across his lips.

"Baby I can't, you see Mark's here."

"That's why I brought Kim to keep him company." Dro looked over Isha's shoulder and Kim was talking with Mark but staring at him. When they made eye contact, Kim slowly ran her tongue over her lips, "Hey Dro, welcome home!"

"Hello Kim." Dro just smiled before he made the introduction, "Mark this is Kim if you don't already know."

"No, he don't know. I don't just give my name to anybody plus I never did the white tee thing," Kim interrupted.

"Oh Dro, I know she didn't just try to play a player."

"I guess you've got your hands full but this here is the lovely Isha, my wife."

"Pleased to meet you both," Mark was puzzled trying to remember where he knew Isha from.

"Mark, we're going to slide up in here real quick, so handle that," Dro looked at Kim.

"I got this, you need anything?"

"You know what boy, you're to…" Kim stopped in mid sentence when Mark pulled out a couple of knots of money and passed them off to Dro.

"Here, do you champ. I got more, it's like we're printing the shit and Dro."

"Yeah," Dro replied, stepping over a bum to enter the building.

"That's handled."

Dro admired the beautiful site of the Hotel suite that was lit by the glow of ten candles. Isha had placed five on each side

101

of the bed. Teddy Pendergrass' *'Come go with me'* played on the stereo. Red and Peach roses covered the king sized bed and made a line to the bathtub. Three bottles of Champagne sat on ice. The smell of imported Issey Miyake flowed out into the hallway which was Dro's favorite scent. The temperature was a tranquil 74 degrees. "Damn baby, how did you have time to do all of this?"

"Remember when I used to come see you for the weekend and on Monday's until you told me to stop coming?" She threw a quick hard two piece to Dro's chest. "Oww girl, that hurt. But I'm glad to see you still got it."

"I don't care, I want it to hurt. How could you tell me something like that? The woman you say that you love, who carried your children...to stop coming to see you?" Dro picked Isha up and carried her to the bed softly laying her down on her back. Looking into her eyes he said, "I'm sorry."

"Dro I needed you. I got this done quickly because they know me. This is where I would and cry myself to sleep night after night when you would decline my visit."

"I needed you also baby but for me to have you in my arms again I couldn't show any weakness or I would have died in there. My family is my heart and there is nothing I wouldn't do for ya'll. That made me human in a concrete jungle filled with the most infamous animals. So to survive I had to become one of them. Somewhere I lost myself while at the same time I pushed you away trying to lose you also. But you remained my foundation that refused to move and that's what kept me grounded knowing that you were ready and still with me...thank you." Dro kissed her while slowly removing her clothes until she lay completely naked. He scooped her up into his arms again, becoming more aroused by the scent of her Dior Homme perfume before sitting her into the warm water. Dro relieved himself of his clothing as Isha watched his every move. The sight of his muscular chest and eight pack abs along with the extra pounds he gained set her body on fire. Dro gripped two bottles off the ice as he slid in between Isha's soft legs. She wrapped them around his waist and pulled him closer.

"Matty said I can't drink but he never said I couldn't taste." Dro turned the bottles upside down until he covered

Isha's whole upper body. Then he let his tongue entice Isha as it moved all over her body. The feeling of his lips sucking on Isha's breast along with the friction he applied on her clit, built a sexual desire she didn't know existed. She thought to herself, "He knows my body too damn well." Dro picked her up out of the water like she weighed nothing and sat her on the edge. Taking her legs into the air, he kissed one toe then the next, followed by her ankles. He moved up inch by inch until he kissed every part of her lower body except her sex box. "Please don't stop!" she whispered. "The world couldn't get me to," Dro answered, caressing the middle of her sex box at a nice rhythm in all the right places. He used his finger to massage her clit as he ran his tongue in and out of her love box. Isha locked her legs around Dro's head and squeezed tightly while her body quivered, releasing a rush of hot cum. She slowly released her grip on Dro and fell straight onto her back to the wet tile trying to catch her breath.

"You're not getting away that easily."

"I know but please let me get my air right first." Dro would hear no such thing; he was out of the water and on top of her in a second. He aggressively parted her legs and then eased the head of his manhood into the tip of her walls. Isha stopped him with an arm to his abs. Dro looked into her eyes as she said; "I love you." She removed her arm and closed her eyes as Dro entered her. A loud moan escaped her mouth as Dro gently expanded her pussy walls with every thrust. Feeling that Isha was nice and wet he picked her up and carried her over to the king size bed laying her on her stomach. Dro re-entered her from the back but satin sheets was making it hard for him to get his balance so he pulled Isha by the waist until his feet hit the floor. He made love to her every way possible, slow and deep, fast and hard, then midpoint rough where he squeezed her ass cheeks hard while biting her on the back with each stroke. Isha bit her lip and pulled her hair as she took in the pleasure until she couldn't stand it anymore. Her body started to tremble, "Oh-oh Dro oh, I oh-oh I miss you oh-oh I'm cumming oh-oohhh baby you make me feel so good." At that moment Dro's body became stiff as he released inside her. Isha lay there weak, unable to move.

"Come on woman… round two in the bathtub."

"Now I know why I love you so much."

An hour later Isha dropped Dro and Mark off at the luxurious Plaza-Warwick in center city. "Who lives here?"

"Me"

"Yeah right," said Dro as he took in the sights of one of the top hotels in the city. When they approached the entrance, Brad the door man quickly opened it and said, "Nice to see you made it back safely from your trip Mr. Mark. How was it?"

"Just beautiful Brad."

"That's always pleasant to hear and by the way, if I'm not mistaken I believe Kate has some mail for you."

"Thanks Brad."

"No problem"

Mark gave Brad fifty dollars with the handshake then retrieved his mail from the front desk. "Kate can you please hold all my calls and have a thousand charged to my room, sent Western Union."

"I know, to your two friends as always."

"Yes, but now it's only one, Forty."

"That's Mr. Daniels. I got it."

"Thank you"

They rode the glass elevator to the 56th floor. Mark pushed in his eight digit code then stepped in. "Dro make yourself at home because my home is yours really and that room in the back on your left hand side is yours along with everything in it. Now if you don't mind, a player got to go and wash his ass from all that running." Mark locked the bath room door and pulled out his iPhone. "Yo, he's here so hurry up."

Dro was amazed by the apartment as he moved from room to room. The living room had two inch wall to wall carpeting that felt like air under his feet. The black, white, and gold furniture consisted of two sofas, six chairs, and a wedge wood coffee table that was all designed by Creston. The exterior lighting with the gold and black draping gave the room a mysterious look. The dining room had several Deco paintings on the wall with an antique custom made blatt Billiard pool table sitting in the middle of the marble floor.

The side stair case led to the theater room where a four piece black and red lambskin recliner chair rested in front of the 100 inch screen that hung from the ceiling. Dro returned back up stairs and stopped in front of the room that Mark said was his. He put his ear to the door and listened for any movement. Certain that no one was present; he opened the door cautiously. When he stepped in, he thought he was in New York on Fifth Ave, from all the designer accessories that were everywhere with the tag still on them. Beneath the bed were shoes from one side to the other by name, like Alessandro Dell Aegua, Armand Basi, and Neil Barrett. Dro opened the door to the walk-in closet and pushed the red button on his right. He watched as over eighty suits moved passed his face on hanger. Dro picked out a cream colored silk linen suit, black linen shirt and black gator shoes and a cream Trilby, all by Louis Vuitton. There were two walnut wooden boxes sitting side by side on top of the dresser. In the first box was twenty-one pair of glasses, of all designers. In the next box was the jewelry to match, from iced out watches, chains and rings, to smooth plain and classic. Dro laid a Marc Jacobs watch and glasses next to the suit. He turned the water on in the room shower then stepped in.

Walking down the hallway, Dro was surprised by the fact that the clothes fit him perfectly. Mark heard the door close. "Here he comes now, so be ready." Shawn slid his gun from his stomach over onto his hip then reached behind his back just before Dro entered. "That's what I'm talking about champ, you look open casket sharp." Dro looked from Mark to Shawn and back again, feeling that something was off center. He sat in the chair that positioned his back against the wall before he spoke, "See, this right here is my taste, plus it fits like its tailor made."

"That's because it is, you don't think after all the times we got our shit tailored together in the joint that I would forget your numbers?" Dro smiled as he watched four sweat drops roll down the side of Shawn's face. The room temperature was a comfortable seventy degrees so Dro knew that there had to be another reason for Shawn to be sweating like that. Mark picked the room phone up and dialed four digits. "Yes Kate, can you have my car out front in ten minutes. Oh my bad, the blue one, thanks."

105

"I'm going to the bathroom and then we're out." Mark cut his eyes at Shawn and then disappeared down the hallway. In the bathroom, Mark heard the sound of four hard rumbles followed by glass being broken. He raced to the living room and was shocked at what he saw. Shawn was out cold, face first next to a demolished glass coffee table as Dro had his hand gripped tightly around Shawn's black 45, pointed to the back of Shawn's head.

"Nooo.... Dro! What's going on, what happened?" Dro faced Mark but kept the gun locked on Shawn. "You tell me, it's your man? Mark, I love you like a son but don't let that money make you cross me because it's not going to be easy."

"Money? Cross you? What the hell are you talking about?" Mark questioned.

"You know what the fuck is going on," Dro's arm started to shake as he gripped the gun tighter. "I saw you give him the eye and as soon as you left he stood up to talk about how he got something for me, and I saw this," Dro pointed to the gun. "On his hip and when he turned to the side, I tried to break his face." Mark busted out laughing so hard, a tear escaped.

"I don't see nothing funny, I've haven't been out of jail 24 hrs and I'm about to bag your man."

"Dro you're bugging, you sure he wasn't going for this bag?" Dro watched Mark with a hawk's eye while he gripped a bag from beside the sofa. "The man wants to be a part of our boxing team. I've been teaching him some moves late night at Matty's when I can find the time but I told him he had to ask you and he thought if he got you something, it would be easier. So he got these off of eBay," Mark handed the bag to Dro. Dro slowly opened it to see a pair of black on black boxing trunks. "I think that they belonged to Frazier or Tyson, whoever it was they had them on when they won the title." Dro sat the bag and gun down on the carpet and helped Shawn to the sofa.

"And Dro, don't you ever disrespect me like that. I love you like the father I lost and I can't wait to find and I will the moment that angel makes his move but until then, crossing you is like crossing me. And Shawn, I told you to watch the jab" Mark said. "But he sucker punched me," Shawn rebutted.

"So."

17

On the way to the A-One privately owned sports bar, Mark gave Dro all the information he could pick up since he'd been close to Bo and Gotti. "Now you know all the hot blocks and small businesses that do the main numbers. I've been playing the kid Bo like Blackjack you know, pushing all the keys for him and I still don't know any of his stash spots but you won't have any problem with that. Because Bo doesn't even have a clue we're on to him."

"On to him?" Dro asked.

"Yeah I believe he's the one."

"Why?"

"Because when I said you were coming back everyone was on deck but him and the fact that's how he moves, on some one man power shit. Making it seem like it's all about A-One then he turned around and tried to make a side deal with me. Talking about tell Gotti and Shawn that I'm no longer dealing with A-One, that I'm going solo. Then he would supply me on the side at a cheaper price but he'd keep all his money to himself. That's a snake. You should have seen his face when I said I couldn't because Shawn's family and I never cross family."

"Yeah, we don't get down like that," said Shawn as he cut his eyes at Dro while rubbing an ice pack against his swollen face. "Dro I know it was him."

"What about Gotti?"

"I've been watching him closely too but he don't say too much around people, plus he has this unorthodox style of how he plays the background and lets Bo look like he's running everything. But believe me, Gotti's on every coin they make and anything of importance must go through him but he always deals on the up and up." Dro sat in silence for twenty minutes, letting everything run around in his mind before he asked, "Where are they having the party for me tonight?" Both Shawn and Mark turned and looked at Dro, whose head lay back relaxed, resting on the head rest watching the movie Immortals.

"How'd you know about that?" questioned Mark.

"If I have to cut the grass to see the snakes, I got to know everything."

"At Soldi II..."

"Just like Boggy said it would be," Dro said smiling.

They stepped inside the sports bar looking as if they were three models instead of men on a mission. Shawn's attire consisted of tailored black dress pants with a light pink and white pin striped button up Armani shirt. He also wore a Black Armani suit jacket that matched with his soft Gucci loafers. His pink and yellow diamond watch and chain added just the right touch. Mark took the classic approach with his Thomas Burberry brown pants and jacket, white polo shirt, red gold Rolex and a vvs eight carat diamond rope.

Bo, Gotti, and Mall lounged in their personal booth when Gotti spotted them. "Over here Dro!" Bo and Gotti rushed to their feet to embrace Dro. "It's been a long time partner, but I'm glad to have you back."

"Thanks Gotti"

"Nigga get off your ass and stand the hell up and show some damn respect. This man is one of the main reasons you can get money with us now," screamed Bo at Mall who shot up to his feet, mad at himself. "My bad Mr. Dro, I'm Mall, pleased to meet you."

"Did anybody ask your damn name?" Bo questioned.

"It's okay....Mall, is it?"

"Yes"

"Bo, take it easy on the youngin," said Dro. "Nah it's just the fact that they forget too easily that we were their age and they don't have to go through or do half the shit we did to see a dollar. Let alone get a dollar but he's tough sitting here ice grilling somebody, matter of fact go sit over there," Bo pointed to a small two chair table in the far corner. "It was nothing big, let him stay," Gotti pleaded as they all took a seat. "Nah, I want to see one of these tough young punks punch me in the mouth now go on get and on your way over there, tell one of them bitches to send a few bottles of Champagne over here. This is a celebration."

Mall slowly walked across the floor thinking, *"How could I be so caught up in my feelings to show my emotions like that?"* A month after Pretty Tony went missing and a thousand questions to Isha all ending with the same story, Mall believed it had to be Dro's work who sent someone out of A-One to kill or kidnap Pretty Tony. So when he heard Dro was coming home soon, he did what he had to do in order to be a part of Bo's circle. Even if it was to be a yes man, but now the wait had come to an end and he wanted answers.

They all raised their glasses in the air while Bo gave a toast. "This is to the next champ and the many nights of stacking this money together, A-One!"

"A-One," they all said together before drinking the glass straight back. Bo continued, "Dro how does it feel to be back in the game?"

"I won't really know until I'm tested."

"You don't have to worry about that, you will be tested." Dro's muscles instantly tightened as he looked at Bo and Gotti. Tension was in the air. Mark slid his hand unnoticed, inside his suit jacket letting it rest on the handle of his chrome forty five. Dro stood to his feet and asked, "What was that, I don't think I heard you right at all."

"Follow me I can show you better than I can tell you."

Bo started for the exit with Shawn and Dro behind him, then Gotti with Mark bringing up the rear. Shawn slightly nodded to get Dro's attention; once they made eye contact Shawn cut his eyes at Bo then moved his lip so Dro could read them. "I'm going to steal him." Dro shook his head "No" then moved his lips to say, "Be easy, I got him." Bo stepped out into the crisp night air where a white stretch Mercedes limousine sat parked out front. The words *'Welcome Home Champ'* were written in bold red letters hanging from a banner on the side. Dro was caught off point when Bo opened the back door and said, "Yeah, you'll be tested."

Shawn pulled his gun quickly when twenty of the most beautiful women of all shapes, sizes, and colors stepped out of the limousine. They stopped right in front of Dro. "Whatever you want from who ever, it's yours. This is the new A-One Dro and we have become a corporation. And you're a CEO and we're glad to have you back my nigga."

109

"That goes the same for me too Dro, if only Rell was here it would be just like old times."

"Well let the old times begin because Rell's right here." Dro made a fist and hit his hand over his heart moving it in a circle motion.

"You never lied," Gotti gave Dro a strong hug. Bo walked back into the bar and said, "Mall bring your dumb ass on, we're out."

18

Club Soldi II was so packed that the security guards refused to let anymore people enter unless you had heavy juice. The three parking lots that surrounded it were covered with luxury cars from one end to the other, making it easy for the black tinted Lincoln Navigator sitting on 24 inch rims that was really an undercover surveillance truck, to blend in.

Detective Brian and Detective Michael from the 39th station made sure that they were receiving the sounds and pictures loud and clear from the device sewn into the material of officer Dell's shirt and belt buckle. "One-Two, One-Two."

"That's it, you ready?" asked Det. Brian as he removed the head phone from his ears. "Ready as I'm ever going to be," answered Officer Dell. "This is your fifth time in there and you still haven't come back with nothing on Roc or the club. The city is ready to shut down funds to this operation if we don't come up with something soon. So stop all that damn partying, drinking and showing off that ice acting like you're one of them and bring me something to lock that son of a bitch up on!" Det. Michael demanded. "Take it easy on the man Michael, we all want Roc as badly as you do but Dell here is doing his best and if there is something going down in there, like the Confidential Informant stated, he will find it." Det. Brian had been watching the drug trade in the city for over twenty years from the Black Mafia to the next generation of Junior Black Mafia, then the Young Guns, now Roc. So he knew how bad Det. Michael wanted Roc, he also understood that money was power and it wouldn't be easy.

Inside, undercover Officer Dell showed his already stamped hand to the two 400 lb. bouncers and then stepped into the third floor V.I.P. box. He adjusted the gold Gucci framed glasses that had a built in PRF-13 receiver which gave access to his eye sight to the detective's working the surveillance monitor in the truck. Dell was a twenty seven year old, 5'll" two hundred pound undercover cop in his fourth year, transferred from NY. Being that today's target is a much younger hustler, Dell moved rapidly from officer to drug task force agent, then undercover specialist. He made over 30 successful busts until one day his

111

field team jumped the gun and took down a drug Kingpin before the deal was made, blowing his cover, and almost ending his life, after several attempts on it. The Department forced him to transfer to Philly. Dell promised to never trust a field team again. "What's that going on to your left?" asked Det. Michael. Dell turned his attention there to see over sixty people standing in a circle as two men stood in the middle. While he moved closer, through people he could see there was a three layer white, green, and gold cake in front of them. The green was a painted hundred dollar bills and the gold was a dollar sign with the words 'Welcome Home Champ'.

"Dell, you have to move the red headed woman on your right over about three feet to her left because she is blocking the shot. All we can see is her back side and what a lovely back side it is." Dell continued to move until he was at the front, standing next to Mark. "Brian look at this, isn't that Dro the boxer with Bo? I'll be damned," questioned Det. Michael.

"Yes but he's no longer in the game," answered Det. Brain.

"Then what the hell is he doing back with A-One?"

"It looks like a welcome home party," stated Officer Dell.

"I didn't hear you, what did you say?" asked Mark.

"Nothing I was just clearing my throat," Dell respond.

"Dell don't waste any time with them, we'll get them sooner or later. Move around and try to find Roc."

Dro cut the first piece of cake when Isha entered with Kim. Isha's beauty captivated the room in her sky blue DKNY dress that hugged her every curve just right. She could feel all the eyes on her body as she crossed the floor. Usually it would have made her feel uncomfortable but not tonight, she couldn't care less because her man was home. She walked right by Bo without a word and put her arms around Dro's neck, missing the touch of his lips on her. They kissed, "Baby I don't understand why you rented an apartment and can't stay at home with us, your family."

"Love, how many times have we been through this? But for the last time, I can't afford for anything to happen to ya'll while I'm in them streets. Plus I'm on parole to that address, so if I wanted to turn back baby, I can't. Believe me; I am going to miss you and the kids every minute we're apart." Dro kissed her softly on the lips, then he looked deep into her eyes before continuing, "Promise…it will be all over real soon."

"I know but that doesn't mean I have to like it." They laughed and danced for hours together as Dro moved around the room getting to know the rest of the A-One team.

"I see you haven't lost a step, you're as light on your feet as ever."

"You haven't seen nothing yet."

Dro elevated Isha's right arm and spun her in a 360 degree circle before dropping her so low that her head was four inches off the ground. Bo looked on from a distance in a booth with pure displeasure written on his face as he downed his fourth bottle of Remy X.O. He was with four females and Mall but not paying them any mind.

"Bo look, isn't that the guy you've been trying to get to talk to you?" asked Mall while tapping Bo's arm rapidly, excited to be in the presence of the man walking across the floor. Bo coming back from his abstract thoughts, snapped, "What the hell are you pulling on my damn arm for?" Mall just pointed. Officer Dell was dancing with a cute red bone about 5'7" who looked like Lisa Raye when Det. Michael screamed into his ear, "Stop all that damn jigga-booing and get over there, it's him." Dell looked up and couldn't believe his eyes after several trips to Soldi II coming up with nothing; this could be his big break.

"Excuse me beautiful but I have to use the restroom."

"But the song isn't over!" she replied. Dell ignored her as he smoothly walked off in the direction of the three men. Dressed in a three piece double breasted suit, Roc with Manny and Billy D right behind him, tapped Dro on the shoulder just as the song ended. "Excuse me; I believe you need to speak with me?"

"Yes I do Mr. Miller."

"Please, call me Roc."

"Okay Roc, can we talk somewhere private?"

"If needed," Roc answered.

"Most definitely"

"Alright, come with me."

113

Dro excused himself from Isha, "Love I got something very important to take care of so here, take my keys and I will meet you back at my apartment."

"But baby do you know who he is? That's the medication man for all these dope heads around me," Isha stated.

"Yeah."

Isha rushed back to the booth where Kim and Mark were talking and gripped her blue Fendi purse, then rushed back. "Here take this and be safe." She passed over the gun her father bought her many years ago. "No you keep it; I'm going to be fine." As Roc departed, his eyes roamed around the crowd and immediately paused when he saw Kim, *"Where have I witness that face?"* he tried to recall...then it hit him, "Black!" Roc's mind flashed back to the night he had Black face to face with death when he and his team invaded Kim's home in search of the man who at that time was only known by the name Solo; it was a night that changed Kim's life forever. What started out as a quiet night with Black the love of her life ended by means of blazing gun fire, with Black trying to take out Roc's team and Roc's team closing in on him, Black ended up being held hostage in an attempt to get information and forcing him to give up as much detail as possible about Solo. Roc made sure that Black knew who really held the power and that getting to the head of the Get Money Click would soon come as he fired two shots.

Kim was awakened by the sound of gun shots that night, which turned out to be the initial exchange of gun fire between Black and Roc's team. Startled and confused, she jumped up making sure that it wasn't a dream. Hearing another shot, she grabbed her gun and crept from her bedroom heading down the stairs cautiously and entering the living room. Once she made sure no one was there, she headed toward the kitchen just as Roc stepped out of the darkness eating a bag of potato chips. Kim's gun was aimed on him in seconds and ready to fire, but not before she heard, *"Bitch drop it!"* Buff, one of the men on Roc's team, had his gun pressed to her head.

Roc had called out through the patio door, *"Black, I got somebody that needs you for a minute."* From that moment on, Black knew that he was in a world of trouble and pleaded for his wife's life, even if it meant that he'd lose his own. Roc interrogated him, gathering every bit of information Black could provide about Solo.

The gun fire that proceeded was short lived and so was Black when Manny, silenced him for good. They spared Kim's life, knocking her out cold before making sure none of their finger prints were left behind. Roc hoped his decision to let her live was the right one as seeing her face seemed to open a new chapter in a book that was already finished.

Upstairs in his upper office that over looked the club, Roc sat behind a big cherry oak and marble desk watching the third dimensional surveillance screen, when four fast knocks followed by two pauses made contact with his door. "Come on in," Roc said as he remained seated while Manny, Billy D and Mark made their way into the large office with Dro following behind. Manny looked at his watch and then touched the second screen on the left; giving the sign. Roc now knew the men came unarmed, if not it would have been an indication of disrespect.

"Please, have a seat." Mark and Dro rested on one of the two soft black leather sofas. Billy D stood behind Roc while Manny stayed in front of the door, making sure that no one entered or left. Roc continued, "It came to my attention earlier today by an old friend of ours, Meshane that you would be here and needed to see me."

"Yes and thank you for taking the time out to see me."

"Don't worry about it, this meeting was needed more than you know so what is it that I can do for you?" Roc asked.

"A few years back, I had to kill a man out in front of your club."

"I think I do remember, oh yes with all the bad news coverage D.A. Earl Dash was trying real hard to close me down. It's a shame he still thinks he runs this city," Roc effortlessly spun his chair around, turning his back to Dro and Mark. His eyes scanned over the twenty seven, 10 inch monitors that were overseeing the club ground. Then he proceeded, "I'm sorry to hear about your situation, if it helps....I did visit the hospital on several occasions. Me and Rell have a friend in common and I was hoping to catch him there really badly but we'll meet again. That's another story though," Roc smiled for the first time in weeks at the thought of revenge. But if he had learned anything

115

from Billy D, it was that patience was a virtue. So like wine, he would wait for the taste of revenge would only get greater.

"I was wondering if I could obtain the surveillance tape from that night to see if I missed anything or anyone. If you don't have it, I understand because a lot of time has passed."

"Don't worry yourself about my foundation, we're all together. The question is if you do find someone on the tape, your plan is to make them disappear correct?"

"Exactly," Dro replied sharply.

"It will be for whoever had something to do with my uncle getting crossed," Mark added.

"Okay, that being said," Roc stood before saying another word and walking around the desk to stop right in front of the both of them.

"If I give you this tape, then I'll become a conspirator to your actions and I don't have the time to find out if a nigga can hold his water."

"What the fuck you trying to say...that we're going to snitch?" asked Mark as he tried to get to his feet, fighting the strong force of Dro's tight grip keeping him in his seat.

"Calm down and chill out," Dro demanded as Manny and Billy D were at Roc's side instantaneously when Roc waved them off. "Let him go because if anyone knows what I'm talking about, it's him right Mark?" Dro locked eyes with Mark for a few seconds which seemed like hours before he released him. If Dro's eyes could talk they would say; Mark was all he had left and if they have to die there...so be it." Mark quickly got up and stood face to face with Roc and said, "Look man, I don't play both sides of the game, and I feel disrespected that you said something like that."

"Mark Listen good, I'm only going to say this once. First, if I were going to disrespect you it wouldn't be with words...that's for kids. Actually I was giving you a warning of what the end of four quarters is going look like if you did. Second, hot head, always ask yourself first if you're prepared for war with an enemy you know nothing about, which means you don't know enough, now step over here, and let me show you something."

116

Roc stopped in front of the surveillance monitor with Mark and Dro on each side of him. "See here, this is the man you have been observe here with on several occasions, I believe his name is Shawn." Roc touched the right upper corner of the screen. Then on eight cameras, adjust to a close up on Shawn. Roc continued, "Your man looks fly in that suit and but that's not the interesting part. Always remember it's what you don't see that has brought our leader in the game this far. As you said, you play on one side of the game."

"Without question," mark remarked. "Well let me show you my triangle offense. You see the two men talking to each other, two tables across from Shawn on his right?"

"Yeah"

"Now look straight ahead on the opposite side to the middle of the bar, you see the lovely Nicky, who resembles LisaRaye?" Mark nodded his head yes. Still, he didn't understand where all this was leading. "Here at the top of the screen," Roc pointed at two more men standing a few feet in front of Shawn that seemed to be in a heated debate. "This is where I need you to pay close attention." Roc touched the screen again and eight more monitors gave a close up of the others, "Isn't this your beautiful wife? She apparently is upset with someone."

"What does she have to do with this?" Dro asked, frustrated. "Billy D, if you would?" On call, Billy D texted three letters into his Blackberry. Moments later the two men stopped debating then smoothly walked off and took a seat at the other table where the other two men were as they moved to the bar. Nicky approached Shawn with a smile before taking a seat next to him in the booth. Dro's heartbeat sped, watching as the other monitor showed the same type of movement but the handsome man that was just dancing with Kim a song ago, pulled Isha away from her argument and onto the dance floor. Roc let the situation set in before he spoke, "Right now I have ten undercover cops in my club that believe I don't know they're here. Five that don't care that I know they're here. This is to say that all Mr. Billy D has to do is push four numbers into that phone and your man Shawn can keep his fly suit on for eternity and that goes for your lovely wife also, and there still wouldn't be any arrest. I'm revealing the bottom section of my mask young buck because when I was coming up, I was like you in some respect, hot headed gung ho, always ready for the physical and only one fourth prepared mentally. But I was blessed to have an old head, the great Mr. Holmes that cared enough to look out because he saw something in me to pull me aside. And for that I currently understand would die for him. Like Mr. Nate did for Dro and I know he would do the same."

"For sure."

"Then I judge you correctly ...and Mark, he's now trying to do the same for you. So remember this when you move out for Rell, yes this is a game but everybody in it isn't playing physically but knows how to win like Phil Jackson. Mr. Billy D?" Billy D pushed in eight more digits, then the man followed by Nicky quickly excused themselves.

Dro was astonished by how much information Roc knew about his personal life as if he was following it step by step. Roc dialed four numbers. "Make a copy of the boxer shooting and have it to me as soon as you can." Dro shook Roc's hand, "Thanks again Roc for everything and sorry for any inconvenience we may have caused you."

"Don't mention it, this is all for our friend we now have in common, just be safe because every person will be tested for their past no matter how far away from the game he believe he is."

Mark looked Roc in the eyes before taking his hand and said, "Thanks man, I respect that. I was out of pocket not knowing it could be that easy to touch my loved ones."

"Now you know and knowing is the whole battle. I don't know what the fuck G.I. Joe was talking about. I will have any tape dealing with your friend to you in a few weeks."

19

*E*arly Monday morning, Dro lay awake next to an unconscious Isha. He slowly eased his way out from under his lover, never taking his eyes off of her, hoping she wouldn't awaken. He exited the room in the same fashion. Dro showered and shaved before choosing today's outfit. He felt comfortable that a light gray suit and white shirt with a blue tie would do just fine for this part. As he stood in the mirror he said to himself, "This is missing something....I know, a touch of class." Dro rushed over to his jewelry box then stepped back in front of the mirror. The rimless Dior eye glasses and Mimum watch with an iced out Bezel put a sense of power to his appearance.

"Hello my name is Steven," Dro said while parking the B.M.W on the corner of Ninth and Chestnut St. then checked his watch to make sure he wasn't late for his 9:00 appointment. With ten minutes still to go he took two deep breaths then exited the car. He stopped at the buildings double doors and said to himself, *"Come on Dro, you can do this. What was all that planning and practice for? It's now or never, so get it together. White mans world, you will let me in!"*

Dro looked up into the clear blue sky. *"Don't worry main Man I got this man,"* he entered with a smile of confidence as he looked for the desk that read 'Patterson.' Once spotting it, Dro approached the velvet rope as he neared a blond haired woman, about 5'7" with the name tag that read Kelly who was blocking his path. "Excuse me sir, my name is Kelly and welcome to The Bristol Bank of the Nation. How may I help you?"

"You wouldn't happen to be Mr. Patterson the manager of this bank would you?" Dro asked with cockiness.

"No sir, I'm not."

"Then it would be nice if you would run along and tell him that Steven Yurman is here. CEO of Air Perfections Jet Company and I don't like to be kept waiting."

Kelly quickly went to the nearby desk and picked up the phone, "yes, can you please tell Mr. Patterson that a Steven Yurman is presently waiting on him." Kelly covered the receiver with her hand. "Mr. Yurman I'm sorry, Mr. Patterson is in a meeting that seems to be running a little late."

"I don't give a damn if he's running a mile, it's 9:05 and if he's not here in ten minutes I will take my millions to another bank."

As Kelly talked on the phone, Dro hoped he didn't overdo it. Five minutes later, Mr. Patterson came dashing through the doors. "I'm terribly sorry to keep you waiting Mr. Yurman. I told them to notify me as soon as you arrived. If you'd like, would you please step into my office?" They moved down the hall and entered the office. "Mr. Yurman I wasn't aware that you were trying to open up that large of an account with us at Bristol when I spoke with your assistant Kim."

"That was my whole intention Mr. Patterson."

"Please, call me Tom."

"As I was saying, Mr. Patterson the reason you didn't know is because I needed to see how you handle everyday business before you knew I was a millionaire."

"Once again, let me say that I'm sorr-,"

"Save it Mr. Patterson," Dro cut him off, feeling the moment had come to close the deal. Dro stood up over Mr. Patterson who remained seated. "At Air Perfections Jet, we believe in hard work. It's because of hard work that we made over twenty million in Beijing so far this year and we're climbing, which brings me here. My company is thinking about buying some land out in King of Prussia where we plan to build another plant in the U. S. This would make me millions, the city of Philadelphia millions, hell the whole damn tri-state will eat off of this project and hopefully The Bristol. But after today I feel my people have to investigate The Bristol some more before I put 30 million into an account here. A man only has his word because I started my business with a hand shake so the hundred thousand you talked about with Kim will be in your bank by Friday."

"Thank you Mr. Yurman and I promise Bristol will help your people with anything they need to know to help with their investigation."

Dro walked out of the bank and pulled out his cell phone to make two calls. "Hello C.O. Dickenson"

"Yeah, what's good Dro?"

"I need you to get Basil on a secure line for me. How long will that take?"

"Not long, call me back after 4:00 count. We should be good then."

"Alright I'll call you then."

Dro dialed the next number. The caller picked after several rings, "Who's this?"

"Dro"

"Dro? I don't know nobody named Dro."

"I'm calling to pay Meshane's $50 sprint bill."

"Oh that service has just been reconnected. Now just tell me where you want me to send it as long as there's a four way enter section and it will be there in four to eight hours."

20

A few weeks later inside his condominium located in West Philly, Bo continued to pace back and forth in a panic as sweat covered his face and clothes. He again dialed Maria's number and could only reach the voicemail. Bo was now past the point of frustration and gripped the phone tightly, yelling into it, "If this is how you want to play, fuck it.! If I'm going to lose everything I worked for, so will you. Get ready, I'm on my way over there right now and I'm telling him everything!" He slammed the phone off and grabbed his car keys from the table. *"This bitch thinks she can just let this happen to me... well I'll show her."*

Bo raced for the front door when his phone began to ring. Not recognizing the number, he answered with a scream, "Who is it?"

"Who do you want it to be baby?"

"Maria, why the hell aren't you answering my damn calls?"

"Because I'm busy," Maria answered calmly.

"Busy? Bitch my business is being ripped apart and I need answers and you're telling me you're busy? Yeah...with that nigga's dick on your lips!"

Maria took in a deep breath and eased it out slowly to keep her cool, letting Bo's disrespect slide because he knew too much to be tipped off to her true intentions until the time was right. "I'm sorry baby; I didn't know you were under so much stress."

"You fucking right, my profit is down 32 percent and I have lost ten men in the last month alone."

"Okay baby, just calm down and tell mommy what happened so I can find a solution and bring this to an end."

Hearing that Maria still cared about his well being brought Bo to a moment of reflection. "Well it started about a month ago when Mark came into the sports bar and pulled me to the side..."

~ • ~ • ~ • ~ • ~

"Damn Bo, I know I refused your side deal but you go and drop the price on your keys and you didn't tell me?"

"What! Drop the price...hhhaa!" Bo laughed as he continued. "I got the best work in this city and to let it fly for anything less than 28.5 in this drought, I would be just giving my shit away, ha-ha."

"Well if it's not you then there is a new player in town and his birds are flying at two g's less."

"26.5! Come on now, you know that got to be some trash when the real price is 33," Bo responded, waving Mark's statement off while starting to walk back to the party. Mark grabbed hold of his arm firmly, "Nigga do you think I would be standing here questioning you about some bullshit?"

"No, not at all," Bo answered, scared while looking at Mark's enormous hand clenching about two thirds of his arm; not wanting to be on the end of Mark's wrath like so many other people he witnessed. Mark followed Bo's stare, apologizing, "My bad Bo," he said, removing his hand.

"No problem," Bo readjusted his silk shirt while smoothly stepping back two feet to put space between them.

"All I'm saying is that I heard this new team is about their money and will body bag something quick and I'm just making sure you're on point because I'm down with A-One for life."

"Mark, look at me...do I look worried?"

"No"

"Then you shouldn't be, now go ahead and enjoy the party." Bo watched Mark until he was across the room before he signaled for Gotti. "Yeah, what's up, why you not out there doing your thing?" Gotti asked, moving his body to the live music.

"I will, but let me ask you this...have you heard anything about some new move makers in town?"

"No, why? Fast money done slowed up?"

"Not that I know of, why would you say that?" Bo questioned, confused. Gotti shook his head from side to side while pulling Bo closer so only he could hear. "Because if it is they're coming for one thing, money, and we're the ones getting it so check your backyard and if you find kids not playing with you no more…it's true."

"Okay, I'm on it," Bo rushed off when Gotti stopped him. "And Bo, if you find something, you better deal with it before I have to."

"No, no I'll handle it."

Bo made his way to his back office with Mall who was fighting hard to keep up as he took order, "Mall, right now I want you to call all our top shipment buyers and if anyone has dropped their purchase, I don't care if it's by one key in the last month; I need their name on my desk ASAP."

"You got it," Mall replied, pulling out his blackberry.

"Hey Bo, wait! You got a minute?"

"No, not right now Mark," Bo slammed the office door leaving Mark standing alone staring at the cherry oak. Mark slowly smiled and whispered, "Damn, he looked worried."

An hour later, Bo dialed Maria's number and received no answer just as Mall placed three names on his desk. "Bo, these all have dropped by 30 keys or more."

"What! That's over 90 keys, that's impossible for me not to miss…are you sure?"

"Really, it's not because this is how Pretty Tony told us to bait the Italian in."

"Say that again"

"You heard me right," Mall confirmed.

"So, Pretty Tony wasn't being shook down by Caesar?"

"In a way, but no," Mall smiled, remembering his friend's street smarts as he continued, "See there was this kid that came back from Cali with better and cheaper product than Caesar but without power he was nothing. Tony knew this and ordered us to continue to buy from Caesar with our up front money while at the same time, we were cutting back on the work he was tossing us on the side like they did here." Mall pointed at one of the several papers he slowly placed on the desk in front of Bo. "Ray here was the first to cut back by three keys, followed by Ruff, then Slow Motion, all doing the same play. The next week, which by the time the move maker had gained some momentum and your men's pick up's had dropped off another ten."

Bo shook his head up and down in agreement while scanning over the personal files he now held that only he and Maria knew existed with the numbers matching Mall's statement. "As the end of the third week neared, your soldiers started to complain about how they really can't handle the extra work you're giving them but they would take half moving them down to fifteen. The reason was only to give the move maker time to get the drop on you." Bo closed his eyes while leaning back in the chair, letting out a deep breath as he remembered each man's excuse by heart, followed by Caesar's words, "Tony I came to believe that you can handle the extra 30 keys."

"Bo, Bo," called Mall, tapping his shoulder.

"What!" Bo yelled, with anger now covering his demeanor for the disloyalty he had been shown. "When is your next drop off?" Bo looked at his Rolex and said, "Today, about a half hour ago." Just then, Bo's phone began to ring. He gradually brought it to his ear, "Hello?"

"Bo it's me Rick, we've been hit," Rick the truck driver screamed as he was out of breath. Re-closing his eyes, Bo asked, "What happened?"

"It was the black van, the black van….they got everybody." Rick's voice trailed off into a whisper as the picture of him being forced to the ground again went through his mind. "Rick to hell with that crying shit! What happened to the shipment?"

"They got it, everything…it's like they were waiting on us but I don't know how? We got three different routes and we don't know which one to take until Gotti gives us the call."

"Because you were tagged fool!" Bo screamed, slamming the phone shut on Rick as he was speaking. He then started to pace back and forth. "I can't believe someone had the ball to steal something from A-One, this can't go down lightly at all."

"You want me to go get Gotti?" asked Mall, while heading for the door. "No, no don't. I'm the boss of this shit and I'll handle it as soon…" The sound of his phone again ringing interrupted Bo. Reluctantly, he picked up the phone and said, "Hello"

125

"Bo what's up with this? Ya'll don't want to do business with me no more?"

"Ruff, what are you talking about?" Bo questioned, lost.

"Come on, you don't have to play me, I know when I'm got. So I'll come clean, I was buying some small work on the low at a good number only to make some extra cash but never would I let you go baby. You're my main man."

"Knowing this, why would you think I'll cut you off?"

"Because the guy you sent said there will be no more business done with me and A-One from here on out," Ruff explained.

"What guy?"

"The one in the black van"

Enraged, Bo tightened his fist and screamed, "Hhhhaaa" before asking, "What's the name of the new connect?"

"What?"

"I said give me the fucking name of the new connect, you fat piece of shit!"

"H-h-he goes by the name of The New King."

"We'll see," Bo hung up the phone infuriated. "Mall, get five men and make sure they're heavily armed with heat and meet me out back now!"

On the way to the heart of North Philly, Bo gave his men the plan. "Listen, I need all of you on point because we're about to take it back to the foundation of A-One." He cocked back his 9mm. "So if anything gets in the way of this shipment, drop them and let their family put them in the ground." Bo grasped his Nextel and chirped the shipment driver. "David, where you at now?"

"I'm five minutes away from the location."

"Okay, stay sharp, I'm right behind you about fifteen minutes out."

Twenty minutes later, Mall drove the tinted B.M.W. wagon to the tip of 29th street to what seemed to be normal. "Bo, where's your man at? If it's on lets get it poppin," stated Aziz with his forty five in hand."

Chirp. "David I'm here, where you at?"

When no answer came, Bo said, "Man this shit doesn't feel right. Aziz, you and Paul get out here and work your way

126

down through the block. See if anyone looks out of place while I circle around and drop Mitch and Samson off at the other end. This should give us all enough time to meet up at the destination." Bo pointed to a four story warehouse that sat in the middle of the block.

After doing just that, Bo and Mall exited the car. Bo scanned the area with a sharp eye when a man known by the name Slow Motion appeared from the warehouse door. He gradually moved with his unique slow dip and bop, walking towards the BMW with drops of sweat forming at the corner of his face.

"What's up baby, did you see David?" Bo questioned, breathing a sigh of relief.

"Yeah," Slow Motion nervously answered.

"So where is he?"

"In here...I mean in there," Slow Motion pointed to his chest while looking behind him toward the building.

"So everything went well?"

"Ye-ye-yes. They're just waiting for you."

While Slow Motion explained the details, Mall perceived that something seemed a little suspect and began to look him over closely, making Slow Motion even more nervous. Slow Motion's hands and face began to sweat. Mall began to circle him, suddenly spotting a red dot locked on the back of his head. Mall kept his cool and played along, taking his place next to Bo, thinking of Slow Motion's words while continuing his motion for a sign. "Yes, they're here...that's it." Mall noticed that the third button on Slow Motions polo shirt was black and the rest were yellow. "That's got to be a wire," he thought quick just as Slow Motion said, "Let's go the money is inside."

Just as he turned and Bo started to follow, Mall quickly kicked Slow Motion in the side and removed his gun from his waist at the same time. "Get low, it's an ambush!" The sound of two shots suddenly pierced through the air, the first bullet slammed into the front fender of the B.M.W. as the second just missed Bo's head. Mall got down and returned fire in the direction of the shots, giving Bo time to free his weapon. Aziz witnessed the exchange of bullets just as Bo raised his gun and squeezed the trigger, blowing out the warehouse window. The action made his blood pump to be a part of it. He dashed down towards them at top speed, pushing people off to the side with Paul right beside him. "Move the fuck out the way!"

At the top of the block, four men lowered their masks over their stone faces as the older one said, "The revolution begins today," before bringing the engine of the black van to life. He pushed down hard on the gas. Mall raced to the opposite side of a Jeep for cover as shots came from another window, aimed to kill. Aziz, now two feet away from Bo yelled, "Get the one on the right, I got the left!" while forcing his forty five automatic to echo through the block. He landed several shots, hitting a man in the chest, knocking him from the window. Screams rang out and Bo quickly locked on the other man when he noticed out of the corner of his eye a black van pulling to a stop and several men exiting with their guns drawn. He changed the direction of his target when suddenly a bullet crashed into his shooting arm, knocking his gun loose. Mr. Nate eased out the driver's seat, giving out orders with his 357 mag, finding his target and hitting Mitch in the neck.

"Let's move Soldier 2, I need you to cover the rear. Soldier 3, you get the man behind the truck and Soldier 4, you grab the target, he's coming with us and remember we only kill if we have to!" Mr. Nate smiled again, taking aim but this time it was Samson's blood he wanted. Samson panicked as the gun blast aimed for his heart became too close for comfort. When Mitch's body collapsed in front of him, he thought, "I got to get the hell out of here. Roc is only paying me to watch Bo, not to die for him." Looking for a way out, he dashed for the side alley.

"That's good coward, run," whispered Mr. Nate while his eyes followed along with Samson. Bo was now pinned in between two cars with blood pouring from his arm as Aziz with two gun's firing in every direction covered him. He reached for his weapon that was lying behind the B.M.W.'s rear tire, "Got it," Bo slowly rolled from off his knee careful not to be spotted. He focused on the back of Soldier 5's head and pulled the trigger. The shot bucked wildly right, due to the fact that Bo couldn't control the power of the gun with his non shooting hand. Soldier 5 quickly turned around looking in the direction of the shot, just in time to see Bo vanish behind the car. "I got your ass now!" he said while cautiously creeping along side the car until he came to the rear side bumper. He then swung his gun around on Bo, "I got you!"

"No!" Bomb-bomb, "I got you!" replied Mall as he pulled back the trigger knocking Soldier 5, off his feet. "Come on Bo, we got to get out of here now." Mall pulled at Bo's arm. Bo scanned the area until he made eye contact with Aziz who was keeping the masked men at bay. "Okay, on three with my count," Bo said as he pointed with his good hand to a short cut about thirty yards off to their right. Aziz nodded and moved his lips to say, "Go" while simultaneously letting bullets fly from his right palm, followed by his left. He switched hands with a precision that made it seem like he was throwing the shots while walking in reverse, covering their escape.

Mr. Nate also observed Bo dipping low between the cars and slowly closed the distance between them with his gun locked on the tip of Mall's head. His finger crept back on the hammer and suddenly Soldier 5, appeared with a shocking look upon his face before he crashed to the ground. "Noooo, abandon mission! Save team!"

The men returned Aziz's fire as they all moved toward Soldier 5's still body. Seeing the opening, Bo took off trailed by Mall with Aziz coming behind him before dashing down the alleyway. Slow Motion lay still under a car as he watched the masked men circle Soldier 5.

Dro bent down and asked Shawn, "Soldier 5, can you hear me?" Dro smacked him hard across the face, "Come on, you can hear me!" he repeated following with another hard hit when Mark "Soldier 4" protested, "You don't got to hit him like that, let's get him in the car and to a hospital." With no regard for his words, Dro hit him again; "Smack!" then again "Smack!"

"Come on!" Dro yelled. He then raised his hand back to strike him again when Mark grabbed a hold of his wrist. But Dro, being much stronger, broke free and smacked him three more times. "Okay, okay I'm up....Mom I'm up," said Shawn, disoriented. The sound of Shawn's voice brought a sigh of relief to the men. Dro stood up and ordered, "Now get him in the van, we must move quickly!" In the van, Mark said, "I'm sorry Dro, I didn't know..."

129

"Come on, there's nothing to be sorry about, we're men with hearts so it's only right for you to feel pain for your fallen soldier but he was unconscious from the bullet cracking the plate in his vest, sending the plate deep into his chest. I had to bring him back before he went into a coma."

Back on the block, Slow Motion eased out from under a car as he continued to watch the van disappear and said, "Damn that was close." The sudden sound of a gun being cocked echoed in his ear before feeling the barrel on the back of his head. "I said, I'm the new King of this shit, now come the fuck on!"

~ • ~ • ~ • ~ • ~

Bo shook his head to remove the memory. He looked to his arm that was still sitting in a cast and screamed, "Maria, they almost took my damn life and in the last three weeks they've gotten more of my fucking top customers. I need to know what to do and it has to be soon because Gotti can't find out they exist until the time is right!"

"Calm down baby, have you tried to call a meeting with this guy who's calling himself the New King?"

"Yes and I feel that things could get out of control, this guy is so cocky that he said he wanted twenty thousand and a key of raw from us to just speak to his assistant."

"Damn, this man has balls...he's making my pussy wet and I haven't even met him yet," Maria thought to herself before saying, "So what did Dro have to say about it?" *I know his ruff sexy ass is not having it,* Maria continued to think while waiting on her chance to get with Dro. Bo interrupted her nasty thoughts, "Dro? Fuck him and what he has to say! I built A-One to what it is today and I don't need no help, we're going to deal with this situation like we did the rest."

"You're absolutely right baby; I don't know what I was thinking."

"Now that you're back with me, what're we going to do?"

"Pay it"

"What?" Bo questioned in shock.

"Pay it...whatever the cost to meet him because we can't ever win a war without getting to know our target. While you're doing that, I'll put a plan together to end this."

"See, that's why I love you Maria, you're a get down and dirty bitch, so when are you coming to see me?"

Maria disconnected the phone without responding, thinking, "If Only you knew the half."

21

A few days later, after circling the block several times to make sure his actions would continue to go unnoticed, Dro dressed in all black repeatedly checked his watch until it read 5:26 am before lowering his mask tightly over his face. He then exited the rental car. The passenger started to follow when he ordered, "No, you stay here, I'll be right back."

"Okay, but if I hear anything that sounds like a shot, I'm coming," said Mark as he watched Dro's back until he could no longer see him in the darkness. Dro raced with his body tucked low through the woods when he came to the edge of the yard of his target. He paused with his gun gripped tightly to listen for sounds around him. Once satisfied that he was alone, Dro slid through the hole in the gate he cut. After several attempts to gain entry, he found an unlocked window on the second floor. He pulled himself quickly through it and slowly closed it shut behind him. Dro recognized the place he was in to be the dining room, "It won't be long until I eat here," he said hopeful, as he looked at the Oakwood table. Dro moved cautiously down the hallway and up the stairs, rechecking the time, 5:47 am. He stepped into the bathroom.

Moments later he exited, trying the first door on his left, "Locked...damn!" He quickly moved to the second door and found the same. Confused, with his hand wrapped firmly around the third doorknob, Dro held his breathe as he eased it to the right, gradually the door popped open. Dro was relieved that Mr. Nate didn't forget his part of the plan. He watched the two bodies that laid in bed sleeping, thinking on what he was about to do to their lives and it upset him. Dro shook his head and suddenly his watch alarm went off at 6:00 am, advising him that it was time. He approached the bed with each step having his heart in pain for having to do things like this. "Come on, wake up, I know you hear me. Now come on get up." Dro roughly jerked the covers off of them one at a time. "Come on Dad, let us get five more minutes, pleeease," pleaded Dashon as he tried to pull the covers back over his head. Rasheed thought he heard his father's voice and slowly removed the sleep from his eyes when he spotted Dro. Jumping from the bed he gave him a big hug, "Daddy! When are you coming back?"

"I'm here now tiger."

"No I'm saying at night to read me a book again like you always did before I went to sleep."

"Yeah and to take me to see you fight at Matty's" said Dashon, joining in on their hug.

"Listen, come here and have a seat next to me, it's time we have our first real men talk."

"Yeeaahh," they both screamed.

"Ssshhh, you got to keep quiet, what did I tell you."

"That we can't let Mommy know you're here," answered Dashon.

"And why?"

"Because as men we always do what is needed to keep a smile on the face of the women we love and if mommy sees you she'll cry."

"Like me," Rasheed added.

Dro took a deep breath, knowing that the time had come for this conversation and still it didn't make things any easier. Letting it out slowly, he began, "You do know I love you two with everything that I am and I would never leave your side unless I had to without a choice?"

"We know Dad," said Dashon.

"Ssshhh, be quiet, right Dad?" corrected Rasheed.

Dro could only smile at his two soldiers. "And even though I can't help it, as a man and your father, I can always admit when I'm wrong. And boys...I was wrong."

"Ooohh Dad you was wrong!" said Rasheed.

"Yes, but it wasn't in my actions son, because I would do it again a million times if I thought it would save your Uncle Rell but it was what I didn't do that was a mistake."

"How Dad?" questioned Dashon.

"Because I didn't try to help a friend see a better way until it was really too late and for that, I was taken from your life, which I promise to never let happen again. But for Daddy to read you a book every night and to let you see me knock people out," Dro threw two playful jabs at Dashon's chin. "I just need ya'll to watch after your mother and..."

133

"We know Dad, to keep her smiling," they said together.

"That's right...and our family will be back together in no time."

"Are you sure Daddy, because I miss you so much too," Isha said as she wiped away her tears. She had been listening through the cracked door for five minutes until she couldn't hold back her need to touch Dro.

"Yeah Mommy!" screamed Rasheed as he watched her wrap her arms around Dro's neck and give him a kiss on the lips. "Okay, that's enough of the eye hustling here. Now you two go get dressed." Dro handed them both ten dollar bills before they raced out the room. "Thanks Dad."

"Now that they're gone, come with me," said Isha while opening the door, pulling Dro down the hall.

"I'm sorry baby but I can't."

"What!" A look of pure surprise covered Isha's face as Dro released her grip and started to walk.

"So that's it...you're just going to leave me here alone again, wanting your touch hopelessly. This shit isn't fair." The words again hurt Dro more than doing the time itself. He stopped on the steps and turned to face Isha with his tear coated eyes and said, "You say these words as if my love hasn't been yours since the first time I saw you. Like my pain isn't real, because I do my best to conceal it only so it won't add to the suffering. But if you need to see it, here."

Shame and sorrow along with a deeper love immediately filled Isha's heart as one of the strongest men she knew stood in front of her with the feelings he tried so hard to hide, now revealed. "Baby please forgive me, I didn't know what I was saying...I'm sorry," explained Isha as she went to wipe away Dro's tears that now steadily flowed down his face. He stopped her, "No, don't...this is only the reality of our life until I can get closure for Rell."

Without another word Dro disappeared down the stairs, he exited the back door to find Mark standing there with his gun cocked. "What are you doing here? I thought I asked you to stay in the car."

"I know but you're twenty minutes over your usual time, plus they finally made the call."

"When?"

"An hour ago."

"Now it's about to get fun," Dro smiled as they walked off. Mark spotted Isha standing in the window waving bye and thought, *"Where do I know you from, sexy."*

22

*A*n hour later across town, Kim cruised through Center City on a relaxing morning. She was on her iPhone explaining, "I got this."

"You sure?" the male voice questioned.

"Yes, I know what I'm doing."

"But you know this is very important."

"I know, damn," Kim looked into the rearview mirror at the leather suitcase resting on her back seat then continued, "Don't worry. Remember this isn't my first time."

"Okay Kim, hit me when you're done and remember…"

"I know Dro, don't say anything to Isha."

"That, and?"

"Not now, Kimberly Bruston is about to enter the building." Kim parked and gripped the briefcase while checking her blond wig, making sure it fit just right. She entered The Bristol Bank, walking at a nice pace and yelled, "Kelly, please tell Mr. Patterson I'm on my way."

"No, wait Ms. Bruston he's not here today." Kim never stopped walking as she moved her hips from side to side like she was worth millions, while saying to herself, "If I didn't know that I wouldn't be here."

She quickly entered the plush office and took a seat in the soft leather chair. Her name echoed off in the distance. Kelly, leaving the person she was attending said, "Someone take care of her," and raced along side Kim from behind the teller station. "Stop, you can't go in there." Seconds later, out of breath, Kelly stood next to Kim and with her best fake smile said, "Ms. Bruston what brings you here today?"

"The meeting I have with Patterson…you did tell him I'm waiting?"

"No, there must be a mistake, your meeting is not until tomorrow at 9 am sharp Ms. Bruston."

"Excuse me, bit… I mean Kelly, is it?"

"Yes"

"And you are his assistant?" Kim continued to question.

"Yes I am."

"Then it is you my dear, who has made the mistake because you personally stated that I should be here today at nine sharp," Kim said in an uppity voice to sound like Kelly before returning to her own voice, "See" Kim showed her burned out blackberry that read, *"Deposit money at Bristol at 9:00 am"*

"That says today Ms. Bruston but..."

"There are no buts," interrupted Kim, standing to her feet and placing a finger into Kelly's face. "I don't know how you feel about Mr. Patterson but I won't and will not disobey Mr. Yurman's order."

"I'm sorry, did you say Yurman?"

"Yes, Steven Yurman, CEO of Air Perfections"

As the name hit her ears, Kelly closed her eyes wondering how she, *Ms. Perfection* could screw up something so important. Knowing she had to come up with something quick, she said, "Oh, now I remember. He told me to make sure you're well taken care of until he gets here." *"God I hope he picks up his phone,"* Kelly prayed silently.

"Well Kelly, you can start by overseeing the counting of this two hundred and fifty thousand that should be placed in two trust funds for Dashon and Rasheed Brown. Half in each, this is not to be touched until they reach the age of twenty one with the 5.6 value package that will make it worth two million a piece at that time. It's a present from Mr. Yurman so I need you to make sure it's done right." Kim handed the brief case full of money over to Kelly. "Okay Ms. Bruston, I'll see to it right this moment."

Kim took a seat patiently until she heard the door close firmly. Then she was back on her feet instantly, running around to the desk and putting her fingers to work. She typed in several buttons on Mr. Patterson's computer. "Where is it? Dro said it was here," she continued, coming across a register investment on an Audi - Ai for 300,000. "This has to be it, Audi-Ai, yeah right Audi A-One funny...and what car costs that much by them anyway." Kim hit the mouse, entering into the file which revealed several more investments with bigger cash amounts. "Now I must find the connection to the investor." She scanned through various windows, when suddenly she heard foot steps approaching. *"Come on Kim, you got to get back to the home page.*" Sweat began to form on Kim's face as she tried to find her way out while the foot steps became louder. "*Damn, where is it?*" The doorknob being turned brought a wave of panic over Kim's body. Knowing she was as good as caught, "I can't let Dro say I told you so."

Kelly pushed the door open quickly and placed the tray of drinks she was carrying on to the wooden table and yelled. "Ms. Bruston what are you doing?" she asked, catching Kim.

In Upper Darby, Dro checked his phone again to see if he had missed Kim's call due to Mark's loud car system. Mark noticed the look of concern on the face of the man he now respected more than anyone and said, "Dro, be easy…she'll get what we need. Remember I'm the one who brought her in." Mark moved his hips as if he was sexing the air. "I hope so because she can't keep her eyes off of me and if Isha catches her, we're both dead."

"Yeah, you know how women are; they always want something they can't have."

"And once they do get it, many can't handle the true heart of a man. I wonder what Malcolm X's wife said when she saw him in the window holding that AK," Dro questioned, looking up into the sky like it would answer him. "She probably said, '*Damn my husband's a rider,*'" Mark laughed.

"No, she probably didn't say anything, already understanding her man. Know that whatever he does that may bring them discomfort had to be done to bring them ease."

"Come on Dro, enough with that deep shit, we got work to do," Mark shook his head as they moved along side the two story apartments. Coming to a stop at the basement door he stated, "Between you and Mr. Nate, I don't know who's the deepest."

Just then, the door flew open with Mr. Nate's warm smile behind it. He greeted his two soldiers with straight eye contact and a firm handshake. "I'm glad you're here Dro. In my time I have brought a lot of people from the streets over to the revolution but I don't know about this one, he's nuts for real."

"Where's he at?" Mark inquired eager to see his friend.

"He's up stairs doing God knows what."

138

Mark headed for the stairs with Dro saying, "Don't worry Mr. Nate, I got him." Dro gave Mr. Nate a half hug and another handshake then continued, "Thanks for the help, I don't know how I would do this without you."

"Me either because I wouldn't let you. Oh, and Mark..."

"Yes Mr. Nate," Mark paused on the third step from the top.

"I'm the deepest by far."

Upstairs in the center of the living room, Dro couldn't believe his eyes as Mark burst out in laughter. Shawn was sitting on the sofa laughing also, to the point where a tear escaped from the corner of his eye. They all watched Slow Motion who was strapped to a chair with his leg and hands tied behind his back. His clothes had been removed from his body, all except for his boxers that were taped open at the fly. A rope was wrapped tightly around his neck that ran up into the air through the ceiling light, down the wall and connecting to a man's ankle that lay on the opposite couch with his legs in the air as he smoked a blunt. He was screaming, "See, this nigga here is what you call a live puppet. Watch my act Shawn," the man quickly puffed on the blunt until the tip became cherry red then dropped the hot ashes into Slow Motion's fly.

"Aaaahhhh," Slow Motion kicked his feet wildly as his head shot backwards from the pain. At that very moment, the man slammed down his leg with the rope on it making it lift Slow Motion's small body out of his seat, hanging him in the air by his neck. "Dance nigga or die."

Slow Motion's body bucked in every direction as he fought to touch the ground, feeling he was getting closer to death with each second. His face started to change colors to a dark red when the man quickly raised his leg sending him crashing over the chair. "Shawn, for my next act we're going to play hangman, you ready?"

Without warning, Slow Motion was back in the air, "Forty let him down."

"You lucky bastard, I really was trying to kill you while I talked."

Forty smiled then swiftly released his knife that he'd brought from prison, and cut the rope. "And what you got on?"

139

asked Dro. Forty looked over his dirty sweat pants, Timbs and hoody, nonchalantly and said, "My clothes."

"What happened to the stuff we left you at the apartment?"

"It's there"

"Then why don't you put them on?"

"No disrespect and shit, but this is for Rell and it's still a war, there's nothing pretty about it."

"Point taken solider, point taken."

"On the other hand, Dro your man Bo met our demands of forty thousand and two keys."

"What! It was only supposed to be ten thousand a half key to test his personal work," Dro asked.

"Hey, inflation baby…fuck it." Dro just shook his head. "Don't worry, I got this sucker. The meeting is set up for next Friday as you requested. And here's the sample you needed with a little bonus." Forty gave Dro the keys of cocaine before tossing six thousand dollar knots around the room. "Mark, that's yours, Shawn, Mr. Nate you take two, one for yourself and another for Ace. This be me," Forty slid a large bank roll into his pocket then continued, "Dro this is for you and one for Rell's sister."

Dro was impressed with Forty instantly but not by his words or his actions. It was the feeling of ambition he got from him that let Dro know he would make it just fine. Dro went over the plan for the meeting, "Ace is going to be Forty's wing man on this one while the rest of us will play the shadow until…"

Dro's phone interrupted him and he looked at the caller ID, recognizing the number he quickly said, "Excuse me fellas, I must take this. Mr. Nate will you please finish the rest?"

"No problem, now you men sit up straight and you Forty, put out that funny ass cigarette. Men, many wars have been won through out centuries by discipline alone and discipline starts with integrity for oneself. If we can't respect ourselves, never will we respect someone else's life," Mr. Nate screamed. Dro stepped out the back basement door and questioned, "Kim, you alright? What happened, did you get it?"

"Damn Dro, have some faith in a bitch, you know I played my part but only after Mr. Patterson's assistant caught me on all fours with my ass in the air like I was waiting for you to come and take it."

Dro paid the comment no mind as he listened to Kim go on, "I played it off like I could feel the baby kicking. You should have seen me I had her running around getting me help while I downloaded his whole file then tucked it into my 32 D's and five minutes later, I walked out like nothing ever happened."

"And the money?"

"It's done"

"That's great in case anything happens to me my kids will be straight; meet me at my place in an hour because if what Scotty is saying is true then Friday is going to be a short meeting." Dro smiled looking up at the sky and said, *"I told you I got you, we cry together we die together, we chill together we kill together. Now we will build together."* He sped down the road in need of answers.

23

At 8:05 am Isha was on her way to drop the kids off at school physically, but mentally she was still with Dro as his words played back in her mind again and again... *"Baby I'm here and I'm not going anywhere. You hear me?"*

"Yes, but I need you now Dro...alone, to myself for once."

"Mommy, daddy's not here," said Dashon as he watched his mother continue to talk to herself.

"But I'm going to need you to be patient with me"

"Nooo, no, no Dro! You can't keep doing this to me. I've been second to your friends our whole life and the moment I thought I was done with them, you pull this."

Isha's hand's trembled with frustration while driving as she expressed her feelings, trying to get an answer to the pain she felt inside. *"You know what; fuck your nine hundred and something days of hell. What about me and my hell...ha!"* To find a true answer on Dro's behalf, Isha's mind thought back to Dro's tearful eyes as he said, *"You say these words as if my pain isn't real because I do my best to conceal it only so I won't add to your suffering."*

The statement once again took the anger out of her soul instantly. She still could clearly see the sincere pain that was hidden in Dro's face with every word. *"I know you do baby. I'm sorry...I don't know what has come over me but I'm going to make it up to you,"* said Isha, dropping the kids off. Picking up her phone, with a new found spirit, she smiled and said, "Hey Larry"

"Yes"

"Tell Thomas that I'm not feeling well so I won't be coming into work today." Not waiting for a response, Isha disconnected the call. She headed to New Jersey's Monmouth Mall, which just happened to be Dro's favorite. Inside, her first stop was the shoe store where she purchased the most extraordinary Esquivel Alligator wing tip shoes. Her next stop was Norman. There she had found a cream suit that would fit Dro to the tee. Their also was a peach and white shirt that she

142

knew would go just right with his skin complexion and she had to get it. Stepping out of the store she stated, "Now, it's time for desert."

At Victoria's Secret, Isha's hands browsed through several pieces of lingerie and with the help of the manager, she found a tight see through red teddy with a matching red and gold thong and bra. "That's the one!" Isha said, as soon as she laid eyes on it. "Would you like me to bag this up for you?" the manager asked. Isha replied, "Actually no, I'll need to buy a long coat because I'm going to wear this out."

Isha pulled up to Dro's street an hour later, singing Mary J. Bliges' "24-8." She began to circle the block for the second time as Dro instructed when she suddenly spotted a vehicle that looked familiar out the corner of her eye. It sat parked a street over. "I know that isn't!" Not wanting to believe the feeling her gut was giving off, Isha pulled beside the car studying every inch of it from bumper to bumper. "No…she wouldn't do this to me. Why am I bugging?" Isha threw her car into drive and slowly pushed on the gas pedal. She pulled off saying, "Fuck it, I got to know."

She slowly raised the spare key ring that Kim gave her and pushed the button. "You dirty bitch!" Isha pulled off, leaving Kim's car alarm blowing and head lights flashing. "If this is how ya'll want to play, then let the revolution begin," Isha said while looking at her reflection and wiping away her tears with both hands. "This is the last time I cry for you Dro." She grabbed the bags that contained the items she had just purchased for Dro and tossed them out the window. Quickly, Isha dialed several numbers on her phone with a male voice answering, "Hello?"

"It's me, now shut up and just listen," she demanded.

Inside his apartment, Dro and Kim for the tenth time read over the A-One documents trying to figure out the true meaning behind the numbers and letters that they saw. "Dro I still don't get it, if you're saying that all the companies that start with B and O represent Bo's side of the money and the one's that say G and O represent Gotti's money, then that leaves the Ai investment as their team money, am I right?" Kim questioned with a puzzled look. "Yeah, if you look at the rhythm of the deposit, first it's the A-One here." Dro pointed to the top of the

143

paper with a pen and drew a tree with several branches. On the very top branch, he placed the words A-One investments. "See, every deposit goes in effect once the money hits for this one."

"I know that Dro, what I don't get is if Bo run's A-One like he says he does, then why is Gotti's deposit almost double his?" Kim continued to inquire. "I don't know, maybe he gave more," Dro tried to explain. "No, I was thinking that also but if you look at the first series of deposits, they're all the same until the fourth and then…"

"Gotti's became a little bigger than Bo's each time," Dro said, finishing off Kim's thought.

"How did I not see that before?"

"Come on Dro, I was in your math class and you know if it wasn't for me you would never have passed," Kim laughed.

"Okay smart ass. If you know everything, what are all these numbers, 1, 15, 3 mean?"

Kim was about to answer as a loud knocking sound came from the door that stopped her. Dro's mind quickly tried to figure out who could it be as he whispered, "Kim go hide!"

"What?"

"You heard me, now go!"

"Are you for real?"

"KNOCK-KNOCK," this time the sound was much harder. "Yes I'm for real, hurry up!"

Kim shot Dro a look that said, *'Nigga have you lost your damn mind.'* "Pleeeaase," Dro said while giving her his best puppy eyes. "Okay but you owe me and I want mine."

Dro quickly hid the documents prior to answering the door. "Who is it?" he asked but received no response. The knocks at the door resumed. Dro tried to look out through the peephole but it was covered by what looked to be black tape. The action forced him to remove the black 45 mm from his back. Kim's body became hot as she ran her hands over her hardened nipples while watching Dro through the cracked bedroom door. *"Damn…he's gangster."*

Dro quickly yanked the door open and within a second he had his gun locked in the face of the man standing there. Boggy smiled, he looked pass the gun to find Dro's eyes and said, "I would lower that if I were you."

144

"You're right! Nigga I'll give you one second to tell me who you are and why you're at my home before you become another statistic." Boggy, with a calm voice as if the situation couldn't bring him death asked, "So you don't remember me?"

"Hell no"

"That's the way it's supposed to be," Boggy said, breaking eye contact and looking to his right. Dro followed his stare and came face to face with Lil Mac's P39. "You heard the man, drop it!"

"For what, you shoot me I shoot him...that's the way it should be. I can die with that," stated Dro turning his attention back on Boggy, tightening his grip on his weapon just when Boggy gave him a light head nod to look behind him. "Nah, I'm not going for that one nigga," Dro said instead of turning around. He stepped forward until his gun was an inch from Boggy's face. "The man said drop it and I mean now!" a voice demanded off in the distance. "Please Dro, drop it."

Hearing Kim's cries, Dro let out a deep breath as he lowered his gun. "Okay that's better, now take this." Boggy finally brought his hands out from behind his back to reveal a black box. "This is the video that you asked Roc for and more if needed. Men, lets roll."

Lil Mac concealed his weapon and said, "No hard feelings Dro, it's always safety first."

"I understand but damn, ya'll had to do all this?" Dro complained. Mohammed kissed Kim softly on the check and eased five hundred dollars into her palms. "You're innocent in this." He let go of the hold he had on her neck. "I'm sorry for any discomfort I may have caused you sister but a man always does what he has to do."

Kim looked at the money she held then screamed to Mohammed as he exited the porch. "Don't worry about it baby, as long as you pay how you weigh you can come back anytime handsome."

"Kim, get in here," Dro pulled her by the arm from out the doorway then slammed it. "Girl you need to stop playing cause if something happened to you I wouldn't be able to live with myself and I know Isha couldn't either."

145

"You know what, I'm sick of this shit," Kim gripped her purse and jacket and headed for the door. "Dro, when you can treat me like the grown ass woman that I am, and not your teenage sister, then call me." She turned and opened the door and said, "Oh and the numbers 1, 15, 3 are the day each individual made his own deposit. A-One starts it off on the fifteenth followed by Gotti on the first then Bo on the third."

"Government check day," Dro thought out loud, now understanding a bit more. "So if you're trying to stop them, most likely the transaction is done by wire and that means Dro, you're going to need a hacker."

"A what?"

"You're a smart ass, you figure it out!" Kim slammed the door behind her.

Dro smiled at Kim's statement while placing the disk into the DVD player but it quickly disappeared when Rell's face suddenly appeared on the screen as they all exited the truck in the parking lot of Soldi II.

24

*I*n the meantime across town in his personal office, Gotti sat behind his desk with his feet up in the air, resting on its corner. The smokes from his Cuban Havana cigar danced on his tongue while he listened to his connect, "Gotti, the reason I'm down here in person is because I'm hearing things about A-One. I'm not one to listen to hear say when it comes to my money, I need to hear it from the horse's mouth," said Tywan who stood with his hands wide on the desk. His six foot one frame towered over a relaxed Gotti. On sight, one would never know that Tywan was one of the five major suppliers in the city; dressed in his no name blue jeans, white sweater and white Nikes. On his wrist, was a plan Timex.

Hearing no response, Tywan questioned, "Did you hear me?" Gotti blew the smoke out into the air, missing Tywan's face by nearly an inch. He sat up straight in his chair looking Tywan in the eyes and said, "What things?" before taking another deep puff.

"The things like A-One might be losing the strong hold they once had on this side of the city or why it took you an extra week to make this month's payment." Gotti, with an expressionless face retorted, "You know Tywan, you hear a lot of stuff." Tywan waited for Gotti to continue but when he didn't, he screamed, "See, this is why I don't talk with you about business. Where the hell is Bo at?" Tywan looked at his watch. "He's over twenty minutes late."

"Here, you call him. This line is secure, so you can stop beating me in the head about my business because as long as you niggas are getting paid, you need to shut the fuck up!" said Gotti. A smile crept on his face while thinking to himself , *"Yeah, I said it pussy and I dare you to say something, that's right keep on dialing them numbers cause you know if it wasn't for Meshane, I would have been took your shit."*

Tywan dialed the last three digits to Bo's phone number also thinking to himself, *"I know this clown didn't just say what I think he did. His mouth is getting looser by the second. I told Roc to let me shut it the first time. But no, he said never to let a*

147

small piece of pride in my heart stop me from feeding my whole body. Well, I'm starting to get full really quick."

The sound of the phone brought Bo out of his zone as he noticed the secure number on his caller I.D. and stopped in mid stroke. He slowly removed his hands from the soft, thick ass they possessed. "Bo, what are you doing, I know you better not stop," yelled Maria who was bent over with her hands tied to her ankles.

"But it could be..."

"I don't give a damn who it is! You begged for me, you either yoouuu wa-waaant iiiitt or that's it damn! Pleeaasse right there!" Maria closed her eyes to enjoy the pain as Bo began to pick his speed back up, ramming himself into her harder with each impact. "That's it you bastard, fuck me!" Bo kicked her feet in some more which effectively made her ass rise higher in the air. Then in one smooth motion he grabbed hold of her shoulder pulling her roughly back towards him as he slammed his stiff manhood up into it. "O-o-o-oh you mutha a-a-a-hhh," Maria screamed with pleasure. Sweat started to cover Bo's whole body as he stroked away as if he was a wild animal enraged, forcing each inch of his dick deeper into Maria.

"You know bitch your going to stop screaming at me!"

"Oooohhh, no not my ass. Stop, o-o-h shiiit it feels like my ass is going to burst!" The sound of Maria's cries became louder than ever as he slid the last inch of his throbbing rod inside her. "Noooo!" Lost in his own thoughts, Bo said to himself, *"What, you dirty hoe. You think I forgot you put me to the side for him? Not giving a damn about my feelings. Well take this ass hole the size of a flash light back to him!"*

To get in deeper as if it was possible, Bo positioned himself over top of Maria's ass while wrapping an arm around her waist as his free hand squeezed her right breast. Maria bit down hard on her bottom lip, taking the impact from every individual stroke that felt like it was shaking her spine loose. She slowly moved her hips to the left with his push to ease her pain, catching Bo's rhythm. Maria's pain interlocked with her own anger could only make a little drop of pleasure. A hot sensation raced through her body, "Oooh" she began to pick up her pace,

148

making her ass become wet with her juices coating Bo's shaft as he slid in and out.

"Ooooohh it hurts" Maria moaned loudly. *"I know, you no good hooker!"* Bo said again keeping his thoughts to himself. Maria felt herself about to cum and yelled, "Let my waist go-o-o, ohhh damn." Releasing it, Bo watched as Maria pushed off of her toes and fell face first onto the bed, leaving her ass out in the open. "You want it, now take it," Bo closely observed Maria's facial expressions while the tip of his manhood disappeared inside her. "Yesss baby, take all of it," Bo wanted Maria to feel pain the same way he did for her. So without warning, he jammed the rest of himself through her, "Aaaahhh!" He pulled it back out to the tip, only to slam it back again. He savagely repeated this action until the echoes of Maria's hysterical cry vibrated the walls. "Ooh shit I'm cumming, shit Bo I'm cumming." Maria squeezed her ass cheeks tightly as hot cum escaped her body. She could feel Bo was about to explode as well and demanded, "Pull it out on my ass; I need to feel the heat from inside you!"

Bo did just as he was told, "Aaaahh."

"Now untie me." Free, Maria quickly grabbed hold of the two pair of leather straps from out of her toy bag and raised them in the air, "Your turn!" Bo was lying on the bed pinned down on four points when Maria reappeared into the room fresh out the shower with a tray in hand. Placing it on the night stand next to the bed, she engaged eye contact with Bo and whispered, "I love you," while thinking, *"You coward, I took my pain now let's see if you can do the same."* She slowly touched the screen of the stereo and the words of "Pain is love" filled the air. She seductively moved her hips from side to side in the center of the floor. Maria inched closer with each step to the bed. At the end of it, she ran her hands over her naked body down to her clit. She began to play with it, making herself extremely wet and turned on. Maria tasted her own juices while stepping onto the bed, towering over him. Bo looked up hopelessly becoming once again lost in the beauty of Maria's body. "Damn, I love this woman."

She rested on Bo with her knees on the bed. She placed his limp manhood under the outer lips of her love box. She gently kissed from his ear down to his neck as her right hand slowly made its way to the night stand. Then without warning she poured the bubbling hot honey all over his chest. "Aaaahhh, get it off of me!" Bo's body bucked forward nearly tossing Maria from the bed. "Shut up!" she screamed and licked up his stomach when she suddenly bit down hard on his nipple. "Oh, you bitch," Bo tried to break free as he looked up at Maria with a mischievous look upon her face. She gripped his manhood tightly before roughly jamming it into her mouth. Her teeth scratch the tip as she ran them down the length of his rod. Hearing Bo yell out in agony made Maria's body tingle, letting her know she was about to cum. She aggressively began sucking his manhood, moving her head up and down making it hit the roof of her mouth with each movement until it became rock hard. Maria stood up and turned around cowgirl style and started riding him wildly. She dropped down on him with no regard while squeezing his balls. Bo threw his head from side to side to fight the pain from Maria's ass once again crashing into his stomach. His phone started to ring for the sixth time when she yelled, "You can get it cause I'm cumming!" Seconds later Maria removed herself, leaving her juices covering Bo's manhood and balls. Then she quickly slid two fingers inside her ass before pushing them into Bo's mouth, catching him off guard. "Aaaahh!"

"The next time you take something, make sure you eat it first!"

"You bitch!" Bo screamed, spitting the taste from his mouth. Maria undid Bo's right arm and on her way to the shower said, "You do the rest your damn self."

Bo immediately brought the phone to his ear. "Hello?"

"Bo, where the hell are you?" Gotti screamed.

"Oh, oh my car broke down but they fixing it now, I'll be there about a half hour."

"Man I don't want to hear that lying shit, you with that mystery bitch ain't you?"

"No, I swear," Bo tried to explain when Gotti cut him off.

"What'd I just tell you…but we'll speak about that later. Someone wants to talk to you. Here, this nigga said his car broke

150

down and he got a new Benz." Gotti laughed handing Tywan the phone.

"What it do, Bo?" At the sound of Tywan's voice Bo closed his eyes knowing this conversation was yet to come and he still wasn't prepared with an answer.

"Yeah, Tywan what you doing there?"

"We had a meeting scheduled, remember?"

"Damn, my bad Ty, I forgot. Listen I'll be there in no time."

"No, don't worry about it; this one is on me because it seems like you two can't remember nothing," Tywan said, looking at Gotti. "But the next time you forget the day my money is due, it will be on you." Tywan let the phone fall onto Gotti's desk, thinking *"Fuck what Meshane talking about."*

Gotti looked on in shock as Tywan slammed the door behind him. He picked up the phone thinking, *"I hope I'm not underestimating this clown,"* before saying, "Bo, you there?"

"Hey"

"Get here, it's time we talk."

Bo disconnected the call, letting out a deep breath as he fell back on the bed. Maria could clearly see the stress this whole ordeal was having on Bo. She moved onto the bed, resting Bo's head in between her legs and said, "Cheer up Bo, today I think I found out who's behind this New King." Bo quickly reopened his eyes.

"You do?"

"Yes, but we will need a few of your soldiers to pull this off."

"Okay…anything."

25

*F*our day's later, on a Friday at 11:30 pm inside his dressing room at the Wells Fargo Center Dro tried Isha's phone once again and reach her voicemail. "Baby this is uncalled for, no matter what we ever went through we would always talk it out together, not on a machine and I'm not going to start. I love you and the kids and if you can make it here, I would like that. If not, I understand."

The moment Dro pushed end on the call; Matty grabbed hold of the phone and tossed it to Mark. He then hastily taped up Dro's hand. "Look at me kiddo, I don't know where your mind is but I need it right here! With me." Matty smacked both sides of Dro's face. "You hear me, outside these doors is your first step back toward the title and everybody is watching, like you requested invitation only. But every T.V. and big promoter is in those seats for you. So right now I need for you to take what you want out of life and that's to be the champ. If you don't want it, you take the gloves off now and to hell with it." Matty released Dro's hands and stepped away from the table. The sound of Matty cursing brought Dro out of the thought of missing his family, who he hadn't spoken to since the day he refused to sleep with Isha. Now every door and window had been sealed shut with the locks changed.

Dro raised his head to look into the face of an uncertain Matty as he then recalled their previous conversation. *"I don't know Matty; I think it's too soon for me to get back in the ring."*

"Too soon? Your family's future is in your hands, literally and you come to me with this shit?" Matty yelled.

"I know but now isn't the right time."

"Then when, you ungrateful bastard?"

"I don't know but soon." Dro answered, headed for the door when Matty replied, *"Okay if that's how you want it. Fine, but I'm not going to waste another minute of my time with you."* Matty picked up a box and began removing pictures from the wall. *"Man, what you doing Matty?"*

"What I should have done when you first came home talking this crazy talk. I want you out of my gym and off my wall.

152

I don't want to see your face because I don't look at you the same any more!"

"Why?"

"Dro you don't get it do you? See, you were never the best but it was your will to become it along with being a workaholic. That got you by while you were in the ring with the more skillful fighters. But it was your heart that let you over come them and I don't see that person anymore."

"Okay," Dro said as he stopped Matty's hand from taking off the photos of him winning his first fight. "Set up the fight."

Dro now understood Matty's look and got up from the table. He stopped next to him, "Matty, I'm really sorry if I made it seem as if I wanted this any less than the first time you put that old ass tape on my hands."

"That's all we had"

"I know old timer, but as they say, actions speak louder than music!"

A smile came to Matty's face while he pushed play, bringing the surround sound system to life. Shawn and Mark stood still and looked on; being that this was their first time seeing Dro prepare for a fight. Nas' "Hero" blasted with Dro standing alone in the center of the floor bobbing his head slowly to the rhythm. The more his body started to feel the music, the faster the pace of his head moved. Noticing it was time, Matty stepped up and removed Dro's robe and just as he threw, two sharp right jabs then a short left upper cut, he bobbed his head to the right while slamming a left then right jab to the imaginary body. Dro's feet moved in sync with the groove of his hands. He back pedaled with a light bounce then quickly stopped and pivoted to his right, throwing several punches to the upper body. "He's heating up," screamed Matty,

Dro bounced in reverse in a circle when he bumped into Shawn and Mark, "My bad Dro," they stated as they rushed for the corner. "Your bad, it's too late for that, shoot it," Mark with a nervous laugh said, "Come on Dro, you got it."

Seeing that the attention was on Mark, Shawn eased into the corner. "I'll give you five seconds...one...two...five" Then

153

without warning, Dro slapped Mark on his chin. "I said shoot 'em."

"Okay, let's go" Mark slipped out of his corner man jacket as Dro yelled; "Matty set the clock for five minutes."

"What about the speed bag?"

"This is my bag," Dro answered, throwing two fast jabs just in between Mark's now up defense, slapping him again. On contact Mark rolled to the right with the momentum of the jab. He then dropped low sending a loud slap to Dro's sweaty mid section, followed by an uppercut to the chin. Dro saw the body shot coming but the need to feel pain overruled his reflex. The power of the impact along with the look of determination on Mark's face forced Dro to react as he caught the uppercut in the air and said, "That's all you got?"

He faked a jab at Mark's head who in return threw a sharp left then a right hook that caught the tip of Dro's head. Mark responded, "No, there's more."

"I can see," Dro quickly back pedaled as if to retreat which made Mark rush in to cut off the short space they had. Then suddenly Dro shot back inward, Mark's reflexes made him throw the right jab to put pressure on Dro so he could reset his foot position. But the instant he did it, Mark knew it was the wrong move. Dro stepped in as his arm went past him leaving Mark's whole body open. Dro began to shoe shine on Mark, throwing several punches in a circular motion up his body, stopping with a light tap on his chin.

"That's one," Dro said as Mark nodded his head in agreement before stepping back and giving Dro a short bow in victory. The two touched hands and were right back at it. Mark flashed Dro a smile on the outside but inside he was feeling full of anger at himself because Dro had told him over a thousand times, *"Never let another fighter dictate your fight plan."*

"You got me Dro, but I have a few moves of my own." Mark slipped three of Dro's jabs, and then instead of his usual flat footed fighting style, he began to bounce from side to side, left to right and back while dipping all in rhythm. Dro flashed Mark a smile, happy to see his capability to learn on his feet, when a straight right crashed into his lip that made him even more pleased. A loud knock came to the door with Forty being

too preoccupied with watching Mark step up to Dro's call for work. He just opened the door without turning away from the fight. Mark landed another right that made the whispers move around the room asking, "Who is this corner man?"

"What's his name?"

"Who does he fight for?"

"This guy is holding his own."

Dro, feeling the momentum of Mark's assault building with each jab, decided to work on his defense. He slipped several punches before blocking three wild shots to his body. Still smiling, he yelled, "I said work!" He caught two more punches in mid air. Mark threw another set of combinations that Dro again rejected. He thought, *"Why can't I hit him?"* Mark let another jab fly. Dro once again looked over Mark's shoulder to observe the T.V. in the corner showing the fight scheduled before his and spotted a man on his back being counted out and stated, "Time to go."

Dro dropped his hands to the side of his body and swiftly began to move his head like a snake, in and out as his defense. He quickly rushed in, "Don't panic," could be read off his lips by many in the room but he was only speaking to Mark, who started to back pedal with the bounce. "Wrong move, when you're attacked you always stand and fight."

Mark caught the message and tried to stop on a dime but it was too late. Dro's open right hand landed across his face, knocking him off balance to the floor. Dro extended his arm helping Mark up as flashing lights and applause filled the room. Dro turned to see Roc, Billy D and over twenty reporters in the corner, standing behind Matty, who had the biggest smile that Dro had ever seen on him. Matty motioned with his lips, "We're back baby, we're back!" before speaking out loud, "That's enough of the pre-show ladies and gentlemen, if you don't mind leaving so Dro can get ready to show you all why he's the best."

"Matty you can at least tell us when you started to use slap boxing as warm up training?" one reporter questioned. "Well who is the man with him, is he a professional? Come on Matty, tell us something," screamed another reporter as Matty eased the door closed on him. "Let's get ready to rumble!" Matty, proud as any man could be, led the way to the ring with

155

Mark at his side. Dro walked in the middle, in a zone while Forty and Shawn followed behind with the sound of Drake's Headlines playing. Dro's opponent was Mitchell Roger, a.k.a. "The Tank." Who was ranked number ten in the world by the WBF stood at 6'2" and outweighed Dro by twenty pounds with his 240 lb. stature. Dro entered the ring looking through the small crowd in search of Isha. He found Nate and Mrs. Smallwood seated with Rasheed and Dashon on his right. To their left he noticed Bo and Gotti having a heated conversation as Ace, with a grin upon his face sat two seats behind them with a reporter pass around his neck and listening to their every word.

Not seeing Isha, Dro turned his attention back to Matty. "Dro, I'm sorry I couldn't get you a few touch up fights first but you're hot news kiddo and by you waiting to let me put a fight together, they wouldn't let me have anyone unless they were ranked in the top ten." "Then you should have gotten number one," Dro corrected, then without another word, he stepped into the center of the ring. "That's my nigga, no games and nothing but pain," laughed Forty.

Standing toe to toe with The Tank, who tried to scare Dro with his hard looks, stating, "I'm going to make you wish you never got out the can." Dro smiled as he replied, "Stop faking, you know you don't want to fight me because you know I'm going to break your shit. Don't you?"

"Ladies and gentleman, this is Robert Moore and I'm Jasir Johnson for C.V. Sports T.V., coming to you live from the Wells Fargo Center."

"Jasir it truly is a sad moment for boxing fans everywhere that they can't witness close up what's sure to be an electrifying event, what do you think?"

"I must say, at first I had my doubts after the whole Mike Tyson let down once he went to jail. But with the look in that man Dro's eyes as he smiled at The Tank, along with the extra pounds of muscle he added that made him a certified heavy weight contender...this is sure to be a good fight."

The sound of the bell started the first round. Dro came out looking light on his feet, throwing a jabs of his own. For the first five rounds Dro paced himself to study his own strengths and weaknesses; realizing his jab timing was off and his foot movement had slowed down as he listened to Matty, "Dro you're doing fine. Just remember to breathe and you have to keep your guard up because your jab's off." Matty threw a short hook at the air, showing that he still had it and continued, "And he knows it. I need you to double your jab for the set up then, blam! Slam that over hand right dead on him. He keeps stepping in because your feet are lacking their speed but that will make up for it." "Ding-ding."

"The sound of the bell must have given Dro some real energy, wouldn't you say Jasir?"

"Yes, undoubtedly. Look at how he's working that jab. Oh my god, ladies and gentlemen Dro just landed a hard left upper cut to The Tanks body that made him stumble back. Dro isn't giving him any time to regain his composure. He landed another body shot before going up top to The Tank's head."

"The Tank is protecting himself very well"

"Yes, but I don't know how long it will last if Dro keeps picking him apart, landing combinations to his unprotected parts."

"Jasir, what is Dro doing?"

"It looks to me like he's going into the center of the ring, calling The Tank out"

"Indeed he is and The Tank is making his way there." Dro held his hand out for a fair start then winked.

"Do you think this could be a mistake on Dro's behalf, Robert?"

"I don't know, The Tank does in fact outweigh him but I guess we're sure to see…here we go."

Dro launched his assault with a series of punches that The Tank blocked with skill, when suddenly Dro's right hand slammed hard into his face, followed by a left uppercut. "Oh no, my God he's off his feet! This is unbelievable." As The Tank was falling, Dro quickly threw a short left hook to the head that connected putting The Tank out. "7, 8, 9…it's over ladies and gentleman. Boxer Dro Brown is officially back and he looks better than before!"

"Yes, I must say this was a great match"

Dro raised his hand in victory as his family rushed into the ring. He bent down catching Rasheed and Dashon in his

157

arms. Isha wrapped her hands around his neck, placing a big kiss on his lips. "Why didn't you wink back? You know that's our code when there is something in front of us, no matter what, together we can beat anything." Dro stated. "I know but my mind was on other things," Isha shot her eye at Kim who was on the other side of Dro, patting him on the back and smiling.

26

*T*he next day, back behind the walls of Graterford Penitentiary, Scotty's voice echoed through the tier as he yelled, "Rell's sports, place your bets. Rell's sports," while he walked through, passing out his own gambling tickets to the crowds of men. Scotty's life had changed dramatically since Dro made him a part of his plan. Dro now made sure he received two hundred dollars each week with the promise that he would stop getting high and if so, a twenty thousand dollar bonus would be waiting after his fourth clean urinary test is given to C.O. Dickenson. That was two months ago. Scotty's mind was back to its old sharp hustler ways.

"Scotty let me get the Lakers over the Suns and Portland over the Sixer's for a two pick parlay for twenty and twenty."

"Okay fly Ty, but have that money when this ticket blows up because it's sure to be a loser going against Philly like they're sweet." Scotty took the rest of his bets then continued on with his mission at hand. He stopped in the middle of the lower level tier on D block at cell 225 and peeped in. He saw a man with his T.V. tuned to the morning news while he read over the stock market section in the Wall Street Journal. Scotty dressed in freshly pressed brown uniform pants, crisp white t-shirt, white airs and a gold chain, lightly tapped on the door. "Come in," said Basil, looking up to see who came to visit him. He immediately smiled upon seeing his old friend back to his ordinary self. "Hey Scotty, nice to have you drop by."

"Morning Basil," Scotty took a seat next to Basil and quickly turned the T.V. to a rerun of Goodtimes. "Why do you always replace the news like you don't need to know what's going on in the world today?" Basil questioned, folding up his newspaper and giving Scotty his full attention. "Basil, you need to wake up, you're living in the nucleus of news baby. Never could those crackers tell you what you really need to know. Yes, the five o'clock news can tell you that little Ray-Ray was shot this morning at 3 am but here behind these walls, a half an hour after Ray-Ray's body goes still, you'll know who did it, why, and where to find them. Or at least where to look." Scotty's voice trailed off into a light whisper as he thought about Rell and the revenge that was so close to that he could taste it. Which brought about a change of subject, "But the reason I came down here is because C.O. Dickenson is having something like a sickness in his computer and he can't get it out. You being the computer man, I know you know somebody who could help him."

"You mean a virus?"

"Yeah, that's it"

"Let me ask you this Scotty..."

"Go ahead"

"When did you start looking out for C.O.'s?

"Come on Basil, you know me. Fuck a C.O., cop, and the warden, fuck the law itself. I'm doing this for me. The sucker caught me with a few tickets and two thousand in cash. But if you don't want to tell me, to hell with him, I'll take the write up. Plus I need some hole time," Scotty screamed seriously, knowing that if Basil didn't bite the bait that he would surely go to the hole for something just to keep his word. "I couldn't let you do that. Listen, there's this kid named Victor Harrison aka the wiz who used to fix our computer back in the day. He was the best, just Google him and he will do anything for a price."

"Thanks Basil, I owe you one."

"Scotty, just stay yourself and we're even," Basil responded.

Scotty got up from the bed and while exiting he stated, "Plus with an ass like Thelma's, who needs the news." Basil turned to the T.V. and said to himself, "Hey... that is nice." He once again thought of his past wife. Scotty eased the cell door shut and quickly transformed his cool relaxed self into the hyperactive fast talking city slicker that he was in the 80's. He moved deeper into the back of D block which was nicknamed North Philly, where three of the five main lights had been knocked out, giving off a gloomy alley look. People stood around hiding in the shadow, selling anything that would let a weak man feel he could escape the reality that they were in a living hell. Scotty hated to revisit this section, for it was as if his veins could still smell the dope that many of these men had in their pocket.

160

"Hey Scotty, what you don't know me no more?" Scotty disregarded the voice and continued to walk when Big Alan called his name again. This time with much more base and demand that people turned to look in his direction. "Scotty! Ain't this a bitch! Now all of a sudden you're getting a little bit of money, and you don't know Big Al no more when just a month ago I had you stealing these people's whole damn kitchen for a bag."

Anger filled Scotty's soul as he stopped in mid step, with a crowd of laughter filling his ears. Scotty began to think, *"Don't do this now Scotty, this is for Rell and you have things to take care of so please keep your cool and start walking. Don't turn around."*

Scotty placed one foot forward followed by the next, and then his left side began to speak to him, *"What the hell are you doing Scotty? What happened to Rell happened because he was trying to straighten out who ever disrespected him and he wouldn't stand for you letting this fat, sloppy, motherfucker that's half your age get away with this."* Scotty slowly started to spin on his back heels until he came face to face with a 6'3", 320 lb Big Alan, who stated with a big smirk, "Now that's better old head. I'm glad to see you're back on your feet but you can still speak to the soldiers in the field that never lost their stance."

"Yeah, nigga's be walking around here with their heads up in the air like their shit don't stink," echoed from the crowd. "Hey Scotty, you're running around here with that weak ass ticket," yelled another person. "I know one thing, if I hit he better have my money or that's his ass," someone screamed from the back. Laughter again filled the air as Scotty let his eyes roam the crowd, locking on the faces that stood out before resting them back on Big Alan. "First off, you didn't have me doing a god damn thing joker! In the worse moment of my life I never asked none of you suckers for anything," Scotty said, moving his head counter clockwise to make sure his point was understood, then continued, "When I had my addiction I took, not stole from the same fucking people my loved ones pay their hard earned tax money to imprison me. And as far as speaking to you, what's your name? Poison, DOA, Polo, D-wade. All I knew was the

161

name of the dope you had. If I'm not getting high, why the hell would I speak to you?"

Laughter exploded as Big Alan's smirk disappeared. He stated with seriousness, "I know you're not trying to disrespect me Scotty?"

"Nobody's disrespecting you joker, you're disrespecting yourself by reminding a man of his weakest point in his life, then refusing to recognize the man that now stands before you. But before I let you try to make me any less of a man than I am, you will have to end my sentence today."

At the sound of Scotty's response, several men circled him with Big Alan saying, "Calm down, you're right O.G. I was out of pocket, it's just that when you used to come around and we would kick it, I kind of dug you with the Black Mafia stories and I respected you as well. I guess I should have asked when we could kick it again about back in the day."

"Anytime youngin, as long as it's not down here because this place brings back too many good memories." Scotty smiled spinning back on his heels while thinking, *"Damn, that was a big kid. I must be losing my damn mind."*

At cell 112 the sweet scent of Blue Nile flowed out onto the tier as six men sat around a table engaged in a high expense poker game. Scotty eased into the cell. "The bets on you Joe, what you going to do?" screamed Earl. "Yo, come on with all that D.C. shit, my name's not Joe or Moe...its Butch Gravy," stated Gravy firmly, who was already down twenty five thousand as he slowly spread his cards apart to study them once again before asking, "What's the bet?"

"Five thousand on you Gravy, what you going to do?" yelled Blue, the youngest man in the room. He was 23 but over and over again he proved he could hold his own. "Hold on rookie, you got to be patient to get this money I'm dropping; let me see what's on the board." Gravy looked at the eight and four of hearts that lay in the center with three cards still to be flipped and with only a matching set of fours, he said, "I call."

"Aawww damn. If you called I know something can't be right. I fold," said Jerry while slamming his cards into the dead wood. "You did the right thing because this man is setting you up. I call and raise four thousand, that's nine stacks to you

162

Meshane," yelled Blue, without any expression on his face. "Oh it's on me," smiled Meshane, looking at the pair of aces he held in the hole. "Yeah Moe." Meshane instantly raised his head making eye contact with Earl. "My bad, I mean Meshane it's on you."

"Okay, help me understand this Blue, because it seems like my math is falling off in my old age. He bet five, you added four which makes it nine to me"

"That's right."

"But that would leave me with odd money and I can't have that, so why don't you drop another eleven and make it an even twenty?"

After the words left his mouth, Meshane couldn't care less if he won the pot or not. He grinned, pushing the money all together. For his victory was seeing the puzzled look upon Blue's face when he realized he surely didn't have it all figured out. "Damn shorty, ya'll just want to take all of the out of towner's money?" questioned Earl who was from the south side of D.C. "Hey nigga, we want some of that money you got from the mayor," screamed Meech. "Well I call because he had a lot of it," Earl laughed. "Me too," stated Meech. "I believe it's on Blue." Meshane pushed on only to add to Blue's discomfort. Blue's eyes studied the face of every player in the room. Realizing that his pair of sixes may not be enough, he whispered, "I fold." This made Scotty, who understood Meshane's need of power; bust out laughing as he watched Meshane control the young man's action.

Gravy flipped the next card, showing another ace giving Meshane trips. Meshane was about to raise the pot when he suddenly heard someone laugh. Seeing Scotty, he smiled while tossing his cards to Blue, "I fold."

"I knew it, I let this nigga bluff me," Blue thought, mad at him self. He slowly peeped at Meshane's cards while watching him exit the cell with Scotty. Noticing the winning hand he looked up in shock, whispering so that only he could hear, "I'm playing with a man that's crazy."

Outside the cell, Scotty started to speak, "I jus-," when Meshane cut him off by placing a finger to his lips. They began to walk and he asked, "Scotty how is the weather today?"

"I'm not sure."

"Well I think we need to find out."

In the yard that was the size of a football field, Meshane waited until they were on their third lap before explaining, "The reason we needed to talk out here is because the feds got my cell bugged."

"Again?"

"Yeah, you know how it goes but this time they put it in the wall. So as soon as the quarter changes, I'm going to rebuild the wall"

"Why do all that when you can just change cells?" Scotty questioned confused.

"Then that would be as if I bent and if I bend then that means I can break. Never could that be Liz's son plus cell 112 is where the players dwell," Meshane smiled.

"But later for that, what's happening with my man Dro?

"That's the reason I'm here," Scotty became silent until they passed the gun tower then swiftly removed an iPhone from his pocket and slid it into Meshane's palm. "Man, what I need with this? I got ten of these." Scotty didn't respond but instead he checked his watch and said, "30 seconds."

"What?"

"10 seconds"

"Man why the hell are you playing ga..." The vibration stopped Meshane from speaking and he gave Scotty a puzzled look. "Answer it!"

"Hello"

"You said all a man has is his word, so here is my word of helping you keep yours to get rid of your pain." At that moment a picture appeared of a nude man on the screen with his toe tag that read, *'a rat lays here.'* Meshane smiled with a sense of pride rushing through his body. He remembered the day he told Dro the sad story of how his once true friend gave him this time to live in hell for five long years. Meshane continued to smile while reliving that very moment...

The sound of Meshane's three story stone home's basement door slamming, followed by the echo of two sets of foot steps declining the stairs made his reflex kick in. Meshane eased the 45 mm free that rested in between the seat cushion next to

164

him. He patiently waited to put a face to the sound. The sight of his partner Danny with a big grin on his face was all Meshane needed to see to release his gun. He took another slow sip of his drink as Danny and his company took a seat across from him.

"Danny, is this the man you speak so highly of?"

"Yeah Shane, this is Carlo, Carlo this is the boss, Meshane."

"I've heard so many good things about you Meshane, there shouldn't be any reason we both can't be much richer after this meeting."

"That's good but I never heard of you," Meshane paused, looking Carlo dead in the eyes for a drop of discomfort. "Come on Shane, I brought him here because he checked out in every corner of the map and you know I'm not going to bring nobody to you unless they're cool."

"I hear you Danny but it's just the amount of work that he's trying to get off that makes me wonder why I haven't heard his name in another conversation like in Mexico or Texas, anywhere other than this one."

"Believe this Meshane, I'm the real deal," Carlo assured. Danny leaned in and whispered, "Yeah Shane, we get this hundred and fifty keys from him while it's a drought and if you don't like the vibe then fuck him...we don't deal with the clown no more."

"Okay Danny. This is your call but if you're wrong about Carlo that means I was wrong about you and there's only one way to make it right. And that's my word..."

Meshane now studied the picture, "Good old Danny. You should have known any man that has to tell you what he is can never be real."

"Hello, hello?" echoed Scotty tapping Meshane on the shoulder while pointing to the phone. "Oh!" Realizing he was day dreaming, Meshane placed the phone to his ear and yelled, "What's happening Cannon?"

"Nothing too big, you know me, just lending out my body so some real men can live through me."

"True indeed"

"I just wanted you to know that you're gone but never forgotten by me. Tell Scotty I got him next."

165

"Point taken young Cannon and thanks for leading by example, this time I am forced to be a follower."

Meshane heard the phone go dead and without a pause he slammed it down on the concrete breaking it into pieces. "Never will they have a drop of evidence to stick on Dro if I can help it. Scotty, have somebody clean that up after putting it on fire."

Two hours afterward, Scotty sat at the desk in his cell going over his gambling books during the mid day count time. The C.O. now doing the mail dropped two envelopes through the cell bars. On sight Scotty said to Ryan his celli who was watching T.V. on the top bunk, "Baby boy, you got some love from them streets again?" Scotty knew it wasn't for him because he never received mail. Ever since he lost Rell and wasn't there for him when he needed him most, he believed he didn't deserve to have anyone there for himself either. He refused to write or let anyone visit him. After a year of trying, his loved ones slowly stopped.

Ryan got down and grabbed his mail. Puzzled, he quickly opened it not recognizing the name of the sender. He began to read to himself;

"Dear Mr. Ryan

I am Sam Clinton Esq. Attorney at Law. I am aware that you do not know me but I was paid by a person I believe is a friend of yours, Dro, to represent Mr. Scotty Hurst. I have been informed that he will not read his mail. Dro stated that I should relay this message to you and that you would make sure he received it. By way of a secret source inside Graterford Penitentiary, I was able to get my hands on Scotty's original file that dealt with the stabbing of Brandon Alexander and I believe that we might have a chance of overturning his conviction. I'm going to need his help, starting with Scotty letting me visit him on the third of next month. If I do not get a response, I will take it as his refusal of my help."

Ryan couldn't hide his excitement, he yelled, "Scotty! Look, my appeal came through. I may be going home, look...look!" Scotty quickly grabbed his reading glasses and said, "Let me see kid, cause I'm sick of seeing you here anyway." He laughed in a playful manner as he began to read.

Ryan read Scotty's lips on every word until his smile faded away. Once finished, Scotty raised his head and whispered, "You can't trust these people. All they want is money, plus I lost my hope when I lost my son." Scotty ripped the letter up and tossed it into the trash. He sat back down at his desk, lost in a daze as his soul cried inside at the thought of another chance at life. Mentally Scotty knew he couldn't take one more defeat or it would be the death of him. Ryan watched Scotty closely out the corner of his eye, not wanting to be caught staring. His heart was in pain also for the man he saw go through so much. Scotty went from being a prideful father coming off every visit with his son, to an addict, to at last...a killer with life.

Then one day after walking the track with Dro, Ryan noticed Scotty had a new objective. Now he believed his strong friend was scared to fight. Deciding it would be better if Scotty was alone to deal with his thoughts; Ryan started to exit the cell when he stepped on the other letter that was addressed to him from his girlfriend Kat. Reading it, he was surprised to see Dro's name.

"Hey Baby,

A man named Dro came to see me. He said he was a friend of yours and that he owed you some money as well. I got the three thousand you told him to give me and the baby. Ryan, I love you. When we are always starting to do bad, you always find a way to come through for us. He also sent this letter and said give it to Scotty."

The next page read:

"Dear Scotty,

If you're reading this letter, you truly can't understand the integrity you have placed in the heart of Rell because never would he say he was a friend of mine and not mean it! Therefore, if my father, that I love wholeheartedly, were in jail for life, he would do everything in his power to make sure he wouldn't die there. So bet your ass that's what I'm going to do. Now get your shoes shined, clothes pressed and ready for a visit."

Ryan slowly wiped away the wetness in his eyes while thinking, "Damn, I spoke to Dro a few times and that was only when he came to see Scotty and he remembered my family." Ryan was brought from his thoughts when a sudden drop of wetness touched his neck. On instinct, he turned around reaching for his knife to find Scotty standing over his shoulder reading also with tear filled eyes. He stated, "You know he's right Scotty." Without responding, Scotty exited the cell slamming the door as hard as possible, leaving Ryan standing there.

27

*L*ater that night, on Roc's number one Block, Kim watched the bathroom wall clock closely, 9:10 pm. Not wanting to be late for her 10 o' clock meeting she quickly exited the shower, grabbed a towel and paused in front of the full length mirror that hung from the door. She checked her reflection and ran the towel over her swollen breasts, then down between her legs drying herself off.

Being turned on by her own beauty, she stated as if she was speaking to someone else, "Bitch why you keep doing this to these boys when you know they can't handle you!" She smiled seductively as she turned around to give her backside the test of approval. With her hand raised high in the air, she quickly let it go smacking her ass while closely watching it shake wildly in the middle without losing its firm shape at the top and bottom. Kim then used her ass muscles to make it clap together several times in three different rhythms. "Yes, they're certainly not ready for this here."

Kim wiggled herself into a skin tight gold and black dress that matched her Dior bra and panties. Lastly she coated her body with a fragrance of Sexy Honey before walking toward the living room where the scent of exotic weed smoke and laughter was through out the air, while several young men dressed in ACG's and army fatigue sat around Boggy like they were his personal army while playing Call of Duty: Modern Warfare3.

Making her presence known, the whole room became quiet as their eyes took in the sight of her curves. Kim smiled at Boggy who faked that he was becoming jealous. He looked around the room into the eyes of his men, observing nothing but lust while they drooled over his woman. Jumping out his seat Boggy screamed, "What the fuck ya'll looking at? This bitch is like my money...off limits." At the sound of the base in Boggy's voice, the men dropped their heads without hesitation. He gripped Kim by the arm, "Look at you, loving this shit."

"Boggy, if you don't get your damn sweaty ass hands off of me!" He released Kim and she quickly ran down the hall until he wrapped his hands around her waist pulling her closer to him. "Damn baby, where you going in such a hurry?"

"Let me go, I have to meet my grandmother to take her to get her medication, nosey," Kim answered looking at her watch, 9:36. She tried to break loose but Boggy refused to let go of the hold he had on her and whispered in her ear while running his tongue along the tip of her earlobe, "So you're just going to go without giving me a taste?"

"Boy what you need to do is eat out cause there ain't no way you can handle another shot of this after what I just put on you," Kim backed up into Boggy, rubbing her backside into his lower mid section and making him hard. "True, true, that you did baby. But can your man at least get a quickie?"

"No Boggy, I have to buy her medication."

"Then buy it bitch, I just gave you 9 ounces that should be more than enough to grab a case and pay me."

"No, that money's for my Gucci boots," Kim said once again trying to break free. She stopped fighting the moment she saw the large bank roll of money in Boggy's right hand. "Here, take this loan and get her a live in Nurse for the month but if I don't have my money back by Friday I'm going to bust your shit." He slid his left hand up her dress pushing her thong to the side, feeling her wetness. "Now bend over and let daddy do you in." Kim knew that messing up her appearance after she accomplished perfection was out of the question. She grabbed Boggy's wrist, "Come on." Kim pulled him down the hall into the kitchen. There, several nude women were packaging cocaine into ounces, quarters, and halves. "Get out now! Everybody move!" Kim pushed Boggy up against the stove while dropping to her knees and taking his dick deep into her mouth until her lip kissed his balls. She tightened her throat muscles around the tip of his head as she slowly moved her head back and forth, an inch at a time. Kim looked Boggy in the eyes while kissing his balls with each motion. The feeling of his dick rubbing against Kim's tonsils before sliding down the back of her neck made Boggy go crazy. "Damn girl...slow down and let me enjoy you. Damn, you feel good."

Kim paid his request no mind while increasing her speed. She gripped his shaft firmly to get her rhythm and she could feel that Boggy was at his peak so she began to suck on his balls, quickly jerking him off, when Fox entered the kitchen. "Yo, Boggy when are... oh, my bad." Kim stopped while still making eye contact with Boggy and said, "You know that's going to cost you, right."

"You could have asked my young buck to stay girl, I know you like riding the Amtrak." She laughed, "Boy you're crazy," Kim began working her tongue and hand simultaneously in a groove that made Boggy cum in seconds as he laughed with the thought, *"Now...go kiss your man that you're in a rush to see, hooker."*

Kim stepped outside placing an extra five hundred dollars into her Gucci purse before checking her watch again, 9:43 pm. "Damn, I'm good."

A half hour later, Kim drove down 10th and Walnut Street. She parked in the middle of the block as several men stood directing the massive traffic with their own sign language to deceive police infiltration. Kim's' tinted window slid down with a few men deciding to try their hand.

"Hey love, it's about time you stopped to give me a moment of your time," said a young man.

"Excuse me main man that be me. Tell him sexy...you came to see a true player," cut in another man.

"Yes, I did," Kim answered.

"See, now back up and give me some space." The second man made his way to Kim's driver side window with her asking, "So, can you go get him?"

"What?"

"Your boss, the true player. Can you get him for me?"

"Ho...ho...hold up. You heard what she said," stated Sam, the neighborhoods once (O.G) turned fiend. He quickly rolled from the steps rushing to Kim's aid. "Just sit tight miss, I'm going to get him right now. Just sit tight, I'll be right back." Sam pushed his weak legs as hard as he could to the third house from the end, where he was sure he would be taken care of well for his deed. He knocked three times on the door with his special tap. "Come on in Sam," screamed Shawn.

Out of breath, Sam asked "Where's boss man? I need to speak with him?"

"I'm right here, what you want Sam?" questioned Shawn as he sat between the legs of a pretty woman braiding his hair. "I know, I know but I need the other boss," Sam's body shook with anticipation for his next fix. "He's up stairs." With no time to waste, Sam turned and was halfway up the stairs in two large steps. "Damn, that old bastard can move fast!" Shawn laughed to himself.

Sam was quickly out of his sight as he spotted a light on in the back room. He approached the slightly cracked door and noticed Mark reading the book, *The Great Leader of Color.* Sam's ashy knuckles tapped on the wooden door. "Hold up...come on." Sam walked into the room now seeing Mark sitting up watching the Lakers game. "Sorry I had to interrupt you boss. But I had to just clear the whole block to get them young suckers away from that pretty girl that be dropping you off a few streets over, with the good hair."

"Damn," Mark stated, shocked. "How you know all that Sam, you be watching me?"

"No boss, more like watching out for you cause I got to keep you out here. You're one of the last true hustlers that pays a man at the price of what he does and not at the price of where he is at the moment." Sam looked at the floor too ashamed to keep Mark's stare because he hated what he had become.

"That's because we're all men Sam."

"You better know it. Now let's go get this beautiful woman."

Outside in the perspicuous night air, people moved in every direction and Sam said, "Boss, I don't know how all these people got back out here. You want me to clear it again?"

"Nah Sammy, be easy. They don't know any better."

Kim unlocked her door and waved for Mark to get in when he demanded, "Lower the window." The window came to a stop with Kim giving Mark her best puppy eyed look and asked, "What's wrong baby, you don't want to come with me?"

"What's wrong? First you're late. Second you're here where I told you not to come looking for me. Which to my enemy you have just made yourself a part of me and you know I'm beefing."

172

"Well, I'm a big girl and I can handle anything that comes with you as long as I can have you."

"That's great to hear Kim but when you get the first one right, get back at me. And take care of my old head Sam for running to get me before you go."

"What!"

"You heard me, pay the man."

Sam quickly slid his head and open hand into the window, "He's talking about me beautiful, now come on and pay me, I work hard out here."

Kim roughly opened her purse and slammed a fifty into Sam's palm before speeding off from the curb. "Mark, Mark wait," she screamed driving along side him. "Go ahead girl, I don't know what kinds of men you deal with but if you're looking for somebody where you can say anything to, there are a hundred of them out here. If I was you I would start over there," Mark pointed to the men standing in the middle of the block. "Cause I pay them the most."

"Baby, listen…I'm sorry." As the words entered the air, Kim couldn't believe she had actually said them. *"I know I didn't,"* she thought while proceeding to plead, "Please Mark, just give me a chance to explain. My word means everything to me, especially when I say them to you. I just got pulled over, that's out of my control." Mark stopped and said, "Girl, if you're making this up…"

"I swear! I'm not," Kim quickly replied.

Meanwhile at the top of the block, two men sat parked patiently waiting, hiding behind tinted windows in a black Buick. They passed a half empty bottle of Brandy back and forth when Tracy the passenger yelled, "Come on, let's go. They're pulling off." The driver eased into the road creeping down 10th Street. Tracy was a little tipsy from the drink but still on point. He watched their surroundings closely when he suddenly locked eyes with an old man that seemed to be following their car all the way through the block until he gestured for a man that looked to be his next customer. Tracy paid the man no attention and demanded, "Speed the fuck up and make sure you don't lose them!"

173

Inside the car, Kim continued to explain, "Mark I can't believe you really weren't going to come with me."

"Yeah, cause you're playing a game that I don't want to play no more."

"And what game is this?"

"The game of hearts," Mark answered seriously.

"Baby I wouldn't play with your heart"

"True... but only because I won't let you. I know there are a few brothers around here with their heart out of their chest from you and your games. I believe that's what really turns you on, to have control over people who consider themselves to be so strong that they can boss others around like me."

"Come on Mark. You got me all confused with them other women you used to dealing with."

"Do I? Then why when we first met you wouldn't give me the time of day, instead you watched Dro with lust in your eyes until I pulled out them g's?"

"Nigga if you saw all that then why did you sleep with me?" Kim yelled.

"To get even," Mark said as his face turned cold.

Kim thought back to how painful her body felt the morning after they made love, thinking that Mark was just into rough sex, now she knew the truth. "So that's why every time, after we went out you came up with an excuse to leave instead of going to bed with me?" Kim was puzzled, not wanting to accept that she could possibly be rejected for this long. "Never would I have to give an excuse for my actions," Mark smoothly corrected with a smile that infuriated Kim. "Don't you dare sit there and try to judge me because you don't know nothing about me. And who the fuck are you to say something, you're a damn drug dealer."

"Never would I try to judge anyone Kim. I'm in your presence because I like you, but I do know I could never enter your body again until you release that pain filling your heart." Kim's mouth was on fire to respond with an ego crushing remark but all she witnessed in Mark's eyes was sincere concern so instead she asked, "How can you tell?"

"Because in a lot of ways we're the same. I used to feel that the whole world owed me something. When I lost my father,

174

the pain I felt at the time was too much to endure alone so I wanted everybody around me to feel pain also." Kim watched Mark intently as his eyes showed genuine emotion. "So when it came to women, I would trash them with no regard for their hearts. I ran trains on them with my friends until I crossed them too. How could I care about their feelings when I didn't have any? In the midst of my destruction, a true blood friend that had been through the same struggles tried to pull me out of mine and I couldn't see it."

"You're talking about Rell aren't you?" Kim whispered, slightly afraid but more turned on by the seriousness that Mark expressed. He motioned his head up and down to answer and said, "I believe you feel the same about the loss of Black. Now I'm just doing what Dro did for me, and that is not giving up on you." Silence replaced his voice as Mark watched Kim try to hold back her tears when his phone began to ring. "Hello. What! Are you sure? Okay…one." Kim noticed the change in Mark's voice and questioned through her sobbing, "Is everything all right?"

"Fine, I just forgot to drop off something so make this next left while I call and let them know we're coming."

Now only three cars back, Tracy screamed, "Yo man, what the fuck are you doing? She's going left, not right!" as he aggressively cocked back his P89. "I know but she had her blinker on to go right."

"Man shut up and drive. When they stop anywhere, pull along side them and they're out of here." Nikko, the driver fell two more cars behind Kim, who made another left. "Man, it looks like the bitch is driving in a circle."

"I don't care if she's driving in a triangle, when they hit the brakes you be there!"

Kim picked up speed and made a left onto 11th St. like Mark instructed. "Pull in that space right there behind that last car at the end of the block."

"Yo, yo…they're parking, ease right up on them!" Tracy said, releasing his second gun off his waist. He slowly opened the door and held it in place to look as if it was still closed while the car gradually approached its target. Mark exited the car looking around the extra quiet block that came to life instantly

175

with several men appearing on both sides of the street from abandoned homes.

Shawn made eye contact with Mark while Sam who stood at his side yelled, "See, that's the same car right there, I told you!" The moment Mark's head motioned back upward from giving the signal, Shawn raised his gun. Inside the car Tracy leveled off his weapon, prepared to shoot through the front window shell at the sight of Mark stepping out onto the sidewalk. "I'm telling you, if this nigga tries something I'm going to give it to him faster than Dominos!"

"Chill family, they don't even know we're here. Let's just do what we're paid to do and we won't need the back up." Refusing to believe that, Tracy kept his eyes on Mark when he noticed a slight head nod. "What the fuck!" escaped from his lips as he quickly turned his head to match Mark's stare and came face to face with Shawn and Sam's pistols. They both exploded with fire, the shots shattered the side window. The slug found its target on Tracy's upper neck with the second crashing into his chest. On reflex Tracy pulled the trigger, blowing a large hole through the windshield and making a spider web crack moving through it that made it hard for the driver to see.

Nikko panicked at the sound of the gunfire and pushed down on the gas while ducking low with the blast of bullets peering through the car's frame over the car system. "Tracy do something!" Nikko screamed while pulling at Tracy's shoulder to get his attention. Tracy's door flew open and his gun fell to the ground. "Man, get your gu..." Nikko paused, seeing all the blood that covered his hand. He was afraid to look at Tracy in the eyes, knowing he was already gone. Nikko released Tracy's shoulder to grip the steering wheel tightly with both hands and hit the gas even harder, focusing on his escape when the body fell free from the car.

Shots slammed into the back of the trunk, suddenly bringing Nas' song to an end and leaving only the sound of the engine roaring to the max. "God please help me get out of here, please!" Nikko prayed. He picked up his head to see the road and what he saw made him pee on himself. Kim watched Mark with a hawk's eye through the passenger side mirror. He dipped up the street as she questioned herself, *"Why does he have a gun?"*

176

The answer came vibrating through her ears, "Oh shit! They're shooting." Kim slid down in between the driver's seat and the gas pedal while several more shots echoed. She remained there motionless until the call to know that Mark was safe overwhelmed any feeling she had, even for her own well being. She slowly brought her head up to glance over the rim of the driver's head rest and spotted Mark standing in the middle of the street with a car racing full speed toward him. At that moment a million thoughts went through her head, "Why ain't he moving? Is he hit...God please don't let him be."

The car inched closer with Kim yelling, "Mark moooovve!" Mark heard the cries in the background and reacted by squeezing the trigger while stepping forward with each shot. He hit the driver dead center in the chest several times. Nikko's body jerked violently with the car spinning out of control and crashing into two parked cars. Sam smiled as he remembered his old roots and ran up on the car unloading his clip into the driver side door. "I work hard for mine, scumbag!"

Shawn dashed to Mark's side asking, "You alright?"

"Yeah but we need to get these bodies out of here and have the fiends push the car off the blo..." The sound of screeching tires coming to a stop at the end of the block made Mark stop and turn to see a man with a gun in hand pointing at Kim's car. Mark realized what was happening and screamed, "Nooooooo!" rushing to the car at full speed. "Boom-Boom-Boom" The shooter's hand jerked with each shot as he spotted Mark coming from his large shadow quickly moving down the sidewalk and yelled to his partner, "Lets go!"

"Hold on I'm going to kill him too!"

"No, he's not on the list!"

Mark reached the car pulling Kim into his arms as Sam and Shawn flew passed him firing shots at the shooters car as it took off down the street. "Hold on baby, you're going to be just fine," Mark gently laid Kim's bloody body onto the passenger's seat before putting the car into drive and rushing to the nearest hospital.

28

"*D*ro if there is more you need, it's only a push away," Roc's voice stated at the end of the disk just before the screen went black. Dro stopped it after watching it for the seventh time. "There's something I have to be missing," Dro pushed start to replay the disk once again when it hit him... "For me to understand, I must be one with you." He grabbed his jacket and rushed out the door.

An hour later he parked on a corner in North Philly, Dro recalled Rell saying, "*So we all posted up at the top of the old graveyard.*" Dro took a deep breath and looked out the window, viewing the graveyard before exiting the car. He paid the people around him no mind and walked to the left side, stopping at the tip of the one way street. Again listening to Rell's voice continue, "*Caesar rolled up in a new Audi A8.*" Dro bent down and let the dirt run through his hands while he visualized Rell standing in the same spot. Dro thought, "Where would be the best place to cover a vic from every direction if I knew Caesar had to come this way?" Scanning the block, "Right there!" he said as he walked and posted up on a blue truck in the middle of the block as he played back the scene to get into the mind state of his best friends.

A short distance away on the opposite side of the street, several men stood around an EXT watching a fight on the 42 inch plasma TV placed in the back. "Man, he's killing this joker," screamed Bill. "Chill, it's only the third round. My man always heats up in the fourth," responded Seam. "Chill! You better tell that nigga he's fighting to chill or he might not make it to the fourth round," yelled Martin as everyone started laughing. Simon approached the crowd and lightly tapped Martin on his shoulder while giving a nod to slowly follow. "Yo, this man got to be super human to take an ass whooping like this before he heats up," commented Bill. Martin continued to laugh while stepping off to join Simon who was standing with a face of stone. "Simon what' up...is everything good?"

"Why don't you tell me what you done did now?"

"Nothing," Martin answered nervously, thinking, *"I knew I should have killed that clown."* Speaking of the man he robbed last night.

"Then why is he here?" inquired Simon pointing to Dro, who seemed to be talking to himself while moving his hands aggressively in every direction.

"Oh shit! That's Dro," Martin said remembering what Dro did to pretty Tony.

Simon knew he noticed a drop of fear in Martin's expression but decided he would let it slide for now. "Yeah, and we need to find out for what reason. Now have Bill and Tim slide up on him with Seam backing them."

"Simon that's a suicide mission, Dro will rip them apart with no problem."

"Well tell them to grow a beard and wrap a blanket around them because they're going, now send them!" Simon demanded before he turned and cut through the graveyard. Dro was on his knees running his hands over the ground while repeating the words of Caesar, "Because we wouldn't want to mess up this pretty snow out here."

Bill walked past and sat on the blue truck behind him. A second later Tim eased up on Dro and asked, "Ay main man, what you doing in this dangerous part of town by yourself?"

"It's all nice and white and we want to leave it like that"

"What?" Confused, Tim looked from Dro to Bill and back and yelled, "Nigga what you say?" Dro stood up bumping Tim out the way as if he wasn't standing there and headed up the street. The force made Tim fall up against Bill who gripped a fist full of Tim's shirt holding him back. "Man, get the fuck off of me; you see what he just did? I'm going to kill this bird ass nigga!" Tim screamed trying to break free. "Hold up people, do you see who that is?"

"I don't give a fuck…Simon said get him out of here and that's what I'm going to do so come on."

"Okay player, we're going to do that but look at his face and tell me where you know him from."

Tim quickly looked over Dro's features as Dro stopped a few feet away once again talking to himself. Tim suddenly

179

looked toward the truck realizing where he saw the crazy man. "Oh shit! That' the boxer on TV, ay...ay...ay...Dro!"

"Yeah, does A-One ring a bell?"

"Man did he hear me...what should I do, say I'm sorry?"

"No just relax Tim, he's leaving but raise your gun and act like it jammed cause you know he's watching." Simon was indeed watching through a pair of binoculars from the far side of the large graveyard thinking, "*I wonder if he knows.*"

Dro pulled up to the same small row house where Rell tailed Caesar. Getting out he examined the yard and porch. Closing his eyes, Dro let his mind state float back to when he used to put work in with A-One. *"Let's move!" Dro screamed, jumping out the van with his mask pulled down tightly on his face and his palms filled with a P89 automatic. "Bo, we'll cover the front, you get the left. I'll hold the right down. Rell you and Gotti take the back, we move in on ten."* Dro slowly reopened his eyes and ran his hand over the left window frame hearing Rell say, *"Bo, hit the front!"* "The same way I would have done it," Dro headed to the back of the house when he paused to look at the large right window, puzzled.

Out back Dro crossed the length of the yard stepping out into the alley. "This had to be their back up escape route." The vision of where the stolen car would be parked with its engine running appeared before Dro's eyes. He strolled to the back door pulling out a piece of metal along with his weapon. "I picked the lock and then slid into the kitchen," directed Rell. Dro heard the lock pop as he dropped the mask over his face. He eased in through the kitchen. "I bent down low in the doorway that led to the living room with Gotti following me," Dro raced into the dining room moving as if Gotti was his point man. He rotated his gun from side to side. "Everybody get on the floor," Dro whispered as he walked into the living room thinking, "Caesar's body had to be there." Suddenly a man came from the right side of the room yelling, "What the hell are you doing in my house?" Dro turned to face the furious man who upon witnessing the mask and gun, anger quickly turned into fear. "Okay, okay take anything you want but please don't kill me!"

"I'm not, but you just gave me everything I needed to know." Dro reached into his pocket and placed six hundred dollars on the table, "I'm sorry for any trouble I may have caused you." the elderly man slowly picked up the money, mystified at what had just happened as he peeped through the blinds to see Dro race up the street in reverse missing the masked man's license plate.

After twenty minutes, Dro pulled into the car lot of D's auto. The moment he exited, a salesman was at his side in seconds. "How are you doing sir? I'm Ron, is there anything I can help you with today?" Dro tossed the man ten grand and his car keys as he said, "Yes, I would like to test drive a Tahoe from four years ago...no names, but I'll say this, if I'm not back in two hours, that's all yours." Ron looked at the money and then at the 750 BMW and said, "One minute while I get the keys."

Behind the wheel of a black Tahoe, Dro raised the phone to his ear, "Tywan I need you to do me a favor." Tywan waited patiently outside on a quiet street in the center city business district in the passenger seat of a plane Cadillac STS when he noticed Dro turning onto the block and hit the lights. Dro pulled right beside him as he watched Tywan calmly drop the tinted window, thinking, "This is one cool young cat."

"What's up slick?"

"Nothing champ, I seen that fight they aired it today. You look good."

"Thanks, what's up with what I asked you. I know it's a little much. So if you can't do it I understand."

Tywan responded with just a point of his finger. Dro turned to find a white man standing at his window dressed in a mechanics uniform that read, "David's Repair." Dro knew there had to be a misunderstanding and quickly asked, "What is he here for? You do know what I asked you to do?"

"Believe it or not I pay attention to every word spoken to me whether it be a ten year old kid or a ninety year old woman...you never know which one will take your life. Now let the man have your truck and come ride with me, we need to talk." Dro watched David adjust the seat while sliding in his Rick Ross CD and pulling off before getting in the drivers seat, "I guess I'm driving." Tywan smiled. Dro started the engine and was about to pull out as Tywan held up his hand to stop him. Seconds later out of no where two of the same looking Cadillac's

181

pulled up and Dro slid in the middle of them. Dro enjoyed the powerful engine as he tried to keep up with the car in front of him. They eased on the expressway doing 95 mph.

"Make the right now." Dro quickly turned the wheel hard, leaving the first car bumper and rushed onto the off ramp while the third car stayed hot on his tail. "Keep your eyes open Dro because at this turn the light will be turned on in the kitchen of the projects and the roaches will appear."

"Which way?" Dro asked quickly approaching the Hunting Park double exit. "Not yet."

"Not yet? Nigga you better say something." Not paying Dro's request any thought, Tywan looked through the rearview mirror until they were a couple of feet away from the guard rail when he screamed into his Nextel, "We're moving left." Dro made the turn speeding up to 125 mph to just miss hitting the water truck. He looked to the right to see the third car off at a distance, moving fast down the right side. Tywan tapped his shoulder and pointed to the mirror where Dro saw a car slamming into the large water barrel and losing control. The car fish tailed as a Ford crashed into its side. A Saab maneuvered around it followed by another car. "What are you waiting on, for them to catch us? Let's go!"

Moments later Tywan and Dro sat at a table in an African Restaurant as Dro questioned with his heart rate returning back to its normal pace, "What was all that about back there?"

"Oh that was nothing, just the Feds."

Dro had to laugh at the young man's cool demeanor. "That's all?"

"Yeah baby they came with my condominiums, cars and women." Dro liked Tywan, not only because he was willing to help but he also understood the life he was in and what came with it, and that was rare. "What is it you got to talk to me about?"

"Dro, please don't take this the wrong way. I know you're a man and you don't need it but I do. The moment you find out which one crossed Rell, which I pray was the both of them; I ask to be brought in. As a man that wants to win and what I mean by winning is to stay free. To do that I must follow the lead of the wisdom of my mentor and fuck what I feel emotionally because that's the reason so many people are doing life behind a wall that will hold the captured forever because it shows no emotion. By forgetting that they weren't the reason they had made it this far," Tywan paused to let his statement sink in to let Dro know the words were for him also. "So please don't hesitate to ask for anything because any person that believes they can bite the hand that feeds them needs to have their whole head missing," Tywan smiled quoting Roc but genuinely believing in those words. "Thanks, if there is something I can't handle, you got that. But know this…A-One is my family for life and whoever didn't disrespect, I will protect them with it."

"That's respectable"

The two shook hands when Tywan's phone chirped. "Boss, it don't fit."

"Got you, I'm on my way."

After their meal, outside Dro stepped to the driver's side of the Cadillac. "Leave it," Tywan said. "Leave it? Then how the hell are we supposed to get back?" Dro questioned while still opening the door. "Dro I know you've been gone for some time so I'm not going to hold this one against you but will you follow me?" Tywan started to walk without waiting to see if Dro was coming. What Dro didn't realize was an APB (All points bulletin) was already out on all red Cadillac's by now. Dro made it to Tywan's side as he began to explain while removing his huge key chain, "You see this, I call it Larry Bird because it holds the key to thirty three cars which are placed through out the city and they all have high profile engines and tinted windows. So I can watch my enemy without them seeing me which in turn places my eyes behind the mask," Tywan grinned. "The trick is to always be parked on a one way street so you…"

"You'll see your tail coming from the next block over before he gets the jump on you," Dro finished, cutting off Tywan. "Yeah but I was just going to say, to see who's behind you." They laughed.

Two blocks over Tywan quickly jumped in the driver's seat of an old Benz 300 E and raced down the street straight through a stop sign listening to Jeezy's *"I Put on for My City."* They slowly moved down an alleyway stopping in front of a small metal gate that was painted to blend in with the brick wall around it. Anyone who didn't know it was there would never have seen it. Tywan hit the high beams twice while pumping the brake lights in a rhythm that Dro couldn't catch. Then suddenly it seemed that the wall opened up in front of his eyes. Surprised, Dro looked at Tywan from the corner of his eye, *"What's next?"* They eased into a car garage with Dro answering his own question, "You just forced me to step up my game."

Exiting the car Dro saw several cars being worked on. "Come on, this way." Following Tywan's lead, Dro noticed five forest green Acura RL's with their front bumper and doors removed. Next to them were five GMC black jeeps raised high in the air with their bottom cages stripped from its frame as large gray packages were being placed in its outline. On Dro's left sat ten egg shell white S 550 Benz's with their engines and trunk missing. Tywan watched Dro scanning his surroundings for a moment then lightly tapped him on the shoulder whispering, "That's not about you, this is." Tywan opened the door to a small room, stopping next to the Tahoe where David sat behind the steering wheel listening to music. David noticed their presence and quickly exited, "What's the problem D?"

"The problem is that it don't fit."

"You sure?" Dro interrupted.

"I can show you better than I can tell you," David ran off and returned with a 13" touch screen computer monitor and placed it at the back of the open truck. "See, this is the best way that three men in a rush would have done it." Dro shot Tywan a look to say, how the hell does he know when David caught it, "Come on Dro. What do you think I'm stupid? All I had to hear were the numbers with the year of the car and the rest was easy." Dro didn't respond as he stepped closer to get a better look at the 25 bricks of cocaine with stacks of money neatly on top of it. "How much?" Dro questioned. "350,000 and I really pushed that if you notice."

David walked to the front of the automobile with Dro beside him, "You can see the tip of the money sticking out over the rim of the seat and that's all hundred dollar bills. Now here's the other way." David touched the screen. "Here we have brakes, wheels, and rims with each representing the size and shape of a key. The wheels will be the size of three keys in one. You know BNF really stole that from us, the rim being the amount of five." Dro watched the screen as several different three dimensional combinations appeared, thinking of Rell, *"In the end we were looking at 25 bricks, 800,000 in cash. We put the money in the back of Gotti's Tahoe...he lied to me but why."* David cut the monitor off and said, "As you can see."

"It's impossible," Dro stated, concluding David's sentence. Tywan saw the sudden anger on Dro's face and said, "David, brake this down and meet us out front in ten."

Outside with Dro behind the wheel, Tywan stated, "I know this is your mission so I must stay out of it. But I do care and somehow your mission and mine are somewhat the same."

"How's that?"

"At times I think I'm staring into a tinted window looking for something I can't fine when it actually turns out to be my reflection in the glass. I'm looking at"

"What?" Dro, questioned confused while watching Tywan who didn't respond raise his head and suddenly the lights to a black wagon up the street come on. In seconds it stopped in front of him before they raced from the street. Back in his BMW, Dro turned onto the back block where Rell was robbed and his phone rang, "Hello...what? Kim's been shot?"

29

As Kim's heartbeat weakened, Isha's spilled from her pen into her journal:

"Dear Dro,

My love for you has been beyond lust since you first wrapped your arms around my shoulders to protect me. That moment was as if you put a shield over my soul, guarding it from anyone but you. I must admit, I was scared in the beginning and I refused to trust. Then your precious love comforted me. I started to like what I feared, catching myself smiling for no reason...but only for the fact that you have inspired me to let go of my resistance and my love has become so deep that words couldn't describe it.

It was great to have a person that understood my moods so I wouldn't have to explain my pain. Then slowly you began to forget that I was the one holding the door open to the stolen car while driving for you to get away. It was me who snuck you into the basement of my parent's home to use my father's neon light to read your first blue print when Bo and Gotti were too scared. My father made sure my heart didn't run with fear; instead it moved to make you happy. How could you do this to me when you promised you would never break our trust? Liar! Liar! Liar! Why?"

Isha's tears covered the paper making it hard for her to write but her anger forced her to continue. *"In the time of your distrust, my heart cracked as I felt every piece of it painfully drop from my soul, fading away in the wind. Never will a moment of betrayal go uncounted for in the revolution. I pray that your mistake was worth my pain and yours. This is the beginning of you..."* Isha's pen stopped as Mrs. Smallwood rushed through her bedroom door, "Isha come quick!" Seeing Isha's face, Mrs. Smallwood says, "Oh baby, I'm sorry...you must already know." Isha moved her head up and down while wiping away her tears. "Well come on we have to hurry and get to the hospital, they said Kim's not looking good."

In the emergency room waiting area at Temple Hospital, Mark sat away from his crew, alone in a daze thinking, *"If they weren't after me, then why Kim?"* The words from the gunman's lips moving in slow motion just as he pulled the trigger said, "This is for Pretty Tony." Which confused Mark even more, "What did she have to do with that?" he said quietly. A light tap hit his shoulder caused him to pause his thoughts. He stared into the eyes of a man he had never seen as his uncontrollable anger made him shoot to his feet, ready to strike anyone. "What the fuck you putting your hands on me for?"

"Because you can't just sit here, you must stick to the plan brother," the man calmly responded as he stood in a suit and bow tie. "What! Who the hell are you?"

"I'm a friend of Nate's from Temple 27 and that's all you need to know. Now go, we'll handle this." The man pointed to another man also dressed in a suite and bow tie that was holding the door open. Mark made his way while looking around the room and noticed six men. "So where is Mr. Nate?"

"Follow him."

Outside Mark spotted the bulge on the hip of the two bow tie men posted on each side of the door. The head lights of an Expedition flashed twice in the darkness which caught Mark's attention he made eye contact with a person he knew but the face they now wore he never witnessed. It was then, as he wiped the moisture from his eyes that he realized Dro had finally returned to his old self. *"Now, it's going to be hell on earth."* Mark approached the truck with its bass vibrating off the ground. He slid into the back seat to see his loved ones were ready for war. Mr. Nate sat in the driver's seat and Dro was in the front passenger's side seat, speechless with a look that said one word, death. Shawn was silent, also loading his 40 caliber with hollow tips. Mark slammed the door and Forty, who eased over next to Shawn, quickly passed him a 45 automatic, mask, and a vest. The tension in the air was so thick inside that Mark thought he could see it as he said, "Yo, where we..."

"Sshhhh," everyone in the car responded. Mr. Nate said, "We have talked long enough," before turning up the only rap music he ever listened to, the lyrics of Public Enemy began to put him and the others in a zone, *"I got a letter from the government the other day, I opened it and read it and it said they was suckers; they wanted me for their army or whatever. Picture me giving a damn, I said, never!"*

Mrs. Smallwood pulled into the emergency room parking lot just as the Expedition started to pull off. "Mom isn't that Dad's special truck? What's going on, he hasn't driven that since he first came home." Mrs. Smallwood raised her head looking in her husband's face the moment he drove by and said as she exited the car, "No baby, that's not him, now come on lets see about Kim." Isha's eyes followed the truck until it was no longer visible. "I thought that was him, why would she lie. They got to be up to something." Isha checked for the extra set of keys, "But what?"

After an hour, the black Expedition pulled beside a blue sedan with the windows lowering. "What it look like?" Dro asked. "They fire bombed their car 11 blocks away. Then Sam followed them here that's when he called us," answered Forty. "Sam, how many people is in the house?"

"No disrespect to you, I'd like to talk with the boss."

"What!" Dro stated, puzzled.

"I'm only speaking with the boss. People are about to die and it's about to get serio…"

Mark dropped his window holding back his laugh while looking at Dro's face turn red. "I'm right here soldier." Sam's face lit up saying in a hyper voice, "Boss, I'm on point, the two shooters went in that house right there." Sam pointed to a two story house on the left. "And they're still there; Ace went around back to see if he could get a better look." Hearing the man's voice, Mr. Nate yelled, "Sam Mayo, is that you?"

"Ssshhh, damn! What the hell is going on boss? What kind of people are you putting in work with that they be screaming out people's government name?" Before Mark could say anything, Mr. Nate was out the truck with his mask on and the rubber handle of his Mack 11 gripped tightly, making it to the sedan and placing it in the center of Sam's face, "This kind," he whispered.

"Go ahead and pull the trigger sucker. I've been dead!"

"I'm sorry to hear that"

188

"Don't be, they said life's a bitch and I fucked her twice," stated Sam, looking the masked man in the eyes. Mr. Nate removed the mask and said, "Same old Sammy."

"Nate! That you...I should have known when I saw Ace that you were near ya'll been riding together for years. You see one you see the other and you're still the same. Always ready for war, just like back in the day."

"I'm sorry to break up ya'll family reunion but I'm ready to get it popping. Mark, take care of your man and let's go." Dro slid on his black B. Jackson gloves he vowed to never use again.

"Ace, you see anything?" Dro questioned into his earpiece.

"Nothing, we're going to have to do this in the blind."

"Okay, stay still. We're on our way."

Everyone quickly exited with Mr. Nate giving them their position. "This structure is a basic row home. Forty, I want you and Shawn out back with Ace." Dro, while listening, spotted Sam standing at the rim of the circle and gave Mark a head nod in his direction. Mark understood and pulled Sam off to the side and said with shame in his voice, "Here you go old head, thanks. We can handle it from here." Mark eased ten hundred dollar bills into the palm of Sam's hand. "Thanks boss but I want to ride on this one. I can feel it in my bones. With me, Ace and Nate, it's like old times and boss I really need this to feel good about myself again. Who knows, it could be the new start I've been waiting on."

"I know Sam," Mark lowered his head looking at the ground, not wanting to look a fallen soldier in the face as he rejected him. "But you can't."

"Here, don't do this to me. This is my chance to get even for all the wrong I did. Please...that was a good girl, fast but good. She didn't deserve that and God knows it." Mark felt the money slide back into his hand and raised his head to finally look into Sam's face. He then removed his 9mm from his hip, "Here, take this it's new and it shoots better than that old thing you got."

Returning to the circle, Sam yelled, "Nate, don't forget me...I'm riding." Dro whispered into Mark's ear, "What is he talking about. No disrespect but your man's a junkie."

189

"Come on Dro, let him represent."

"What if the same thing happens, who's going to co-sign for him, you?"

"No, I will." Mr. Nate interrupted. "I've known Sam for years and if he says he's ready, he's ready."

"Alright, it's your call."

As everybody moved into position, Mark and Mr. Nate began to count down, "10...9"

"Yo! Dro," Mark said.

"What?"

"8...7..."

"I forgot to tell you that"

"5...4"

"The man who shot Kim said that the hit was for Pretty Tony before pulling the trigger."

"2...1"

"What!"

"Zero"

The Door blew into a thousand pieces and Mark dashed through the smoke using it as a screen. He dropped low having Dro right on his heels, aiming his weapon high in the air. Inside the home, Mall sat on the couch watching the movie *"Taken"* while Simon poured them another shot of Cognac. Suddenly a ball of fire appeared before their eyes, knocking the door off the hinges. Simon let the bottle crash to the hardwood floor and flipped the table up on two feet for cover. Dro aimed right for his head and pulled the trigger. Mark went left and locked on Mall, letting his gun loose, Mall quickly jumped over the couch to retreat with a bullet missing him by a hair. Mall returned fire with the same gun he shot Kim with as he headed for the stairs. The wood chips landed on the top of Simon while he watched Mall make his move, *"I got to get the fuck out of here to!"*

Simon raised his gun, slamming his hammer repeatedly into the chamber, firing at Dro while backing into the kitchen for escape. Sam looked into the window and screamed, "Now!" On cue, several bullets ripped through the back door into Simon's body and head. Ace smiled blowing the smoke off the tip of his gun and whispered, "Man down."

190

They eased in the kitchen with Sam noticing the blood slowly coming from the back of the man's head, he didn't know but if he did he still couldn't care less. To him this was war and they each chose their side. He let his foot fly, kicking the man into the face while passing on his way into the next room. Dro scanned the living room with his finger in the air. He made eye contact with Sam who returned the nod and quickly posted on the side of the stairwell. Dro counted down from three with his finger, 3-2-1. At 1 Sam popped out into the opening and Mall let four bullets off at his frame. Sam dropped low and returned fire while creeping up the steps. "Yeah, you want me!" Mall screamed firing wildly at Sam and forcing him in reverse. This gave Mall the space he needed he dashed down the hall crashing into the back room where Keith Sweats' "Right and a Wrong Way," played loudly as a light skin woman rode Bo's manhood cowgirl style with no regard when "BOMB!" The door slammed hard against the wall. Bo's reflex kicked in and he summarily pushed Jane off of him to grab his gun from the night stand. He rolled from the bed and peeped over the rim of it. Mall squeezed more shots into the hallway then reloaded as he screamed, "Man, I don't know what the fuck is going on I think it's him."

"BOMB–BOMB" He put pressure on the trigger again.

"But the meeting is in two days."

"Man, fuck a meeting. They want blood now!"

"BOMB-BOMB"

Mall's main focus was to keep his enemy at bay. Bo quickly threw on his sweat pants and thought of his next move. Mr. Nate crept up the stairs next to Sam who stood in the second room doorway firing. "Watch out!" Mr. Nate cocked back the Mack 90 with the double hand grip that released 60 shots in three seconds. He pulled the trigger with the kick from its power making him slightly off balance while sending the whole clip through the room's door and wall. "Ruuunn!" Mall yelled at the top of his lungs diving under the bed for cover. Dry wall rocks and glass picture frames exploded everywhere. Jane was seconds too late to respond when several of the shots rattled her body. "Oh shit!" Bo ran in retreat, lifting the window and rushing onto the roofs where he heard a horn in the distance coming from a car up the block, the lights were flashing. Bo ran three roofs

191

over, and then jumped down in to a neighbor's yard. He hurried for the car, praying that it wasn't a set up.

Back inside, Mr. Nate's weapon kicked back empty as Sam moved by him having Dro on to bring up the rear. Sam kicked open the door with his gun locked and a need for respect. He wasn't sure if it was for Kim or his soul when he spotted Mall's body halfway through the window. He aimed down at a ninety degree angle, *"BOMB-BOMB"* hitting Mall in the legs first to stop the escape. "Aaaaahhh!" Shots followed through the window that hit Mall's back and head.

"I work for mine!" Sam laughed. Dro yelled, "Cover me!" He roughly pulled Mall's lifeless body back out the window. Stepping on the roof, Dro watched a man hop into a car and close the door. "Come on Maria, move." Dro stood still until the car eased off the end of the block. "Nah, it couldn't be."

30

12:00 a.m. the night of the meeting, Gotti stood in his bedroom in front of his mirror with his woman aggressively tightening the bullet proof vest around his body. She then placed a button up Armani shirt over top of it. Gotti slid the chrome 380 down in the middle of his back and glanced into his own eyes, "There can never be a new king while I'm still here."

"You got that right baby, now go show 'em I'm going to wait here," the woman said planting a soft kiss to Gotti's lips. Without another word, Gotti stepped into the dining room where Bo, Dro and three another A-one members sat at the round wooden table. The tension in the air was so thick that the men could feel it on their skin as Gotti asked, "Are ya'll ready?" On cue everyone retrieved their weapons from off of the table, checking to make sure they were fully loaded. Bo stood up and stopped next to Gotti stating, "You know you don't have to go with us. I said I can handle it and I can."

"What!" Gotti screamed through tightened teeth. "Nigga, if you don't sit your ass down! I done lost over five hundred thousand in this bull shit and you're speaking about you can handle something?"

Bo slid back down in his seat keeping his fire filled eyes on Gotti. The rest of the men looked on in shock because they never witnessed anyone talk to Bo like that. Gotti looked around, pleased that everyone's appearance represented top of the line class as he requested. He knew people were more inclined to relax when they knew a person had money, believing that they would think twice before showing action for they had more to lose. *"Tonight, they would be so wrong,"* Gotti thought before speaking out loud. "Bo, is everything in place?"

"Yeah, we have five men outside the building watching our backs from the moment we arrive and exit. The others will be inside unseen, giving us eleven men in total that are ready to move if something were to happen."

"What you think Dro?" questioned Gotti.

"That it will be a night to remember."

"Good, now let's go meet royalty."

Upstairs, the woman watched, hidden by the darkness through the windows as the four cars pulled away from the house and slowly said, "Got you."

The cars came to a stop in the Soldi II parking lot; Bo was the first to exit. He quickly looked for his men's positions and as his eyes roamed over them one by one they gave the sign that everything was clear. "Men let's begin."

They navigated through the luxury cars looking extra sharp with an air of confidence that caught the attention of everyone they passed. The man walked in front of a tinted Porsche truck sitting on 24" rims and was actually an undercover surveillance truck to blend in. On sight, Det Michael pushed his oversized head phones off of his head and did a double take to make sure he was seeing what he thought he saw. "No longer in the game my ass, once a thug...always a thug," Det. Michael said under his breath and pulled Det. Brian away from the surveillance monitor. "What now, Michael?"

"Look," Det. Michael pointed at the crew now crossing the street to Soldi II.

"I'll be damned," Det. Brian shook his head not wanting to believe the kid Dro, who he once knew for letting bullets fly in these streets a while back, was now out running them again. But the long years of being on the force taught him a lot of things and one was that the look he saw on these men's faces meant nothing but business. He removed the receiver and let out a deep breath, "Office Dell, regain your position by the entrance, you have four men coming your way. Could be..."

Silence filled the air when Det. Dell questioned through his hidden microphone. "Didn't receive, copy. Could be what, repeat copy." Closing his eyes, praying that he was wrong, Det Brian answered, "Could be possible suspects."

"Forizzle, I'm on them," Detective Michael looked at Det Brian with a puzzled look, saying, "Forizzle? What's that, a black thing?"

"Not now Michael"

"I'm just saying, we might have left him undercover for too long."

"The kid's fine."

Inside, Gizelle walked right past Officer Dell alongside two large security guards and said, "Jihad, let them through. They're with me."

"But Roc said don't let anyone else in, no matter who it is." Dro was once again glued to the beauty of Gizelle as he watched her take charge by removing the velvet rope. "Gentlemen, right this way." Bo caught Dro staring and lightly gave him a nudge in the side with his elbow. "Stop it champ, you know who she's married to?"

"No, who?"

"Roc...and that boxing shit won't work with him."

"Well, I'm starting to like him more and more every time I hear his name." Dro remembered Roc's high tech security system and had to fight hard not to stare at Gizelle's lovely backside as she continued to lead them to the top floor of the V.I.P. section. "Here you go fellas."

Confusion covered all the men's faces but one, as they were shown to their four large tables lined with bottles of champagne chilled on ice. The moment they took their seats, four women appeared with trays of food. Gotti said, "There must be a mistake, we're here to meet with someone and have a few drinks, that's all."

"And that you will, along with whatever else you want. But mistakes, I don't think so. We don't make too many of those...if any. Bo, Gotti, Dro, A-One, it's nice to see you again and like I said before, whatever it is you may want, it's on the house because even though Rell may not be here physically, he will always be here at Soldi II in our hearts."

In his back office Roc watched the center screen as Gizelle walked away with every eye at the table watching her exit when he heard, "Damn she's phat!" Roc smiled while spinning his chair around to face Forty and asked, "You like that?"

"You damn right," Forty answered, getting hyper.

"Would you like me to set you up with her?" Billy D stood behind Roc and slowly moved his head from side to side praying that Forty received the signal he was sending because he was beginning to like the kid. Forty could feel the friendly atmosphere change while noticing Manny out the corner of his

195

eye ease in front of the door. He returned his stare to Roc and said as the vision of Gizelle enlarged with each step on the screen, "Nah, I'm cool. I like my bitch better."

Roc again smiled, liking Forty's style himself. He tapped the desk twice and just like that the mood was back to normal with Raja relaxing, Manny smoothly stepping back into position. Ace sat still next to Forty on the couch and being from the old school, he knew danger was just on his life but before he could react it was gone. He tried to figure out the source when a knock came to the door, followed by one of the most beautiful women he'd ever seen.

Gizelle entered the room, "Fellas," she said before kissing Roc on the lips. "Honey, the men are in place and their drinks and food are laced with a small does of naprosyn. Once the intake reaches its peak it will put them out for at least two hours. The girls are counting and when the time is right, they'll make their move." Roc pushed the chirp button. "Mark, you heard that, you're window is two hours on Forty's go."

"Copy," he responded. Gizelle started to leave but Roc stopped her, "Love, before you go I would like you to meet a new good friend of mine. Gizelle, this is Forty the new King. King this is my wife Gizelle."

"Nice to meet you Forty," said Gizelle. Forty looked at Roc and then at his men, then to Ace and back to Roc, embarrassed and stated, "I'm sorry, I didn't know I..."

"It's alright she has that affect on me too," Roc interrupted. At the sight of Forty's facial expression, Gizelle yelled, "Roc, I know you're not playing that game on this kid."

"You know I wouldn't do that."

Gizelle gave Roc a suspicious look and questioned Forty, "Baby did he ask you if you would like to meet me?" Roc slowly moved his head up and down hoping that Forty would pick up on it. Forty answered, "No," with a smile. Roc closed his eyes shaking his head from side to side. "Thanks baby, that's all I needed to know. Everybody in the world wants to protect Roc because he's a good person, even myself. But you should have said yes and I wouldn't have believed you." Gizelle gave Forty a big kiss on the cheek and continued to walk out the door, "But that good person will be sleeping in his back office tonight

196

fellas." The moment the door slammed everyone in the room started laughing.

"Roc, I didn't know."

"Its cool young buck, you passed your first test by doing exactly what you were supposed to do, now go out there and play the role to a tee."

"Okay, but this is no act. That be me."

Out in the V.I.P., the group, One More Chance had just ended their session saying to the crowd, "Thank you, we like to dedicate our act to Wayne Perry, Cool C and Mumia Abu Jamal, and everyone on Death Row or serving life in prison. Because everyone in the world makes a mistake, why can't they change and have one more chance...thank you." The crowd gave another round of applause and Bo said, "Yo, they were alright. I think I'll get their ringtone."

"Man to hell with them. Where is that nigga that been messing with my money at?" questioned Gotti. "I think that's him right there," said Dro. Forty activated the phone on his hip before moving through the crowd aggressively bumping people out of his way as he passed. He stopped next to Bo with four men standing behind him; and said with his hand extended, "I believe you're here to see me."

Bo started to rise from his seat when Gotti placed a hand on his shoulder, "Let me." Gotti and Forty sized one another up by the firmness of their handshake. Forty looked over Gotti's shoulder and said, "I know I don't have to kill all these people to shut A-One down."

"Not at all," Gotti gave the head nod and everyone parted a few feet away while Bo, Dro and Gotti remained seated. As Forty and Ace took their seats at the table, Mark was across town with a team of five men listening to their every word through his blue tooth as he picked the lock to A-One's main headquarters. "Got it!" The door slowly came open with Mark waving everybody in. "I want us in and out in twenty minutes flat. That means we have to turn over everything from top to bottom then put it back because no one is to know we have been here until the time is right."

The men separated and Mark took the last masked man by the arm and whispered, "You come with me." They quickly took the stairs to the back office. "There you go, now do your magic." Victor's aka the Wiz hands swiftly began to move over the computer keys then hit enter. 'Access Denied' flashed across the screen. He made several more attempts with different pass codes and received the same response. "Fifteen minutes," Mark screamed into the close circuit walkie talkie. "That's the time you got left wiz, to get in there and get what I asked you for or I'm going to have to leave you here." Mark removed the 12" knife from his hip and hid it behind his back. Victor couldn't see what the masked man concealed in the pitch black room. He tried to use the glow of the screen to get a peep but was still unable to see although he recognized the sound of steel as it left its hack. Sweat began to soak Victor's mask and gloves as he thought about how he wouldn't even know the face of his killer. He stood at the end of a dark alley when the black van pulled up with four masked men in it as the driver ordered him to get in. Victor was hesitant at first but for fifty thousand in cold hard cash, he placed the mask over his face and jumped in. He now kicked himself as Mark yelled, "Ten minutes!" over the airwave.

"Kid, what's taking you so damn long? I heard you were supposed to be the best."

"I am but this is an updated system that was just put on the market within the last two months. Whoever owns this computer really doesn't want you in it."

"Does that mean you can't get in it?" Mark asked, tightening his grasp on the handle of the knife.

"No, it means it will just take longer." Victor pressed enter and the computer screen read, "Welcome Gotti." His eyes quickly lit up like a kid in a candy store as he surfed through A-One's files. "I'm going to plant a motion virus, give me your phone. From now on when ever they access this computer, you will receive every letter that's input."

"That's nice but what about their accounts?" questioned Mark, getting right to the point.

"They're right here. All three of them."

"Three?"

"Yes"

"I thought it was just Bo and Gotti"

"No there's one more person"

198

Back at Soldi II, after finishing their meal, Gotti waited until the waitress removed the plates before he began to speak, "I came here tonight to find out what is it that has to be done for us both to eat off of the same plate. War costs money and I'm in the game to make money."

"Speak for yourself," Forty smiled interrupting. "Since this war started I have made nothing but money, along with gaining some strong customers. So you tell me what you will do to remain eating." Bo's face turned red hot as he yelled and jumped to his feet, "You clown ass nigga, do you really think you're going to keep eating now that I saw your face?"

"Bo, sit down"

"No Gotti, fuck this lame if he wants war."

"Bo I said sit down and I'm not going to say it again."

Bo did what he was told. Gotti then calmly stated, "Sorry for my partner's outburst."

"It's understandable. I do that to people when I'm on their ass," Forty paused to meet Bo's stare and said, "And to answer your question, yes I do, until I'm full."

Dro saw that the meeting was heading in the wrong direction and spoke up, "Men we're here to get an understanding so there won't have to be no more blood shed. So let's not let our pride get in the way of that." He quickly directed his eyes to Forty giving him the message to chill. "Yeah, listen to your friend," said Forty.

"King, can I speak to you for a second?" undercover officer Dell moved in closer while watching Ace pull Forty off to the side and began to whisper in his microphone debriefing it. "Seems that they're having some kind of disagreement by the looks on some of these guy's faces. I'm now going to try to get closer to use the PAR 14." Dell slid and pointed the listening device located in his class ring, in their direction. Ace's voice came clear into Det Brian and Michael's headphones. "Listen young cannon, be easy. You can't go too hard. We need them to at least stay for another 40 minutes to give the team enough time to hit the two other spots."

"Where are they at now because when the time is clear, I've got something for that loud mouth nigga Bo!" stated Forty.

199

"They just gained entry into Gotti's apartment, leaving your new friend Bo for last. Now let's have a seat and remember, be easy."

"You're right Ace," Forty answered. Det. Michael quickly removed his headset and as his pulse began to race he asked, "Did you hear that?" Det Brian was already on his walkie talkie, "64.com dispatch."

"This is dispatch, copy"

"This is Det Brian, I need you to locate the last listed address to a Roberto a.k.a. "Gotti" Powell and send several cars there immediately. I believe there is a burglary in progress. Men are believed to have a 190 so proceed with caution."

"Car is in route, requesting back up, copy"

"Dispatch car 82 assisting"

Inside Gotti's plush apartment, Mark dashed into the den yelling, "Ten minutes!" before rummaging through the desk drawers, finding nothing. He continued to move through the china closet when, "Soldier 1, I think I got something you need to see." Mark stepped into the master bedroom and stopped just over Victor's shoulder. "What is it, Wiz?"

"Look, I traced this maze here and I believe I have your third person," Mark looked at the screen closely. "Man, I don't see anything but a whole lot of numbers."

"That's what you're supposed to see. What it means is what you need to know and that's why I'm here. I must say, they did hide it well. Look at these nine sets of twenty digit numbers. Then take the third, first and sixth out of each one and repeat it three times, you got?"

"A phone number," Mark interrupted.

"So you do know about computers?"

"No, I saw that number before but I just don't know where," Mark said, searching his brain for answers.

"Well, let's find out," Victor quickly typed in the number. "And it belongs too…"

I'll be damned," Mark was stunned as the woman's picture flashed on the screen. The anxious voice of Soldier 2, bassing through the speakers brought him back to reality. "Soldier 1, I believe we may have company. Soldier 3, thinks he heard something moving outside, come quickly!"

"Alright, everybody get prepared to exit in heat motion because we must and we will make it out of here."

Outside, the police lights lit up the hours of darkness as they surrounded Gotti's house. Car 82 was the first on the scene with Officer Roger exiting saying, "Chris stay here and cover the front while I go and check out the back." Car 15 pulled into the driveway and two policemen with their guns drawn asked, "Officer Chris, what's the situation?"

"Sssshhh, be quiet and cut off them damn lights. You'll have us out here like sitting ducks," Chris screamed at the two hyper rookies as he thought, *"Why these two?"*

"Oh shit! Everybody get down," screamed Officer Dave, ducking and pulling his partner James down beside the car. "I think I saw someone with a gun in the window." Officer Chris unlatched his weapon, telling James, "At the count of three I want you to run as fast as you can across the lawn to the back of the house to assist Officer Roger while we cover you."

Officer Chris could see the fear in the rookies face as he pushed James hard in the back yelling, "Run!" He raised his walkie talkie and said, "Heads up Roger, help is coming your way an armed suspect has been spotted, and we're ready to move on your go." Chris and Dave posted up on each side of the front door waiting on the call. Back inside, Victor looked out the upstairs' window as Soldier 3 screamed, "Come the fuck on, it's time to move!" They raced together through the hallway and down the steps where Mark stood with the rest of his men in the living room and said, "I didn't spot anything but that doesn't mean no ones out there so heat motion is now in full effect."

Soldier 2 quickly removed the back pack from his shoulder, opening it and snapped the three pieces to the AK47 together and screwed the silencer in place. Soldier 3 loaded a black 36 shot tech 9 while Mark who now held a 45 automatic in each hand, stated, "Soldier 3 you and Soldier 2 protect the front, Wiz you get in the middle in front of me. I'll cover the rear.

Outside Officer Chris braced himself against the wooden door and whispered, "Listen rookie, I'm going to ram the door in, you just make sure that if anything moves, you pull that trigger…you hear me?" Dave nervously shook his head up and down as he grabbed his revolver with both hands. "Go!" Chris backed up ten feet dropping his shoulder and running full speed into the door. The door caved in with Dave right behind it. He rushed across the threshold and opened fire. Several shots went up the stairs after the escaping suspects. Roger shook his head as the rookie took aim at the wind as he spoke into the walkie talkie, "Dispatch, this is Officer Roger, the house is clear." The call went over the air wave with Det. Michael yelling, "Damn! They got away."

Det Brian paid Michaels' complaining no mind and inquired, "Dispatch what's the most recent address you have on a Kevin a.k.a. "Bo" Johnson?"

"That is First Avenue located in West Philly. We'll have a car just drive by if you'd like to see if anything looks out of place."

"Copy"

Det Brian then demanded, "Dell stand down and meet us out front now!" He jumped into the driver's seat while Det Michael asked, "Brian, where are we going?"

"I know why they didn't catch the burglars"

"Why?"

"Because they were at the wrong one of his houses but if I'm not mistaken, we tailed this Bo character to an upper class house not too far from here. I believe we can beat them there."

"Then what are you waiting for, lets get these sorry bastards off the street," said Det Michael.

Back in club Soldi II, Dro ran his hands over his face trying to hide his laughter while he listened to Forty, who walked around the table telling his side of the story. "See, Bo I didn't want to declare war on you but I learned when I was just a nappy headed kid, if I didn't have nothing to give the other kids, they would never give me a piece of their turkey sandwich and I would go hungry too ashamed to use my ticket for a free meal. My family didn't have money so one day when my stomach was growling and I refused to sit around them kids another minute hoping that they would throw me some scraps," Forty's voice got louder as he began to get hyper with each word, "I said to myself, King if they don't want to give it to you nicely, then you got to take it ruffly. You know after a week, I had every G.I. Joe and He-man action figure in a two block radius. That's when I answered myself saying; you could be good at this King, if not the very best."

"No disrespect King but what the hell does this have to do with us?" Bo questioned.

"Everything"

"Explain please," Gotti asked while calmly studying everything about Forty's appearance that he could. From the way he walked and talked to how he moved his hands. "It would be my pleasure," Forty responded just as Jeff approached Gotti and pulled him off to the side and whispered something that only they could hear. Moments later Gotti returned to the table saying, "Excuse us king but something has come up and we'll have to do this some other time. Thank you fellas." Before Forty could comment, A-One was leaving the V.I.P. section with Dro looking until he locked eyes with him. Gizelle broke their stare stepping in front of Forty and said, "Roc wants to see you."

Behind his desk with his feet rested on its corner, Roc pushed the button on the remote control surfing through the club. He possessed the power to monitor every inch of its inside as well as an half of a block in every direction outside. He released his finger spotting two waiters in the basement wine cooler. The nervous look on the one man's face caught his attention. The man stood as if he was looking for something while blocking the view of the fake camera that hung from the ceiling while the other waiter began stuffing bottles of Ace of Space into a large book bag right in front of the real hidden camera. A second later, Roc saw his intercom light flashing stating, "Now he stays on his job," before answering it. "Yes Patrick"

"Roc, quick...go to camera six, I have two waiters."

"I know, let them have it."

"But Roc..."

"Just save those tapes. Like always I promise it will be worth its weight in gold in due time."

Roc continued to surf when he noticed three women that looked as though they were about to fight at the bar on the second floor and stopped. He watched a lovely lady in white throw a wild hang maker at the quiet woman in a blue dress standing a few feet away from her. "The one in the white is nice, but you know if she would've connected that punch she would

203

have to answer for her impudence," Roc said to Billy D moments before his bouncer rushed the scene breaking up the fight before get could get started. "Yeah, but that was the old Roc, the new you has come a long way in your intense training. I'm even more impressed by your train of thought. I never would have predicted when I gave you the option of good or bad that you would have picked to change Dro's life for good with the disrespect shown to you. But you did and doing so you now not only can distinguish how to think five steps ahead. I have taught you how to increase that by two giving you the knowledge to be seven steps further then your enemy without using one of your own hands. Now our friend is none of the wiser that you made Meshane's evidence disappear from the DA's offices. Therefore making him in debt to you so he would really cut into him while Dro thinks it's the other way around genius. I guess what I'm trying to tell you is you're almost ready for the best." Billy D stated. "You think so?"

"Yes, now it depends on how Dro's hunt plays out if you will ever be ready. For it was your decision to ride with him so if he fails so do you?" The two looked at each other for a second as a hard knock hit the door. Manny led Ace in the room with Forty right behind him. Roc looked to Raja, lightly nodding his head. On call, Raja texted three letters into his phone. Roc then addressed his guess "Forty my friend, how'd the meeting go?" When there was no response, Roc repeated, "Forty." Ace bumped Forty in the side, making him break his stare from the screen on two women half naked in the V.I.P, "Yes Roc?"

"I said why was your meeting so short?"

"That's what I need to know because they ran the hell up out of here too fast for something not to be up."

"I was thinking the same thing," Roc said hitting a different button that lowered a 42 inch T.V. screen from the ceiling. Coming on, it showed a still picture of Gotti with Jeff. Roc pushed play and Jeff's deep voice came clearly through the surround sound system. "I'm sorry for the interruption Gotti, but our police friend called saying an all points bulletin went over the air that someone was breaking into your house in West Philly."

"What! Are you sure?"

"Yes and they're believed to still be there."

Forty immediately started dialing Mark's number when Roc stopped him. "Wait, there's more." He clicked to Officer Dell on the screen.

Across town, Mark picked the lock to the basement door to Bo's condo. Once inside, he gave the sign to move. His team eased out from the shadows of darkness. Three men searched the first level from end to end as Mark and Victor looked for Bo's laptop. After gaining access to his computer which Victor now did in seconds, he stated, "The same information is here but there has to be a connection like AI 2390."

"Come on, not the computer talk again."

"Oh, I'm sorry. I mean a sister laptop."

Mark lifted up the large bed frame finding nothing. He then searched the closet while Victor stood in the middle of the floor with his hand on his chin. Mark, with sweat racing down his face removed the carpet from the center of the floor and screamed, "Don't just stand there, help!" "Ssshhh, I'm in my zone dude." Mark just shook his head and turned to move the main desk when Victor said, "I got it." He then walked over to the bed placing his hand inside the pillow case returning with a Dell laptop.

"How did you know?"

"If you look at the rooms size and add that with the environment of electronic devices placed through out..." Victor stopped in mid sentence seeing the confusion on Mark's face and said, "Let's just say he was in a rush to put it away from whoever came and visited him today."

"Can you crack it?"

"Do you have to ask?"

"Then do what you do," Mark ran to join his men on the second floor where they raided every room as his phone vibrated. He recognized the number and answered on the first ring, feeling something was off. He removed his gun from his hip asking, "What now Forty?" After receiving the update, Mark walked through the back room and stopped at the window. Carefully, he stayed hidden in the dark and eased the blind back an inch, "Yeah they're here," Mark said, hanging up the phone. He watched Det. Michael race across the back to disappear behind a large tree. Mark quickly motioned with his hand for Soldier 3 to come and then whispered as he pointed, "We have company, look to the second tree on the right. That man is not alone so don't lose him while I locate his friends. Keep this on the low from the white boy because if they're cops like I believe and we have to finish one, he must go too."

"I got you but I don't see nothing." As the words left his mouth, the home phone began to ring. "Should I answer that?" Mark asked smiling, before rushing through the house giving each of his men their instructions. "Guard the window and look for any advancement."

Outside Officer Dell posted up on the side of the house. He covered Det. Michael who made his move in position to cover the exit. "I'm in," said Michael into his walkie talkie while adjusting his eye to the darkness. "Copy that, I'm in position," added Officer Dell before easing down beside a large air conditioner until only his eyes could be seen. Det. Brian lay on his stomach in the gravel driveway and used the house as a shield. He listened to the house phone for the fourth time before he responded, "Fellas I'm in position but I don't like the feeling of moving in the blind. I'm going to try to move in for a closer look, over." Det Brian did a survival move, using his elbow and knees to move across the grass and stopped near the large living room window. "Michael, I don't see any movement on the first level, what you got? Copy."

Det Michael took another look around, scanning the area from left to right and as he grabbed his walkie talkie to respond he noticed a slight movement out the corner of his left eye. He sprung in the direction of the movement, locking his weapon on Soldier 3, catching him off guard. "Michael, is everything alright, copy?"

"Drop the gun before I shoot!" Det Michael screamed with his hands shaking. Soldier 3 stared into the eyes of the man he believed to be a cop and let his Mack 10 drop to the ground and said, "You know you can walk away from this right?"

"Shut up and walk towards me with your hands raised, slowly."

"I guess you didn't hear what the man said," Mark stated while walking out from the shadows of a tree to Michael's right side. Det. Michael realized he'd been tricked and closed his eyes as Soldier 3 removed his weapon and walkie talkie. "That's it, nice and easy. We wouldn't want to have Marshall Law in the city if you did something stupid and I have to kill a cop."

Undercover Officer Dell sat debating as he watched the two suspects move in on Det Michael. *"I should let them kill this racist cracker...but if I do, it will go in my file that he died on my watch and that will slow me down from making Captain. Maybe next time, Michael."* With his 9 mm gripped tightly, Dell eased out from between the A.C. and moved toward the back of the house while he radioed Det Brian. "B, Det Michael has been captured by two armed men and it appears as though they're moving him to the far side of the yard."

"What! I'm coming," Det Brian jumped to his feet running for the back yard on the opposite side of Officer Dell's position. He stopped by the large bush at the tip of the yard to see Michael being handcuffed to the back fence. As he found the distance between him and Michael to be about 30 yards, Det Brian decided that in order for him to get a for sure kill shot, he needed to be ten feet closer. "Dell, cover me I don't think we've been spotted but I'm going in."

"Repeat that," Mark interrupted through Det Michael's walkie talkie, then continued, "This is what you're going to do Det Brian and Officer Dell, yes he told us everything. So if you want to see him alive again, slowly walk out into the open where I can see ya'll. You get one minute and counting." Thinking fast, Det Brian picked up his cell phone and dialed, "Hello Dell, it's me. This is what we're going to do..."

"Shoot our way out right, because I'm not going out there. That's suicide B."

"Fifty seconds," came over the airwave.

"Dell, I don't think so. If these men were cop killers Michael would be dead already. They're trying to find a way out."

"Forty seconds"

"I hope you're right Brian."

"Thirty seconds"

"Put your spare weapon into the center of your back and follow my lead."

207

"10, 9, 8," Mark continued to count down as he watched the two cops step out in the open. "Now drop your weapons!" As soon as the guns hit the ground Victor asked, "Now?"

"No, wait...now turn around," Mark directed, looking over his shoulder to see the van come to a stop four houses over. "Now!" Victor quickly dialed numbers on Mark's phone that made the security lights all come on at once, blinding the officers. "Now run!" Shawn, held the door open for Victor and Mark while they dove in and said, "Damn, that was a close call!"

"You're right Wiz, now it's time to end the show." Victor pressed four more numbers which activated the silent alarm."

"In two minutes they will be surrounded by there own men at gun point and if one of them makes the wrong move the way these cops is scared they as good as dead," laughter filled the air as the van raced down the block.

31

A week had elapsed and Dro again watched in disbelief while he analyzed the face of the third person in A-One. "Mark, with everything we've got are you sure it's her?" Dro questioned, hoping for answers that didn't come. "Yes, we followed the money and she was with it."

"Then where is she at now?"

"Our people have been on her since we found out. You want them to bring her in?"

"No, take me to her."

An hour later in an apartment complex located in West Philly, Mark eased the B.M.W. along side a black tinted jeep with Shawn dropping the window. "Where is she?" Mark questioned firmly, knowing from the first time he saw the woman that something wasn't right.

"In the second condo on the left but she has company."

"Bo or Gotti?"

"Neither, it's a white guy in a tie and slacks."

"It doesn't matter," Mark replied, removing his gun while opening the driver's side door.

"Wait!"

"Come on Dro, I know it just became more personal with her now involved but this is still about finding out who did this to Rell."

"You're right but something just doesn't feel right," said Dro before turning to Shawn and asking, "What other information did you get from the apartment?"

"This is the closest we could get because it's a gated community and the security guard wouldn't let me or Ace in, even after I offered them money."

"I bet I can get in, how many guards are there?"

"I don't think so Dro," Shawn said with a hint of certainty.

"I didn't say that," Dro corrected.

"Then who did?"

The back window rolled down and a voice said, "Me."

"Sam! What's up?"

"You know me, just riding with two bosses."

"You really think you can get in?"

"Have you ever seen me sleeping on the street?"

"No"

"Well I lost my home ten years ago," without another word, Sam exited leaving the men speechless. He moved across the parking lot with a structure of confidence as if he lived there for years while his eyes searched for any weakness. The tinted fence made it hard for Sam to estimate the space between it and the building just in case he had to make a run for it. He crept passed the large window of the main entrance and waved at the two guards sitting inside. "Gentleman."

"Who was that?"

"I don't know I think it was the man from 3B"

"John"

"Yeah, that's him"

"I don't know. I'm going to check it out."

"Suit yourself. I told you who it was but hurry up so we can finish the game."

Pat stepped outside and looked from left to right and then went back inside. "What happened, I thought you were going to check it out?"

"He's gone."

Sam listened to the lock reconnect with its base before easing out from down beside a parked car. *"Rookie,"* Sam mumbled removing a small metal square case from his back pocket that made his hands shake just by touching it. He slowly opened it with his soul calling out. *"Please daddy, just one more time."* "I said no more, I'm with good people again and I can't let them down," Sam stated, fighting himself. He looked passed the needle and rubber tie he hadn't used in weeks. He had promised Nate and Dro he would quit. Sam's eyes stopped at the long jimmy key he was looking for in the first place and quickly grabbed it before slamming the case shut. *"I got to get rid of this shit,"* Sam wiped the sweat from his forehead as he stepped out from behind the car and speed walked to the left side of the main office just beating the rotating camera by seconds.

Inside the jeep that all four men now occupied, Shawn said as he watched Sam attempt to pick the lock to the side emergency exit with the camera rotating back toward him. "Ten grand says we will have to bail him out tonight."

"Why'd you say that?"

"Look at him Dro. He's sweating, he's nervous and shit."

"Oh, you mean he's the same way you were when I met you?"

They all began to laugh. "Aaahh," Shawn tried to answer when Dro cut him off, "Bet! And make sure they're all hundreds." Sam's hands shook repeatedly while he tried for the sixth time to jimmy the lock. He watched the camera that was closing in on him fast. *"Come on Sam, you can do it. You can't let them down,"* he said to himself. Again, he forced the key back in roughly turning it left and right. *"Come on baby, open up for daddy. I can't let them down."* Sam listened for the popping sound of the lock giving way. The camera was now within inches of him. "To hell with this, I can't let myself down!" He dropped the key to the ground and kicked the door frame until it cracked open and he rushed in. "What the hell was that?" asked Pat, raising from his seat. "Man, I didn't hear anything and you didn't either. You're just trying to run from this beating!" yelled Tim. "You just deal the cards, I'll be right back."

Sam approached the top of the stairs hastily while hearing an echo of a walkie talkie.

"Are you sure?"

"Yes, it looks like someone forced their way in. I'm going to check it out."

"Wait Pat; let me lock up first to assist you." Without responding, Pat said to himself, *"Yeah right fat boy."* He walked through the door to see broken wood chips on the ground. "Somebody's here, now which way did they go?"

Sam watched the security guard as he paused at the cross path, praying that he didn't choose the steps. "Damn," Sam knew if he was lucky and the rookie checked the second floor first, his window of escape would be three minutes, if not sixty seconds top. With his back against the wall, knees bent and his head tucked low, Sam walked quickly to apartment 3D. He stopped near the window and peeped in, spotting a pair of black slacks, shoes and a bra. *"This cracker's getting his tip wet."* He then

211

quickly placed his ear to the center of the wooden floor and heard footsteps under him. A smiled appeared on his face, "Rookie."

Back on his feet using the same case, *"Please daddy, one more hit!"* "I said no!" Sam gained access to the apartment. He looked around while slowly tip toeing up the stairs to the sound of soft moans that came from the back room. The upstairs was a three bedroom, one bathroom structure. In seconds, Sam was on the run. He went into the first room and rushed straight for the jewelry box but caught himself, *"Come on Sam, you're not here for a robbery, you've got money."* He closed the box and then looked through the closet and drawers while locking certain things he saw in his memory. He moved down the hallway and laughed as he listened, "Oh John, give it to me. O-o-h John, yes." *"She's faking,"* Sam mumbled. After going through the other rooms, he returned down stairs to the living room looking for anything out of place but found nothing. He began to leave, "Fuck it," he said, "Some habits are hard to break," and then he turned around.

Mark was becoming impatient out in the truck, tapping his fingers on the steering wheel and yelling, "That's it; he's been gone long enough. I'm going to get him. I ain't letting him go to jail on my watch." Mark pushed the door open just as Ace spoke up for the first time, stating firmly, "Get your ass back in the car. How dare you underestimate the soul of a true soldier?"

Slamming the door, Mark replied, "Never would I do that. I just want the best for him."

"And that is to let him prove himself because only then will he feel equal enough to return to the fly Sammy the Gun I once knew and will soon know again." Ace grinned while pointing to Sam dipping back across the parking lot with the same confidence but the level was now much higher. Sam smiled at the thought, *"I still got it. Always send Sam on a mission and he'll handle it."* Then, Sam saw Pat approaching and asking, "Excuse me sir, can I speak to you for a minute?"

"No, not really but if you have to"

"I just want to ask you a few questions"

"Okay, shoot. Heeeyy, don't walk up on me like that. What is it, son?" Sam turned on his old man act in front of Pat as he threw two slow playful punches.

"Where are you coming from?"

"Oh, I was just trying to buzz Mrs. Johnson. When you see her, tell her Barry came by to take her to bingo but I can't be late son." Sam turned his straight walk into a limp and headed to the truck, "Rookie."

Inside the truck, high fives made contact with Sam's back and palm while they cheered him on. "Okay Sammy, I see you're still as smooth as ever when it comes to the pigs."

"Ace, you know a rookie can't hold nothing on me. Not even my jimmy hat." They all laughed while Mark circled the block. "What did you come up with?"

"Well, the man she's with is named Jonathan McClusky; he's 36 and married with two kids. His mistress is the one we're after. He'll be taking her to a play at eight."

"Hold up Sam...how do you know all of this?" questioned Shawn.

"Cause he made reservations."

"Yeah, but how do you know?"

"Oh, I got these," Sam pulled out the man's blackberry and wallet that he'd removed from the man's slacks.

"Well I guess we need to change," said Dro, taking out his own phone and beginning to dial.

Later that evening around 7:30 pm out in front of the Magic Theatre of Arts, Mark and Dro pulled up in a stretch limousine. They both wore tailored tuxedos with reverse colors. Dro's was laced with a white jacket and slacks with a silk black shirt and gator shoes. Mark was the same but black with a white shirt and shoes. A dark red bowtie gave them just the right touch that was needed for the night's event. The driver rushed around the car to open their door. Dro was the first to get out, stepping into the cool night air as his shoes sunk into the plush red carpet. He looked around with his heart filled with pride, loving the sight of so many black people coming together and smiled making his way through the double glass doors. He handed the man their tickets.

"Gentlemen, welcome to the play *"Silent Cries of a Thugs Love"* by Yusuf Woods. If you will, please follow me. The V.I.P. section is right this way." On the way to the stairwell leading to the upper balcony, Mark grabbed Dro by the arm asking, "Man what are you doing? Didn't you see the sign Forty gave you back there?"

"Yeah I saw it"

"Then why didn't..."

"Your seats gentlemen...and please enjoy the show."

Mark placed a twenty into the man's open palm then waited until he was gone to continue, "Then why didn't you let him grip her when he had her?"

"Because she was only going where she needed to be. Plus I heard this is a good show." Dro lowered his dark LV glasses over his eyes then pointed at the four seat section with two seats already taken by their target and her company. Laughing at Mark's shocked reaction, Dro said, "After you." They took their seats seconds before the lights fell and then the curtain began to rise.

On stage, a beautiful woman vacuumed her living room floor hesitantly and stopped when the phone started to ring. *"Not now damn it. I hate it when someone calls while I'm cleaning. But I better answer it because it's probably your father,"* Sarah *said, speaking to her one year old son sleeping on the sofa. Answering the phone with a smile, she cheerfully questioned, Malik is that you?"*

"No bitch, it's me and he just left here," a voice *answered. With her smile quickly turning into a hard mask, Sarah firmly said, "Halle, what did I tell you about playing on my damn phone? Malik don't want you and he never will."*

"I knew you would say that you dummy. That's why I left a mark of my passion on his chest while he was nailing me to the head board, ha-ha."

"Liar!" Sarah shouted and slammed down the phone. The noise was so loud that it woke Malik Jr. who began to cry. She quickly rushed to his side and took him into her arms, placing him against her chest to the sound of her heartbeat. He was suddenly relaxed. "Yes baby, mommy loves you." Jr struggle to keep his eyes open and lost the moment his father

stepped through the door. "Honey, I'm home. What's for dinner?" Malik placed a long kiss to Sarah's lips. She smiled and looked him deep in the eyes as she replied, "Chick, macaroni and cheese, rice and whole corn. Have a seat while I lay sleepy head down and then I'll heat up your plate."

"See Dro, a woman's mind is always cooler than a nigga's," whispered Mark.

"Yeah but their bite is much colder also," Dro answered.

Sarah returned with Malik's dinner; slowly placed herself on his lap and began feeding him. She calming asked in between bites, "How was your day baby, did you work hard...what did you do?"

"Nothing big, you know the same old thing."

"No, I don't know. Enlighten me." She smoothly handed Malik his tray.

"Thanks baby"

"No problem," she watched Malik raise the fork to his mouth then roughly ripped open his buttoned shirt. "You nasty motherfucker!" Sarah screamed, seeing the reddish marks on Malik's left nipple. She pulled back her hand and slapped him across the face. "Girl, I know you didn't!" Malik said as he dropped the plate and jumped up off of the sofa. Sarah was faster as she also stood quickly to her feet while pulling the knife from her back pocket and placing it to his throat. With tears running down her face she questioned, "I didn't do what? Disrespect you like you did me, our family...why Malik? Make me understand, why!"

"Okay baby, I will. Just put the knife down," Malik raised his hand to meet Sarah's knife-held wrist. "Malik, I swear on everything I am, if you touch me I will cut your whole damn head off."

"Okay, okay baby. Just listen to me first. I need you to understand this has nothing to do with you. You have been more than any man could ask for in a wife. It was my insecurities as a man, a husband and father. Ah-ah-ah, I'm just so screwed up." Careless of the knife at his neck, Malik lunged forward forcing Sarah to remove it but not before leaving a scar across the side.

Feeling fed up, Malik rested his face in his hands on his lap. The sound of weeping could be heard as Malik's body jerked

215

back and forth. Confused, Sarah removed herself from the couch and got on her knees in front of him and with both hands she slowly brought Malik back to a sitting position. With tears beginning to fill her eyes, she said, "Now is the time to be the man I married and talk to me."

"It's gone," Malik replied softly.

"What?"

"I'm sorry baby. I tried to tell you, I'm sorry."

"Okay but I'm listening now"

"Everything was in jeopardy"

"What's everything?"

Malik stood to his feet and started to pace the floor, "Everything...you, the baby, the house, the car, everything"

"Don't put this off on us. We weren't going anywhere until now."

"Why not put it on you ... the definition of a man is defined by the woman he holds closest to his heart."

"To hell with you Malik."

"You say that now but when I told you we needed to cut back on buying stuff, did you? No! You had to have that new Coach bag. The car's getting old Malik," he said in his best voice to imitate Sarah. "And it was only a year old. Well, we didn't have it."

"How not? I got it and what you make, that should be easy for our company."

"You still don't get it"

"No, I don't Malik and what does that have to do with you cheating and me getting half?" Sarah yelled while moving her neck and head with every word. Malik now looked her in the eyes and began to panic he laughed, "Half...ha-ha, yeah you can have half. Go in the kitchen and get the scale under the stove and you can have half of this brick of cocaine right now. Don't look shocked, the company fell five months ago. I'm a thug now and Halle comes with the hustle."

The curtain slowly lowered, ending the first scene. The announcer stated there would be a five minute intermission. "That's my cue baby. I'm going to freshen up and I'll be back in a second."

"Well, I'm going to go with you," said Jonathan, pulling out her chair while laying the fur over her shoulder. "I'll take that," stated Dro holding his hand out for the fur. "I think not," Jonathan protested when Mark eased to his side cutting him off while opening his jacket to show him his forty five automatic. Mark whispered, "I think so." Taking the fur, Dro smoothly wrapped it around her tightly. On contact, the woman turned to thank him as her hands covered her mouth with surprise.

"Dro"

"Shy, may I have a minute?"

"You can have four but I got to get back to see the rest of the play because Yusuf is just amazing!"

"Yes, it seems he knows the heart of a man and there's not too many of those guys left."

In the gallery, feeling no bad tension, Dro decided to take another approach. "Shy, I must say, you're looking lovely tonight."

"Thanks, Mr. G.Q. himself. Too bad I couldn't get you to feel that way fifteen years ago."

"You did, I just knew I couldn't handle you back then Ms. Prom Queen."

"Point understood."

"May I?" Dro interlocked his hand into Shy's arm. As they strolled down the long hall, he asked, "So, what have you been up to Shy? I haven't seen you in some time."

"Yeah, like fifteen years."

"It's been that long?"

"Dro you know I left in the middle of the school year"

"I almost forgot the fight," Dro remembered the moment clearly. *"That's what I want people to believe."* Shy's voice became low to the point where Dro had to struggle to hear while she continued, "But I left to give birth and I lost the baby. I was too ashamed to come back until two months ago."

"The reason I asked is because of this," Dro handed Shy the file. He studied her face while sliding his hand into his front jacket pocket and making eye contact with Forty and Ace. They slowly approached on both sides of the wall that was covered with historical paintings. Shy's eyes read over the words at a pace that Dro could follow. Then they suddenly became larger,

217

moving much faster where he no longer could keep up. On the second page of three pages, Shy looked up at him then quickly grabbed her cell phone while backing away from him in a hurry…as if he was on fire. "Where did you get this? Hello, police, yes I need the police," she bumped into a man in pursuit of her retreat. "Oh, I'm sorry sir," she said. Dro stood still with the distance growing between them as he watched Ace say, "No problem, I was coming to meet you anyway." He removed the phone from her ear and placed it to his," I'm sorry sir, there was a misunderstanding. We thought someone was stealing our car but it was my son. Okay, thank you officer."

"Let me go or I'm going to scream!" Shy demanded. Dro gave Ace the signal to release his grip and said, "Suit yourself but you will need closure and now is the time. So please finish." After completing the file, Shy asked, "Why would someone want to hurt me?" She looked around before continuing, "It's evident that you guys mean business."

"That's what I was hoping you could help us answer."

"Those dates are three years ago and I was nowhere near here let alone any SEC Bank, look," Shy pulled out her North Carolina driver's license that was renewed only weeks ago.

"I'm sorry."

"Don't be, I just had to know what I feel in my heart was right. Let's get back to your seat before the show begins."

Returning to the edge of the balcony, Dro laughed seeing Mark with his gun to Jonathan's side and talking like they were old friends. "This nigga Sef is deep, the way he be spitting that shit, right cracker?"

"You know it, bro."

"Ho-ho-hold up, watch your mouth with that bro shit."

Dro showed Shy to her seat, kissing the back of her hand and said, "Don't worry, this will all disappear…I promise. Let's go Mark." Mark looked from Dro to Shy and then back to Dro as if to say what happened. "It's not her, come on."

"But it said…"

"What it wanted you to think"

"But what about the rest of the play?"

"Come on Mark, we're the ones who just got played but I think I got one more quarter left." Exiting the Magic Theater, while praying that his thoughts were wrong, Dro dialed. *"It's time."*

32

*A*cross town at the Plaza Hotel, Gotti sat in a back booth in a dimly lit restaurant arena. "I'll have another Jack Daniel straight, no ice." "Coming right up." He continued to wait for his guest to arrive. "Here you go, sir." Without hesitation, Gotti turned the drink straight back. The high Cognac burned his chest on contact with his thoughts traveling to how stupid he was to entrust Bo to handle this situation from the beginning. "These bastards done broke into my apartment, and then pissed on my bed. No, this shit is personal and I'm about to see why. Mystery woman my ass." Gotti stood there with a devilish smirk pulling out a chair for his guest. "Waiter, bring us a bottle of your best champagne. Neshonda, I hope you didn't have a hard time finding me, this is the best hotel in the city."

"I couldn't wait to see the inside"

"So you've never been here?"

"Yes, I have driven by it a million times but to actually be sitting here…" she paused to take a moment and look around at the beautiful structure and said, "It's amazing."

Gotti smiled while thinking, *"I know it can't be this easy."* He dug into his suit jacket pocket and pulled out a white envelope, gliding it across the table just before the waiter returned. "Sir, this is Don, eighteen forty…"

"I don't give a damn what it is, just open it this is a celebration."

"Pop!"

"You heard that?"

"Yes"

"You know what it is?"

"Wine"

"No, that's the sound of a new beginning for you."

Neshonda took the envelope and asked, "What's this?"

"Open it"

"Oh my God," she responded seeing the five thousand and began looking around nervously, thinking someone would come and take it. Gotti gently placed his hand on top of hers. "Relax and take a deep breath. That's it…now lets toast." He touched Neshonda's shaking glass and said, "This is to your first day on the job with me."

"I got a job! Thanks but I hope I don't have to carry them white squares taped to my chest again but I will if I have to though."

"I would never have you do that baby"

"Then wait a minute…what job?"

"I need you to tell me all that you know about Bo, so I can throw him a surprise party. And just give a little heads up on the side, can you do that?"

"Yes," Neshonda slid her chair next to Gotti's and reached for his zipper when he grabbed her hand, "Let's start with Bo."

"Oh…he likes it when I bend over and he's hitting it from the back while I massage his balls."

Gotti shook his head in disbelief of the thought that Bo would ever have someone of this nature in his presence. *Told him there was a lot he didn't know about his friend.* "Why don't I just ask you some questions and you answer them the best way you can?"

"Okay, but are we going to eat because everyone else is eating," Neshonda once again looked around the crowded room at the plates of food covering the tables as she licked her lips. "You can have whatever you want, waiter, now let's start. Give me the name of every friend that you think should be invited to the party."

"Okay, that's uhh-uh…Mall, yeah Mall and uh," Neshonda's eyes roamed, spotting a waiter and yelled, "Over here!" *"Bomb-bomb,"* the sound of Gotti hitting the table hard with an open hand turned her full attention to him instantly," Oh my." Gotti, threw tightened teeth asked, "And who else?"

"Nobody, I only know Mall, he's the one that comes to my projects to get me and I told him to watch himself next time because Ricky and Artie said when he comes back frontin' in that Benz, they're going to take it. I don't know why they be hatin".

"I don't think he will have to worry about that no more. Where did he used to take you?"

"To a big white house on Kin…Kin,"

221

"Kingston Street?"

"Yes, that's it," Neshonda smiled.

"Excuse me, are you ready to order?" asked the waiter. *"Thank God,"* Gotti thought to himself before saying, "Yes, give her your best of everything." *So I can get this dumb hood rat away from me.* After the food returned, Gotti asked several more questions while he watched Neshonda stuff an appetizer then an extra big main meal followed by dessert down her throat. "So you're sure you have told me everything without missing anything so that he'll have the party of the year?" Neshonda belched and fanned her face, "Excuse me that always happens when I have shrimp."

"Just answer the question."

"Yes, that's it"

"Check please"

The waiter approached as Gotti stood up and quickly grabbed the check from his hands. He tossed the tip on the table. "That be you"

"But sir, you don't have to do that, I can't take it from you."

"I know kid but I want you to have it."

Without another word, Gotti's gator shoes made their way down through the plush rug. Neshonda was confused by his haste departure and stuffed the last piece of apple pie in her mouth before rushing off in pursuit of him with her tight fitting jeans making her wobble from side to side. "Hey, wait up baby." She caught up to Gotti when he was placing his Black Card on the counter. "Wait baby, slow down. I know you in a hurry to get all of this, "Neshonda ran her hands over her breast and thighs, "But you can't get it without me."

"Woman if you don't get the hell away from me. I done fed you and got your pockets fat but I'll be damned if I give you a wet ass."

"Excuse me sir, this card has been rejected."

"Forget you nigga and that fake uppity ho ya'll be chasing after!"

"What!"

"Sir, this card isn't working."

"There has to be a mistake, the card has no limit."

222

Neshonda walked out the door and Gotti quickly searched his wallet, pulling out three more cards and passing them to the desk woman before dashing after Neshonda. "Wait, don't go."

"No, you didn't want this, go talk to that skinny girl. Oh I forgot! She's with Bo at the moment." Neshonda turned her back on Gotti and raised her hand. A taxi slowly pulled to a stop beside her. "I don't understand, wait who are you talking about?" Gotti questioned as his voice became louder with sweat forming on his hands and forehead. Neshonda looked over her shoulder and smiled at Gotti's discomfort. She pulled the back door open and started to get in the taxi when Gotti's large hand gripped her wrist tightly. "I'm only going to ask you one more time."

"Stop! You're hurting me."

"So tell me"

"The girl you was standing with yesterday in the…"

"Sir, sir, wait! I'm sorry but none of these cards are being accepted."

"What?" Gotti turned to face the woman. Neshonda pulled free and jumped into the back seat screaming, "Driver go, go!" The taxi took off down the parking circle. "Yes, I also thought there had to be a mistake sir, so I called the bank and they stated that all these accounts have been closed out. "How! I don't understand."

"Well some how the money that was backing your cards is all gone."

"Bitch you got to be kidding me, what are you saying…I'm broke?"

"No, I'm not saying that sir, what I'm asking is do you have cash to cover your bill?"

After paying the bill, Gotti made several calls all over the city to investors coming out with the same reality, that he was broke. He yelled, "Listen to me; I don't give a damn if your whole family is sleep. Get your ass up and meet me in twenty minutes before I put them all to sleep for a long damn time!" Gotti hung up the phone and tossed it onto the passenger's seat. He looked in the rearview mirror questioning himself while driving through the double gated community, "*What the hell is happening and why of all times now? I knew I couldn't trust that nigga."* Moments later he walked onto the 21st floor and observed several moving boxes lined along the wall. Shaking his head, he said, "Look at this scared ass nigga." In anger he knocked hard on the wooden door making it vibrate with each pound. "Hold up, I'm coming," a voice yelled. Swinging the door open, Bo asked, "Why the hell are you banging on my door like that?"

"Because I wanted to, now move."

"Oh, Gotti…I didn't know it was you. What you doing here?"

"I get it now; you didn't think I knew about this new apartment of yours. Yeah, look at you…scared to death." Gotti walked into the dining room, bumping Bo out of the way as if he wasn't even standing there. "Scared of what? I just thought it was time to buy something new."

"I know it just so happens to be a few weeks after somebody breaks into our homes," Gotti took a seat on the sofa and threw his feet up on the china design coffee table. "It's not that."

"Yeah, I know Bo, I know." Picking up the remote, Gotti looked around the half finished room realizing the condo had to run Bo a pretty penny. "Well I hope you paid for it in cash."

"Why would I do that and have the feds on us in minutes?"

Gotti stopped the channel at the Home Shopping Network and said, "I need some plates. Go ahead and order them for me."

"Plates?"

"Yeah nigga, now here…" Gotti dialed the number on the screen and handed Bo his phone and waited.

"What! I don't understand."

Gotti smiled, happy to know it wasn't Bo that crossed him as he eased his right hand free from the gun in his right pocket while he watched Bo fish for another credit card. "Don't bother, we're broke."

"Huh?"

"Just come on."

On a quiet street in Center City, Gotti killed the lights and pulled into a dark alleyway just as a black and white police cruiser turned on to the street. Inching down low in his seat, Gotti glanced in the rearview mirror when Bo asked, "What are you hiding for when we're legit?" "Man, if you don't get the hell down here. I don't give a rats tail if we're legit or not, we're black in Center City after business hours. We're going to jail." Bo slid down right before the cop car moved past. "Come on, let's move." Gotti checked both directions before stepping out onto the side walk. He speed walked to the third building on the right and Bo followed close behind. "You stand right there."

Bo hid while Gotti tapped on the door. Seconds later the blinds slightly opened with the sound of the locks being unlatched coming behind it. "Come on, hurry!" Nervously the man's eyes looked out into the darkness to make sure they weren't followed. Closing the door, he asked, "Mr. Parker what's so important that you..." Before the words could fully leave his mouth, the butt of Gotti's 45 automatic cracked into the side of Mr. Patterson's face.

"Coward, where's our money?"

"Aaaahhh," the force of the blow knocked Mr. Patterson off his feet. He began to plead, "Stop, stop...there must be a..." Without warning, Gotti backhanded Patterson across the face. "Okay, okay I'll show you the money." "I know you will, or you're a dead man. Now get up." Bo roughly pulled him to his feet by the collar of his shirt while dragging him to his back office, kicking the door open. He slammed Mr. Patterson hard into a rolling chair. "Now show me," Gotti demanded. Mr. Patterson was holding back tears typing in the code. He could see his own blood drop onto the keys. He hit enter then pushed away from the desk, clutching his head, "There's your money."

Gotti looked at the screen, and then his hand again found its base, *"Slap"* at Mr. Patterson's mouth. "Man, this has nothing but zeros on here."

"What!" Bo pushed Gotti out of the way in disbelief of what he was seeing. He quickly pulled Mr. Patterson from the chair, "Now fix it!" "B-b-but I don't understand how this could be? No one has access to this computer but me and the code is locked in my brain," Mr. Patterson tried to explain. "Fuck what you're talking about, my money is gone and you better find out who has it, now!" Bo cocked back his gun and placed it to Mr. Patterson's head. "Noooo, don't! I think…"

"What?"

"I mean, I know someone," Mr. Patterson quickly googled the name of the Wiz. Every link headline read 'Deceased'. Bo's fingers tighten around the trigger. Gotti pulled him off to the side, "Listen, if this cracker don't come through tonight, how much time do we have to get Tywan his money?"

"Until the day after tomorrow."

Gotti closed his eyes, feeling a headache coming on and knowing there was no way that they could again be late with their connects money without going to war. Reopening his eyes he ordered, "For now we're going rock for rock, block for block, everything goes down to the oil, tens and twenties until I can feel this nigga's money."

"But what about us, if we p…" As Bo began to dispute, Gotti's phone rang. "Now what!" Gotti said before answering it, "Who is it?"

"The man with your money and if you want it back, this is what has to be done…"

33

Outside of the Temple Hospital, obscured by the raindrops that covered his front windshield, Dro sat parked while Roc informed him, "It's handled, the last pieces have been pushed into play and the stage is now set."

"I know, I have to take care of my part but I don't know if I can," Dro said, revealing his true feelings.

"Dro, to say that your fears don't exist is a fear in itself. It's only when you admit them that shows you are human, making you able to conquer mankind. All you have to do is take the first step forward and your heart will do the rest."

"Well listen for the ground to start shaking because I'm walking."

Dro ended the call, looked to Mark and asked, "Are you ready?" Mark took in a deep breath, then slowly released it before answering, "No, but this is as ready as I will ever be." They entered the hospital where the air was silent and rode the elevator to the tenth floor. Dro was the first to step into the large hallway with his heart pounding. He stopped in front of room 339, "It's now or never," he stated before tapping on the door. Dro started to enter and noticed that Mark wasn't with him.

Turning around, Dro found Mark sitting on the floor of the elevator with his hands wrapped tightly around both legs and his face covered in tears. Dro saw that he was in pain and lowered himself next to Mark, calmly speaking, "Let it out solider, I know it's hard to deal with because nobody wants to see their loved ones stuck in a hospital bed. But it's our support and love that helps them get better."

"True, true, but I can't...I feel like the pain has come from my own hands and if I wasn't such a hard ass my heart would be paralyzed over some fucking money!"

"Mark, your sorrow and pain is well justified. Every person should feel that he or she is the protector of their people but that can't stop when we miss one. We must continue to strengthen one another."

"He's right son. When my husband of twenty fives years had his stroke, I couldn't stand to bring myself to see the strongest man I ever knew in such a weak state," confessed a woman in her mid sixties who had over heard their conversation as she waited for the elevator clear. "I'm sorry to bother you two but if you don't mind."

"Oh no," they said jumping to their feet.

"Thanks"

Dro helped the lady onto the elevator. Saying their goodbyes while the door closed, Mark reached his hand out and stopped it. "Wait Miss. If you don't mind, may I ask what happened...did you ever go see him?"

"No son. But he got well, then left me for another man."

"Ma'am, we're sorry to hear that he became gay."

"Please! God no, Larry would never do such a thing. He died two years later and went back to his Lord. That's the man almighty I speak of. So go see your loved one because you'll never know when their soul will be set free.

Inside room 339, Dro fought to hold back his tears knowing he had to show the heart of a man in order for Mark to follow. The sight of the weak human laying in the bed with I.V.'s attached to their veins made it hard for Dro to believe it was the same person they knew. The two slowly inched closer on each side of the bed until they reached the head. Mark observed the face that once showed youth and health now showed wrinkles and gray hair, forcing him to take several steps backward until he bumped into the wall. Dro was lost in his own thoughts and eased his hand to interlock with the person lying in the bed. A single tear escaped his eye, falling onto the face of Rell and his eyes suddenly opened. This made Dro pull away but Rell's firm grip of his hand stopped him. Rell wasn't able to speak so he used the little strength that he had to squeeze harder, letting Dro know he wanted him to stay. Dro returned the pressure as the two hands trembled. "I know homie, it's okay...let it out," Dro said, wiping the tear that rolled down the side of Rell's face before stating, "We cry together, we die together, we kill together, we chill together."

Rell let go and hit his hand recklessly against his chest due to his loss of nerve functioning. He repeated the act until his hand landed over top of his heart, where he then moved it in a circular motion on the spot. "I love you Rell, I'm just sorry it took me so long to become the man I needed to be in order to get here." A hard moan came deep down from Rell's throat as he tried to respond. He reached his hand out to the dresser with it flopping back and forth while Dro continued to explain his actions. "I know I was wrong, I should have been the first one here. I just couldn't bring myself to see you like thi…" Without warning, Rell made the lamp come crashing to the ground." He began to buck forcing his body two inches high off the bed to clamming back down. "Stop Rell, stop before you hurt yourself," Dro screamed and grasped Rell by both arms. Rell's feet continued to fly, almost kneeing Dro in the face. Dro quickly changed positions while gripping Rell's right leg and arm, ending with his left side going wild. He looked up at Mark for help, but Mark shook his head no, from side to side. Dro couldn't understand Mark's puzzled look of fear.

Dro was trying to keep Rell calm when the door swung open and a Nurse and man in a white coat came in, "Stop it sir! Please step away from the bed. You shouldn't be touching him," the Nurse stated and moved Dro out of the way to rush to Rell's aid. She gently wrapped her arms around his head pulling him to rest on her chest as she slid halfway in the bed with him. She then began to caress Rell's hair, speaking in a soft tone, "Be calm baby. I'm here; it's going to be alright. Just relax."

Rell's movements subsided with each stroke of her hand until he sat completely still. "That's it baby, relax. I've got you." Rell closed his eyes, and his breathing returned to normal. Dro looked on in amazement at the Nurse's actions and questioned, "Miss, what's actually wrong with him. Is there anything I can do to help?"

The Nurse just smiled, giving Rell more words of encouragement. "Baby, be at peace with your soul and rest." She then turned to Dro with the smile disappearing instantly, "Yes, you can get out! It's your presence that is bringing him discomfort. I don't know how you even got the information about this new room. Do you Dr. Woods?"

"No, I don't Nurse Salle, but I see that you have everything under control here so I will continue with my rounds." Dr. Woods exited the room. Dro was still confused, asking, "B-b-but Miss, I just got here."

"I'm sorry but I haven't seen that much anger in him since he lost control of his hands a year ago."

"But he was moving them when I came in"

"Yes, they are nerves within his arm that he uses at times to make a point when someone doesn't understand our communication system. But it is extremely painful so if you don't mind, please leave."

Dro, whose face was now covered in tears, took one last look at Rell before giving a head nod to Mark to follow his exit. Nurse Salle eased out the bed and placed a soft kiss onto Rell's forehead. He gripped her hand reopening his eyes. Rell's upper body shook as he tried to open his finger to point.

Out in the hallway, Dro squeezed his head tightly with both hands and screamed, "Aaaaahhhh….fuck, why did it have to be him and not me!" Dro threw punches, making contact with the wall. Mark saw the blood stains on the paint and pulled Dro back, "Come on, that's enough champ. We did all we could."

"Never could there be enough until this is finished. Did you see him, that wasn't my brother, my friend, that wasn't Rell! But I'm going to find out who took him away from me and I got a clue who it is. Now come on." Mark flinched as Dro waved him on, seeing the intensity in his emotions.

At the elevator, steam rose from Dro's head. He aggressively pushed the button to the basement when a voice yelled, "Wait, sir there was a mistake!" Dro stepped back into room 339, recognizing that the balloon and flowers that covered the back walls were now pushed to the side revealing several pictures. Dro's eyes roamed from his left, where a framed photo of him and Rell standing together the day he returned home at Soldi II. On the opposite side, there was one of him with Rell and the kids at the Eagles game. In the center stood a picture of Rell and Isha standing in front of Rell's Tahoe. "Sir…sir" The touch of the Nurse's hand got Dro's attention and he looked at the envelope she held out toward him. "I'm sorry; he was actually trying to get to the dresser for this."

Dro gave it a closer look, seeing the words, *"To the Champ."* written on the front. He recognized Rell's hand writing, ripped it open and began to read:

"Dear Dro,

230

By now I understand you don't want to hear from me since all my letters were returned. Damn homie, I never thought we would come to this but your actions are understandable. Never should I have crossed the line of our friendship by putting your family in harms way, because of the need to have you by my side again to watch my back. I needed to feel comfortable again as I moved with snakes in my grass every where and I'm sorry. I know I promised in my last letter that I wouldn't write again, that I would respect your wish to be left alone. Now it's a month later and I'm starting to feel this funny feeling in my left and only good arm. Dr. Woods told me what was happening but it's a long name, I can't spell it. In short, my arm wont' be working too much longer. I guess they really fucked the old boy around good. I am not mad because when we had our turn, we burned their ass up every chance we got. It's only right we lose one. So please don't be apologetic for something that was destined to happen. Don't start talking that soft, I'm sorry shit and I love you mess. Taking away from the rule we set as men. I swear, I'll lose it."

Dro paused, looking up from the paper to see Rell's tearful stare placing his hand over his heart again, now understanding its meaning. He moved his lips in slow motion to say, "Yes, the heart of a man." Dro began reading again:

"Dro, I need you to know in your soul that never in anyway did I try to hurt you. With each second I lay in this cotton casket losing control of myself, first my whole right side, then my left leg, now this: still in all, there wasn't a moment that my mind wasn't clear about my intentions. I don't want to be seen like this, so weak. But I have to put my pride to the side. I'll wait until they free you from your barbwire casket so that you, my only real family can close mine.

Dro suddenly shot his tearful eyes at Rell, whose eyes were now dry. Rell's arm began to shudder before slamming it across his chest, flopping it in a circle. "Rell, stop it baby. You're hurting yourself," Nurse Salle said. "What do you mean he's hurting himself?" Dro asked, watching Rell, who continued to pay the request no mind. "His arm muscle is officially what he's using, what little remains of its tissue that is left to connect to his shoulder that is ripping with each motion."

231

Not breaking eye contact, Dro moved his head up and down, making his own circle. He was unsure if he noticed a smile on Rell's face or not as he rolled over, laying his head back on Nurse Salle's chest. Dro finished the letter:

"If the answer is yes, Boggy has made it possible but you're the only one that knows the words to free me. If you have forgotten them, this is how I'm supposed to live. Either way, we come from Allah, to Allah we shall return.

Sincerely,

The last of a dying breed...Rell

P.S. Tell Rasheed to stop getting B's in gym class.

Once Dro was done with the letter, he pulled out a lighter and placed the paper on fire prior to dropping it into the metal trash can. He paused next to Nurse Salle, bent down and kissed Rell in the center of his head. "Don't worry; my soul understands." Dro stepped back, wiped his eyes and waved Mark on, who slowly inched closer to the bedside, "I can't," he said, and then rushed out of the room. "That's it; Rell has been through enough for one day. If you don't mind, can I speak to you outside," the Nurse asked.

Closing the door gently behind them, Nurse Salle questioned, "You do know he loves you right? I truly believe that if it wasn't for you he wouldn't have made it through this far. Despite what everyone thought, he did. I would like to thank you for giving me the pleasure of meeting such a strong man. In many ways he reminds me of my grandfather, just in such a young body with his integrity and spirit. I can't lie. I'm going to really miss him but if going with you will make him feel better, so be it."

"Excuse me, I don't understand"

"What Nurse Salle is trying to say," interrupted Dr. Woods as he walked up behind Dro, "Is that Rell stated that once you came, you would be taking him home. You know, two faces one tear."

"What did you say?" Dro asked turning to face Dr. Woods. "That you'll be taking him."

"No, after that?"

Nurse Salle looked on in confusion, seeing the visitor's eyes suddenly become distant. Dro's thoughts flashed back to the

232

sexy lips of Gizelle, the manager of Soldi II, as she spoke those words to Rell, *"Oh, before I forget, Boggy said there will always be two faces one tear."* Then he quickly shifted to Roc's statement, *"I'm sorry to hear about your situation. If it helps, I did visit the hospital on several occasions. I even put a doctor there to look over him."* Dro's last indication was that of Tywan's expressions *"Dro at times I think I'm staring into a tinted window looking for something I can't find. When actually it's my own reflection in the glass I hunt."* Dro smiled realizing now that the answer he was chasing after was always with him, "You're right, I must take him home because as always, we cry together, we die together, we chill together we kill together."

"Nurse Salle, will you start the paperwork while I go prepare the patient," Dr. Woods patted Dro on the shoulder, "You did the right thing, son." Dro watched Nurse Salle's hips sway back and forth walking down the hall. "Rell, you always did know how to pick them." Then a loud beeping sound came from behind Rell's door. Within moments Dr. Woods emerged yelling, "Nurse, everybody come quick the patient is going into cardiac arrest." The medical staff rushed passed Dro as he whispered, "Rest in peace, homie."

Dro met up with Mark downstairs pulling him by the arm. "Why didn't you speak to him?" Mark replied, "Because I couldn't."

34

*B*ack at Graterford Penitentiary, inside the gymnasium, Meshane sat in the back bleachers waiting on the basketball game to begin and asking for bets across the stands, "Yo Bo, put that eleven hundred you owe me on the white team."

"Bet, but we can double up cause you know I don't like winning short money."

"It's done, say no more," Meshane answered as he scribbled the number on paper. "Earl, what you going to do, D.C.?"

"I like the black team for a grand, Joe."

"What did I tell you about that Joe stuff...but it's a bet."

"Doe," yelled Meshane, who continued to call out names, "I'm cool Shane, I don't want to do it to you like that. I like you for real and you just giving your money away," replied Doe. "Nigga don't do me no favors, if you see me and a bear fighting, help the bear."

"Okay, but I'm going to throw honey on you first because you're sweet as bear meat. That's only after I put this two stacks on black."

"Bet"

"Meshane," whispered Scotty, sitting next to him looking down at his shirt like he was minding his business.

"Yeah"

"Listen, you haven't been down here to see this team play in preseason but the last time these two played, your team lost by ten points."

"It should have been fifteen but I got this," Meshane stood back to his feet and called out a few more bets while he looked over the crowded, asking, "Is there any top players I missed?" "Yo, Shane let's bet six boxes of Newport's?" a young man asked.

"No you flea, I only bet cash Bug."

"You the flea."

"Suck my ass Lame," Meshane said, as he stared down Blue. "Blue, my main man...I know you're not going to pass up on this. The black team is from Richard Allen and that's your part of town, right play boy?"

"Without question...that be me and we're known for getting money but there's something about this that seems too easy and that's far from anything dealing with you."

"Boy, you're not no philosopher, you're a convict. If you're scared though, say it and I'll get one of the guards to bring you a dog."

People in the stands began to laugh and Blue thought, *"I'm getting sick of this clown's jokes."* "Fuck it, I'll take the bet for 5g's but I want 5 points," Blue smiled. "Don't do it Meshane, I'm telling you," again whispered Scotty. "Bet," Meshane sat down with a huge grin on his face, rubbing his hands together and said to Scotty, "Now that's the one I needed. See, all the other bets were just a set up to get him."

"I don't know Shane, this one don't look too good for you," Scotty stated. Meshane kept a smile on his face. The music began to play when the teams were being led down the tunnel. "I can't really believe an old G like yourself would underestimate me of all people, Scotty. But I'm not going to remove a stripe from you because I know you're a little rusty now. When did you see me miss a game?" Scotty paused, lowering his eyes and trying to recall, "Come to think of it...never."

"See old friend, out of sight, out of mind. That's old game, just recycled. By them not seeing me in weeks, led them to believe that I don't know about how poorly they have been playing when in fact, I'm the reason."

"And why would you do that?"

"I thought you'd never ask. Look at who's standing at the door on your left"

"That's Capt Clark, what's he doing here? Somebody must be going to the hole."

"The first answer is because I needed a favor and the only way I could get it was by winning it out of him because he don't take pay offs. And you know we don't ask these suckers for nothing. Second question is more like getting out." Meshane laughed.

"Getting out...I don't get it."

"Just watch, it's going to be hard to miss. Meshane, you got four C.O.'s in your pocket that I know about. There could be more. What you need a favor from him for?" Scotty asked, knowing the power of Meshane's hand between these walls. "Yeah, but they don't have the power I need to pull this off."

"I'm telling you Shane; don't try to bring them hookers in here covered up because them Muslim's are going to kill you for sure."

"No, I wouldn't do that but I know that plan would have gotten us paid t…" Meshane stopped speaking hearing an outburst of screams erupt throughout the gym. "Damn, them kids is big as shit," said Scotty looking at the two 6'3" and 6'4" players that brought up the rear. Suddenly over half the eyes in the place were on Meshane. Seizing the moment, he stood to his feet with his hand held out wide and stated, "Oh, what's wrong…you niggas don't like the bear meat now that you know the price of it? This is my restaurant, Blue! Yeah, I'm talking to you because you're what it's about. These other cats just caught a ride on a bus to pick you up. Give you five points," Meshane said sarcastically. "I could have given you twenty; you are now looking at the twin towers, so enjoy the show. I'm going to sit back and watch you lose your money, ha-haaa!"

Scotty shook his head while Meshane returned next to him and questioned, "Why are you so hard on that kid?"

"To be truthful I really like the kid's style like every body else. But by being a likable person, you get followers that make you a target of their power. Dig the game, Capt Clark didn't bet me on the game; that would have been easy. See, he's originally from Richard Allen also. A few weeks ago I locked the lame in a conversation on gang warring back in the day and how the loyalty of Richard Allen has changed from his time to big Al's and now. But you know pride's a motherfucker, he began to argue that if you're born and raised there, it will always remain the same."

"Now I get it. Blue's from RA, the team from the RA and you bet him that Blue would abandon them before it's over with?"

"I see the oil I'm spitting is starting to work"

"I got you but where did you get these kids?"

"From Dallas Penitentiary. I had C.O. Dickenson transfer them in this morning."

They both laughed. The game began with the white team taking over from the tip off going up ten at the end of the first quarter. Meshane asked, "Did you think about seeing the lawyer like we talked about?"

"I'm not going to lie, I gave it some thought but I can't trust it"

"Why? I thought you said the lawyer checked out"

"He did. As Dro said the man hasn't lost a case in over ten years but I still don't trust these people, they could put anybody around us wearing a wire like they did that kid Capone. Me, I'm not going out like a sucker because Capone hasn't done anything and I'm guilty," Scotty said with a face of stone. "*And I'm not going to let you,*" Meshane thought to himself before speaking out loud, "I feel you but this man isn't going to keep coming here to see you, trying to get you free and you're turning him down and wasting his time, Scotty."

"I know but when I killed them two people, they were trying to give me the death penalty. Life was a deal and I took it."

"Now it's time to give it back," Meshane responded with a smile appearing as he watched Blue exit the stands in the middle of the third quarter with his team down by twenty five. "Come on Scotty; let's go get something to eat, on me. What I had to do here is finished." They made their way from the stands hearing people scream, "Meshane you think you're slick, you piece of shit!"

"Yeah, yeah, I know. Just have that paper so I can wipe my ass."

"Nah Joe! That wasn't right, how you brought them ringers in here on the real that was some petty shit slim. But if that's how you got to get to a dollar, holla at me. My money is longer than train smoke and I can make it easier for you." Meshane stopped near the exit and turned to face Earl. "What! You nigga's know when it comes to that bread you can't tell me nothing. I done did all that shit from riding in the big missiles to the point ya'll didn't know what kind of car I was in until the following year. The baddest bitches, you name it, that's why I

237

keep that dumb ass look on your face like now. Just make sure you pay it, however if you want to impress me, jump in the air and stay there."

In the hallway leading back to D block, Meshane became serious, placing his hand on Scotty's shoulder. "OG, you know these walls are my ears and I hear that lawyer will be here again in two weeks. I'm asking you to go, if not for yourself then do it for these young cats that now look up to you and show them that they must never stop fighting for their freedom."

"I understand and respect your opinion but I made my bed, now I must lay in it."

"You don't, that's what I'm trying to tell you."

"Well tell that to them two people I have laying in the ground about hope, then I'll think about it. And stop riding me, you know back in the day I used to beat your father's ass and I know the apple hasn't fallen far from the tree." Scotty walked through the double doors of D block leaving Meshane standing alone in shock, being that it was the first time he witnessed Scotty show a drop of emotion for anyone other than himself. "*I guess once you take your mind back soldier, the heart will follow.*" Meshane stated as if Scotty still remained. He then headed to B block to meet his personal chef. Scotty moved to his cell thinking, "*If it's an eye for an eye, then I have to make it a life for a life.*" Scotty's train of thought was interrupted by the scream of C.O. Dickenson calling him," Scotty I've been looking all over for you. The Chaplain wants to see you."

The word quickly spread of the death of Scotty's son through out the prison without anyone seeing Scotty in days. Meshane, along with several other people stopped by to pay their respects, only to be met by a pitch black room. The door was pinned shut with Scotty's knife jammed in the crease of it.

Early Monday morning, Meshane let out a deep breath looking at his watch that read 8:45am. He was praying that he hadn't lost his biggest bet yet, "Come on baby, I believe in you." "8:50am," Meshane continued to pace the tier when Scotty's cell door cracked open. Rubbing his hands together, Meshane quickly walked over until he spotted Ryan coming out and the door slamming behind him. "Scotty wait, it's me!" When no answer came, Meshane asked Ryan, "What is he doing in there?"

"I don't know, I just sleep there at this point, look at me, I can't even see." Ryan stepped back so that Meshane could look at his mismatched pants and top. "Damn, Scotty done lost his mind," commented Meshane. He looked at his watch again, 8:55am, thinking, *"Sometimes you just got to pay it."* He saw Blue who was across the tier smiling as he pointed at his watch. Just then the cell door swung open and a clean shaven Scotty walked out with his uniform freshly pressed, and a black gator belt and shoes. "Look at you play boy, you're open casket sharp...where you going?" Meshane inquired. "It was an eye for an eye; they now have my son... that makes us even." Scotty moved with a new found stroll as he listened to Meshane's voice trail in the background. "That's right player, all you got to do is get there." Meshane started to dial Roc as he stopped next to Blue, whispering in slow motion for Blue to read his lips, "Pay it."

He placed the phone to his ear with a smile of triumph. "You know that just going there isn't enough to win, he must sit down and tell that white man he hates the story that could get him the chair."

"Listen Blue, I'm hard on you for a reason and in the end, you'll understand why. But if I don't ever tell you anything else to live by in life, remember this...never bet against the heart of a man."

Scotty slowly declined the individual steps leading to the visiting room. He wiped sweat from his forehead, realizing, *"You got to be on point Scotty. Watch everybody around you. No one can get too close. Make sure you look the cracker directly in the eyes and if he flinches, kill him too".* Scotty patted the plastic knife he taped to the bottom lining of his uniform jacket. He slightly turned the door knob to the right then stopped. *"Wait, what if I panic and just start stabbing people. I don't want that to happen."* Instantly Scotty's subconscious other half took over his mind. *"But if you do, fuck it...there's nothing worse than what we've already got. We're here for life Scotty."* Once again he turned the handle to peek through when suddenly the door swung open. "Your visitor is waiting."

Scotty looked Capt. Clark up and down as he pointed, thinking, *"What is he doing here."* "Don't just stand there, go."

239

"Oh, oh my bad," Scotty's legs felt like bricks walking into the visiting room for the first time in over six years. He looked around the room and a smile appeared. He quickly turned back to Capt. Clark, who said, "I don't see nothing funny and tell Meshane I'm going to get his ass in the end."

Scotty disregarded the statement and strolled pass the sign that read, "This section is closed." He headed toward a man in a pin striped suit that had his back toward him. Scotty, with his hand extended said, "Excuse me, Mr. Clinton...oh shit, you're black!"

"Have been all my life but don't tell the man, he might not ask me to lunch again." They laughed taking their seats.

Scotty stated, "This just might work."

"Oh it will, if we have to pay for it," Mr. Clinton said firmly.

35

*J*ust before nightfall, sitting in a lounge chair with his feet up, Sam oversaw the steady movement on 10th and Walnut St as he handed out the bundles of work to the block runners. "Here Sam, I'm done," said Aaron anxiously counting out the money from his last package while looking over his shoulder at the many cars flowing into the block. Sam calmly took the money and placed it in an old potato chip bag, then tossed it to the ground. Seconds later, a kid riding a skate board at top speed came through and picked it up without stopping. Once seeing the money was secure, Sam faked like he was stretching and stuck his pinky out half way, giving the code sign to the man in the window of an old abandoned house across the street that Aaron was to receive five bundles, two more than his last flip. "Thanks Sam, I'll have that car this week then I can get all the ho's."

"Save your money for..." Before Sam could finish, Aaron was already across the street heading through the path that lead to the back of the house. Eric stood off at a distance waiting on his turn to re-up with envy and hate in his eyes. He couldn't stand the fact that now he had to take orders from the same person that used to wash his car for a bag. As he approached Sam, he thought, *"Look at this reformed junky in my spot like he owns the world, when last month he probably would have given up his ass for a bundle. It's okay...Dro made Mark look past me this time but I'll be here when you relapse pussy and I'm going to treat you like the addict you are."*

Sam spotted Eric out the corner of his eye and turned to face him with a big proud smile. "Eric, my main man...I see you out here doing it, running to cars and shit, getting at that big money."

"Yeah," Eric smirked with fire in his eyes.

"Yeah, true. Not too many people can move with the speed like you with that swiftness you use moving in and out the street."

"I hear you. Why don't you just give me mine and let me get back to that wonder bread that's flowing out there because not everybody can lay around and get money like you," responded Eric, not wanting to be in Sam's presence a second longer than he had to. The kid on the skateboard raced from the opposite direction on cue, grabbing the money. Sam said, "You damn right, this spot here is for chiefs only, not Indians."

"Is it?" Eric questioned with a slight laugh.

"Without a doubt, if I'm sitting here in it. I done beheaded so many damn young fire starters and brave hearts that when I was stuck out there on my peace pipe, the roughest spear thrower couldn't handle me. But now that I'm back, I wish they'd stop letting off smoke signals and say what's on their mind." Sam stood to his feet sending the cue of three fingers, cutting Eric's bundle in half. "Sam, you made a mistake, my number is forty, not twenty."

"I know but if you don't think I belong here then take the rest and I'll show you the difference." The two stood face to face with Sam now out weighing Eric by ten pounds but lost to him by two inches in reach. "Sam you got this all wrong. I just want to do me."

"And so do I," said Sam looking Eric in the eyes before continuing, "So until you respect me as a full man or I show you something less than that, I'm going to do the same by you. Now be happy with half the work so you can see how it feels to have to work twice as hard to be something you already were." Without speaking any further, Sam stepped out into the street and raised the remote, hitting a button as the lights to a tinted Qx4 came to life. Jumping in the driver's side, he chirped Shawn, "Young Cannon."

"Sam, what's popping baby?"

"Dark just fell so I'm on the move for boss again. I need you back on the block until I get back."

"I'm coming out the door now."

Sam laid his seat back then slid the 9mm from his waistline and placed it on the dash board just when he spotted Shawn coming down the house stairs. Making eye contact, they both gave a short nod while Sam was pulling into the street. "Oh, young cannon, watch that nigga Eric. I just demoted the clown for trying to be me, plus he talks too much. If the Feds come at us, I know he's going to break." Shawn began laughing so hard his stomach started to hurt. He was watching Eric mean mugging

242

Sam's car while it drove by. "What happened, ahhhaaa," Shawn questioned holding his belly. "Let's just say I'm back at it," Sam replied, hitting the horn as he sped off down the block.

A half an hour later, he turned the lights off, slowly pulling up to the back side emergency exit of Temple Hospital with the car still running. He looked around; making sure nobody witnessed his activity. Once satisfied, he flashed the lights twice before lightly tapping on the brakes. Moments later, Sam opened the door about a third of the way and then a man dressed in all black slid out from between the bushes, dashing to the car. Sam hit the gas pedal before the man could get half his body in the car. "Damn Sam!"

"I'm sorry Dro, but if I'm going to be riding around with fifteen years on my hips," Sam's eyes looked to the gun on the dash, "To feel safe, we got to stick and move because I'm too old to have a man half my age or less telling me when to eat, sleep and shit. So it can't be nothing more than excuse me officer, I'm sorry for speeding, here's my license and give me my ticket. But the moment I hear, *sir can you step out*...right there I'm firing, Boom-Boom!" Sam explained; feeling that there was no other way.

Dro saw the chrome 9 mm automatic and said, "Oh, you're an armed career offender, I feel you. But I just keep five on my hip." Dro lifted his shirt to reveal the black forty five. They both laughed to hide the reality of their statement. In a city where death had become more common than a job, Dro knew that even though he didn't want to, as Roc stated for him to have a chance at a normal life again, he must carry a gun for now. "So, how is that pretty girl holding up?"

There was no answer, and Sam took his eyes from the road to look for the reason. "I said what happened with K..." he paused when noticing that Dro was only there physically but his mind was elsewhere as he stared out the window in a daze. Sam understood the pressure that was upon Dro's shoulders from their talks and knowing the same disloyalty showed from his own action. He decided to leave him be and give him time to think, Sam slid in his Maze CD. "*It's going to be alright young cannon, I'm with you.*"

Meanwhile, Dro's mind was focused on the reason that he and Sam had been on several late night stake outs for the last few weeks. He again prayed that the feeling in his chest was wrong but with each passing moment, it kept getting stronger. It began the second he dropped Mark off after leaving the hospital, slamming the door, Mark asked through the opened window, "Are you going to be okay?" Dro slowly nodded his head up and down, saying, "The stage is set. Now I must play my part."

Pulling off, Dro drove for hours rationalizing until he came to a quiet street in South Philadelphia. Hastily, he made his way up the front steps, ringing the door bell twice. A woman in her fifties appeared and when she spotted Dro's face she quickly opened the door and wrapped her arms around his waist while laying her head on his chest. "Baby, I've been so worried about you. Please just bear with me as I hold you." Dro could tell that Mrs. Smallwood was sobbing as her grip tightened. He gently brushed her hair back out of her eyes and she raised her head to look at him. Mrs. Smallwood asked, "You alright?" Dro softly kissed her on the forehead, "I'm fine." "That's good to hear, now come on." They moved down the hall with a voice calling, "Honey, who was that at the door?"

Stopping in the doorway of the kitchen, Dro answered, "It was only me," catching Isha and Mr. Nate by surprise. "Don't just stand there soldier, come and have a seat. Honey, make the boy some food." Dro never moved as he watched Isha looking at him with disgust before turning back to the morning paper that she was reading with Mr. Nate. "No, I just came to see her...Isha, you got a minute?" Isha paid Dro no mind and continued to read. Mr. Nate covered the paper with his large hand, "Isha, what's wrong with you, this is the father of your children. You owe him that much...Isha!" Mr. Nate gave Isha a look that said, "Child, if you don't get yourself moving."

"Okay, damn," Isha slammed both hands on the table and stood up. "And watch your mouth in my house."

"It's mine," she replied, grabbing her purse while heading out of the kitchen.

"I don't give a rat's ass whose house it is, as long as I'm in it you're going to keep your mouth clean around me!"

Isha walked by Dro without saying anything as he declared, *"Actually it's my house."*

"Kiss my ass Dro!" Isha stomped her feet all the way down the hall. Dro still didn't move, refusing to chase after any woman. *"Isha, I know you're upset with me by the way you've been refusing to return my calls but I didn't know it had come to the point where we started to disrespect each other."*

"Disrespect? Ha!" Isha stopped in her tracks and walked up to Dro until her mouth was an inch away from his chin. *"What was disrespect is what you and that bitch Kim did to me!"*

"Isha! What did I say about your mouth, girl. I'm not playing with you."

"Don't worry daddy, I'm leaving."

Dro stood there in shock, starting to understand why the suit next to Kim's' car fit to a tee. The sound of Isha slamming the door made Dro jump...

"Boss, boss...we're here, boss," Sam yelled, again tapping Dro's shoulder to get his attention and bringing him out of his thoughts. "Wh-what is it Sam?" "We're here boss, I checked the surroundings like always and no one's here but the back door is unlocked," Sam explained anxiously. He was hoping this would be the night that whatever Dro had planned went into play. "What now boss?"

"We wait."

"Right"

Dro continued to look out the window at the street while beginning to reminisce again.

Dro was dressed in his Sunday's best black suit, walking to the podium that was placed just above Rell's casket. He gradually moved his eyes over the crowd from left to right looking for any sign of guilt. He was sure that whoever crossed Rell was inside the church. Dro's eyes paused at his far right where a private section was reserved for family and loved ones only. They continued to roam over the first chair that was empty followed by Rell's sister, whose face was covered in tears while Mark sat beside her and caressed her back. He spoke words of encouragement, through his own silent tears. Roc and his team sat in the back while Bo and Gotti sat in the next two spots. Bo

245

looked as if he hadn't been to sleep in days, sitting with his legs crossed, lost in a daze while looking at the gold and black casket that was aligned with flowers that would be Rell's final resting place. Gotti on the other hand seemed nervous for some reason, Dro thought, following his eyes, searching in every direction, but why?

Then a light grin eased from the corner of Dro's mouth, hearing Tywan's statement in his head, "If they don't have my money in a week...I'm going to take it out of their ass. Starting with that nigga Gotti." The end of the week just happened to be yesterday. Dro's smirk quickly formed into a smile with the sight of his family. Isha sat with Dashon on her lap refusing to look at Dro. As Rasheed who were seated in Mrs. Smallwood's lap, waved excitedly, "Hey Dad."

"Ssshhh, young soldiers. This is a time for quiet," demanded Mr. Nate. "Dad, hey," Rasheed said again, preparing for his grandfather's backhand that never came. Dro faced the crowd and began, "I guess I should start by thanking everyone for coming to show my brother, my friend, our friend...his last respects. Even though he is no longer with us physically, he will remain respected...this I promise you." Dro stopped for a moment to let his threat sink in before he proceeded. "Rell was a good person to many people and he was always there when you needed him. I remember when we were in boy scouts together and he s..."

"Stop, don't do this! Move, get out my way, stop!" Dro heard the commotion and stopped to see the crowd separating. "Stop, he's not going out like that!" a voice yelled in the distance with Scotty stepping out from the edge of the crowd with two sheriffs five feet behind him. He made eye contact with Dro and said, "We can't do him like this Dro. I know you mean well but my son was a gangster and the record must reflect it."

Scotty gave Dro a big hug and whispered in his ear, "I know they're out there and this may be my last time out here so I'm going to give them something to listen to." 'Bomb, bomb' Scotty hit the microphone twice. "Is this shit on?" "Yeah uncle, now do you," yelled Mark proudly. He saw Scotty dressed in a suit looking good as his handsome old self for the first time in years. He was twenty pounds heavier with his hair dyed black and Armani on his back. Roc give a short nod and Scotty proceeded, "I'm going to start by saying it be what it be. My son didn't die, you nigga's killed him but standing here is not a saddened man looking for a fucking hand out and tears. Here stands a man driven by revenge that is owed to a coward who wasn't man enough to let my son know he was even a foe. Well, I'm here to say it's war...so be sure to know I'm yours." The words from Scotty's tightened teeth sent the crowd into an uproar as the two sheriffs started to head for the podium. Roc and Boggy stood in their path, blocking them. "Let the man finish and everything will be just fine."

Dro looked out into the crowd again, finding two more empty seats, thinking, "Where did they go and why..."

Just then, Sam shook his leg, "Boss, snap out of it...he's here." Dro adjusted his eyes back to the present moment to see a man exit his car and use his key to enter the house they were staking out.

"What do we do now boss?" Sam questioned.

"We wait."

"Right, right."

Dro laid his seat back slowly until his eyes were level with the dash board, letting out a deep breath, recalling the moment when...

Dro shut the door to his apartment after seeing Scotty off and hearing the good news that the court had granted his motion to reopen his case. "I hope you win old head, I hope you win." Making his way to this favorite chair, Dro again studied the surveillance tape of the night Rell was shot at Soldi II to the end with Roc's voice stating, "If you need more, it's only a push away," Before the screen went black. "I know I'm missing something, but what?" Dro went to rewind the disk and pushed play instead. The screen came to life with Dro looking on, puzzled as he watched Roc tap him on the shoulder. Dro raised the volume and listened, "Excuse me, I heard you need to speak with me?" Roc questioned. Remembering the moment, Dro inquired, "What's this got to do with it?" as he continued to watch himself say, "Love, I got something important to take care of, so here, take my keys and I will meet you back at my apartment.!"

247

"But baby do you know who he is?" Isha asked.

"Yeah"

Seeing Isha rush back to the booth made Dro laugh as she tried to hand him her gun. "No, you keep it; I'm going to be just fine." Dro watched him and Mark leave the screen. Isha returned to a back booth where Kim sat with a man handing her a glass of champagne, asking, "Excuse me love, may I have this dance?"

"It depends"

"On what?"

Kim raised the glass to her lips, tasting her drink and said, "Rozay, oh yes you may." The picture showed Isha alone sipping on a drink when a drunken Bo slid beside her. He began to whisper something into her ear. Dro jumped up from the chair to turn up the sound but Bo's voice was too low for the hidden microphone to catch. All of a sudden a loud 'Smack' was heard and Isha's voice said, "I don't give a damn what you tell him. My family is back together and there is nothing you can say or do to break it up!"

"Come on, I wouldn't do that. I'm just saying."

"You're not saying nothing! Now get the hell out of here before I tell Dro."

Isha threw her drink in Bo's face before snatching her purse and heading out the door. Dro sat there numb, wondering what their fight could have been about..."What did he say?"

The blinding lights of an oncoming car with their high beams on brought Dro out of his thoughts and he heard Sam say, "Get down boss." They both ducked while watching the car pass through the side view mirrors. "Its okay boss, you can get up. No, hold up...it's turning around." Dro closed his eyes and Sam stated, "Boss, it looks like our friend is having company. What you want to do now?"

"Call in the team."

36

*M*oments earlier inside of an old Buick Regal that drove slowly down 51st and Master, Gotti lay across the back seat gripping the handle of a P89 automatic as he screamed orders to Slow Motion. "Make a right at the stop sign and turn down the alley on your left."

"But Gotti, we have already been through this whole area, twice."

"I don't care, this is his playground and I'm going to find him before he gets a chance to find me," said Gotti, speaking of Tywan. He sat up straight to get a better look around. "If you say so, I'm with you just make sure when we're done with him, I get those keys you promised me for helping you get back the money he owes you."

"Now, do I look like the kind of person that would play you?" Slow Motion shot Gotti a look through the rearview mirror to say, *"Nigga please,"* before turning down the alley. They didn't find anything so they continued to drive through what Gotti believed to be Tywan's territory for another hour. Slow Motion pulled to a stop asking, "Gotti, are you sure this is where he gets down at? I've only seen hand to hand corner hustlers out here and we don't mess with these suckers."

"Well we do now, pull up on them right there," Gotti pointed to a group of men standing at the end of the block dressed in Polo boots and hoodies passing a blunt in a circle. Slow Motion drove up near the curb. "Gotti, don't do no dumb shit because these young bulls are not playing, they kill everything and anybody...cops and all. They especially won't hesitate to do us."

"I got this, just pull over."

"Alright," Slow Motion stopped and Gotti dropped the back window. "Hey fellas, any of ya'll know a guy that moves by the name of Tywan?"

Upon hearing a stranger's voice, within seconds the crowd had guns pointed at the car. "Hold up, be easy. Don't shoot...I'm just trying to see an old friend about some business, that's all."

"Get the fuck out of here now before I push your shit back to the white meat!" stated a kid in a red Philly's cap that couldn't have been any older than nineteen. He was holding a Mack 11 tightly in his palm. "No, no...let's rob the vic and take his car," said another kid that ran out into the street, locking his 9 mm on Slow Motion and boxing them in. Slow Motion looked at the large barrel pointed at his head and his mind began to run wild, *"Oh shit...it's going down. I told Gotti's hard headed ass! But I'm not going to let these young pussies finish me off. I'm running him over and getting the fuck out of here."* Slow Motion's hand moved towards the gear shift. "No! Chill, Mo. I got this," Gotti whispered from the side of his mouth before yelling out, "Hold up fellas, I come in peace." Gotti quickly stuck both arms out the window, "It's just that Roc said that I wa..."

"Stop! Nobody fire," ordered a man who looked to be the leader of the crowd. He stepped from the middle of the circle and started to walk toward the car. Gotti knew he now had their full attention while slowly removing his arm from the window, leaving one hand in sight resting on the window. The other hand reached for the weapon that was on the seat and placed it to the door frame. Gotti was thinking, *"If I kill the leader, the rest will follow. So if you don't bite the bait, kid you're out of here."*

The young man stopped at the edge of the sidewalk, leaving a few inches between him and Gotti then asked, "What was the name that just came from your mouth?"

"Oh, Roc...that's my old head. Why, have you heard of him?"

"No!"

The moment the man's response came, Gotti knew he was lying. He played it off and continued, "Well, he just dropped word to me to get at his young bull, Tyron, it's important but you know he don't like dealing with the small shit!"

"You mean, Tywan?" corrected the kid as he let out a cloud of blunt smoke into the air, making sure to keep his eyes on Gotti. "Yeah, yeah. So you do know him?"

"Not at all. I remembered it from when you first said it. Being that this is my block, if I hear someone going by that name, who should I say is asking?"

250

"Busy"

"Okay Busy. Now if you don't get yourself out of here within 30 seconds, I'm going to have these young wolves turn your whip into the first drop top Regal."

"Enough said. Mall, u-turn and get us off this man's block."

Slow Motion's hands trembled nervously turning the wheel, praying that they would lower the guns from his face. He then quickly stepped on the gas, racing up the block. "Thank God. Gotti you can think on your feet, I thought we was goners. But why did you call me Mall?"

"Just be quiet. Hurry up and circle the block."

"I'm not going back down there, are you crazy?"

Gotti heard enough and raised his gun to Slow Motion's head, "If you say another word without doing what I tell you to, I promise you'll wish I had left you back there. Now, like I said...circle the block, kill the lights and park on the street on the next block over." The leader waited until the car's rear lights could no longer be seen before pushing speed dial on his cell phone. A woman answered, "Drug Abuse Education, this is Jane how may I help you?"

"Yes ma'am, I think I might be having a relapse, can I speak with a counselor please?"

"Yes, one moment."

"This is counselor Ed, how can I help you sir?"

"It's me Red. You just had some nosey jokers come around here asking about you."

'That's nothing new, who was it this time...the feds, DEA, ATF?" questioned Tywan, really not caring but knowing the rule to never underestimate anyone.

"No, it was some cat about 220, going by the name Busy."

"Never heard of him"

"Me either and I would have bagged and tagged him but he threw O.G.'s name in the air also."

"What?" screamed Tywan, now giving his full attention.

"That's what I was thinking when he said he had some kind of message for you."

"You sure he said Roc?"

251

"Positive"

"Was he alone?"

"No, he had some guy named Mall with him"

"Mall…Mall, wait a minute, that nigga dead…"

'BOMB-BOMB' Two shots speared through the night hitting Red in the neck and head, dropping him to the ground instantly. The phone fell from his hand as Tywan's words echoed into the night, "Gotti, you dirty bastard…it's all fair in the time of war."

Down the street, Gotti tossed the hot gun into a brown bag. They left the scene with him explaining, "That's why I called you Mall, now he knows it's one for one because I know he had something to do with Mall's death."

"But Gotti, what if he…"

"What if he what?"

"Nothing…but don't you think you should call Bo and let him know what you just did?"

"No, I'm going to call him and let him know what we just did." Gotti dialed the number, letting it ring a few times before disconnecting the call. "Better yet, take me over there."

Inside Bo's home, he laid two rose scented candles in the center of the lovely decorated dining room table. He stood there for a moment to look at it and made sure everything was set just right for this special moment. Next, he ran over to the air conditioner, turning it on high to feel the cold chill, "Perfect," he said, pushing the button to the remote control that turned the fire place on. Bo adjusted the flame level as an impatient female voice called from a back room, "Bo, I'm not playing, if you don't come and get this damn mask off of me…"

"Okay, I'll be right there baby," Bo dashed to the coffee table to get a basket of orange, yellow and pink rose pedals to place through out the room. Locked in the back room, Maria had a sleeping mask over her face with black tape covering the eyes so that she couldn't see. Maria once again tried the door knob, as if something had changed in the last ten seconds. "If this pussy don't come on…Boooo!"

"What?" the door opened.

"You better get this shit off my face…that's what."

"I will, in just a minute." Bo softly kissed Maria's lips before taking her arms and guiding her through the living room to the end of the dining room where he removed the mask. "Oh my God, it's beautiful!" Maria jumped into Bo's arms, giving him several kisses. "You did all this for me after all that I put you through?"

"There's nothing I wouldn't do for you"

"Good answer," Maria smiled. She unfastened Bo's belt buckle and dropped to her knees. Bo closed his eyes, feeling Maria take his manhood deep into her mouth. He was lost in the lustful moment as Maria licked over the skin of his balls with no hands. Then he caught himself, "Stop, stop baby."

"What...you ready to cum already?"

"No, I just want everything to be right for our special day," Bo answered, pulling her to her feet and placing her in a seat at the table. "What's so special about it?"

"Just wait here. I'll be right back." Bo started to rush off when Maria stopped him to ask, "What are you supposed to do?"

"Oh, sorry," Bo gave Maria a passionate kiss, ignoring his vibrating phone in his pocket until he was forced to come up for air. Maria looked at Bo, ran her finger over her lips and said, "That's right, taste it." Bo walked into the hallway and quickly checked his phone while looking over his shoulder to make sure Maria didn't catch him. Seeing that it was Gotti's number, he began to laugh, *"Now who's the scared joker...ha-haaa!"* Bo knew more about computers than Gotti, so he understood Mr. Patterson when he said, "Your money's here but it's not here. I just have to find how and where they moved it to."

Still silently laughing, Bo envisioned Gotti's confused face when he asked, "So are we broke or not?" *"Ha-ha,"* Bo had put so much money to the side that he knew that he was going to pay Tywan on his own until the money was found. He just wanted to see Gotti sweat for a few days. Bo returned to the dining room with a large plate full of Maria's favorite food only to find her completely nude with her feet spread out wide on the edge of the table as she poured a glass of wine over the lips of her love box. "I decided to go straight for desert," She slowly began to move her fingers over her clit in a counter clock wise motion until she became nice and wet. She made her three

253

fingers disappear inside herself, "Are you just going to stand there until it turns into pudding?"

Bo dropped the plate of food on the floor. He scooped Maria up into his arms and carried her to the fireplace, laying her on the floor. Bo looked down at her, seeing her eyes beautifully glowing from the reflection of the flames. He bent down asking, "Want a ride?" Maria responded, "You know it, sexy." Maria wrapped her legs tightly around his neck. Bo stood lifting her into the air to where only her fingers touched the floor and began to enjoy his meat by roughly sucking on her clit. "Oohh-ahhh," she softly moaned. "Wait...o-o-ohh, bend over some," Maria demanded. Bo followed until her palms became flat, giving him more balance. "Now you can put your tongue in it!" Bo used his lips and tongue like magic, mastering the art of love making taught to him by Maria. He lightly bit down on the side of her pussy lips, tasting her love juices.

Off in the distance a bumping sound stopped him, "Did you hear that?"

"Yeah, that's my stomach, letting you know I'm about to cum for you!"

"No, I'm serious..."

The noise occurred again, this time with much more force. Maria was the first to recognize its source, "Oh shit!" She released her legs in a hurry, rushing to get her clothes that were lying on the chair and her 9 mm. "Don't just stand there, check the camera!" she screamed. Bo struggled to get his last pant leg on and hopped over to the T.V. to hit the screen and saw a man dressed in black racing across his basement floor and heading for the stairs. "Baby, someone's here."

"No shit!" said Maria, ripping the tape from the mask and recovering her face again. She had just her pants, shoes and bra on, running from the dining room through the living room to the main hallway. Maria moved from side to side like her father taught her to be prepared for anything.

"No, this isn't real, we ne..." Bo saw that he was now alone, "Now I know why I love her." He gripped an extra clip before chasing after her. Maria reached the top of the stairs and listened for footsteps. She couldn't hear anything so she shot passed to get to the far side window. Looking out, she gently

254

raised it up halfway, stuck her weapon out and pulled the trigger rapidly. "Take that, pussy!" Maria yelled as she watched multiple shots crash into a man's upper body and knock him off his feet. She then slammed the window shut and turned around coming face to face with Bo, "How many of them are there honey?"

"I can't tell, I just bought this house. The cameras are only working on the first floor and the basement."

"You're telling me you have two unsecured floors with people trying to kill me?"

"You! No, Maria it's just a little misunderstanding over some money I owe. But don't worry, I'll handle it."

"Ooh Bo watch out behind you!" Maria yelled while raising her gun. Bo quickly turned around and fired, not missing a step from his A-One days, placing a large hole in the empty wall when abruptly the back of Bo's head exploded. *"Only if you knew the half,"* Maria watched Bo's body bleeding in front of her then stepped over him to head down the hallway, "I told you to watch your back, coward!" She grinned, continuing to speak to herself, with her voice becoming deeper as if she was someone else, "Now, let the party begin," she closed the door behind her.

Seconds before, Dro screamed, "Move!" into the two-way receiver while he covered Sam's back. Sam slid through the basement door. "Soldier 1 and Soldier 2 are in," Dro informed, running up the wooden stairs, meeting up with Sam. "Soldier 3 and R...Aaaaahhh," the sound of shots came over the airwave mixed with a deep scream. "Soldier 4 are you alright? Stay still, we're on our way."

"No Soldier, continue with the mission. I got Soldier 4 in my sight," said Mr. Nate. He pulled Ace through the kitchen door that he just kicked in. Ace laid on the cold tile taking in deep breaths through his mask. His shirt and jacket were soaked in blood. "Soldier 4, tell me where you're wounded."

"I have...two shots in my arm and...one in my lower chest. But give me a minute to catch my breath okay and I'll be fine." Ace started to try to get up but Mr. Nate reached for his bullet proof vest and pulled him back down. "Just be cool Ace,"

Mr. Nate picked up his walkie talkie, "Soldier 6, what's your location?"

"I just reached the second floor on my way to meet Soldier 5 in the middle as planned."

"Well that changed. I need you down here now to assist Soldier 4," screamed Mr. Nate while unbeknownst to him, Ace was already dead.

"But what about Soldier 5?"

"There are no buts; a man is down so get here. Soldier 5 you hear that!" Mr. Nate demanded.

"I do and I can handle myself if there's something up there, I'll find..." *'BOMB-BOMB'* The same sound of shots repeated. Dro yelled, "Soldier 5, say something!" He was praying for a response and one came, "Or someone will find you." A muffled female voice said through the walkie talkie, finishing Soldier 5's statement. Dro closed his eyes, not believing what he'd just heard.

Outside, Mark hid in the darkness covering the front door to make sure no one came in or escaped. He once again heard the vibrating noise of gun fire and wanted to leave his position but for the thousandth time, he remembered what Mr. Nate said, "A soldier never abandons his post, no matter what happens. There is no one part of a plan more important than the other." Then the silence came from Shawn's radio, followed by an unrecognizable voice, "Fuck that. Soldier 7 is on his way." He rushed the door, ramming his shoulder into it and busting in. He questioned, "Soldier 1, where you at?"

"I'm on the second floor attending to Soldier 5"

"How is he?"

Silence

"I said how is he?"

"He's fine," Dro said. He listened to Mark let out a sigh of relief then motioned to Soldier 6 with his finger to his lips to remain quiet while using his free hand to shut Shawn's lifeless eyes. Sam stood over Dro with two guns in hand letting his eyes scan every direction until Dro ended his short prayer. "Dro let's go and get this bastard." Dro jumped up setting his sight on Soldier 6, "Go see to Soldier 3 then get back here. I'm going to have a body for you to look over, come on Soldier 2." Dro and

256

Sam moved from room to room. Sam kicked the doors in with his gun dropped low, covering Dro who rushed in with a need for blood.

Maria was only a few feet away watching their every move, just waiting for the moment they approached her position. *"Keep coming boys, and I'm going to put you where you need to be."* She spotted Dro appearing in the hallway, now inches from his death. "Soldier 2, there's nobody in there," Dro said, speaking of the last room. "But they have to be, we came only seconds after the shot."

"Then they're in there," Dro pointed in the direction of the living room, "Let's do it!" Sam retightened his grip on his pistol, leading the way with Dro right behind him. Sam spotted Bo's dead body, "Dro, look!" Sam bent down to check Bo's pulse, hopeful that Dro's friend wasn't gone. Dro screamed, "Nooooooo!"

All the while, Maria laid and waited on the top steps using half of Bo's body as a shield. She smiled, thinking, *"This can't be true."* Seeing Sam bend down toward her, she swiftly brought her hand out from beneath Bo and fired, "BOMB-BOMB' two shots blasted through Sam's head that knocked him back towards Dro. Maria jumped to her feet, catching Dro off guard while he fumbled with Sam trying to get his balance. She swung her gun around to stop at Dro's head and her finger pulled back on the trigger as she immediately switched direction to the stairs and fired, 'BOMB-BOMB'

"Ah-ah you bitch!" said Mr. Nate. He received a shot in the side of his neck but mentally refused to let the pain finish him. Mr. Nate returned fire using his body as a barricade to keep Mark at bay, who tried to rush passed. The hesitation of Maria's fire was enough time for Dro to make his move. He rushed Sam back into the last room to place him on the floor. His blood began to pump with rage to the sound of several more shots ending in a scream coming from Mr. Nate. "That's it," Dro ran back out into the hallway with his gun raised and ready for blood. He spotted his target, aimed and fired. The shot missed Maria's face and she turned in the direction of the shot, meeting the eyes of Dro. Maria had the same villainous grin and blew a kiss to Dro before taking off up the steps that led to the third floor. Dro ran after her but stopped to see what she was aiming for then he saw Mr. Nate lying down with his back up against the banister as Mark tried to stop the blood that was coming out of his neck. Dro crept back down the steps in reverse with his gun still pointed forward. As he got near Mr. Nate, he asked, "What's it look like soldier?"

"The plan remains the same as always, no survivors, no retreat, now go get that crazy bitch!"

Speaking into the walkie talkie, Dro said, "Soldier 6 what's your status?"

"I just placed Soldier 4 in the car, now I'm making my way back to the house."

"Okay, listen," Dro handed his radio to Mr. Nate, "Tell him your location soldier. I'm going to bring you the girl who did this to you!" Dro then shot a look at Mark, hoping that he made sure Mr. Nate would be fine before heading up the third floor steps.

There were two sets of eyes outside moments earlier that observed Soldier 6 closely as he helped a man across the grass that looked to be wounded. Slow motion said, "Come on Gotti, we can catch them off guard," his hand reached for the door handle when Gotti grabbed him by the back of his neck. "Boy, if you don't sit your ass down."

"But they're coming from Bo's house"

"Yeah and they're going to that black van," Gotti pointed. Slow motion watched Soldier 6 lay Soldier 4 in the back seat and slam the side door. On sight, he remembered the day it slowly came down his block with five men dressed in black, like now and jumped out. Slow motion reopened his eyes, he didn't want to relive the moment a second longer. He removed his hand and said, "Then again, you're right. We should chill and wait until it clears out."

"Oh shit! Look, it's about to hit the fan!" stated Gotti. He pointed to the third floor window where all the lights suddenly started to go out. Maria went through each room killing the lights until it was completely dark then she checked her ammo and saw that there were only eight shots. Maria reached for her extra clip, "Damn, I must have dropped it," she said, cocking back the hammer. *"This will have to be enough."* She stood off at a distance of the stairway entrance, listening for footsteps.

Dro tightly squeezed Mr. Nate's hand one last time then made his way patiently up the steps with his back against the wall, one at a time. Then the hallway went pitch-black, he felt that it was a set up and knew he had to think fast. Maria heard him coming closer and estimated her enemy was now only a few feet away so she ducked into the shadow with her gun pointed at the only entry and waited. A look of madness lay under her mask when she saw the outline of her enemy's body racing out from the entrance as it dove for cover. She pulled the trigger, hitting her target several times dead center in the back. Her pistol stayed locked on her motionless victim. She bent down to turn the body over and said, "Now, face me pussy!" she roughly gripped the body, "What the hell!" she held up a black shirt connected to a bullet proof vest. Quickly placing the vest on, she captured a sudden movement from the corner of her eye just as Dro charged her body and knocked her gun loose. They landed on the carpet with Dro on top. He wrestled with Maria until he had both her wrist held tightly. "Stop, I don't want to hurt you if I don't have to."

Maria's struggling stopped and she laid still looking at the masked man, "It's too late for that," she slammed her knee into his balls, "Haahhhh." Maria rolled out from under Dro and leaped for her weapon that was lying in the center of the floor. Dro's pain shifted to panic real fast as he saw Maria nearing with the gun. He knew his fate if she was to make it while he was re-gripping his forty five. Dro stretched his arm out and kicked off the ground with all his might. He jumped at Maria, caught hold of her ankle and pulled her towards him. Maria started to lose her balance when her feet began to slip from beneath her she went down face first, busting her lip and chin. A light cry escaped with the blood pouring from her lip. Maria tried to regain her focus but began to feel her body being forced backwards. Still not willing to give in, she kicked as hard as she could and broke free to grab her 9 mm. In the same motion she turned and had it aimed at Dro's head in seconds. He was now standing with his gun at her heart while they stared at each other as if in search of one another's soul for a reason.

259

Dro broke the silence, "Why…just tell me why?" Maria laughed deeply at the sound of the question. "Ha…if you only knew the half of it."

"See, that's where you had me. I only knew half to begin with but now I think I have figured it out."

"Never! The plan was flawless and after I kill you, none will be the wiser."

"It was until you underestimated one thing."

"And what was that?" questioned Maria, slowly stepping in to close the gap between the two.

"My heart"

"Ha…and how is that?"

"The day you planned to kill Rell, you never thought I would risk everything that I own to stop it from happening"

"Oh, how little do you think one knows you? If Bo would have done his job like he told him to, you wouldn't have been there. Poor Bo, but what can I say…it's hard to find good help now a days." "You know they say that the true definition of a man is defined by the woman he hold closest to his heart." Dro said as the impact of Maria's own words made him think back to that very moment.

Rell slid his chair away from the table and said, "It's getting late fellas and I have to make some moves early in the day so ya'll go ahead and enjoy yourself. I'll catch ya'll in the AM."

"Come on with all that, we came together so we're leaving together," said Dro, who was feeling uneasy. They made their way through the crowd toward the elevator with Rell at the lead and Bo tapped Dro on the shoulder, "Here Dro, go get the Jeep because I'm pretty fucked up and I don't think I can drive." Without stopping, Dro kept his eyes on Rell and responded, "Nah, get Gotti to do it."

"No, I need you to do it because he might crash my shit, please." Dro now considered that maybe he knew then. He was ready to answer when Gotti took the keys from Bo's hand, "Come on nigga, I got it…"

"Dro, please don't tell me you're shocked that the great, we cry together, we die together would cross him. Now, welcome to the real world, ha-ha," Maria continued to laugh at

Dro's puzzled expression. "So it was him that crossed Rell and you being the forth person on the mission, it wouldn't be hard for you to know the exit route."

"You still don't get it"

"Maria pulled the trigger sending a bullet past Dro's face. The loud sound rang in Dro's ears yet he refused to flinch while keeping their stare down game alive. Maria noticed a strong connection beginning to move her feet counter clockwise. Dro gave a light head nod then back pedaled clockwise, she screamed, "Hell with the set up, but yes I was there on the ground too but this shit is about you in more ways than one!"

Downstairs Mr. Nate finally made it to his feet with his arm wrapped around Mark's shoulder. He heard a shot go off, "Oh God, not Dro!" and removed his arm from Mark and sucked up the pain, "Let me go, boy." Mr. Nate started up the stairs with Mark right on his tail. Approaching the top, Mr. Nate gave a four finger signal that told Mark to halt as he witnessed the head nod from Dro. He slowly backed into the stairwell and listened to the woman becoming more hype with each second. Mr. Nate thought, *"I hope Dro knows what he's doing because a bitch with a gun is nothing to play with. But if he doesn't...I do."* He readjusted his grip on his weapon. Maria screamed, "This shit is about you!" The reality of the words felt like the world fell on Dro's chest. "So you used me to use Mr. Nate to kill Pretty Tony for you?"

"Yes, but for you. I knew you would come home looking for answers so I gave you what you wanted but no, that wasn't enough for Dro. You had to keep digging." Mr. Nate heard his name and the disloyalty that came behind it. He raised his gun but Mark held his arm to keep him at bay. "So you're the one who gave me Shy?" Dro questioned. "Yeah, to hell with that bitch. You always did like her so you got her. Is she dead? Better yet, don't tell me...I already know the answer, Bo said it but I didn't want to believe you really got soft!" Maria squeezed the trigger, letting another shot fly by Dro's head but this one was much closer. Mr. Nate was fighting to get free as he saw how close Dro just came to death, "Why doesn't he just pull the trigger and end this madness?"

Dro wasn't fazed at all and asked, "But why Kim...she hasn't done anything to deserve to be lying in a hospital bed with a hole in her face?"

"That's why...revenge is never a good motivation to kill but Mall wanted to bring death, anything for his friend Pretty Tony. And the person who set him up is still alive," Maria shook her head in disgust.

"I guess you can't explain your madness."

"What!"

Dro stopped moving in a position that placed Maria's back to Mr. Nate. Dro responded to plant his seed, "I asked you why, not for his reason. Mall's actions were from loyalty...it's sad but in some way it's understandable but you on the other hand, you did just the opposite." Maria became silent, looking as though she was lost in thought. Mr. Nate felt this was his moment. He let the gun from the arm that Mark held fall. Mark released him to retrieve it as Mr. Nate removed a 380 automatic from his waistline and aimed. Dro looked at Maria's face and thought he saw tears in her eyes behind the mask. He now felt that this was his chance to get her to put the gun down, though he stopped when he spotted Mr. Nate's old trick go into play. Dro screamed, "Noooo!" as he dove. Mr. Nate fired, 'BOMB-BOMB-BOMB' the two bodies crashed to the ground, both laying still. Mr. Nate rushed them with his gun aimed and following the head of the flash light as it roamed over the large pool of blood. His heart began to beat faster; he fell to his knees listening to see if Dro was still breathing, "Thank God!" He looked for a wound and felt his hand become covered in blood. With his knife, Mr. Nate cut Dro's shirt off from the back, locating a gun shot would in his lower back. He tried to roll Dro over to stop the bleeding but Dro's hold on the woman's waist was too tight. "Son, if you can hear me, let go so I can get you some help....son?"

For a few moments there was nothing but silence then Dro finally responded in a soft whisper, "Nooo". Mr. Nate was shocked at his answer and believed he'd heard Dro wrong. "Come on Dro, you're losing a lot of blood." Mr. Nate again tried to break the grip. "No," Dro said once again. Now knowing he heard correctly the first time, Mr. Nate ripped the mask from the face of the still woman. "Oh my God, nooooo!" Mark stood above Mr. Nate and saw the face. He quickly radioed to Soldier 6, "Dr. Woods we need you up here now." He pulled a tearful Mr. Nate out of the way and spoke, "Dro you must let her go before she goes into a coma." Dro slowly released his hands. Mark immediately began hitting on the woman's chest hard, "Come on…come on," he slammed his hands again harder into her chest. The woman coughed loudly and started to open her eyes, "Are you hit?" Mark asked. "Hit, what are you talking about and where are my clothes?" She looked around, confused but quickly found a familiar face and said, "Daddy, why are you crying?" She got up and ran over to him when she saw Dro and her heart began to fall.

She lowered herself to the floor, scooping Dro up into her arms, "What happened to him? Don't just stand there bitch, get some help!" Her voice suddenly deepened as if person was speaking as she continued, "No, let him die for his disloyalty." Then it returned to normal, "Lord please don't take him away, he's all I got." Mark appeared at Mr. Nate's side leading Dr. Woods and stated, "Nate, we got to get out of here. What do you want me to do?"

"You're right, clean up any prints then burn this house to the ground. I'll meet you at the van in five."

"Got you," Mark took off.

"And me," Dr Woods questioned.

"Dro's shot, and the bullet went in and out of his side, I can close that. I need you to handle her because I can't this time; it kills me to see this happening again."

"I understand," Dr. Woods said with a large smile and gentle tone. "Hi Isha Maria Smallwood, it's me, Dr. Woods, you do remember me don't you?"

"Yes, are you here to help Dro because he was baaaddd to me?" she pushed Dro hard in the back of his head.

"No, don't do that. He will be good from now on. I promise but may I ask you a question?"

"Yes"

"Why haven't you been taking your medication?"

"I have even more then before," Isha grinned devilishly.

Outside, Slow Motion and Gotti passed a blunt of kush back and forth while sipping on some Remy 1738 parked deep in the cut like they were at a drive in movie. They watched Mark with his eyes filled with rage carry Shawn's body to the van as it pulled off. Slow Motion was still a bit nervous about Gotti's plan and asked, "Do you think that's all of them?"

"Look at your scared ass"

"I am but you're sitting here like you didn't just see that man carrying bodies out of there like trash," answered Slow Motion.

"Man, I don't give a fuck if he was carrying missiles. But if it will make you feel better, we'll wait ten minutes before going in to see what's left."

Slow Motion passed the blunt to Gotti thinking he may have smoked too much as he tapped Gotti's arm and pointed to a ball of flames that seemed to keep getting higher when a shot came crashing through the passenger side window nearly hitting Gotti. "What the fuck! Man, get us moving!" yelled Gotti. He quickly lowered his head as he watched out the corner of his eye a man looking like a bum squeezed the trigger, "Let's go!" realizing they weren't escaping; Gotti looked to the right to find Slow Motion with a blunt in his mouth, dead. He pushed Slow Motion out the car as the dome light gave up his identity just as he jumped in the driver's seat. Gotti dropped the car in reverse; he returned fire while swearing to put an end to the people for making him do what he said would never be done...retreat.

37

*T*hree weeks later, with his strength only at eighty percent, Dro headed out the side door of Temple Hospital accompanied by Mark and Dr. Woods saying, "Dr. Woods thanks for everything. Again, if it wasn't for you, I don't know how my family would have made it."

"No problem. Any friend of Roc and Boggy's, has to be a friend of mine. I'm sorry your wife couldn't come with you but as you know she has a medical condition, Multiple Personality Disorder (or MPD). It's a psychological disorder where a person possesses more than one developed personality therefore I must keep her at least another week or so until I'm certain there are no signs left of the five deadly personalities she took on while refusing to take her medications."

"Deadly personalities! Are you sure Doc? Up until now my wife has never committed a crime in her life."

"Indeed, but sadly to say, Isha's parent's have and the reality of them being in a Federal Detention Center moved your wife to search for the reason why. After our talk which I can't go to deep into because of the privacy law, I learned some years back she always had the desire to know the reason why she was without a father for more than a decade. In finding out, she started to study the F.E.D.S magazine."

"I'll be damned... she read them every month or she goes online to do it, but what does that have to do with anything?" Dro said, not seeing the picture. "That's where she developed her personalities; through the stories of some of the most dangerous and cold hearted people to ever walk this earth. While the law may have thought they put some people away for life in a cell, they were actually once again free... living through your wife..."

"*Dr. Woods, please report to the E.R. immediately, Dr. Woods please report to the E.R.*" A voice echoed through the hospital's intercom interrupting Dr Woods. "Fellas, if you'll excuse me, I'll see you later. Oh and before I forget, Dro pray...always. That's what you do without me, it works better." Dro gave Dr. Woods a head nod in acknowledgement then walked Mark to his car. "Mark, are you alright? It looks like you lost some weight since the last time I saw you."

"Yeah, I'm fine. I've just been running you know, ha-ha...trying to keep in shape. You know Matty said he'll have a fight for me next month," Mark answered before slamming the door of his car and starting the engine. Dro remained outside with a sense that something was different about his friend that he couldn't put his hands on. "Dro are you sure you don't want to take a ride with me to clear your mind for a few hours?"

"Nah, this walk is good enough."

"After all the shit that she just put you through, you still can't leave her; can you?"

"No, but I learned something from all this?"

"And what's that?"

"That Yusuf was right when he said the true definition of a man is defined by the woman he holds closest to his heart."

"I hear you," Mark laughed. He lit a match and placed it to his lips.

"Mark, when did you start smoking weed again and why does it smell funny, is it laced?"

"I know...I know you don't have to say it, it's a bad habit and I shouldn't be doing it but with everything going on with Shawn dying and shit I just wanted to relax." Mark took a deep pull, closing his eyes and let the white smoke enter his lungs and held it as Dro's words went in one ear and out the other. "I don't care how bad it gets, what you're doing is not the answer." Mark blew the smoke out, feeling it recharge him. He turned his glossy eyes to face Dro, putting the car into drive, "I suppose Sef is correct because the closest woman to me is my mother and the bitch is a junkie... but it is what it is. So I guess she defines me, ha-haaaa. Fuck it, we're put here to die, it is what it is."

"What did you just say?" Dro asked, hearing Rell's voice replay in his head *"It's the one who says "it is what it is," all the time."*

"I said it is what it is, I quit before and I can do it again. If not, fuck it...it is what it is."

Hearing those words once again, Dro fought the pain that raced through him from his gun wound as he reached for his weapon with disgust, betrayal and revenge acting as one, moving through every vein in his body. Just as he reached for his gun, Mark's foot stepped on the gas. Dro couldn't fight the visualization of Rell flipping around in his hospital bed in a panic as his eyes shot open. "It was because of you bitch!" Dro yelled as he raised his weapon trailing Mark's Benz as it disappeared beside the building heading for the main exit.

"Oh no nigga, you gone die today!" Dro dashed for the hospital door to cut Mark off. His coat flew in the wind as his feet rushed over the cement determined to keep his promise. He slipped through the double glass doors racing down the freshly waxed floor while his eyes pursued Mark's car through the large side window.

Dro reached the elevator pushing the button to the first floor rapidly, "Come on damn it!" The time moved with each second feeling as if it was an hour to Dro. Not being able to hold back his rage to kill, Dro made for the stairwell. He rounded the corner as his eyes searched the huge parking lot for the man that controlled his thoughts for the last three years and was now sure to be dead by sunset. "Got your ass," Dro said with the first smile in a long time visible on his lips. He pulled the stairwell's metal door open taking the steps three at a time reaching the bottom in no time; Dro entered the ground floor waiting area just as mark's Benz turned onto the straight away placing Dro more than a few steps ahead of him. Dro still not content pushed his legs even harder. He was suddenly blindsided by a Nurse reading a patient's folder coming out of a corner room just as Dro made the right turn a few feet from the exit. They collided with the Nurse receiving the short end of the stick as her papers flew everywhere. Dro barely felt the impact and continued to flow with his momentum sticking his arm out to stop his fall while pushing off the ground. He removed the forty-five automatic from his waistline seeing Mark approaching from about twenty yards away. "Dro nooo!"

Everything that came next seemed to move in slow motion as Dro's gun elevated toward Mark's face as he continued for the glass door while his finger tightened around the trigger; he paused at the sound of his name being screamed again. "Dro Nooo!" He barely turned his head in the direction of

267

the source when noticing Nurse Salle with blood coming from her mouth and eye staring up at him as she said, "I know... but not this way dear." Nurse Salle turned her vision to the left where two security guards were rushing into the building behind Dro. "So put that away and please help me up quickly. Don't worry I will cover for you." Dro did as he was told and assisted Nurse Salle back on her feet as he continued watching Mark drive down the highway knowing soon they would meet.

"Oh Nurse Salle are you alright? We received a call there was a man racing through the hospital," asked the security guard

"No I'm fine Paul; I think that call could have been for this fine gentleman who after seeing me fall, came running," explained Nurse Salle making it to her feet.

"Okay if you say so, but are you sure you're alright?"

"If not I don't know a better place to get hurt." Nurse Salle said making everyone laugh but Dro. He was picking up the paper from Nurse Salle's folder when he observed his wife's name. His eyes quickly glanced over the content, "Diazepam!"

"Dro you shouldn't be reading that. What are you trying to do, get me fired?" stated Nurse Salle snatching the file from Dro. "I'm sorry Nurse Salle." She saw the confused emotion on Dro's face and whispered, "Its okay, I know you didn't mean anything by it. You just love your wife... but don't worry she'll be fine. Diazepam is the drug she was on which actually had a counter effect and was enhancing her illness but Dr. Woods caught it and now Isha is on the correct medication. He always did like her, let's just be thankful for Dr Woods."

"Come to think about it, you're right....thanks again," Dro gave Nurse Salle a hug good bye and headed out the door with death still fresh on his mind. Placing his phone to his ear Dro knew there was one person that could find Mark before the sun could rest. "Hello Gizelle..." he said on his way to his car.

Inside his main office at club Soldi II, Roc sat listening to his weekly report of events when the intercom buzzed interrupting his visitor. "Excuse me," Roc said hitting the intercom button, "Yes."

"Roc baby, I know you're in a meeting but I think you should take this, Dro is on line three and I had him on hold for sometime but he sounds kind of upset about something."

"Okay put him through...Dro my main man, how's that recovery coming?"

"Never mind the recovery, it's nothing. Pain will one day stop but death is everlastingly..."

Roc continued to listen with his eyes lowering with each word as Dro's aching voice gave him the details of everything that had taken place lately, ending with Mark's deadly consequences. Roc understood that Dro was nearing the end of his rope and suggested, "I think you should get here." Roc then let the phone rest back in its cradle and leaned back in his seat returning his attention to his guest. Roc had already calculated his next move based off the answer to the third question he would ask, "Sorry for the interruption, as you were saying."

"With Bo dead and A-one no longer able to hold down that side of town, it's wide open for the taking."

"And I'm assuming you're the one to do the taking?" Roc questioned.

"Without question, you just have Boggy sit them bricks out like I've been hearing and tell me a day you want to have your money picked up."

"What about conflict, how would you handle that if you feel there was no other way but to fight?"

"Come on Roc, you know me... if it's on, it is what it i–" Mark's words got caught in his throat at the sight of Roc's chrome forty-five raising up from under his desk as Roc said, "Silent prayers will seal the heart's of warriors so they will return safely back to their maker in which they came. But the spoken words of a fool will reveal in time, the true maggot that crawls within his heart." With lack of hesitation Roc slammed five slugs into Mark's upper body and face with the force that blew him out of the huge leather chair he sat in. Roc gradually stood to his feet looking to Billy D before tossing his weapon. Dro caught it in mid air now stepping all the way into the room. He reached Mark's body, greeting it with shots until the gun kicked back empty. Billy D watched enough of Dro standing frozen with his finger flicking away at a vacant trigger eased the

269

weapon from his palms. "Son it's over, now take a seat and relax we'll handle this small situation. Roc you want me to get Boggy and Lil Mac to deal with this?" questioned Billy D.

"No their plate is already full, have Haffee and Fox do it."

"Okay," Billy D departed in search of the clean up team leaving Roc and Dro alone to talk.

"Roc I can't believe after all that I did for this piece of shit, matter of fact, fuck me…all the stuff Rell's been through for him and this is how he returned his love by disrespecting his own family?"

"Who knows why anyone disrespects anybody Dro, but don't worry you did the right thing. Because that kind of act can't go on without being dealt with. One of the wisest things my father said to me was just after he killed a man who owed him money right in front of my eyes. He said, *"A man who can't keep what he has is not supposed to have it."* Being a kid at the time I took that statement for what it was on the surface although it was much deeper. Any person can acquire money but only few will be respected. My father didn't kill Big Jeff over money… how foolish of me to think it was just about that." Roc reached into his pocket pulling out a roll of hundreds ripping it into pieces aggressively and then tossed it to the floor. "This is nothing; they can have it all as long as my name is good. If my name is superior…and it will be to the death of me, there's nothing that I've once seized that I couldn't have again."

Dro sat and watched Roc's veins pulsate with rage as his body appeared to grow wider with each word and his eyes displayed fury and suddenly turned pitch black. The cold wickedness of his outer shell forced Dro to break his stare for a second; unsure that he was witnessing what he just saw. Dro became more uncomfortable from a strange gut feeling. But not understanding why he stood to his feet shaking Roc's hand. "Roc, thanks for everything you have done for me. I swear I will never forget it. Though it seems that I have lost everything in my fight to find the truth you have be-" Dro paused, "You have been there all along the way to help me. It's been a long day so I'm going to hit the spot and call you later."

"Alright Dro you do that, but hang in there because this is only the third quarter." Dro entered the hallway in a daze bumping into Billy D and kept walking without saying a word. "Hey Roc, what's up with the young cat is he going to be okay?" Billy D questioned.

"Old head he'll be just fine, he just got a lot on his mind right now that's all. Did you see my car keys?" Roc said pulling back the drapes. Dro slid behind the wheel of his B.M.W with his mind going in every direction. He slammed the door shut laying back with his skull relaxing on the headrest as he let out a deep breath. He closed his eyes trying hard to remember where he felt this evil sensation before. Thinking back, sweat drops appeared on Dro's forehead when his eyes suddenly reopened in shock "Oh shit it's him!" Dro said as he struggled to get the key in the ignition with his trembling hand. Making the connection he pulled out of the parking spot seeing Roc with a friendly smile on his face waving bye from his office window.

Dro waved back but his expression was different, because he no longer saw Roc in the window at the moment but instead he saw him with those same pitch black eyes staring at him with revulsion, the very moment that his life turned to hell as the cops surrounded him the night of the shooting. Dro then felt an atmosphere of malice suddenly arrive and he quickly turned to meet it as he lowered the gun to see Roc promising with his lips moving slowly, *"For his disrespect I will destroy everything he knows."* Dro still didn't want to believe that a man he never knew could take control of his life in the blink of an eye, he quickly searched his mind as he saw his life in reverse... The look of fear on Isha's face as Roc approached him in the club the day he returned home took center stage as Isha questioned him in a panic. *"Baby do you know who he is? That's the medication man for all these dope heads around me."* Then it was Roc's statement, *"I'm sorry about your situation. If it helps...I did visit the hospital on several occasions."*

"Isha was speaking about the people in her head. Not the club. And Roc could do it so easily with the help of Dr. Woods giving her the wrong drugs," Dro whispered, hearing the lie told to him by Dr Woods once again, *"While refusing to take her medication."* Dro quickly picked up his phone and started to

271

dial. "Hello, yes I would like to speak with Nurse Salle please it's an emergency…yes I'll hold."

"Nurse Salle speaking how may I help you?"

"You can start with the truth! And if I feel that you're lying, let's just say there won't be anyone that can help you when you get hurt this time. Now who gave Mrs. Smallwood the change in medication?" Dro yelled into the phone. As Nurse Salle identified the voice, her body began to quiver as she visualized the large gun Dro had with him earlier. "Bitch did you hear me?" Dro asked turning on to Broad Street.

"Yeees, I-I heard you sir," Nurse Salle inhaled deeply running her fingers over her flickering eyelids feeling a headache coming as she quickly blurted out the answer. "I did it."

"What? But why, you don't even know her?"

"For Rell."

At the mention of Rell's name Nurse Salle became encouraged as she continued "You don't even get it do you? It was never about her it was always you. But they needed to use her... it's always two faces one tear, so if she cries so will you. But you don't know anything about that either or you never would have left Rell in the street alone after he always had your back."

"Bitch! Someone better have yours cause you're dead when I see you!" Dro screamed stepping on the gas doing sixty across the intersection.

"That's if you see me again, I may be just a pawn in this mission of respect, but now I'm a rich pawn and thanks to Apple, my iPhone allows me to still receive my pages at the hospital even when I'm not there Ha-haa…did you think I was going to stay there after I witnessed that look of madness on your face as you prepared to kill another pawn? You should learn how to mask some of that anger because I would be nothing of the wiser b—" Dro disconnected the call now seeing his nightmare clearly. His foot eased off the gas as he crept to the line of traffic thinking of his revenge as Nurse Salle's words haunted him. "Mask …mask…" Suddenly Roc's voice entered his head. *"I'm revealing the bottom section of my mask young buck because when I was coming up, I was always ready for the physical war but only one fourth prepared mentally."*

"Oh shit the meeting!" Dro shook his head in disbelief "He was speaking to me... not Mark. Warning me to my fucking face that this would happen and I didn't even see it."

"Actually I was giving you a warning of what the end of four quarters is going to look like if you did. Always ask yourself first, if you're prepared for war with an enemy you know nothing about," Dro repeated Roc's words out loud speaking to himself hoping to gain an answer from within. "But I don't know shit about you faggot! I got your name from Meshane...I'll be damned! Meshane knew the whole time." Dro pounded his hand hard on the steering wheel now realizing that he was out smarted from the start. *"Dro, young cannon if you're going to find out who did this bullshit to your homey Rell, you have to go back to where it took place. What's that's club called again?"*

"Soldi II."

"Yeah, yeah that's it; well you're in luck, cause that's my man's spot and I know he wouldn't have a problem with you coming there."

"I don't know Shane."

"Cut it out... I'm telling you to go there when you get out and it will go as smooth as if he planned it for you."

"But!"

"Dro," Meshane interrupted, *"I have never lied to you yet."*

Dro continued to bang his hand, "Nigga if you wanted me dead what the fuck you playing games for? But now it's too late cause I'm coming for you!" Dro threw the car in reverse *BBeeeeep BBeeeep!* He aggressively hit the horn on the black Benz behind him also caught in the rush hour traffic. Dro with his head out the window yelled. "Yo back the fuck up so I can turn the hell around. You fucking foreigner."

"Me sorry sir there no much room and me being new to the country I no drive well. The rules in me country are so different I wish my wife was here she could make it out that small spot," The man yelled back.

"Your wife, that's it... the reason Roc didn't try to kill me yet, is because his is going to try and kill Isha first. *Two faces one tear"* Dro's finger raced over the number as he dialed Isha's hospital room number in a panic as Roc words played

273

with his mentality. *"Dro hang in the there this is only the third quarter….I was giving you a warning of what the end of four quarters is going look like."*

"Fuck you Roc!" Dro yelled while listening to the phone ring for the fourth time. Isha picked up on the sixth ring as Dro watched the funny looking foreigner exit his car, rechecking the space he had to move. "Hello…hello, who's playing on my damn phone…hello?"

"Nobody baby, it's me."

"Then why didn't you answer, and where you at baby you were supposed to be here hours ago?"

"I know Isha, but just listen to me. Do you have any of the medication that Nurse Salle was giving you?"

"No baby, I told you I wasn't going to take it anymore."

"You tell me a lot of stuff but right now I pray you were lying to me."

"I wasn't lying but I do know where some is. Why, are you trying to get freaky with one of my old friends cause that is still like cheating?"

"No! But I need you to take two pills real quick and get the hell out of there…someone's trying to kill you and I think its Roc fo--." *Boom-Boom* there was a hard knock at the window.

"Hey sir, I think I can move by now." The man said speaking English as best as he could.

Dro let out a sigh of relief, shocked by the man's presence. "No I'm okay."

"But you so are not," stated Cyrus quietly when *"Boc… Boc… Boc… Boom – Boom - Boom!"* the sounds of gun fire erupted through the air as Todd and Boggy ambushed Dro's vehicle from the passenger side while Lil Mac rushed from behind. Dro was dead before the third shot hit him, but to be certain Cyrus removed the Ruger from his hip, exploding the driver's side window into pieces as he placed two more in his skull. "Come on lets motion!" Cyrus said running back to Boggy's Benz over the screams of Isha, "Drooo! Drooo!" "Isha was in a state of extreme shock finding what she heard on the other end of the phone so hard to believe. "You will all be deaaadd!!!" Tears streaming down her face and shrills from her cries began to quiet for a brief moment as she uttered the words,

"I define Dro! So Roc…muthafucka, you will soon meet the definition of a man!"

Todd and Lil Mac quickly followed while Boggy slowly walked as if he didn't have a care in the world. Boggy slammed the driver's side door placing the car in drive. He pulled onto the side walk and drove around Dro's car then back into traffic. "No…no what are you doing?" asked Cyrus "We just killed a man, follow the plan and go in reverse. They can't eye us."

Boggy grinned saying, "Come on Cy, I love Roc but I can't do the mask thing. I'm all the way thug and I don't have a cut card. Some shit nigga's need to see because I know I can't dictate what another man will do. A real man will do what the fuck he wants but like Roc said; this here will dictate who the fuck they do it to."

"He's right Cyrus," Todd added. "This is the underworld nigga and cats don't respect anything but death. So at first sight you either feed it that or it's going to feed off of you."

"Enough! I understand the underworld Todd but what about you?" questioned Cyrus.

"My heart can't get no colder. Out here I witnessed whites killing blacks, blacks killing blacks and the economy killing blacks. The funny thing is I used to sit in my million dollar office and give the NAACP a check once a year and think that's what my father meant by making a decision that will uplift my people as a whole. How could I have been so wrong? That money will never touch my people at this level. That has to start within, to build them up to being the kind of person that will receive a check to go off to school. So I'm riding for them to see a better way to the fucking death of me."

Cyrus smiled, "Now you sound just like your father," he said as he dialed Travis informing him that they were ready.

38

*I*nside the dining room of Dro's home, Mr. Nate sat on the end of the table in tears as he listened to Molly Weiss of C.V.T.V. reporting live for *In these Mean Streets* as she informed the world of Dro's death. He listened attentively to every detail, optimistic to obtain anything for his personal investigations. He suddenly sat up straight hearing the echoes of soft foot steps a short distance behind him. "Honey ya'll back...Dashon?" he called out. When no answer came, on impulse Mr. Nate reached for his gun. "Ace Boon Coon I wouldn't do that if I was you because Ace is dead, leaving old Boon Coon alone all by himself," a calm male voice stated, followed by the sound of a hammer being cocked. Mr. Nate let out a deep breath releasing his weapon and said, "I knew you would one day come."

"Is that so?"

"Yes, and I tried to warn Dro that something was suspicious when I heard that Rell was released by a single phone call from the D.A. without a hearing or anything. The move had him written all over it, but Dro wouldn't listen, the bait was too good. His childhood friend, how could he resist? Then like that he was gone, forced into the hands of the cracker to be judged as I once stood."

"Honestly he should have died then; it would have made things that much easier. But everyone must answer for their actions, that's why I'm here for you to pay for yours," the man replied as he moved closer to Mr. Nate with a weapon aimed at the back of his head. "You're here because of a mistake I made over twenty years ago damn it! And I swear to God if I could take it back I would. Just know I never intended to rob Money Man Holmes or Billy D of anything...they were like family to me."

"But you did," the man said, now only inches from Mr. Nate.

"But you don't understand...crack hit Harlem hard and I needed money to get my lil princess and family out of there before it was too late and they were the only ones that really had it like that."

"Then you should have just asked," the man said stepping out in front of Mr. Nate to reveal himself while continuing, "Because that kind of act can't go on without being dealt with."

The sounds of hands clapping forced Roc to hastily redirect his aim onto the source to see Billy D standing in the background dressed in all black with a large smile upon his face "Now you're truly ready, you knew you were going to kill old Boon Coon the moment you read the letter. But if you did, you also knew you would have had to go to war with A-One. So you helped them kill each other," Billy D said. Roc stood up saying, "A man once told me that leadership is the art of getting someone else to do something that you want done because they wanted to do it. But when did you catch on to my plan?"

"Who said it was your plan."

"Don't play with me!"Roc said.

"Ok if it will make you feel better, the moment you asked for your keys your eyes became pitch black… that's when I knew that what ever you told that kid to make him leave like that was only a decoy. You know the eyes never lie… so I followed you."

"Well we are going to have to change that. It's just too bad that Dro said that he would die for him," Roc said as they departed genuinely liking Dro.

"Yeah but a man is only as good as his words."

"Speaking of words don't you think it's time you finish telling me about the Legend of Billy D?"

"I guess I'll have to if you won't let it go."

"Not a chance."

"Ok if I must," Billy D said as his sparkling green eyes inflamed suddenly turning pitch black "See, it was the year 1976 and I was more then a player's playa, I was a handsome gangster and all the pimps couldn't stand me because when Billy D came around it was mandatory to send your dame out of town…."

In days, the sad news of Dro's death quickly flowed through the thick walls of Graterford Penitentiary like the cries of a man that couldn't protect his manhood. While many

277

gangsters hid their pain through silent tears, others showed their detestation for no other reason then that Dro didn't mess with them. "Yeah, I knew they were going to smoke that clown, he wanted to be in everything but a casket. But now he got one," said Q laughing.

"I know babes, where's that upper cut and right jab he hit you with now?" asked Apple, speaking in a girl's voice. "No where, shit...because you can't punch through a bullet, bitch!" In the background Blue laughed at the demonstrations of disrespect while making his way down the tier. He stopped at Basil's cell looking in as he lightly tapped on the metal door. "Go away!" quickly came in return.

Blue thought he saw a tear in the corner of Basil's eye and decided not to push any further even though it was killing him inside not to. He continued to stroll down D block heading to the side yard when he saw Meshane standing outside his cell talking to Earl. Blue thinking now was always better then later detoured in Meshane's direction. As Blue got closer he could see several guards moving around in Meshane's cell. *"They must be shaking the Vic's cell down for all that gambling shit that's been going on. I'm glad I stopped going up there...they say when it rains it pours,"* Blue said lying to himself. The real reason he no longer gambled there was because Meshane beat him out of most of his money. Now he was forced to gamble for jail house money like Newport's and cake. Blue struggled to keep the smile from his face as he spoke, "Damn Shane, I heard what happened to old boy. That's crazy how they did him dirty, shot him all in the face and ass and shit. But I know if you were out there big homie that would never had happen."

"Yeah," Meshane said dryly as he listened to catch Blue's angle.

"Yeah, I'm telling these nigga's that's your walking grounds. But they like, man fuck Shane he was in here schooling Dro, walking the yard with Dro and if he was who he said he is then he should have been able to save Dro."

"Yeah," Meshane said again but this time with a little more excitement now seeing that Blue was playing his best hand ever against him.

"Without question, they're kicking your name down the drain baby. Talking about you been faking it the whole time. Point taken, you had a few whips and shit but they saying you don't want any parts of that action out there. When it comes to that gun play you give them the no look pass and act like you didn't see that shit."

"Excuse me Meshane," a guard interrupted "We're ready for you now."

"Ok I'll be right there, just give me a second to finish up with my main man Blue."

"Alright but make it quick," the guard ordered stepping back in the cell pulling Meshane's TV unplugged.

Blue stared at Meshane closely thinking; *"Now I'm your main man after that nigga's dead."* Meshane returned his attention on Blue saying, "Thanks for the info B."

"Any time Shane but that's just in here, who knows what they're saying on the streets."

"I know what they're about to say, Meshane's home, time to get that big paper popping again."

"What?"

"Oh you haven't heard, I'm out of here... the head D.A dropped my case this morning shortly after Dro's funeral. I guess the next thing they're going to be saying is Meshane fucked my bitch, he's driving another missile and damn he's eating!" Meshane laughed at Blue's shocked expression. Blue was traumatized as he watched Meshane stop at his cell and several guards carried his belongings to R and D.

The words "You son of a bitch," slipped from Blue's lips while thinking back to the day Dro left the prison and Meshane said looking him dead in the eye, *"Nigga you going to be here you're damn self. I need him to leave so I can go, then maybe you can follow."* Blue looked around in a panic hoping nobody was trying to kill him before racing down the block.

Meshane stepped out into the afternoon air opening the cell phone he got from C.O. Dickenson. He pushed the number seven on speed dial as directed; Roc answered on the second ring. "What's happening old timer? I hope that everything went according to plan."

"It couldn't have gone any better if I would have done it myself. But dig, word on the street is that Isha and another girl with a scar on here face is moving around with heat and you're the main target. I hear there's a few others but the thing that get's me is she's asking all the right questions with information that people aren't suppose to have. I also know they're the ones who tracked down Gotti and killed him in cold blood."

"Note taken."

"Ok, now what's happening with them things, I'm trying to start up my phone bill again?"

"I got you; in the third row of the parking lot you will find a gray Benz s55. In the secret sack you'll find fifty squares and two hand guns for your protection. Once finished, get with Mac, he's handling the rock now." Meshane scanned the foundation spotting the brand new vehicle. "Roc I'm on it." Meshane rushed to the beginning of his new life. "The door code is your birthday and the key is under the front seat," Roc notified an excited Meshane as he pulled the door open taking in the smell of new leather. "Man Roc, this thing right here is cold. Now where the hell is the key so I can get this party started?" Meshane said with his head half way under the seat.

"Excuse me Sir are you looking for these?" the sound of keys shaking got Meshane's attention. He sat up to see two female guards standing in the groove of the door as one held the Benz's keys out for him "Yes, love you're a life saver." Meshane reached for the keys when he notice the large scar on Kim's left cheek "Suck my ass Scotty!!!" Meshane screamed at the sight of Isha and Kim's guns rising simultaneously. *"Boom–Boom–Boom."* Each bullet ripped through Meshane's frame as the women worked their way from his leg up to his face sure to it that he would suffer. The smoke from the twin glocks was still thick as Isha picked up the phone out of the blood placing it to her ear saying to Roc, "One day soon you will have to face the definition of a man and then it will be your blood on my hands… Harlem bitch! But my hand is red, not black," Isha licked her finger of Meshane's blood. "I can't wait ha…ha…" Roc laughed disconnecting the call thinking, *"Every time you think you're out, there's always someone that wants to answer to human nature."*

Roc continued to walk through the freshly cut graveyard until he stopped in front of a black and white marble sculpture of an angel headstone that belonged to his father. "Dad this is going to be quick because I'm in kind of in a rush... I just want you to know that I have done what you have asked of me. Mac is now a rich man who in the past two years has ran my business just as well as me if not better, with the help of the same people I had and now he owns it. So at this point dad I must say we're even. Today ends the chapter of me watching out for the blood of my brother."

Roc bent down placing a single white rose at the base of the headstone that symbolized peace and closure then continued, "From this moment on I must find the answer to my own destiny because I will possess the *victory of the mind* by any means necessary, and that I now promise you." Roc headed back through the trail with unmarked thoughts of killing Adrian Cortez as the sound of a hard engine came to a screeching halt on the grass a few feet before him. He looked up at the sight of Mr. Nate's tinted black van just as the side door was sliding open. Though a surprise attack didn't shock him, thinking of the Legend of Billy D, it now actually turned him on. Roc quickly pulled his weapon stating the words of Mr. Holmes, *"Now we'll continue to fulfill whatever is meant to be of your destiny...* you're damn right we will." Roc rushed the front of the van aiming at the driver to see Billy D smile at him saying, "Shit, the man owned me money...how else was I going to get paid?" The open side door to the van revealed Haffee, M. Easy Mohammed, Raja, Boggy, Manny, Todd, Cyrus, and Travis. "Come on, get in we've got a corporation to steal."

THE END

ORDER FORM

Please make checks/money orders payable to:
Master Expressons Publications
3 Germay Dr, - POB: 1654
Unit 4 Wilmington, DE 19804
For book order inquiries only call: 215.792.3915

Allow 2 weeks for shipping/delivery.
$15.00 per book, plus $2.00/shipping & handling per book.
Orders can also be placed at www.MasterExpressions Publications.com

PREORDER NOW
UnforgivableBlood: Forgotten Secrets of a Family's Ruin-**(82S) $14.99**

AVAILABLE NOW
Blood of My Brother - **(71B) $15.00**
Blood of My Brother II: The Face Off - **(72B) $15.00**
Blood of My Brother III: The Begotten Son - **(73B) $15.00**
Blood of My Brother IV: Behind the Mask - **(74B) $15.00**
Legend of Billy D: The Awakening of a Don - **(121L) $15.00**
Alexandra: Echoes of His Sins (eBook only on Barnes & Noble and Amazon.com).

The Definition of a Man - **(122D) $15.00**
Heavy Lies the Crown – **(2214H) $15.00**
Your Name: _____
Address _____
City _____
State _____ **Zip Code** _____

Enter Book order number(s) from above **or** circle title(s):

_____

Total number of books ordered _____
Total Amount Due: $ _____